P9-BXZ-811

Batista, Paul A.

FIC
Bat   Manhattan lockdown

B 11)
DUE DATE   7/16   8 27
                               26.95

DB

MAHOPAC LIBRARY
668 Route 6
Mahopac, NY 10541
(845) 628-2009

MANHATTAN LOCKDOWN

Also by Paul Batista

Death's Witness
Extraordinary Rendition
The Borzoi Killings

7/16
o/p
$27-

MANHATTAN LOCKDOWN

PAUL BATISTA

MAHOPAC LIBRARY   FIC
668 Route 6   BAT
Mahopac, NY 10541
(845) 628-2009

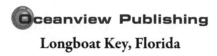

Oceanview Publishing

Longboat Key, Florida

Copyright © 2016 Paul Batista

All rights reserved. No part of this book may be reproduced in any form or by any electronic or mechanical means, including information storage and retrieval systems, without permission in writing from the publisher, except by a reviewer who may quote brief passages in a review.

This book is a work of fiction. Names, characters, businesses, organizations, places, and incidents either are the products of the author's imagination or are used fictitiously. Any resemblance to actual events, businesses, locales, or persons, living or dead, is entirely coincidental.

ISBN 978-1-60809-197-3

Published in the United States of America by Oceanview Publishing
Longboat Key, Florida
www.oceanviewpub.com

10 9 8 7 6 5 4 3 2 1

PRINTED IN THE UNITED STATES OF AMERICA

For Hazel, Nelson and Alma

MANHATTAN LOCKDOWN

CHAPTER ONE

Cleopatra's Needle rose above the acres of summer trees. In the glittering June sunshine two of the four sides of the thirty-six hundred-year-old Egyptian obelisk glowed in the light. It was the first time during the three-hour party that Roland Fortune had the chance to look out over the park's thousands of trees, the green expanses of the Great Lawn where hundreds of men and women were sunbathing, and the heights of the grand apartment buildings that lined Central Park West.

Sarah Hewitt-Gordan touched his arm. "They were geniuses, weren't they?"

"Who?" He looked at her. Even in the intense light her face was beautiful.

"Olmsted and Vaux."

"The rock group?"

She laughed. "If the networks only knew what a comedian you are, you'd have your own show."

Smiling, he kissed her forehead and turned to the crowd on the roof garden of the Metropolitan Museum of Art. Most of the guests at his forty-seventh birthday party were under the white party tent. The murmur of voices, the tinkling noise of glasses, and the music of the band.

This was Roland Fortune's third year as the mayor of New York City. Raised in the Bronx, he made certain that ten of the eighty guests invited to this early Sunday afternoon party were from the neighborhood on the Grand Concourse. But he also made certain that the other guests were the people he'd cultivated and who'd cultivated him in the fifteen years in which he rose as a member of the city council, then as a congressman from the South Bronx, and now as mayor; actors, writers, television news anchors, baseball and football players, other politicians.

And Sarah Hewitt-Gordan. She'd spent almost every night with him at Gracie Mansion since they first met a year earlier at a party at the Asia Society on Park Avenue. The daughter of a retired major in the British Army, she had graduated from both Eton and Cambridge. She was a partner at Goldman Sachs.

His closest aides, Hector Suarez, who had been with him since his city council days, and Irv Rothstein, his press secretary and a former *New York Times* reporter who joined him when he ran for mayor, had warned him against public involvement with a woman who had the style and accent of an English aristocrat, not to mention the tony name Sarah Hewitt-Gordan, "with a fucking 'a' instead of an 'o' in her last name," Irv said. "And the hyphen is going to kill you in Bay Ridge."

"Not a chance," Roland Fortune answered. "Look at her. I'm the envy of every guy in New York, especially the Italian guys in Bay Ridge. And besides, I love her."

Since it was early Sunday afternoon, guests were steadily coming and going. New people had arrived during the few minutes he and Sarah spent overlooking the undulating beauty of the park. Bill Cunningham, the eighty-year-old society photographer for the *New York Times* whose photographs of famous people at parties appeared in the Sunday society page, was slipping like an elf among the guests. He had already taken pictures of Robert De Niro, Michael Bloomberg, Tom Wolfe, and others. As Roland Fortune entered the shade under the festive tent, he embraced Matt Damon, and Cunningham unobtrusively pointed his old-fashioned Leica at them.

Roland Fortune was exuberant.

* * *

He felt the concussion just as he heard the first explosion. As broken stone and concrete instantly ripped the party tent to shreds, he fell to his knees, pushed down by a stunning wave of sound and force just as powerful as an avalanche. Suddenly there were bodies on the ground near him, covered in the same white dust and stained by vivid red blood. Even though his ears rang painfully, he heard screams and moaning, shouting and the words, "My God, my God." Now there was no sun, just an opaque drifting mass of dust laden with shards of glass. He found it painful to breathe. Dirt filled his mouth. He rubbed his eyes to dislodge the debris. It felt as though the grit was cutting the corneas of his eyes.

He stood up. He tried to shout Sarah's name, but he gagged. As he moved with his hands in front of him like a man in an unfamiliar black closet, he was propelled to his left by the second thunderous explosion. Something struck his left shoulder. At first it felt like a punch. He put his right hand on his shoulder, groping. He touched a tear in the fabric of his jacket and then the warm, sticky blood. Feeling a freezing flush of fear throughout his body, he tried to lift his arm. The pain was excruciating. He screamed. His own voice sounded as though he were underwater. He barely heard it.

He didn't want to fall again. He feared the people on the ground were all dead. He had a sense that if he went to the ground, he'd never rise again. He staggered like a damaged boxer but stayed on his feet.

In the aftermath of the second explosion there were no sounds: no screams, no sirens, no voices, not even the sounds of birds.

That eerie silence lasted only seconds. A hand grabbed his right arm. It was as if a lifeguard pulled him from a drowning downward spiral. He came face to face with Dick Maguire, the leader of his security detail. "Stay on your feet, Mayor. Stay on your feet. You can move. Follow me."

"Where's Sarah?"

"Keep moving, keep moving. Don't stop, don't stop."

"Where's Sarah?"

"Let's move, move."

They reached a security door at the edge of the roof garden. It had been blown open. In the stairwell the air was slightly clearer. Roland, who had been smothered by the swirling dust outside, began gulping for air. When he tried to sit on the steps, Maguire held him up against a wall. "Catch your breath, Mayor. We can't sit down. We've got to get out of here."

"What happened?"

"Forget it. Got to get out."

Roland Fortune was an athlete. He ran almost every weekend of the year in Sunday morning races in Central Park, along with thousands of other runners, and that strength, and his fear, supported him as he moved down the stairwell.

Two other members of Roland Fortune's security detail were waiting for him and Maguire when they burst through the emergency door on the museum's main floor. Screams, frantic movements, roiling clouds of dust. Centuries-old statues were toppled and broken, stained-glass windows shattered. Maguire and the other security men, bracing Roland Fortune up and hustling him along, were the only people with any sense of direction. They were headed to the rear wall—once all glass—that faced the lush greenery of the park's gorgeous nineteenth-century interior. Everyone else was moving erratically. They were dazed. There were bodies all over the floor. Fires were burning on marbled walls and floors.

And then there was a third explosion.

Every pane of glass on the rear walls shattered into countless shards. More and more dizzy and unfocused, Roland felt himself lifted through a gaping space in the wall. Outside, on the sloping lawn, the world seemed almost peaceful while he was eased gently onto the grass. Just as he passed out, he smelled the rich, moist odor of the grass and earth. And of blood, his own.

CHAPTER TWO

GINA CARBONE, THE commissioner of the New York City Police Department, began eating the rich antipasto her mother, that magician of food, had created for the family's annual start-of-summer get-together. Gina loved the texture of the cheese wrapped in carpaccio, the succulent slices of tomato, and the tang of the marinated artichokes.

The flagstone patio of the family house on Staten Island overlooked Fort Wadsworth, the Coast Guard base that resembled a small New England college campus and the glistening expanse of the Verrazano Narrows Bridge. As a very young but observant girl, she had spent hours watching the bridge being built. It seemed to evolve out of air, gradually materializing like a spider's web. Her father was an ironworker who spent six years of his life on the construction crews fashioning the stunning span that arcs like a filament for two miles between Staten Island and Brooklyn. They lived so close to the Staten Island side of the bridge that her father was able to walk to and from work each day, carrying his gunmetal-gray lunchbox. She still thought of him whenever she saw the graceful arc of the bridge.

"Auntie," her thirteen-year-old niece Elena said, "Mom says you had a date last night."

Gina was uncomfortable with the way Elena, her favorite niece, was changing. She had a small silver stud embedded in her left nostril. Gina had been tempted to tell her that it looked like snot, but she restrained herself. And now she noticed a tattoo in the shape of an eyelash on her niece's left wrist.

And, of course, Elena had taken to teasing about her unmarried aunt's love life.

"I did," Gina said.

"But you got home before midnight and he didn't stay. Like what's that about?"

Gina Carbone spent at least one weekend each month at this three-story house where she'd been raised. The third floor had been converted into a separate apartment for her, complete with a state-of-the-art communications center. Gina felt deeply comfortable in this familiar home, redolent with the smell of slow-cooked food and her older brother's cigars. She went to the early Sunday morning Mass at the Church of the Assumption, the granite church where her father had taken her every Sunday morning until she graduated from high school and enlisted in the Army.

"It was a first date, sweetie."

"You didn't even take him upstairs for a drink. I don't get that."

"Elena, you've been looking at too much TV. What channels are you watching?"

"How do you ever expect to get a man?"

Playfully, she raised her voice. "Linda," Gina called out to her sister, "you need to take your daughter to church."

Linda Kotowski—her estranged husband was a Polish plumber who had moved to Jersey City—laughed as she carried more food to the table. "What, and fuck up the nuns?"

Linda, a schoolteacher, was two years younger than Gina. She was a slender, physically softer version of her sister. There was no rivalry between them; they had always loved each other.

It was exactly 1:30 when Rocco Barbiglia, the lieutenant who traveled with her on the weekends, stepped through the door to the patio and said, in a subdued voice, "Commissioner? Can I see you for a second?"

Gina gave a playful slap to the side of Elena's head, as if saying *Wake up, kid*, and rose from the table. She walked past Rocco, who followed her to the edge of the patio. A refreshing sea breeze raised his thin hair.

"What's up, Rocco?" she asked. "Better be important. I was just about to tell my niece how to stay a virgin. I know a lot about that."

"There's been a big explosion at the Met."

"When?"

"Two minutes ago."

"Bombing?"

"For sure."

"People hurt?"

"Lots. The bombs went off on the front steps. A sunny Sunday afternoon. You know how it is, must've been hundreds of people sitting out there. Enjoying the sunlight."

"Bombs? More than one?"

"Three, four."

"Send out the Code Apache order."

Code Apache was the order to close every entrance and exit to Manhattan. There were many bridges, large and small, and four tunnels connecting the island of Manhattan to the Bronx, New Jersey, Queens, and Brooklyn. There were also helicopter landing pads in Manhattan and docks, wharves and ports. Code Apache closed them all. No one was to enter or leave the island. The idea was to seal Manhattan as thoroughly as a ship in the middle of the Atlantic. Only the president, the mayor, the police commissioner, the director of homeland security, the attorney general of the United States, and the chief of staff of the military could issue that order.

"And let's saddle up," Gina said.

A former Marine who had served in the Gulf War and still an agile man, Rocco jogged off the patio toward the unmarked van in which the mobile communication facilities were installed. At the same time Gina briskly walked toward the festive table on the patio. She was fearful and anxious. These were her brothers and sisters and their children and parents, all the people she loved in the world. The city was being attacked, people had been killed, and other assaults might soon happen. The possibilities of injury and death were endless, and there was no way, she knew, to predict whether the people she loved would be engulfed in it. And no way to protect them. Staten Island was in many ways a world unto itself, an island, but not immune.

"Hey, everybody, I just got some real bad news." It took a second for the friendly clamor around the table to subside. "Somebody's bombed the big museum. There are a lot of people hurt. I'm on my way into Manhattan."

*   *   *

Gina was proud of the way she had organized the police department in the three years since her surprise appointment by Roland Fortune. She had spent thirteen years in the Army, first as an enlisted soldier and then as an officer. She had learned principles of management that enabled her to increase responsiveness in the police force into a more military precision. Only a few commissioners before her had ever served in the military. Most of them had been political appointees, and a few had served as chiefs of the police departments in other major cities. She was the first native of Staten Island, and the first woman, to command the NYPD. When she saw that the traffic was already suspended on the two-mile-long

Verrazano Narrows Bridge as her convoy reached it three minutes after leaving her family home, she was gratified. At least the first step of what would be a long day had fallen into place perfectly, just as she had planned it.

Rocco, crouched in the jump seat across from Gina, handed her the secure phone, saying, "It's Billy."

"Talk to me, Billy," she said.

Billy O'Connell, one of the five deputy commissioners, was on duty in the secret underground crisis command center at the corner of West 14th Street and Jones Street in the Meatpacking District, once the place where meat and pork were distributed to city restaurants and grocery chains. The Meatpacking District had for many years been legendary for its complete control by the Gambino family. That grip had long been removed. The district was now best known for some of its new state-of-the-art, expensive apartment buildings and a variety of drug-happy clubs with deafening music for teenagers and trendy men and women who danced all night to hip-hop and rap music.

The main entrance to the center, called Fortress America by those who knew it, was through a former meat warehouse that, at street level, appeared to be a boarded-up after-hours club, Le Zinc. It was a still seedy area of the city where no one would have expected to find a state-of-the-art security center inside a nineteenth-century warehouse.

"The area around the museum's not secure yet," Billy said.

"How many units are on the way?"

"Six more squad cars. And five crews from the 19th Precinct."

Gina knew she had to stay steady and focused. But, as she also recognized, she was afraid. From the mid-span of the bridge, she looked out at the glittering expanse of New York Harbor and lower Manhattan, one of the most remarkable sights in the world. The day was absolutely clear, just as 9/11 had been. What was it about beautiful days and explosions? The Statue of Liberty, the office buildings that fronted Battery Park, the vast expanse of the Hudson River: the scene looked like a postcard or a montage in a romantic comedy. All that was different now was a diaphanous tower of smoke rising from the museum six miles away.

"What's the status of Homeland Security?"

"Alerted. They're closing down the airports."

"Coast Guard, State Police, National Guard, Port Authority?"

"All alerted." Billy's Irish accent was even more intense than usual, a sign of anxiety and adrenaline.

And finally she asked the question she had wanted to ask first. "What about the mayor?"

She had been invited to Roland Fortune's birthday party on the roof garden of the museum. She'd called to tell him that one of her nieces was being confirmed that morning at the Church of the Assumption. That was not true. She avoided Manhattan society parties like a plague.

"Our people are telling me he's dead. Not confirmed."

In the far distance on this endlessly clear day, she saw two police helicopters, gleaming flecks of bright metal, suspended like toys above the tower of thickening smoke.

CHAPTER THREE

GABRIEL HAUSER'S ROUTINE on Sunday mornings was to walk with Oliver, his gentle collie, through the attractive streets in the neighborhood near the museum between Fifth Avenue and Madison Avenue. This was a particularly delicious Sunday morning. The London plane trees lining the quiet streets were lush, the air was sharp and clear, and a breeze shook the newly mature leaves, casting crisp and intricate patterns of light and shade on the sidewalks.

The morning was also delicious because he had slept for twelve hours. He worked fifteen hours every day except Sunday as an emergency room doctor at Mount Sinai Hospital, a cluster of old and modern buildings directly across from Central Park on Fifth Avenue between 97th Street and 101st Street. Because it was close to East Harlem, the emergency room was always hectic on Saturday nights: men, women, and even children who had been shot or knifed or who had overdosed on Valium, Xanax, Percocet, Vicodin, OxyContin, and other opioids, the new street drugs of the twenty-first century.

As he walked on 82nd Street, he could see at the end of the block the colorful crowds on the grand steps of the museum. There were wagons with bright umbrellas where food was sold, the New York fare of hot dogs, salted pretzels, and Italian ices. The food wagons were all aluminum. Their sides glinted in the bright daylight. From the heights of the museum's walls immense banners displaying the names of artists and exhibits were suspended. They undulated in the cleansing breeze. Gabriel wondered if he would, in fact, find among the hundreds of men, women, and children on the museum steps the dark man who had sent him in one of his many text messages that single indistinct picture of himself.

The first explosion came from one of the food wagons. It was a flash at least as bright as the sun. A wall of sound and debris blew toward him, a dirty tsunami of dust and small flying objects of glass, broken stones, and flecks of metal. Still clutching Oliver's leash, he lifted his hands to shield his face and felt the stinging of debris. Oliver wailed, hurt and bewildered.

Gabriel lowered his hands as soon as the hail of small, fragmented objects swept by him. He was able to see the steps of the museum. Bodies were on fire as if self-immolated. The remnants of the food wagon were burning. The banners along the heights of the museum were tattered. A sheet of fire flared on the waters of the long fountain in front of the museum even though, incredibly, the water continued to rise up. Water couldn't quench the flames.

Even though he felt it immediately, he couldn't see the source of the second explosion. His view was blocked by the apartment building at the corner of 82nd Street and Fifth that faced the museum. But he did see another nuclear-style wave of smoke, dust, and debris rushing down Fifth Avenue from the source of the explosion. More bodies in flame, propelled by the new explosion, were littered across the steps. He thought he could hear the crying and shouts of voices interwoven with the bell-like concussive ringing in his ears.

He pulled Oliver into the doorway of a brownstone. Although the dog was not visibly hurt, his trembling and crying were intense. Gabriel double-knotted the leash to the iron railing and tried to soothe him. The dog stared at him with bewildered, hurt eyes. He loved the devoted dog but knew he had to act.

Gabriel ran toward the museum. He had nothing with him to deliver aid to anyone, but he did have his knowledge and his experience as a combat-trained emergency doctor. Just as he reached Fifth Avenue, a third explosion, this one at the north end of the museum, blew him to the ground. He quickly jumped to his feet, like a football player knocked down and immediately rising, and ran across Fifth Avenue to the wide plaza and steps. He saw cars and buses in flames on the avenue and sidewalk. On top of one of the double-decker London-style tourist buses, passengers, mainly the Asian tourists who had visited the city in the thousands over the last six years, were thrown against the railings as it careened down the avenue before toppling over, spilling people onto the street like damaged toys.

He turned his attention to the injured on the nearby steps. Within an area of ten feet there were at least seven bodies, including two children torn to pieces like rag dolls. One of the adults, a woman whose face was ripped apart, appeared to be breathing, but when he knelt over her it was clear she was dead. In his two years as an Army surgeon in Iraq and Afghanistan, he had learned to abandon the dead immediately and seek out the wounded, like Dracula hunting hungrily for fresh blood. He could never help the dead, but he might be able to help the living.

A man lying near the first exploded wagon was moaning. His left arm below the elbow was limp, obviously broken, and hemorrhaging. Gabriel knew that the first essential act with even a mortally injured person was to give assurance—in Iraq he had come to call it "placebo hope." As he took off his shirt to make a tourniquet of one of the sleeves, he leaned over the man. He was sweating, as was Gabriel. On the man's face, just below his left eye and spreading just above his heavy beard from his cheek to his left ear, was a vivid birthmark in the shape of Japan. He was clearly an Arab, probably one of the men who worked at the first exploded food wagon. Somehow, he looked familiar to Gabriel, a vague image in the recesses of Gabriel's anxious mind.

They were within inches of each other, their eyes totally engaged. "You'll be fine," Gabriel said. The man exhaled the breath of the near dead.

But Gabriel knew he could be saved. He twisted the sleeve of his own torn shirt around the man's sinewy upper arm. The bleeding lessened. On his left wrist the man wore a metallic bracelet. It was thick, surprisingly large and silvery, with chain-like links, and sticky with blood. It was flexible enough to remove, and Gabriel did that because it could further aggravate the wounds. He slipped it over the man's knuckles. Gabriel put it into his pocket, thinking he might keep it safe for this injured stranger, a man he knew he was unlikely ever to see again. It was odd, Gabriel thought, that this Arabic man, probably a Muslim, wore an ornament. The Koran forbade it, and in his years in Iraq and Afghanistan, he had never seen a native with even a ring on his finger.

With his practiced hands, he then probed under the man's torn clothing for other wounds. He felt blood on the area above the left kidney and then, probing further, he touched a sharp point from which the bleeding came. He pulled, removing a shard of the aluminum casing of the food wagon. It was so large that when he tossed it away it made a distinctive noise, like a dropped nail, on the stone.

Holding his hand over the wound, Gabriel noticed in the midst of the debris around them an intact bottle of water. He opened the bottle, poured some water into his hand and washed the man's face with it. Responding, the injured man opened his eyes wider and with his right hand held Gabriel's wrist as if in gratitude. Gabriel put the bottle to the man's trembling parched lips, and he drank.

Gabriel propped the man's head on a fragment of loose concrete. Then he heard a woman's voice nearby. She was moaning, "Help me, God. Help me."

He did.

*   *   *

Later that day, after the security footage was retrieved from the debris, the image of Gabriel Hauser wandering alone among the dead and injured was broadcast around the world. By that time the police knew his name. *Gabriel Hauser, the Angel of Life.*

CHAPTER FOUR

As GINA CARBONE's convoy approached 79th Street and Madison Avenue, the streets were wild. Hundreds of people were out, looking in the direction of the museum as dense smoke billowed above it and the elegant nearby apartment buildings. Traffic was at a complete standstill, a hopeless gridlock, a virtual parking lot, and she and her staff left the convoy and walked three blocks uptown to the public school building, PS 6, that occupied the entire block fronting Madison Avenue from 81st Street to 82nd Street. She had ordered that the building be taken over as her command center. There was so much confusion on the streets that no one seemed to notice that the commissioner of the New York City Police Department and a phalanx of uniformed officers carrying M-16s and other evil-looking assault weapons were steadily walking through the chaotic crowds. Some people in the crowd with cell phones held aloft were recording her.

She made her way to a classroom on the northern side of the building. She was able to look down 82nd Street toward the museum. Through the leafy trees she had a glimpse of Fifth Avenue and a portion of the museum's steps. Using binoculars, she saw uniformed officers setting up barriers and beyond them what at first looked like multiple cigarette butts scattered on the steps.

They were charred bodies.

Gina Carbone had served in the Gulf War and from helicopters had seen the bodies of dead Iraqi soldiers scattered on the desert.

She had no sense of connection with them. But now she realized that the smoking smudges were people just recently killed by shrapnel and fire. Part of her reputation was built on the perception that she was cool, unflappable, and tough, but she found herself audibly inhaling as though she was on the brink of screaming. *These fuckers,* she thought, *how did they get here?*

Donna Thompson, a black police captain, was waiting for her. Crisp and efficient, she had a sheet of paper on which she had written the information she knew Gina needed.

"How many dead people have I got?"

"Fifty at least," Thompson calmly said. "We've only just now started letting EMT people through the barrier."

"Why so long?"

"We had reports that there might be more bombers inside the museum itself."

"How many wounded?"

"Not many so far. Ten. There are more likely more dead than wounded."

Gina was an NYPD sergeant on 9/11. She had arrived in lower Manhattan six hours after the towers fell. At old St. Paul's Church on lower Broadway, a church surrounded by a cemetery with gravestones from the 1600s and 1700s, doctors and medics were waiting to care for the wounded. It became chillingly obvious as the hours passed that there were very few wounded, just as there were very few intact bodies. Doctors and nurses stood around uselessly. Soon the church became a rest station with water and food for the people working at the scorched place where the towers had collapsed.

"What do we know about how many people were at the museum when this happened?"

"One of the security guards was at a coffee shop on a break. He said that on a pretty summer day they could have as many as three hundred people on the steps, sitting on the benches on the plaza, looking at the pictures and other stuff in the outdoor stalls, just hanging around. Not to mention tourists on the buses, those double-decker kinds. There were five tour buses lined up on the avenue."

Gina was making notes on a pad of paper. She wrote columns of numbers as she listened.

"How about inside?"

"This guy is a guard in the Temple of Dendur on the northern end of the museum. Part of his job is to count as best he can the number of visitors in the area on one of those old-fashioned hand-held clickers. He had a headcount of 350 when he left for his break. Pretty primitive, but at least it's some info."

Gina thought about the slanting expanses of panes of glass that encased the Temple of Dendur where Egyptian tombs and statues were displayed. The shattered glass would have been hurled to the sloping lawn at unimaginable velocity. There must have been sunbathers on a gorgeous day there. Even a fragment of glass could maim or kill. When she wrote down the number 350 on her pad the lead point of her pencil broke. She was that tense.

"And what about the rest of the museum?"

"At any one time on a Sunday there are as many as a thousand people inside, more on a rainy day."

"Anything else?"

"Sure. Every window facing Fifth Avenue in all the big apartment buildings was blown out from 86th Street down to 79th. All of the glass blown inward. There are dead and injured people there. We don't have easy access. They're Fifth Avenue apartment buildings, after all. The security system in every one of these rich people's buildings is better than the Pentagon. Besides, God knows how many of them were at their houses in the Hamptons on the weekend."

Mahopac Public Library
668 Route 6
Mahopac, NY 10541

FIC
OAT
326 2200

Some of the most famous people in the world lived in those buildings, the most desirable in Manhattan, with unobstructed views of the museum and all of Central Park. For the first time that morning, Gina gave some thought to the type of mind that could envision and execute all this. These were people who knew that large concentrations of vulnerable men, women, and children would be clustered together on a day of the week when the city was relaxed and festive, the numbers of police at reduced levels, and vigilance taken down a notch.

And whoever had done this knew the city especially well for another reason: not only would the massacre kill and maim many tourists from around the country and the world, but it was bound to kill and maim rich and famous people in the most expensive buildings in the world. Jackie Onassis had lived for years in a building directly across the avenue from the Met. The bombings on 9/11 killed thousands of innocent people but very few famous ones. The World Trade Center was a place where most of the people worked as clerks and technicians for big brokerage firms and government agencies. Although it was a huge, spectacular target of opportunity, it was not the place where members of the power elite were likely to be killed.

"And what about the roof garden?"

"Not sure, no word."

"I know there were people up there for a party."

"There are trees and plants up there," Captain Thompson said. "It's all still burning, like a forest fire."

Gina Carbone didn't like pretty boys, but Roland Fortune was more than a pretty boy. She first met him three days after he was elected mayor. He had campaigned in part on the need to replace the top people in the police department. She was at least three rungs below that level. He interviewed several men and two women who ranked higher than Gina and who were better educated and with more years of service. But he had responded well to her and five days later he held a televised press conference announcing her appointment in which he described her as a gritty, streetwise, brilliant officer who had vision, integrity, and drive. In private he never tried to charm her. He was a patient listener, often, but not always, endorsing anything she recommended. She admired him. The thought that he was blown to shreds or burned to death unnerved her.

She was on the verge of asking about the physical damage to the museum. But a hand touched her shoulder. "The president's on the line."

She took the secure cell phone. She covered her left ear to avoid any distractions and turned to stare at the elementary school's undersized basketball court. There was an odor of varnish and scuffed sneakers. The gym was hot. There was no air conditioning in early summer and there were too many people in the room. The grimy windows were reinforced with steel mesh.

"Commissioner?" The voice was easily recognizable. Andrew Carter was the most famous person in the world.

"Yes, sir."

"Tell me what's going on. Like everybody else on the planet I only know as much as what I see on CNN."

She wanted to sound authoritative and controlled. "We have as many as three hundred people dead. An unknown number of wounded. I gave the order a minute ago to let our emergency people enter the secure area. We were concerned that additional bombers might still be on the scene. I don't want a situation like 9/11 when the rescuers blindly go running in to help the victims only to become victims themselves."

"Understood."

"The city's locked down, the subways are stopped, tunnels and bridges are closed, police boats are in the rivers, and airports in lockdown."

"What about the air?"

"At least ten police helicopters are up. They haven't been challenged."

"There's a contingent of fighter jets five minutes from the city."

Fighter jets? She restrained the impulse to tell the President of the United States that fighter jets were about as useful as camels. She needed real troops on every corner. This was guerilla war, not Star Wars.

He asked, "Are there other places up there where large groups congregate on the weekends?"

The president, she remembered, was from Los Angeles. Obviously he knew nothing about Manhattan on a summer weekend.

"We have huge concentrations of people on days like this at Battery Park, Riverside Park, Washington Square Park, Times Square. I have units at or en route to all those places and others."

"Do you folks have any information as to who's responsible for this?"

"At the moment, sir, the blunt truth is we have no idea. There was no more chatter or negative information than we have had for years, just the usual low and sustained hum of danger. Do your people have anything?"

"I'm getting information on that."

Gina thought about all the billions of dollars spent on the worldwide apparatus of national security since 9/11, and the president didn't have any information as to the men who carried out this devastating attack. In fact, she knew more than he did. Suddenly she felt impatient, eager to get back to her work, and annoyed that the president was distracting her from the real things she had to accomplish.

She said, "This is a huge failure. I have hundreds of people, maybe more, dead and wounded on my turf and on my watch. I'm going to find out why my people, the FBI, Homeland Security, the CIA, all those security honchos, had no clue this was coming. But right now, sir, I need to organize relief efforts, make sure hospitals all over this island are ready to accept the wounded, and guard against the possibility that there are other lunatics out there right now about to carry out more attacks."

"I appreciate, Commissioner, that you have work to do. We all have work to do."

"Is there anything else I can tell you right now?" She knew she could be abrasive. She detected the impatience in her voice.

"I understand something might have happened to the mayor. We tried to reach him. We were told he may be a victim."

"He was at a party on the roof garden of the museum when the explosions happened. I've had a report from one of our helicopters that there are many dead people on the roof. There are fires still burning up there. There's a lot of foliage up there, plantings of rare trees and shrubs. We've got no information as to whether the mayor was one of the victims."

"That leaves you with a huge responsibility, Commissioner. You're now in charge, at least for the time being. You can't let too much time pass before you have a press conference to reassure the public."

"I'm more interested in telling the public what is going on, what the facts are, what needs to be done. All of that is not necessarily reassuring."

The president was impatient, too, not pleased with the brusque local Italian girl.

"Do your best."

The man is a candy-ass, Gina thought. "Sure thing," she said.

And she hit the "end" button on the cell phone before he did on his.

CHAPTER FIVE

"I'm not staying," Roland Fortune said. "Let's get that IV out right now."

The excruciating pain in his shoulder and back had lessened since the moment he walked through the emergency room door at Mount Sinai, the hospital nearest the museum. He was surrounded by policemen, some of whom had guns drawn. He was the first wounded person to arrive at the hospital, at exactly 1:45 p.m. Covered in blood and grass stains and dirt from the ground where he had fallen at the rear of the museum, he had regained consciousness in the ambulance that raced through Central Park. As he lay on the stretcher in the rocking vehicle, he'd felt the initial surge of relief from pain when one of the medics injected him with morphine.

"Mr. Mayor, you've lost significant quantities of blood," Dr. David Edelstein, a sober man with the weight and presence of a rabbi, told Roland. "Your hemoglobin is low, you're so impaired by painkillers that you'll have trouble walking on your own, and you aren't likely to be able to hold any press conferences or to act in a coherent, focused way. There's a significant risk of infection. You need to be treated."

"Listen: I was hit by a stone, not shrapnel. I was cut, not shot. You run a hospital. I run a city. I can't lie down in a hospital because my shoulder hurts when there is complete chaos out there. There are thousands of people who think I'm dead. Unless they can see me and see that I'm alive and functioning, there will still be this alarming distraction that the leader of the City of New York is dead."

Edelstein's expression didn't change. "I can't worry about that. You and you alone are my patient right now, not the population of the City of New York." He paused. "If you leave, you'll be doing that against medical advice and you will have to sign a form that says precisely that, just like anybody else who walks out of here without the approval of a doctor."

"I genuinely appreciate the concern, but I feel strong and alert enough to step up to do the things I'm supposed to do. I can't live with myself secluded in a hospital bed while there are fires still burning ten blocks downtown from here and the dead are still being counted."

At a signal from Edelstein, two male nurses expertly disassembled the tubes of the IVs to which Roland Fortune was attached. They then placed his damaged shoulder and arm in a sling, fastening it to the fresh clothes that had been brought to him from Gracie Mansion, the spacious Georgian mansion overlooking the East River in which New York City mayors lived during their terms. As they worked on him, he felt a resurgence of the pain and asked for another Vicodin. One of the male nurses placed the pill in his mouth, like a priest giving communion, and he swallowed it without water. Just the act of taking the pill brought him increasing levels of relief from the pain. Like a drug addict worried about not having enough, he put a handful of Vicodin in his pocket.

He watched the television set affixed to the wall just below the ceiling as Gina Carbone began to speak to the world. She stood in bright sunlight on the sidewalk in front of PS 6. "We now know that six hundred thirty-six people are dead," she announced. "There are at least ninety-five men, women, and children in hospitals throughout the city who are wounded in varying degrees, most with burns, many in life-threatening condition."

Gina Carbone had a commanding presence. She was calm and measured. She was an attractive woman. Her raven hair was pulled back from her forehead and tied at the back of her neck. Her well-balanced features and the graceful muscularity of her body gave her the look of an athlete. Roland was grateful for the firmness she conveyed, and he found her Staten Island-tinged accent reassuring, a home-bred New Yorker obviously in command.

She said, "At this point, we're not certain what the final number of dead and wounded will be. We are still involved in search and rescue operations inside the museum. So far we have located at least fifteen wounded inside the building, which, as many of you know, has dozens of separate galleries. We consider it still a place of high security concerns and danger. Too many evil, cowardly, and dangerous men have too many places to hide and opportunities to carry out more evil."

The scene on CNN shifted to the museum's steps. The front of the museum was profoundly scarred. The windows were blown away. The massive stone façade, that heavy nineteenth-century fortress-style front, had huge gouges. For more than a century two immense blocks of stone had rested above the entrance. There had once been plans to sculpt them into neoclassical figures or lions' heads but that had never happened. Now they were toppled.

Incredibly, there was still bright midafternoon sunshine, as on any limpid day in June. And the long oval fountains still gushed water into the sunlight even though flames rose from the water.

The camera shifted back to Gina Carbone. "While no single life is more important than any other, I can now reliably tell you that Mayor Roland Fortune is alive. There have been rumors all afternoon that the leader of the city, who was attending an event at the museum when these despicable bombings happened, was among the casualties. He did sustain what are described as serious but not life-threatening wounds, and he will certainly recover."

Roland's attention was suddenly and fully arrested by the question he heard from one of the reporters. "Do you know anything about the condition of the mayor's partner, Sarah Gordan?"

Roland had repeatedly asked Irv Rothstein, who had arrived at the hospital from his apartment on the West Side an hour after Roland was admitted, where Sarah Hewitt-Gordan was. Rothstein repeatedly had said, "We don't know."

"The confirmed names of the dead are being posted right now on the city's website. Ms. Hewitt-Gordan was with the mayor at the museum event. Unfortunately, her name is on the list of the dead."

Roland Fortune felt his bones turn instantly to water. He couldn't stand. He sat down on the bed and leaned forward, his hands covering his face. Except for the voice of Gina Carbone still speaking steadily, matter-of-factly, there wasn't a sound in the room. When Roland took his hands from his face, he looked at Irv Rothstein.

"Did you know about this?"

"We weren't certain."

"Is Gina certain?"

"She should have told us, Roland, before she went public with it."

There was a sixty-second pause. Irv had from time to time counseled Roland to express more emotion when he was on television or speaking to large groups of people. Irv felt that Roland projected class and intelligence and control under pressure, but not enough *rachmonis*, the Yiddish word for passion from the gut.

Suddenly Roland, lithe and tall, stood up. There were tears on his face. He wiped them away. In a clear voice, he said, "Let's get moving."

CHAPTER SIX

THERE WERE ALREADY thirty patients in the emergency room at Mount Sinai when Gabriel Hauser arrived. Men, women, and children lay on stretchers or on blankets on the floors in the hallways. With shades drawn, the emergency room's cubicles were filled to capacity with the most seriously wounded. He rushed through the ER toward the locker room where doctors changed from civilian clothes to white or blue scrubs, the baggy uniforms of their trade. He saw five of the dead lined on the floor against a wall. Three of them were uncovered. Except for the fact that they were in the torn remnants of the casual clothes of Sunday tourists—the thick-soled walking shoes favored by Europeans, Abercrombie & Fitch safari pants and t-shirts with names and slogans stenciled on them—the bodies were identical to the torn bodies of the dead soldiers in Iraq and Afghanistan: ripped faces, torsos with livid holes, legs cut to the exposed bones.

In the locker room, Gabriel swiftly shed the clothes he'd put on four hours earlier for his Sunday walk with Oliver. He had managed to call Cameron Kennedy Dewar, his partner, to ask him to retrieve Oliver and take him home. He told Cam to stay away from the area around the museum where rumors still swept that more explosives were planted somewhere in the vicinity.

The clothes he had worn were as bloody as the clothes of the wounded he had treated on the horrific steps. He dropped them to the floor in front of his locker as he put on the immaculate scrubs.

His pants were unusually heavy: the thick bracelet he'd removed from his first, badly injured patient was still in his left pocket. Gabriel remembered that the wounded man hadn't carried a wallet. He put his own wallet, a comb, the keys to the apartment, and the bracelet he'd removed from the first wounded person he treated into the roomy pockets of his scrubs. And then he trotted back to the nearby emergency room.

More wounded had arrived in the ER in the five minutes Gabriel needed to change and wash his hands and face. The level and intensity of noise had escalated with the new arrivals. Doctors and nurses were shouting in the din of the cries and moans of the injured. He grabbed the arm of a male nurse who leaned against the nurse's station as if catching his breath, and tugged him toward an injured woman who was in the stretcher closest to him. The ER was now so completely overwhelmed that it was no longer possible to give priority to the more severely injured. It was a random choice. Everyone looked grievously wounded.

In three hours he treated at least thirty people. This was an endurance contest, his body fed on adrenaline, his mind tempered by experience and good judgment. He had spent hundreds of hours in war treating the injured, but there had been only one three-hour period when he was confronted with as many injured as this.

Just as he was finally preparing to take a break outside in the crisp afternoon air of Central Park across Fifth Avenue from the hospital, he turned to one more patient. It was the man he'd first treated on the museum's steps. The birthmark that spanned the area below his left eye to the edge of his beard made him instantly recognizable. There was, too, something else about the face. Fleetingly, Gabriel thought the face had the vaguely familiar features of a man he had seen in the grainy cell phone picture he had intended to use to meet a man he believed was named Silas Nasar, an Afghan. Gabriel had been so engrossed by other injured people that he hadn't once thought about this man. Now it was as though he had come across a person from his long-ago past. And Gabriel was relieved: if the man was still held in the emergency room and had not yet been taken to an operating room or a better-equipped unit elsewhere in the hospital then his injuries were less serious than they had seemed when Gabriel cared for him on the museum steps.

"How do you feel?" Gabriel touched the hand into which the IV needle had been inserted.

The man's lips were still parched. His black eyes were focused on Gabriel. He whispered in clear English, "Pain, the pain is awful."

"We'll give you more painkillers."

"And water, please."

Gabriel remembered that he'd placed water from a random plastic bottle to this man's lips hours earlier. He took a cup of water with a straw from a nearby tray and placed the straw between the man's lips. He sucked greedily.

Finally Gabriel asked, "Do you remember me?"

The intense eyes kept their focus on Gabriel. Although the man didn't speak, Gabriel had a sense that somewhere in that pool of pain there was recognition. Gabriel gripped the man's right hand, trying to give reassurance, comfort. He took the heavy bracelet out of his pocket and gently fastened it to the man's right wrist. He had never imagined that he would be able to return it.

The patients who had arrived with no names, no wallets, no handbags, no knapsacks, and no passports were identified by numbers and letters written in magic markers on their foreheads. Someone had handwritten *Patient X52* on the dark man's forehead.

"You'll be all right," Gabriel said. "I promise."

Patient X52 squeezed Gabriel's hand powerfully. Gabriel, who was not certain he knew Patient X52's name, didn't erase the magic marker lettering and replace it with the words *Silas Nasar*.

CHAPTER SEVEN

GINA CARBONE GAVE the order for the eighteen arrests. Most of the men were in Queens. Four were in Washington Heights in Manhattan. They were selected from the secret Hit List that the police department had covertly maintained during the three years she had served as commissioner. No one outside the department knew that there was a Hit List, and only ten other officers in the department knew about it. Gina hadn't asked for any legal opinion from the staff lawyers assigned to the department for one simple reason: she was certain that any legal opinion would conclude that the creation and maintenance of the list was illegal, that it involved racial profiling, and that it entailed violations of Fourth Amendment rights since the homes and apartments of these men had been secretly examined without search warrants and sophisticated surveillance devices installed in them without any judge's authorization. Roland Fortune knew nothing about it. She had created the Hit List so that she could act quickly if something catastrophic happened in the city she loved, the only city she really knew. She had an innate distrust of Homeland Security, the FBI, the Defense Department, and the CIA. Even of Roland Fortune when it came to this kind of issue. He was in no way a warrior.

The men who were arrested were not brought to Central Booking in Manhattan or the police precincts or Rikers Island for processing and arraignment, the standard routine after any arrest. There was no plan to bring them before judges or assigned lawyers or told what charges they faced. They were all taken in unmarked police vehicles to a detention center embedded in one of the vast, abandoned piers that extended into the East River. The cops who made the arrests had been trained for swift seizure of the men on the list, which was constantly revised as new information developed, and her special secret unit consistently monitored the men on the list to be certain where they were in the event they had to be taken down.

"Any of them cooperating?" Gina asked Roger Davidson.

She and Davidson were in the small girls' locker room in PS 6. The entrance to the room, which smelled of disinfectant, was closed and two sergeants stood outside. There was no way anyone could hear the conversation between Davidson and her. Davidson was a retired CIA agent who was nominally the head of the NYPD's Operation Outreach, the benign name Gina created for the Hit List unit. Like every other member of the unit, Davidson posed as a civilian employee of the department. He was designated as a community liaison officer, an absurd title for a man who in his long career had killed fifty-five people.

"Not yet. But one of them seems to be having second thoughts."

"Which one?"

"The guy who owns the food wagons."

Gina already knew that it was not suicide bombers in civilian clothes who detonated the explosions. The sources of the explosions were three food wagons in front of the museum. One of the department's forensics investigators had reported to her that the wagons were crammed with explosives; even the metal poles that supported the festival-like umbrellas were stuffed with explosives. Someone using a remote device had triggered them—one, two, three. Mohammed Butt owned a business in Queens that provided hundreds of food wagons to street vendors. He had become rich.

"What is he saying?"

"He must be a make-believe lawyer. So far he's saying he wants to get a lawyer, make a plea deal and get immunity."

Gina rolled her eyes. "What a fucking world we live in. A plea deal? Immunity? The fucker must spend his time watching lawyer television shows when he isn't planning jihad and making millions off of no-bid city contracts."

Although Davidson had spent many hours in windowless conference rooms with Gina Carbone, he had never once heard her swear. It added a new and welcome dimension to her.

"What do you want to do with him?" he asked.

"Pull his balls off and make him eat them unless he talks. At least pull his balls off."

Davidson returned her taut smile. Imitating a line Richard Nixon once spoke, he said, "That would be wrong." Like Nixon, he didn't mean it.

Gina laughed, her first laugh since the sunny hours on the patio on Staten Island with her family so many hours ago.

"Promise him anything and everything," she said. "Write it down for him so that he thinks he has a contract. See whether that works."

"And if it doesn't?"

"Be creative."

Davidson gave her a knowing look. He had a license from her to use the skills he had developed during his years in the CIA interrogating Arab men in secret dark prisons around the world. He said, "Creativity is the lifeblood of this business."

"Did you pick up everybody on the Hit List?"

"Except one."

"Who?"

"Silas Nasar. He's a U.S. citizen. In fact, he was born in Bayonne. Only native-born on the list."

"Why is he on the list?"

"I told you a month ago. Don't you remember? He's traveled to Pakistan six times, five times after 9/11, once before. He claimed to have long-lost family members there."

"Remind me. We had to have some other reason to put him on the list. Takes a lot to qualify."

"He owns a big electronics store in Queens. He has a fixation on communication equipment. Not just cell phones and pagers, but GPS systems and tracking devices. He loves innovative stuff, like tracking devices in candy bars. Things that send and get messages and let people know where you are. Jewelry, watches with tiny communicating devices. Even bracelets; my ex-wife would love to be a customer."

"Which one is he?" she asked.

Davidson took out his iPad and delicately touched the illuminated screen. For a large man who had killed people with his own hands, he had unusually long fingers as graceful as a pianist's. His fingers floated over the bright graphics. A picture as vivid as life appeared. It was Silas Nasar. It was a far clearer, better-defined picture than the one on Gabriel Hauser's cell phone.

"Hell of a birthmark," Gina said when she saw the seahorse-shaped blemish.

Davidson said, "He shouldn't be hard to find."

"Then go fucking find him," Gina said.

CHAPTER EIGHT

THE SILENCE WAS strange. Six hours earlier, as he was carried to the blasted rear windows of the museum, there were sounds everywhere—piercing screams, otherworldly moans, out-of-control fire alarms, the crunching of glass and stone under foot. Flowing cataracts of water from the fire prevention system, useless in the chaos. He remembered that he had felt submerged in noise, as if he were drowning.

Now the museum was quiet. There was still beautiful sunlight on its scarred, ochre-colored surfaces at five in the afternoon. The early summer air was gentle. The trees in Central Park were lush. Above the upper edge of the museum a vivid half-moon shined in the blue daylight sky.

Roland Fortune had given thousands of press conferences, he was gifted with the ability to be fluid and informative, often funny, and he experienced some of that hit of anticipation as he walked toward the microphones at the podium at the base of the museum's front steps. He knew this was the most important press conference of his life. Ever since he had joined Gina Carbone and Harlan Lazarus, the Secretary of Homeland Security who had arrived by helicopter just fifteen minutes before Roland reached PS 6, he'd been in increasing levels of pain but hadn't taken any more Vicodin. He didn't want to talk to the world with any slurring or hesitation in his voice or sluggishness in his appearance. He would rather have an edge of pain to keep himself alert. He was in a fresh, beautifully tailored suit.

"This is a day of outrage," he began. His voice had its usual clarity and he was alert enough not to read from notes. "The toll in human blood, suffering, and loss is immense. By the latest count, there are, we believe, 975 men, women, and children dead. One hundred and fifty-three wounded, many of them critically. It's certain that there are dead or wounded people inside the museum, an area we are sifting carefully because of fears that explosive devices may still be implanted there. Thus far, one first responder has been killed when debris in the Temple of Dendur collapsed on her."

Across Fifth Avenue the green and red canopies over the entrances to the apartment buildings were shredded like confetti. Immense American flags were already suspended from many of the buildings, a symbol of grief, strength, and defiance that had spontaneously ornamented the city in the days and weeks after 9/11.

"This great city has again been the victim of a vicious, cowardly assault. This is an unspeakable act of violence that is an affront not just to this city and this nation but to the world. It has taken place on a glorious Sunday when men, women, and children were simply enjoying themselves and the gift of life on an early summer afternoon. I will never rank the viciousness of terrorist attacks. The recent coordinated assaults in Paris were a despicable horror, as were the attacks in London and Madrid after 9/11. At this point, as this monument to civilization still smolders behind us, we have no clear information as to the people or organizations responsible for this carnage. We do know, however, that ISIS, with its social media resources, is claiming responsibility, just as it did in the Paris assaults."

Roland gazed directly into the main camera. There could have been over a hundred million people around the world watching him. "There are things that the toll of horror can't convey. The city and the world have been wounded. People from every continent were here, in this great meeting place of the globe. We believe that men and women from at least twenty countries are among the dead. We grieve for every one of them, for their families, and their friends."

He paused. "Now let's talk about security. More than thirty thousand law enforcement personnel, most of them members of the New York Police Department under the remarkable command of Commissioner Gina Carbone, are deployed throughout every borough of the City of New York. We are executing well-developed and frequently rehearsed containment, control, and retaliation strategies. Although there have been no arrests so far, I can tell the people who are responsible for this that there is no escape from this glorious island of Manhattan, and they will be found and punished."

Nearby a siren began to wail. Roland Fortune tensed up, as if threatened. The reporters glanced in the direction from which the sound was coming, six blocks uptown. Even though there were no spectators on the sidewalk since the area had been cleared, there were some people looking out of the smashed windows of the Fifth Avenue apartment buildings. Roland noticed that they, too, glanced toward the source of the sound.

Roland knew he couldn't let the siren distract him and that he could not hesitate or stumble or appear frightened. He continued, "The lockdown of Manhattan will continue certainly until tomorrow morning, although how long depends on circumstances we can't now foresee. There are centers throughout Manhattan where those who are stranded can receive food and shelter. We have counselors at those sites who are trained in treating shock and fear and grief. Plans for this, as for many other aspects of our response, have been in place and constantly revised for several years. Some of that response you are seeing as the day and night unfold; others you can't see but they are important to our safety."

Roland turned briefly to the magnificent, damaged building behind him. "What you see behind us is one of the monuments not just of New York but of the entire world's civilization. Despite all the scarring you see today, it remains intact, and it will endure. So, too, this most magnificent of all cities in the world. It has been assailed because of its greatness, because of the hope it has always represented for the world, and it will recover from the atrocities of this day."

Irv Rothstein gave him the covert signal—a hand cupped over his left ear that a third base coach might give to a runner on second base—that Roland should wind up the conference.

Roland had long ago come to rely on Irv and focused again on the camera. "Thank you all for being here. We will keep you continuously updated as new information becomes available. Again, this has been a terrible day for this city, the nation, and the world. But it is certain that we will recover. God bless this great city and the United States of America."

CHAPTER NINE

FOR THIRTY VERY quiet seconds they watched the footage on the video screen placed in front of one of the blackboards in the classroom. Taken by CCTV cameras just fifteen minutes earlier, the scene showed the new World Trade Center Memorial, with walls of water smoothly cascading into the pool. Every five seconds the scene on the screen shifted to a view of the memorial from a different angle. They were essentially static images, even though they revealed a live scene, and they were remarkably clear; a high-definition image of the simple and elegant memorial. The tall walls of constantly cascading water shimmered in the sunlight over the smooth surfaces of dark marble.

And then the scene changed, drastically and horribly. The center of one of the walls exploded, and water and stone burst out, a spectacular sight, like a view of an exploding meteorite. One of the sentries near the top of the suddenly damaged wall stepped backward, completely stunned. He was a New York City police officer assigned to the terrorism unit. He was dressed in black and wore combat boots and a black helmet. Like the six other guards stationed at the memorial, he carried an M-16. Within two seconds it was clear that he was hurt and not just startled by the explosion that had shattered the silence. Mesmerized, Roland Fortune, Gina Carbone, and Harlan Lazarus stared as the screen revealed the sentry begin to stagger aimlessly and fold forward. The rifle fell from his hands. His body lurched toward the brink of the wall, and he fell into the pool.

"Jesus H. Fuckin' Christ," Gina hissed.

Then there was a second blast, powerful enough to raise a geyser of water from the center of the pool. Three of the guards dropped to their knees, their rifles raised to firing position. They each pivoted, scanning the suddenly dangerous buildings around them, looking for the source of the missiles that had inflicted such damage on this national memorial. They saw nothing on which to focus and no clear source of danger. They had the discipline of combat veterans and were not going to shoot their powerful weapons without having targets.

Then the scene shifted to another location. Gina Carbone and Roland Fortune instantly recognized the intersection of Wall Street and Broadway, where for three hundred years Trinity Church had stood surrounded by its ancient graveyard. The intersection was four or five blocks east of the World Trade Center memorial site.

The CCTV footage showed two men in civilian clothes as they strode quickly, not quite running, into the desolate intersection. They were casually dressed. A lone cop in street uniform emerged from Rector Street, a narrow lane which formed the southern border of the church's ancient burial grounds. He was surprised to see two men walking rapidly just thirty feet from him. The intersection was otherwise empty. For a moment he seemed uncertain, simply watching the two men move on to the deserted path of Wall Street toward the East River.

Almost in pantomime, the cop finally made a decision. Although the CCTV footage was silent, it was clear that he shouted something. The man closest to him immediately reached into his waistband and took out a pistol. The cop, who was young, was mesmerized. He stopped moving. The bullet hit him in the face. He fell backward from the force of the shot.

The CCTV footage ended.

Roland Fortune was not nearly as experienced with the reality and sight of violence as Gina Carbone. He was standing with her and Harlan Lazarus as the footage unfolded. They were in the midst of diminutive desks and chairs in the second grade classroom of PS 6. The sight of the officer, young, inept, inexperienced, unbelieving in that instant before he died, sickened Roland. He sat down on the desk nearest to him. He asked, "Where are those two guys?"

"We don't know," Gina said.

"Judge, what the fuck is happening?" Roland Fortune had a temper that rarely flared, but when it came, its intensity sharpened every feature of his face. It resembled the hateful glare of the street kids he grew up with in the Bronx. As a street fighter when he was a teenager, the ability to use his fists gave him credibility in the neighborhood and that credibility had protected him.

Harlan Lazarus, a former federal appeals judge who had left his life-tenure job to become the Secretary of Homeland Security, wasn't used to people challenging him. His history as a Harvard Law School professor, a United States Attorney, a judge, and now a cabinet secretary had insulated him from other people's anger and made him expect, and get, homage. He had spent a life surrounded by sycophants. He insisted on being addressed as "Judge." He said, "Do you want to ask me that question again?"

"Sure. How is it that someone can take a shoulder-fired grenade and launch an attack on the World Trade Center Memorial?"

"Are you serious, Mr. Fortune?"

"Serious? What the hell are *you* doing? Where are *your* people? You know what I see? *Our* police helicopters, *our* cops, *our* boats, *our* guns. *Our* dead. What the hell are you up to? It's been seven hours since this all started. How much time do you need?" He caught his breath. His voice rose, "Where the fuck are *your* people?"

Harlan Lazarus glared at Roland. He was entirely bald; he had one of those skull-like faces with no spare flesh, all bone; he was skinny and intense. "We have long-standing plans, Mr. Fortune, that are now being implemented all over the world."

"And what the fuck does that mean? I have a thousand people dead before noon, and now an explosion in the most sacred place of my city, and at least two dead policemen. It's nice to have you fly in from wherever you were, but I haven't heard one useful word from you."

"I don't report to you, Mr. Fortune. You report to me."

"Since when? Forget that pecking-order shit, Mr. Lazarus. I need information. I have millions of people who elected me to run this city. You're lucky if you could get your wife to vote for you to clean the toilet. I'm the one guy people listen to. I'm the guy who has to talk to those people, make them comfortable, give them a sense of confidence. You scare the shit out of people."

"You're completely out of order."

"Save that shit for the courtroom. I want to know where your people are and what they're doing. I want to know if they have any information that this kind of thing is going to happen again."

Lazarus' security detail stepped closer to him, almost imperceptibly, drawn by Roland's anger. Lazarus said, "We're not aware of anything."

Increasingly in pain, sweating in the hot classroom, Roland said, "That's reassuring. You weren't aware of anything half an hour ago, were you? Or at nine o'clock this morning?"

Lazarus was visibly trembling, enraged. "I think this little dialogue is over. There are things that we are doing."

"Like what?"

"Mr. Fortune, they are things that are way above your security clearance."

"What kind of bullshit is that?"

Lazarus' stare conveyed nothing but contempt. "I'm about to let the president know that we have a rogue mayor."

Roland had at least once a month been invited to play basketball with the president, a Rhodes scholar who after two years at Oxford had played for two seasons with the Los Angeles Lakers before leaving for law school at Stanford. Roland had never seen Lazarus at any of those private games in the White House gym. "What is this, the eighth grade? Call him right now. Get him on the line."

"You need another pain pill, Mr. Fortune."

Harlan Lazarus turned away and left the classroom.

Into the silence that filled the room after the door slammed, Gina said, "Roland, we need his help."

"Are we getting it? How often did he call you today?"

"Never."

Roland was now touching his shoulder, as if the act of rubbing it would dissolve the pain. "Gina, I want you to find those two guys. Make arrests. Do you get that?"

* * *

Fifteen minutes later, Mohammad Alizadeh and Ali Hussein, two livery car drivers who had been parked since the first explosion in the chilly shadow under the elevated section of the FDR Drive at the eastern end of Wall Street, were thrown against their shabby Lincolns by heavily armed members of the counterterrorism squad of the NYPD.

Word of the arrests was sent as they were happening to Gina Carbone.

After listening quietly on her cell phone, she turned calmly to Roland. "We've got two arrests. They're wearing what looks like the same clothes as two guys on the tape."

Within ten minutes Roland Fortune was standing in front of PS 6. The Vicodin he had just taken was beginning to work its magic. The throbbing in his shoulder was muffled. He announced into the microphones arrayed in front of him, "A team of elite members of the New York City Police Department's antiterrorism unit has just made arrests in connection with the murder of a New York City police officer near the World Trade Center Memorial. Let this be a signal that we will find, and quickly find, anyone who harms us. And that we *will* stop harm before it happens."

CHAPTER TEN

THEIR APARTMENT WAS on the fourth floor of a classic, five-story New York City brownstone. Its windows overlooked the trees that lined East 80th Street between Madison and Fifth. It was Cameron Dewar who had found the place three years earlier. "Gabe, you've got to get over here," he had said. "I've found the place for us. It's just what we want. It's amazing, my love."

They had dated for only three months before they decided to live together. Cam volunteered to do the work of looking for a home for them. They had agreed that they wanted to rent an apartment in an Upper East Side brownstone and hoped they could avoid living in a new, cookie-cutter high-rise building. Cam, an engaging, attractive man who worked in public relations, knew many people. A friend had told him that the owner of a brownstone wanted to rent to a quiet couple. Within five days he and Gabriel Hauser were in the apartment. They had turned it into a cozy Victorian home. They often called themselves Holmes and Watson and the apartment 221-B Baker Street.

Now Cam whispered into Gabriel's ear. "Gabe, there must be three hundred reporters out there now."

Gabriel had slept for less than an hour on the leather Chesterfield sofa in the living room. Numb with exhaustion, he had come home just as early dusk was gathering. He'd drifted quickly into sleep without even changing his clothes. As he woke, he heard the sound of voices on the street. "What's up, Cam?"

"They found out where you live."

"Who?"

"Reporters. They started calling just after you fell asleep. There are pictures of you all over the news. The police released security footage of the museum just after the blasts went off. You're as clear as day in the tapes and they identified you. *Gabriel Hauser, the Angel of Life*. The tapes show you there on the steps, taking care of people, the only man standing."

"This is a joke, right?"

"No joke. Take a look."

Cam waved the remote at the television set. With perfect timing, an announcer's voice on CNN said, "New York City officials have identified the man on the security tapes we've been showing you for the last several hours, the man who was treating the injured in the immediate aftermath of the museum explosions."

The footage had an uncanny clarity, almost movie-like. It was taken from one of the multiple security cameras installed on the tall poles of street lamps thirty-five feet above the steps. It showed Gabriel applying the tourniquet to the first person he treated. It also showed Gabriel sliding something loose and silvery over the man's wrist. So powerful was the camera that it revealed the face of the injured man. Dead and injured people were sprawled all around him on the monumental stairway. In the silent footage, the food wagons and the stalls where vendors sold pictures of New York memorabilia for tourists were still on fire. The delicate Parisian-style benches and chairs on the plaza at the museum's front were grotesquely twisted. Somehow water still gushed up from the fountains.

The CNN announcer said, "Ever since the city released this security footage three hours ago we've been trying to identify this man, already called the Angel of Life. Police estimate that he was treating the wounded just one minute after the last of the three explosions, at a time when more explosions were likely. This is being hailed as an extraordinary act of heroism."

Cam stood behind Gabriel, both hands on his shoulders. The announcer said, "It was obvious that this heroic man had experience in providing emergency medical assistance. Now we know that he is Gabriel Hauser, a doctor at the prestigious Mount Sinai Hospital just ten blocks north of the epicenter of the explosions. We're told Dr. Hauser is a veteran of the Iraq and Afghan wars, a graduate of Stanford and Cornell Medical School."

Gabriel, without turning around, put his hand over Cam's left hand. Gabriel said, "I don't like this."

They cherished their privacy. They were a close and loving couple. Cam was born and raised in Alabama. After graduating from Ole Miss, he left the South because he was gay and lonely. When he arrived in New York, he had found satisfaction in training in public relations, comfort in living without falsehood and pretexts as a gay man, and love. "I don't like it either," Cam said in his genteel Deep South accent. "God help us. I'll have to learn what it's like living with a hero."

"And how much of a hero do you think I'm going to be when America finds out I was tossed out of the Army for being gay?"

Three interviews followed on CNN with other doctors at Mount Sinai. Gabriel wasn't even certain he knew them. They were asked about Dr. Hauser and, in a strange inversion of reality, as though they were speaking about someone else, Gabriel heard himself described as "compassionate and caring," an "extremely skilled emergency room doctor," and a "courageous man."

He knew he was completely unprepared to deal with the fame that was now obviously cascading over him. He had never sought notoriety. When he and Cam made contributions to groups like the Gay Men's Health Crisis and the Lambda Legal Defense Fund, they asked to be listed as "anonymous."

Gabriel had been through challenging experiences in his life. Even before he enlisted in the Army, he'd led a life he now rarely talked about. His father was Jewish, his mother Puerto Rican. His father had trained as a flautist at Julliard and played briefly with the New York Philharmonic. He was a failed musician who refused to find other work and lived an increasingly alcoholic and embittered life. Gabriel's mother was a flamboyant woman who loved Manhattan nightlife and spent most of the early years of Gabriel's life at places like Studio 54, CBGB OMFUG, and the Mudd Club, those legendary party spots of the late 1970s and early 1980s. She spent her days in melodramatic hugging and praising of Gabriel before she left for what his father called the nightly whoring around. "I'm a concert flautist," he'd shout at her, as though the words meant he was royalty. She'd answer, "You've got your flute stuck up your ass."

As a teenager, Gabriel each day left the chaos of their messy West Side apartment for high school at Collegiate, the exclusive all boys' private school he attended on a scholarship on West 77th Street. He was introverted and a very gifted student. By the time he was in high school he dreaded going home. He managed to find several other boys who were as shy as he was who lived in stately apartments on West End Avenue and Riverside Drive. Their parents had opened their doors to Gabriel, who was intelligent, well-spoken and respectful, to spend the afternoons and evenings studying in their homes.

And when he was fifteen, just weeks after his gorgeous mother abruptly left for a rehab in California, Gabriel had the first exciting experience of his life. Jerome Fletcher was a partner in a huge law firm and the father of Bobby Fletcher, one of Gabriel's classmates. One school night, after a short run in Riverside Park when he was first learning the running that he later pursued throughout his life, Gabriel showered in one of the four bathrooms in the Fletcher apartment. Jerome was in his mid-forties. He had been a track star at Cornell and a serious decathlon athlete who almost qualified for the 1992 Olympic team. He volunteered that spring to help Gabriel train as a distance runner. It was exactly the kind of lonely, demanding sport that Gabriel was born for.

When Gabriel emerged from his shower after that first run in the park, Jerome Fletcher, with muscles in his legs and arms like chain meshing, was standing naked just outside the door. Gabriel realized in the instant before Jerome embraced him that he had found the excitement, comfort, and love he wanted. As Jerome rubbed his heavily veined, fully engorged penis against his, Gabriel was deliriously happy, somehow freed from the craziness of his mother and father, the wrecked apartment, the insanity of that life.

Jerome, in love with this boy who was exactly his own son's age, carried on his affair with Gabriel for two years before arranging to send him to Stanford on a full scholarship. Gabriel felt he had been sent into exile. He wanted to go to Columbia, only fifteen blocks away from Jerome's apartment, but Jerome's wife, Carol, who had learned about the affair between her husband and her son's best friend, insisted that Gabriel leave for the West Coast or she would tell the police and Jerome's law partners about her husband's involvement with a boy. Even though Carol Fletcher had no intention of leaving Jerome, she was jealous and angry. Jerome told Gabriel that his wife was deadly serious about the threat, she had pictures of them together in bed, and copies of sweet notes Jerome had regularly slipped into Gabriel's gym bag. "I'd go to jail for life if the police found out, Gabe. That's the world we live in. We have to do what she wants."

Gabriel spent his first semester at Stanford lovesick and homesick. He was in love with Jerome and called him often at the office. For months Jerome happily took the calls. Then one day Jerome stopped accepting them and stopped sending e-mails and text messages. Gabriel became not only lovesick and homesick, but heartsick as well. The pain was acute; he was obsessed with it.

And then after two weeks of silence Gabriel received an envelope with no return address. Inside was a copy of the *New York Post*. The headline on the front page read, *Deadly Sex Games of the Rich and Famous*. There were three long articles on a murder, in a pay-by-the-hour Bronx motel next to the Major Deegan Expressway in the Bronx, of the leading corporate partner in the whitest of white-shoe New York law firms. According to the *Post*, Jerome Fletcher had been a frequent guest at the motel under the name Robert Smith. He was found strangled with a belt and stabbed fifteen times, mainly in the face. A seventeen-year-old black boy, who had arrived at the motel just minutes after Robert Smith checked in, was under arrest for the murder. He had several prior arrests for prostitution.

Jerome's death was searing to Gabriel. He had lost, violently, a man he loved. He was also angry. Jerome's cruel and abrupt suspension of the letters, e-mails, the texts, and the cell calls had wounded Gabriel profoundly in the two weeks before the killing. Gabriel had never been in love before Jerome and so had never been spurned or hurt in that way. He had no equipment in his life for dealing with a lover's rejection, the abrupt and painful fact of separation; he had written a series of e-mails and texts, even a letter, to Jerome that expressed his longing, asked questions, and begged forgiveness for whatever he'd done that led Jerome to drop him. Gabriel devoutly believed that if anyone would be able to explain to him the vagaries and mysteries of love, and how to deal with the loss of love, it would have been Jerome. After all, Jerome had taught him how to run, how to think, how to relate to and assess other people, and how to spend quiet time listening to music and reading. Now Gabriel had no mentor. And no lover.

And in the weeks before the murder, Gabriel, for the first time, had experienced the torments and pettiness of jealousy. He had no doubt that Jerome had replaced him with another lover or lovers. He found himself imagining what Jerome was doing and how: Where did Jerome and the new boy or man spend time together? Who had been the seducer? How often were they making love?

It was three days after Gabriel read the articles in the *Post* and elsewhere, including the Internet and even the West Coast newspapers, that Detective Talbot called him.

"Is this Gabe Hauser?"

"Yes."

"I'm a detective with the NYPD."

Gabriel felt a rush of anxiety. He was eighteen. He had never once talked to a cop. "Yes," he said.

"Need to talk to you about a buddy of yours, Jerome Fletcher." In Talbot's grating Brooklyn accent Gabriel for the first time heard the scorn reserved for gay men. The sarcastic words, the malicious tone, and the edge of mockery. *A buddy of yours.*

Gabriel asked, "Who?"

"Guy named Jerome Fletcher."

Gabriel tried to sound respectful, even childlike. "He was a friend of mine."

"Listen, Gabe, we know he was more than a friend. We got his e-mails, texts, voice mails to you, the works. Yours, too."

Gabriel said nothing, thinking, *Why would Carol Fletcher give that stuff to the police?*

Detective Talbot said, "We want to help you, and you can help us."

"I don't understand."

"Can you come back to New York? We'll pay for it."

"I've got finals soon."

"Your friend was dangerous, Gabe. You're not the only boy he did what he did to you. Your friend knew other men who liked to do what he did. We want to find them, too. Mr. Fletcher was part of a little club of guys who liked boys."

"What did Mr. Fletcher do?"

"Come on, Gabe. He raped you. He did it to others, including the boy in the motel."

Raped. That word haunted him for years afterwards. When he was in medical school his course in psychiatry described any sex between an adult male and a boy under eighteen as rape and instructed on the troubled, terrible lives that the victims later suffered. Post-traumatic stress disorder, acute anxiety, manic depression, suicidal tendencies.

In truth, Gabriel had experienced none of that. Over time he did wonder what borders Jerome Fletcher crossed to bring himself to stand naked that day after their first run together and to initiate that first embrace, when Gabriel, his young torso almost hairless, was still gleaming and wet from his shower. As an adult, Gabriel never sought out boys, and there had to be some deep-seated reason for that restraint, some taboo that Jerome Fletcher had set aside and that ultimately killed him in a rancid motel room in the Bronx. Even as an adult, Gabriel wouldn't apply the word rape to the two years he and Jerome had passionately pursued their afternoons together, often at the Regency on Park Avenue and sometimes in the West End Avenue apartment.

"I wasn't raped, Mr. Talbot."

He knew he was a continent away from New York and couldn't be forced to return and at that stage in his life didn't want to go back. New York was where his father had in effect barricaded himself in the grungy apartment on upper Broadway. And it was where the places were to which Jerome Fletcher had introduced him, such as the grand Metropolitan Museum, the cobblestone streets of Soho, the cozy warmth of the West Village and the vital, alert men striding on Christopher Street, many of them holding hands. And New York was where Jerome had met his squalid death.

"Sure you were, Gabe."

Before Talbot could go on, Gabriel Hauser hung up. It was an act of courage, defying authority for the first time. *Defiance of authority:* he liked the feeling. He never heard from Talbot again.

Now, as they listened to the broadcast on CNN describing him as the Angel of Life, Cam asked, "What do you plan to do?"

"Sell my memoirs."

Cam chuckled. "I'll write them for you."

"I'm headed back to the hospital. I came home to catch my breath, remember? I have work to do."

Just as he was rising from the sofa, he was riveted by the scene on the television. The police commissioner, a woman whom he and his friends described as the cop who looked like Cher, announced that the police were searching for a man named Silas Nasar, a United States citizen "of Afghan descent."

There on the screen was a picture of the man Gabriel knew both as Patient X52 and Silas Nasar: a face with a distinct, seahorse-shaped birthmark. It was a face, too, he had seen before: a grainy image sent from Kabul to his cell phone not long ago and then on the shattered steps of the Met and again in the emergency room at Mount Sinai.

Gabriel's cell phone had slipped between the pillows on the sofa where he had been sleeping. As soon as he found it he scrolled to the contacts window and pressed the screen for Vincent Brown, who was still in the hospital. Brown answered on the first ring.

"Gabriel, how are you?" Brown's cell had identified the incoming caller.

"Rested. And you? Why are you still there?"

"Hey, man, why leave? Where else can I have as much fun as this?"

"I'll be back soon."

Brown could be sardonic, like one of the doctors on *M*A*S*H**. He said, "Why don't you stay there and rest? I don't think any more patients have come through the door since you left. It's funny, but when there's something like this all the usual street stuff we get just stops. No beatings, no stabbings, no overdoses. Strange way to get peace on the streets. If we had a big bomb going off every day, there'd be no more muggings."

Gabriel asked, "Can you do me a favor?"

"Sure."

"There's a patient we only know as Patient X52. He's the first guy I treated and then I saw him again in the ER."

Brown had an immediate answer. "You signed him out just before you left."

"What are you talking about?"

"A woman claiming to be his sister came in. She talked to you. And that guy X52 walked to the elevator with her."

"Where did you get this? Where's the joke in this?"

"No joke. I saw it."

"Not possible, it never happened."

"Sure it did. You said she told you she was a doctor from Los Angeles."

"This," Gabriel said, "is all made up."

Brown's tone of voice never changed: sardonic, determined, almost rehearsed. "You looked at her. You said 'Fine.' You had one of the nurses bring you the discharge papers. She said her brother couldn't sign them, his hands were damaged. She signed for him. And then they left."

"You're out of your fucking mind, Brown." Gabriel was furious. "Or this is a joke."

For a long moment Vincent Brown said nothing. "You need to remember, Dr. Hauser, who your friends are."

CHAPTER ELEVEN

It was finally dark. Roland Fortune, exhausted, his senses dulled by the fresh Vicodin that spread through his system, sat alone on a wicker chair on the terrace of Gracie Mansion overlooking Carl Schurz Park and the East River. A cool fragrant breeze blew in from the river. In the distance the long expanse of the Triboro Bridge glittered in the darkness. There was no ordinary traffic. Red-and-blue emergency lights rotated everywhere: on the FDR Drive, the bridge, and the Queens waterfront. On the surface of the river, which normally was alive even at night with heavy tug boats and barges gliding noiselessly upriver and downriver, there were only police and Coast Guard patrol boats. Their glaring, probing beams swept through the darkness. An hour earlier, two men had drowned trying to swim from Manhattan to Queens. The currents in the East River, which was not really a river but an immense estuary of the Atlantic, were powerful, overwhelming, controlled by oceanic tides.

There were no lights on the terrace. For the fifth time, Roland touched his cell phone, its light illuminating his face, and scrolled to John Hewitt-Gordan's number in England. Sarah's father had left three messages for Roland since early afternoon. By the time of the last message, John's clipped aristocratic voice had weakened slightly. "Roland, please, if you can call that would be much appreciated. I know you must be hellishly busy."

Roland genuinely liked the man, although they could not have come from more distinct worlds. John had a wry sense of humor. He called Roland "Mr. Mayor," and Roland called him "Mr. Major." It was their way, simply by changing a letter, to get comfortable with each other.

Roland knew that John Hewitt-Gordan loved his daughter profoundly. She was his only child. His wife had died ten years earlier in a horrific car crash. Roland knew he had to speak to him, but he was mentally and emotionally disorganized by the craziness of the day, the lingering clamor of event after event, fear after fear, pain, anger, and the images of dead bodies and the voices of the dying and the wounded.

Tom Greenwood, a police lieutenant Gina Carbone had assigned to lead a squad of armed guards to follow Roland through the night, said, "Mr. Mayor, it's not a good idea to sit out here with that cell phone screen shining. Anybody can see it from a mile away."

In fact, Greenwood and Gina hadn't wanted Roland to spend the night at the mansion. There were hotel rooms, preselected as part of the emergency plans, where he and other high-ranking officials could stay as anonymously as tourists. Gracie Mansion, a cream-colored colonial house completely different from any other building in Manhattan, was a target of opportunity. When he had told her he was headed to the mansion for the night because, he said, it was "home," Gina Carbone answered, "Not a good idea, Roland. The mansion's vulnerable. Impossible to guarantee your safety."

Fixing his stare on the Triboro Bridge, Roland tapped the screen where John Hewitt-Gordan's name appeared. It was the middle of the night in England. He hoped that John was sleeping, oblivious to the vibration of his cell phone or its ring.

John picked up on the first ring. "Roland?"

"John?"

John was a consummate realist. His training at Sandhurst, the British equivalent of West Point, and his thirty-year career in the British Army's intelligence service had infused him with the rigors of truth, candid assessments, and the ability to differentiate between rumor and fact. He asked, "Is it true? Is Sarah dead?"

"Yes." Suddenly Roland felt his throat constrict. "She is. I'm so, so sorry, John."

"What happened?"

"She put together a birthday party for me. It was on the roof garden of the museum overlooking Central Park. She was very happy. And then the bombs went off."

Roland heard this austere, elegant man inhale sharply and sob. Roland quietly asked, "Do you want to hear more?"

"Indeed, I need to hear this, Roland."

"There were three explosions. She died instantly in the first one, John. She couldn't have suffered."

John was crying now, a long wail that Roland couldn't associate with the man he knew. Still staring at the array of twinkling and flashing lights on the expanse of the bridge, Roland just waited. He had to accept this man's pain.

At least a minute passed before John's ravaged voice came back. "Where is her body?"

Roland rubbed his gritty eyes, which were still scratched, dry and irritated from the explosive dust. Sarah Hewitt-Gordan, a woman who looked forward to the gift of life every day, a woman who made him laugh and gave him ideas in the brilliant flow of her conversation, and who made love to him with a wild passion that always astonished him, was now a torn body temporarily lost somewhere in this wounded city.

"No one's been able to tell me that, John. There are over one thousand people who are dead. It's impossible at this point to know who all of them are. The morgues are overwhelmed. For years we've designated places to use as temporary morgues if this ever happened."

More calmly, more like the stiff upper lip British Army officer, John said, "I understand."

"The recovery people probably have no way of knowing who she is."

"I want to retrieve her. And bring her back here."

"Of course."

"Do you have any idea when we will be able to fly there? When the airports will open?"

"There's no way to know, John. Not tomorrow, maybe not for days."

There was a pause. "Roland, my daughter loved you."

"She loved you as well, John."

Roland Fortune heard another profound sob. Then silence. His cell phone pulsed and the screen abruptly read *Call Ended.* He sat in the cool dark, crying.

CHAPTER TWELVE

GINA CARBONE HAD never been to Pier 37, even though she'd authorized building a secret, dark, unknown prison there. Until today it had never had inmates. The skeletal staff assigned to it posed as janitors and maintenance men, and their only role was to make sure that vagrants and kids never entered the pier. The prison inside, as she had ordered when it was installed, had to remain secret.

Gina left PS 6 soon after an armored Hummer had taken Roland Fortune away to Gracie Mansion. His departure had drawn a wave of attention from the dozens of reporters who thronged Madison Avenue, and in that confusion Gina and three of her staff members slipped out a side door of the school to an unmarked Ford. The black car raced down Park Avenue. Forty blocks downtown, it sped into the strange and unique circular roadway that ran through the base of the old Helmsley Building and the towering Met Life Building over Grand Central Station. The curving, dark passageway was like a medieval tunnel, and the driver went at a speed that was so much like a race car that Gina, forced backward in the seat by the tug of the car's velocity, said, "Who's driving this? Mario Andretti?"

There were men with rifles who were almost invisible in the dusk settling over the pier, the East River, and the low skylines of the Brooklyn and Queens waterfronts across the river. Further to the south were the spans of the dreary industrial-looking Manhattan and Williamsburg bridges and then the glamorous Brooklyn Bridge, whose hundreds of suspension wires shined like the strings of an enormous harp in the final light of this bright day.

The main entrance to the pier was a massive roll-up door installed in the 1950s, when the longshoreman's union still dominated the waterfront, the long-gone era of *On the Waterfront*. Its surface was covered with rust and marked with bold swirls of spray-painted graffiti. The car stopped near the rolled-up gate. The gate opened only with manually operated pulleys. Leaving the car, Gina bent forward and passed under the gate as soon as it was high enough. The chain pulleys screeched.

Unlike Pier 37's decaying exterior, the inside glowed with the crafted, high-tech clarity of the inside of a spaceship. Gina walked to an interior door, which slid open noiselessly. There were thirty-two gleaming prison cells. She knew there were eighteen men in the cells, all seized that morning in the coordinated, secretly conducted raids. They were all silent as Gina passed by them. Some of them looked astonished to see a woman.

Her destination was a room whose door was printed with the words "Interview Station." A bearded thirty-year-old man named Abdullah Hasan sat at a table. There were two detectives in sports jackets in the room, each far larger than Hasan. They were unarmed. Hasan seemed to smirk when a woman entered the room.

"You're supposed to stand up when I come into a room," Gina said.

He looked puzzled, as if wondering why anyone would ever stand up for a woman.

"Do you know who I am?" she asked.

Hasan glanced at the two men, obviously looking for answers from them, for sympathy, for intervention. They were men, after all, cohorts.

"Do you know who I am?" she repeated.

He shook his head. There was an arrogance in the gesture, a look she recognized as contempt.

He said, "You tell me." Just those three words made it obvious he was fluent in English.

Gina punched the side of his head. It was a sharp strike. He wasn't wearing handcuffs or restrained in any way. Although staggered by the unexpected force of the punch, he managed to stand up. He scowled at her.

Gina stepped forward. She hit him in the stomach. He bent forward, struggling for breath.

"Don't you talk fresh to me, fella," she said.

One of the guards picked up the overturned chair and eased Hasan into it. When Hasan stopped gasping, the guard poured water for him. In a polite voice, he said, "Drink this."

Hasan did.

"Let me tell you something, Mr. Hasan," Gina said. "I know you know who did this. You're a smart man. We've known about you for a long time. We know you like to do deals. We can do a deal for you. Tell us the truth, the whole truth, and nothing but the truth. Tell us who worked on this with you, who had the idea, who acted on the idea, and where all your friends are now. What their plans are. You help us and we can help you. You give us something and we give you something. We know what a good businessman you are. You're great at bargaining. We have the bargain of a lifetime for you. Give us the truth and you can get anything you want."

Bargaining was indeed familiar territory to Abdullah Hasan. "What do you think I know?"

"Come on, Mr. Hasan. That's not the way bargaining works. You think about where you are right now, and let me tell you what happens to you if you don't tell me the truth. Nobody knows where you are. You don't know where you are. We know. Lots of people were killed today. Who knows, maybe you were, too."

His absolutely black eyes stared at her, barely blinking. Gina, who had for years dealt with street drug dealers, leaders of Puerto Rican and Nicaraguan gangs and Italian Mafia soldiers, recognized that this was an intelligent man. She also recognized, instinctively, that he was the kind of man who might roll over on his cohorts and cooperate. He was a coward, a punk, an opportunist. She actually admired those few Italian, Russian, and Puerto Rican gang members who would never rat on their buddies and would go to jail for years in the crazy belief in the integrity of their silence and loyalty.

He said, "I'm hungry. Can I have some food?"

This was a good sign. He wanted something. Smiling gently at him, Gina said, "Detective, please get him some food." She paused. "Mr. Hasan, remember, we can help you. Just relax. These men will stay with you. Talk to them."

Gina Carbone left the cell.

* * *

A panel truck marked with the words *Jeeves Linen* came to a stop on 61st Street between Madison Avenue and Park Avenue. Engine running, the van idled for thirty seconds near the service entrance to the elegant Regency Hotel. Three men dressed as hotel workers scanned the nearby areas. One of them gave a signal, an upraised hand waving slightly, and the rear door of the van opened. An automated lift brought down to the sidewalk a large bin containing neatly folded sheets, napkins, and tablecloths. As the bin was rolled on its steel wheels toward the open service entrance, Gina Carbone walked alongside it and into the hotel.

With three armed guards, she took the service elevator to the tenth floor. Her room was the closest one to the service elevator on that floor. As she opened the door, she said to the guards, "Did you make sure you put a mint on the pillow?"

It was the kind of quick, joking comment that made the cops she came into contact with relaxed and loyal; one of the reasons why, even as a woman, she had the respect of most of the forty thousand cops who worked for her. The commissioner she replaced was a lawyer from a big law firm, a partner of the last mayor. That commissioner, her predecessor, was a haughty bald guy who was derided as an ineffective, effete snob by the whole force, from captains to the new recruits.

The cops who regularly served on her security detail were so loyal that they never broke the code of silence about her personal life. They knew about Tony Garafalo, who was waiting for Gina Carbone in the living room of the suite. He was the supervisor of the service department at a big Mercedes Benz dealership in Brooklyn. He was married. He had three teenage kids. He had once served eight years in a federal prison after he was convicted of intimidating witnesses who had been called to a grand jury to testify about the Gambino family.

Tony Garafalo stood in the middle of the living room. "Hey, babe," he said.

Tony Garafalo was Gina Carbone's lover.

CHAPTER THIRTEEN

GABRIEL HAUSER WAS jolted out of a restless sleep at three in the morning. The skin at his throat literally dripped with sweat and the soft skein of hair on his chest stuck to his body. Despite the air-conditioning, the bedsheets under him were wet. He reached for his cell phone on the nightstand. Its pulse had vibrated so powerfully that it made the nightstand and even the bed reverberate enough to wake him. The phone's small screen cast a glow on the nearby furniture and walls. Cam was asleep beside him.

Gabriel had received many calls at this time of the night. Not one of them was happy, ever. It was a rule in life that no conversation at three a.m. was ever good. The vibrating cell phone was the one that linked him only to the hospital; it was his umbilical phone, the cord that attached him to work and that could be pulled at any time he was away from Mount Sinai. His civilian cell phone, the one that connected him to his family and friends and the world at large, was in the kitchen, turned off. At the last time he checked it, there were at least twenty messages in it, all of them from reporters at news stations, newspapers, blogs, and magazines. He hadn't taken a single one of those calls or returned a single message. The voice-mail box was full.

"Dr. Hauser?" Gabriel didn't recognize the voice. Had one of the reporters somehow gotten his secret hospital number? Who gave it away?

"Who's this?"

"My name is Irv Rothstein."

The name meant nothing to Gabriel. "You'll have to tell me who you are."

"I'm a deputy mayor. I work with Mayor Fortune."

"Are you calling from Mount Sinai?"

"What?"

"Are you calling from the hospital? This number is only for the hospital."

"No, I'm calling from Gracie Mansion."

"What is it?"

"The mayor wants you to join him at a press conference tomorrow morning."

"A what?"

"He wants to introduce you to the public. To the world, in fact."

Oliver always slept at the foot of the bed and ordinarily stayed still through the telephone calls that came to Gabriel in the middle of the night. Like Cam, who still breathed sweetly and regularly beside him, the dog was familiar with these calls. But he had been skittish and needy since the morning walk and the two hours he had spent, whimpering and terrified, tied to the iron railing before Cam had retrieved him. Now Gabriel saw in the dark Oliver's upraised head and the sweet, trusting eyes staring at him.

"I'm not interested in a press conference."

"You're not?"

"I can't see a reason why I should do that."

"Dr. Hauser, there are so many reasons. The city, the country, in fact, needs to see how a brave American responds to a jihadist attack. The mayor wants to congratulate you. So does the president. What you did yesterday was heroic."

"I don't think so. It was an instinct. I'm an emergency room doctor, and there was an emergency."

"Doctor, this is important. There is no good news anywhere. Like it or not, you're the only good news around. You should share it."

"Doesn't the mayor have better things to do? I know I do."

Irv Rothstein wasn't used to people refusing to cooperate with him and Roland Fortune. "Can I have the Mayor speak to you?"

Cam, his face as handsome as ever, was awake now. The conversation had gone on much longer than the usual three a.m. calls. He mouthed the words, "What's up?'

Gabriel touched Cam's hand, as if reassuring him, and then said, "Look, Mr. Rothstein, this is not the kind of thing I do. If he wants to call me after seven, I'll talk to him, but my answer is going to be the same for him as it is for you. I'm not interested."

"Mayor Fortune is a very sincere, persuasive man. He thinks you're a hero, as does everyone else, Dr. Hauser, and you can lift people's spirits."

"I doubt it, Mr. Rothstein."

* * *

Roland Fortune and Gabriel Hauser didn't speak that morning. At six thirty a hard knock sounded on the door to the apartment. Instantly alert and protective, Oliver stood up at the foot of the bed, barking as he vaulted to the floor and ran to the door. Gabriel woke, his heart racing at the sudden onslaught of sound that jolted him from a deep sleep. Gabriel went to the door. The knocking continued, sharp and insistent. While trying to settle Oliver, Gabriel said, "Who is it?"

"Police, police."

"What do you want?"

"Just open the door, sir."

Gabriel hesitated. His dislike of police, of authority, was implanted in him the precise moment he was thrown out of the Army. And then he heard Cam's voice. "Let them in."

Gabriel opened the door, a towel wrapped around his waist. Cam tossed Gabriel's bathrobe to him. "Here, baby, put this on." Gabriel left it on the floor at his feet.

The lead detective pushed open the door, holding out his badge. He was a sandy-haired man in his late forties, the picture-book image of the Irish cop. Two other men in suits followed him. Plastic identification tags hung from their necks. They were younger, both of them bulked up from exercise, looking like toy action figures.

The leader recognized Gabriel. "Dr. Hauser?"

Gabriel was always icily cool under pressure. Still standing almost nonchalantly in the doorway, still wearing only the white towel around his waist, Gabriel said, "What can I do for you?"

"Dr. Hauser, I'm from the intelligence unit of the police department's counterterrorist division. My name is McDonough. These men work with me."

Gabriel felt a surge of anger and resentment. Four years earlier, when he was in Kabul, a mild-mannered lieutenant colonel politely asked him, "Major Hauser, could I get a second of your time?" He then told Gabriel he was with Army Intelligence, and within ten seconds he said that the Army had uncovered e-mails from Gabriel to Tom Lathem, who had been an intern with him at Mount Sinai and, for a week, his lover. The chubby, bland colonel, who had the demeanor of a bookkeeper, told Gabriel that his duties at the Kabul regional hospital had been suspended immediately and that he was to leave Afghanistan the next day for Fort Leonard Wood in Missouri, where he would be discharged from the Army within seventy-two hours. "You should've been more careful, Major Hauser. This is the United States Army. The same rules are for everybody. We never ask, and you shouldn't have told."

Although McDonough had none of the unctuous style of the Army colonel, Gabriel's annoyed angry reaction was obvious in the tone of his voice. "It's early in the morning, Detective. I don't have a lot of time. And, as you can see, we weren't expecting you."

"Do you need time to dress?"

"I'm dressed."

"We need your help."

"Everybody seems to."

Cam, who had brought Oliver's loud protective barking under control, hadn't often heard Gabriel speak with even a hint of anger. Cam knew how outraged and pained Gabriel had been, and still was, by the way he'd been bundled up and hustled out of the Army by a rigid, vicious policy: *Don't ask, don't tell.*

McDonough said, "Look, sir, we've been looking again and again at the CCTV footage from yesterday. We've been able to enlarge views that had not been as clear before we were able to bring some new technology in. I don't know if you've seen that footage of you wading into what looked like hell." He paused. "You did some great things out there, Doctor."

"Don't patronize me."

McDonough's reaction was increasingly combative. "Sure, understood, so let's cut to the chase. The first man you treated, do you remember him?"

"Of course I do."

"He was an Arabic kind of guy, right?"

"What does that mean, an 'Arabic kind of guy'?"

"From the Middle East? You spent a lot of time there, I'm told."

"I don't know the ethnic background of the people I treat. He was a man. He had black hair and a black beard. For all I know he could have been Swedish, Tahitian, even Irish, like you. What I do remember is that he was almost unconscious and badly wounded and needed help."

"Did he say anything?"

"Say anything? Are you serious? The man had severe lacerations on his arm. A shard of something had penetrated his back not far from his kidney. He'd already lost significant amounts of blood."

"Did he say anything?" McDonough asked again.

"Sure, he said, 'Help me, please.' You'd say the same if you had a shredded arm and lost that much blood. I hear that from a lot of people in my line of work. Including from wounded Irish cops who come into the ER. Some even cry for their mothers. Especially the middle-aged detectives with names like McDonough."

"Did he say anything?"

Gabriel didn't answer.

"Did you take anything from him?"

"You mean other than the wallet with the thousand dollars in it?"

"You know, Doctor, I'm beginning to get a little sick of your lip."

"You know, Detective, I'm already sick of you."

Quietly Cam spoke out from the background in which he had been soothing Oliver. "Gabriel, what's wrong?"

McDonough glanced from Cam to Gabriel. "We saw you take something from him and put it in your pocket. I'll give you this boost for your memory. It wasn't his wallet."

Gabriel remembered the thick chain-like bracelet that he had slipped off the man's wounded left wrist and then, hours later in the squalid ER at Mount Sinai, fastened to the man's right wrist.

"That didn't happen."

"Now, that's interesting. The video shows that it did."

"Listen to me again: that didn't happen."

"Where is it? We need that bracelet. You have it."

"Get out."

McDonough, passing by Gabriel, approached Cam. He handed Cam his business card, saying, "Tell your girlfriend that when he needs our help, he can call or you can. We're not the only guys who want to get to know him."

CHAPTER FOURTEEN

THE SUN RISING over the East River was always dazzling. Its rays appearing on the horizon sent spears of light that sparkled over the surface of the river. The Triboro Bridge's outlines appeared for seconds to be on fire as the new sunlight flooded the river and the sky.

In a loose-fitting bathrobe, Roland stood behind the French doors that overlooked the flagstone terrace and the river. He was alone and knew this would be the only time during the long day when he would have complete privacy. The glare from the new sun and the river was almost blinding, as it often was at this time of the day. During the last three years he had repeatedly come to this terrace at dawn, dazzled not only by the light but by the exhilarating strangeness of his life, the change from the dirty and cracked streets of the South Bronx to this colonial mansion in a beautiful park on the river.

Roland was in yet another new world this morning, and it frightened him. He had slept for five hours, the painkillers not only easing the ache in his shoulder and back but putting him down to a deep level of sleep well beyond the realm of dreaming. But at the moment he woke, thoughts about the wounded city flooded his mind. He didn't for a second think he had emerged from a nightmare in which the events of the last day were all make-believe. It also struck him at that moment of first alertness that he was completely unprepared for this, even though he had regularly met over the last three years with the odd people from Homeland Security to listen to disaster plans. They were like the Stepford Wives of the security world, that new, sprawling industry that, Roland often thought, manufactured fear, not security. They spoke in rapid rote about assets, security perimeters, insurgents, good guys, bad guys. They never varied from a script. They never fully grasped or responded to a question. The plans all seemed like the war games of young boys at play, except that many of those game players were girls, not just boys. And now reality presented something completely different.

On most early mornings, except on the coldest winter days, there were rowers in racing sculls moving steadily downriver and upriver. He was always fascinated by them. The rowers gathered in the pre-dawn on the shores of the Spuyten Duyvil on the northern tip of Manhattan and were already on the river when dawn came. Where did that Spartan drive come from? He'd always admired people who took on things that were hard to do. The serious marathon runner, the long-distance swimmers, the people who worked six-teen-hour shifts in hospitals. He had heard an ultra-marathoner say in an interview, "I do this not because it's fun but because it's hard."

There were no rowers on the river this morning. There were no barges bearing the city's garbage. No tugboats, no pleasure craft. No ordinary river traffic at all. Just the brightly painted Coast Guard vessels bristling with spinning radar devices and black weaponry. Drab-green Army helicopters, drifting slowly, hovered over the water, lower than he ever imagined they could safely fly. He could feel the pulses from the rotors as they flashed like thousands of swords in the brilliant early light. For a moment he told himself that he would do what he had done at this moment every early morning for the last 365 days. He would walk into the bedroom where Sarah Gordan-Hewitt still slept, arouse her, make love to her, and then, utterly refreshed, go about his day.

But, as it suddenly overwhelmed him, she was dead. That sweet, fulfilling phase of his life was gone.

It was time now, he thought, to suit up and show up.

* * *

Just an hour after his time on the terrace, Roland was in an underground conference room at the disaster command center on West 14th Street. There were twelve other people in the room, among them Gina Carbone and Al Ritter, who was Harlan Lazarus' deputy director of Homeland Security, and Constance Garner, the regional director of the FBI. On a large video monitor suspended over the circular conference table appeared the secretary of defense, Roger Fitton, and, on the right side of the split screen, General Malcolm Foster, the chairman of the Joint Chiefs of Staff, who looked like a West Virginia coal miner suffering from black lung disease. He was in full dress uniform. Roland knew Roger Fitton, the defense secretary, a former senator from Montana who was only two years older than Roland and who sometimes played, and played well, in those once monthly, much coveted basketball matches in the White House gym.

Roland abruptly started the meeting. "I have to give a press conference at eight thirty this morning on where we stand at. People need information. So I need to know from you folks what developments there have been overnight, what the real risks are, what condition the city is in, when we can ease the lockdown, and what arrests have been made. I want facts, not fantasies. I like the way Commissioner Carbone handled this yesterday. Remember the old Jack Webb line? *Just the facts, ma'am, just the facts.* I'm not going in front of the world with any bullshit."

Always congenial, Roger Fitton, an inveterate politician, said, "And good morning to you, Mr. Mayor."

Roland gave that engaging smile with which he'd been endowed, like a genetic birthright, in his early childhood. "Morning, Roger. Good to see you." And Roland nodded at the general, who barely nodded in return.

"First," Roland said, "let me hear about risk. Commissioner Carbone? Mr. Ritter? General? Who wants to go first?"

Gina said, "I will." This didn't surprise Roland. He had long ago detected her contempt for the federal agencies that were supposed to have expertise in defending the city. He once heard her say they were "space cadets." She believed her more focused plans for detecting and deterring threats, dealing with actual crises, and finding and punishing the responsible people were far more effective than any confection that Homeland Security, Defense, the FBI, the NSA, and the CIA had put together. She relished the image of herself as the grunt besting all the West Point and Ivy League grads.

"Go ahead, Commissioner," Roland said.

"The level of risk remains high. Forget color codes. We have identified people on the streets who are still out there with the capacity and the intention of doing more harm. I authorized six raids during the night, and they have yielded ten arrests. The raids were concentrated in the East Village, in what we call Alphabet City, Avenues A, B and C."

Harlan Lazarus' deputy, Al Ritter, asked, "Who was arrested?"

"Primarily Syrian and Sudanese Muslims."

"Were any of them the names we gave you?" Ritter asked.

"No, those names were useless."

"What do you mean?" Ritter looked hurt, not angry. Roland and Gina both recognized that he was a stalking horse for the haughty and offended Harlan Lazarus, who was said to be in Washington talking to the president. Roland knew that Lazarus, within minutes of angrily walking out of PS 6 the day before, had called the president to complain. Roland knew, too, that the president had told Lazarus to control himself.

"They were names, just that," Gina answered. "There were no real people attached to them. Your people at Homeland Security didn't even give us real addresses."

"How so?"

"There is no such place as 374 Pleasant Avenue in East Harlem, just as a for instance. There is a Pleasant Avenue. Most Manhattanites don't even know it's there. It's a short, almost anonymous street way over on the eastern edge of East Harlem. The street numbers don't go that high."

Roland said, "Fine, Commissioner, so you didn't have to waste time tracking those names down." He was intervening intentionally. He admired and respected Gina but knew she was territorial, sensitive, and intent on keeping the allegiances of the people who worked for her.

"What else?" Roland asked. "Are these people telling you anything?"

"We've only had them for three or four hours. We're working on them."

Constance Garner, an overweight, stern woman, said, "The FBI would like to help you with that. Nobody told us about this."

"Sure," Gina said, "we'll work that out with you."

Gina was willing to invite the FBI into the universally known prison on Rikers Island where the ten men were being held because they were not the men locked deep inside the pier on the East River. The inmates in the pier were, she was certain, the high-value men, secretly arrested and held in absolute isolation, and she wasn't about to let anyone see or even know about them. They belonged to her.

"The men you just arrested: are there others like them still out there?" Roland asked.

"There are. We think there is a safe house on West 139th Street where a group of men who pretend to be immigrant kitchen workers at exclusive hotels live and work together and have a special mission. I gave an order to take them down just as we were walking into this meeting. They're under arrest now."

General Foster's scratchy voice broke out from the video screen. "Who are these people attached to?"

Gina said, "Not certain. There is the group *People Committed to the Propagation of the Prophet's Teachings and Jihad*. They're known as Boko Haram. The Nigerian terrorist group. They've been operating in Nigeria and North Africa for more than ten years. Very bad people. It might also be ISIS."

Ritter said, "Can't be either of them. They don't have the capability of mounting large-scale attacks here. They're too loose and decentralized."

"Listen," Roland said. "I don't care whether they're from Boko Haram or Procul Harum or whether they're ISIS or Iggy Pop. What matters is what is happening right now. Mr. Ritter, what can I say at the press conference about what Homeland Security is doing?"

"We're implementing the plans that have been in place for dealing with precisely this kind of attack."

Roland paused, staring at Ritter and shaking his head almost imperceptibly, feigning irritated disbelief. "That's really, really reassuring. I'm sure the entire population of the City of New York will breathe a collective sigh of relief to hear that. So let me ask again: What is Homeland Security *doing* right now?"

"We're monitoring unusual communications from sources here in the city and elsewhere. We think we're close to deciphering what appears to be a sophisticated method of transmitting messages."

"And what are the results?"

"Nothing definitive yet."

"Anything else? Where are your people?"

"We're coordinating with the Army."

The mayor said, "Monitoring, coordinating? All of that sounds pretty invisible, doesn't it? We're almost twenty-four hours into this. What you're telling me sounds like the work of spooks chasing spooks, except that the spooks being chased have rifles, grenades, plans." Looking up at the video screen, Roland was genuinely exasperated and making no effort to conceal it. "General, what are *you* doing?"

The hard-bitten general answered reluctantly, obviously annoyed that he had to respond to a question from a Puerto Rican with the strange name Roland Fortune. "There are troops and material support being assembled at Fort Dix."

"Fort Dix is what, General, somewhere in New Jersey, about eighty miles from Manhattan?"

"Logistically, we had to locate and transport elements of the 25th Infantry and 101st Airborne from various other locations around the country. My troops and assets can't be safely deployed without proper support."

"I never had the honor of serving in the military, General, but frankly what you've just said does not make any sense. I don't need tanks and cannons here. I need what you folks like to call boots-on-the-ground. So when do they get here? The reality is that the people who live here will only be made more comfortable if there are men and women in uniforms at every street corner."

"That's futile."

"Is it? I don't think so."

"We also need approval from Secretary Lazarus," the general said. "After 9/11 the watchword is coordination."

"Mr. Ritter, you work for Lazarus. Can you tell me what the fuck is really going on?"

"We'll have an answer soon. Secretary Lazarus is meeting with the president and his folks right now."

Raising his hands in exasperation, Roland said, "This is all stunningly inept. It takes my breath away."

Ritter and General Foster didn't respond. Ritter glared at Roland as the general, almost without blinking, stared from his segment of the split screen. He looked like a photograph, not a man on a live feed.

Roland asked the secretary of defense, "Roger, do you have anything to say?"

"Sure. The general and Mr. Ritter are experts on military issues, but the president is the final decision-maker. As soon as this conference call is over, I'll join a video conference with the president, Secretary Lazarus, and the general."

"Commissioner Carbone," Roland said, "do you have any reaction to what we've been hearing?"

"I have as many uniformed officers with as many M-16s on the streets as I can find, but it's a thin net."

"At least it's something," Roland said.

He turned to Hans Richter, an impeccably organized deputy mayor responsible for managing the day-to-day operations of the Sanitation, Housing, and Health Departments. He was a fifty-five-year-old bachelor who always seemed to be in his office in the Municipal Building across Centre Street from City Hall. "Hans, what's happening from your perspective?"

"Candidly, Mr. Mayor, Manhattan is in a steady state of collapse. Garbage is piling up on every street, normal ambulance service is almost nonexistent. We also have thousands of people who were in the city yesterday only for a day, visitors from the suburbs for the most part. They have no apartments or homes to return to."

"Didn't someone tell me that if we had a Code Apache situation there were shelters with food and other essentials where people could go?"

"We do. But they're overflowing. There are six hundred cots set up in the Armory on Park Avenue, for example. They're all occupied. But many of the other shelters are in neighborhoods that apparently don't feel as safe to out-of-towners. So there are thousands of people who, for the first time in their lives, are living in the parks and streets. We are managing to provide food and water and some, but not enough, sanitation facilities."

Increasingly in pain, suddenly focusing on the image in his mind of Sarah and the recollection of her scent, Roland recognized that his spirit was bruised. He worried that his mood was deflating. Everything seemed too immense and too complicated and too uncertain. He said, "What else, Hans?"

"Food supplies in the stores have virtually vanished. There's been a rush for food, water, and other supplies that's happened with a speed we didn't anticipate. So we're experiencing more and more pleas for food assistance."

"This lockdown can't last," Roland said.

Hans Richter continued. "Even though this is not my area of expertise, I have to also say the financial markets in New York are closed. I'm no economist, God knows, but that's spreading financial confusion around the world."

Roger Fitton, a career politician who himself wanted to be president, spoke soothingly, "Roland, the president is aware of that. He's the decision maker."

"As in George W. Bush, I'm the decider?"

"I hope I'm going to recommend to him that the lockdown be gradually lifted today and tomorrow if the situation begins to stabilize."

"I can't have a city under siege. Even after the Paris attacks there were no sieges. Sieges cause fear, and fear will rapidly unravel the whole fabric of the city."

* * *

From the back seat of the SUV racing from 14th Street to City Hall, Roland saw empty streets that looked like cities in those Japanese-made horror movies from the 1950s in the grip of an invasion from space aliens. Although this was Manhattan on a bright Monday morning in June, there were very few people outside. There was virtually no traffic. The usual congestion of double-parked delivery trucks replenishing the city after a weekend was gone. Stores and diners were closed since they were places staffed mainly by people from the outer boroughs who hadn't been able to cross the river into Manhattan. As the caravan of heavily guarded SUVs rushed down the old sections of lower Broadway, a squadron of fifteen bicyclists on sleek Italian machines and in skintight, gaudy clothing sped on the freshly painted bike lanes.

"I hope," Roland said, "that the TV stations capture that. It might brighten things up more than I will."

Irv Rothstein, on the rear-facing seat directly across from Roland, said, "Weave the bike riders into your speech. Something like these people are vital and undaunted."

"Or maybe, Irv, they're just crazy."

Roland leaned forward to see the lead rider, a woman. Although all the riders had helmets and were thin and hard to differentiate, she had a special, powerful litheness. "By the way, Irv, is the doctor there yet? I want to talk to him before we go on the air."

"Dr. Hauser?"

"The one who did all that work with the wounded people. As the kids would say, that was some brave shit."

"He didn't want to show up with you."

"Did you scare him, Irv? Haven't I told you to learn to make nice-nice?"

"No, I was smooth. He told me he was more interested in being a doctor than a celebrity."

"Did you tell him he can raise the spirits of this city? We need at least one man in bright shining armor."

"He was adamant. I asked if he'd speak to you."

"Get him on the line for me. I'll talk to him right now."

Gina had sat quietly beside Roland since the convoy pulled out of the warehouse building where the command center was hidden. She held up her right hand. "Mayor, don't do that."

He turned to look at her. "We might have time to get him down here."

"We don't want him down here."

"Come again?"

"I'll tell you later."

The convoy made the turn through the iron gates surrounding City Hall. Knowing that cameras were trained on him, Roland jumped athletically out of the back seat of the SUV as if on a campaign stop. He was smiling. But his movement triggered acute pain. He shook the hands of the police officers who were guarding the plaza in front of City Hall. He walked up to the microphones on the top step, looked out at the television cameras, and spoke.

* * *

After the press conference, the mayor, Irv Rothstein, and three other staff members, his political and campaign cadre, watched the replay of the press conference. Just as it was ending, Irv said, "You sure did good."

Roland nodded. He had been well-prepared, not through the angry and discordant voices he had heard at the command center, but by his own half hour, in private, thinking about what he wanted to convey. And he could see in the video that, in fact, he'd succeeded in delivering that balance of reality and optimism he sought. The broadcasters who summarized the conference spoke about his re-assurance, his message of sternness in hunting down the terrorists and preventing further attacks, the need for vigilance and calm, and the steady scaling back of the lockdown to begin to restore essential services.

"You did good," Irv repeated.

CHAPTER FIFTEEN

THE INTERSECTION OF Wall Street and Broad Street in front of the now-closed New York Stock Exchange was one of the oldest in the city. The intersection was created in the 1600s when virtually all of Manhattan north of the Battery was forest and Broad and Wall were only winding trails. The intersection was wide, more of a plaza than just the crossing of two streets. Looming over the northern side was the immense statue of George Washington in front of the Federal Building as he took the first presidential oath.

Over the last five decades, Wall Street had gradually and radically changed. As recently as the 1960s it was still the street of America's financial power. It was lined with the imposing buildings that housed the headquarters of the world's largest banks. Their big corporate flags hung over both sides of the street, a daily ceremonial display of America celebrating its capitalism. The buildings also housed the offices of what were always called the "Wall Street law firms," the legal institutions that carefully served the interests of the banks in whose buildings they were housed.

But over the years those banks and law firms had steadily abandoned Wall Street and migrated to midtown, first to Park Avenue between 50th and 57th Streets and then west to Times Square when it was renovated and made into a corporate theme park, a kind of urban Disneyland. In the wake of the migration uptown, Wall Street now had health clubs, European clothing stores, and fancy cafés. Instead of the institutional bank flags and American flags overhanging the narrow street, there were now banners advertising the health clubs, stores, and Starbucks.

On the morning after the bombings at the Met and the rocket assault at the World Trade Center Memorial, there was no one in the normally packed intersection. The area from Trinity Church at one end of Wall Street to the East River at the other end was cordoned off as a crime scene after the killing of Officer Cruz.

It was in 1920 at the intersection of Wall and Broad that a horse-drawn fruit wagon exploded on a morning when the same intersection was crowded with office workers. Although the statue of George Washington was untouched, heavy fragments from the powerful explosion not only killed dozens of people but tore holes in the monumental stone facades of the bank buildings. Left as a memorial, those deep gashes in the stone facades were never repaired. You could still touch the gashes almost a century later.

* * *

Forty-five minutes after the press conference and only moments after Roland Fortune had reviewed the video of that conference, his cell phone, the one to which only Gina Carbone and six other people including Sarah Hewitt-Gordan had access, rang. Roland picked up the vibrating phone.

It was Gina. "There's been an explosion at the corner of Wall and Broad."

"Jesus, Jesus. How many people did they get this time?"

"Not sure. Maybe none. The place was empty."

"What happened?"

"There's a sports club right next to the George Washington statue. Our information is that explosives were put near the windows of the club, hidden in gym bags that were probably placed there before yesterday or even last night. They were detonated from a remote source today."

"My God, Gina. When is this going to end?"

Gina was tempted to say she lived in the world of facts, not predictions. "We've covered some ground, Roland. They may not be as smart as they think they are. We think this first explosion at the Met might have gone off before they all left the scene."

"So some of them were killed, too? Is that what you're saying?"

"We have a DNA bank with some of the DNA from people we were interested in, traces left on cigarettes or plastic coffee cups that these people threw out on the streets. We're trying to match the DNA from some of the bodies with what we have in the bank."

"So, what, Gina? Let's assume you find a match and that one of the dead men is a guy you had under surveillance. Unfortunately dead men tell no tales."

"But we also think there's a live one who may have been caught off guard when the first explosion happened at the museum."

"Who?"

"His name is Silas Nasar. He owns an electronics company, five or six of those cheap stores that rip off tourists. But he's also, we believe, one of those guys who loves any and all electronic devices. The stores might be a front. We think he's got tons of money and he's able to develop really sophisticated communications devices all over the world."

"And you think he was near one of the wagons?"

"He wasn't selling any pretzels, but it appears he was in the vicinity, possibly making sure all was in place before he made himself scarce."

"Where is he?"

"He was taken to Mount Sinai. You know that film of the Angel of Life? Dr. Hauser?"

"Who doesn't by now? The aloof Dr. Hauser."

"Silas was the first guy treated by the doctor on the museum steps."

"How do you know that?"

"Enhanced videotapes. Right down to the ability to see a birth-mark on Silas' face. It's his distinguishing feature. It's shaped like Japan."

Even though he was in an air-conditioned room, Roland began to sweat profusely. The pain in his shoulder and back, controlled only by the Vicodin that he had not wanted to use before the press conference, had a powerful resurgence. The painkiller's cottony cushioning of his brain and body seemed to reach a certain point and rapidly dissolve. He found the envelope in which he carried the pills in his suit jacket and shook them out onto the table in front of him. He gestured to Irv Rothstein for water.

Roland said, "Have you found him? He must be in a hospital somewhere, unless he died."

"We have surveillance video from the emergency room at Mount Sinai. Believe it or not, the Angel of Life was with him again. We have it on the tape."

"What are you saying?"

"Not certain," she answered. "But they were together for a little over five minutes. They talked. And they exchanged something, what it is, is not clear. What is clear from the enhanced video at the museum is that the Angel took something from Nasar there. And something—a bracelet, a watch, who knows—went back and forth between them a few hours later."

Roland said quietly, "I'm still listening, Gina."

"Our people think they knew each other."

"Where was Nasar moved?"

"He did what you did. He checked himself out. Some friends of his came to get him."

"When I did it a doctor named Edelstein had to sign the release papers, too. Who signed Nasar's?"

"Why don't you take a guess?"

"Don't tell me: Dr. Hauser?"

"It's his name on the form."

"You must have video of Nasar leaving and once outside getting into a car or van with license plates."

"The video ends when he leaves the lobby. For some damn reason the outside cameras were down."

"When the fuck, Gina, are we going to catch a break?"

She went silent for several seconds, and Roland took two, not one, of the potent Vicodins. "The attacks," she said, "have been getting less lethal. Whoever did the explosion at Wall and Broad had to know that few people, or none, would be there."

Roland, who had studied the history of the city he loved, said, "I think you might be missing something. There's a symbolism in the attack there. That is the exact intersection where anarchists blew up a horse-drawn wagon in 1920. There were many people killed. Horses, too, it was still that era. The men who did it were never found. Not a single arrest. No punishment, no retribution. A devastating wound to the city and never any closure of the wound, except for the passage of years. Now nobody remembers it."

"These guys can't be that smart," Gina said. "They don't know history, they know the Koran, they know killing."

"Is that so, Gina? So far they're much smarter than the president, Harlan Lazarus, the general, you and me are."

"I'm not going to let anybody spook me," she said.

"I'm not spooked, I'm worried. They seem to have mastered the art of doing terrible things at times and places of their own choosing."

He realized he sounded petulant and angry. He didn't want to lapse into those rare moments of rage and anger he had felt toward Harlan Lazarus and the general in the last twenty-four hours. "I'm sorry, Gina, I didn't mean to get testy."

She waited. "Not a problem, Roland. The pressure is on, it's hard to prepare yourself for what things like this will make you feel and how you'll react. And especially for you." She paused again. "Sarah was a beautiful lady."

Somehow he had never expected Gina to say anything about Sarah. They had briefly met once or twice. They were worlds apart. "Thanks, Gina. I need to separate my pain and grief over her from my pain over what's happened to this city."

"You have to take care of yourself, Roland. People were in a panic yesterday when there wasn't any word as to how you were and where you were. Have you had a doctor look at you today?"

"Not yet."

"Make believe," she said, "I'm your Italian mama. Go see the doctor."

* * *

Roland Fortune sat quietly for several minutes after the call ended. He had no idea where Sarah's body was. Where had her purse with her license and credit cards been when the blasts tore the roof garden to pieces, or where had those vicious concussions of air and stone and dust blown the purse if she had been holding on to it? Without the purse to identify her, her body could have been taken anywhere, along with the other dead in and around the museum whose names were not yet known. So somewhere in the torn city, he thought, was the shattered body of the woman who just three hours before she died had passionately rose up over him in bed as she straddled him, her naked body absolutely perfect in the dim early morning light in the colonial-era bedroom in Gracie Mansion.

A former choir boy at the decaying and now abandoned Church of Saint Andrew in the South Bronx, Roland Fortune kneeled on the floor next to his desk and recited, in the Latin he had learned at parochial school, *Pater noster, qui es in caelis; sanctificetur Nomen Tuum . . .*

CHAPTER SIXTEEN

GABRIEL HAUSER WAS on the stairwell as he left his apartment building to return to Mount Sinai when six men—four in combat-style uniforms and two in suits—blocked the way.

Gabriel said, "Can I help you?"

"Just get out of the way, sir." Gabriel recognized one of the big blond men who had stood silently behind Detective McDonough three hours earlier in his apartment.

"I asked you what's going on."

"I need you out of the way, sir."

Gabriel stretched out his arms and touched both sides of the stairwell, blocking passage, knowing the gesture was futile, almost comical.

The group of big men didn't stop climbing the steps. As they continued, two of the men in uniform came forward, grabbing Gabriel by the knees and arms and lifting him back up the steps. Gabriel was strong and agile but realized these men were experts in the dark art of overpowering and controlling other people. They had the training of Navy SEALs or Army Special Forces.

As soon as they released their grip, the lead agent said, "Sir, if you do one more fucking thing, we will put you in cuffs and take you away to where nobody will ever find you."

Gabriel didn't move as the bulky men passed by him to the door of his apartment. He heard one of them murmur, "The fucking faggot loved it when we grabbed him."

Gabriel's rage made him shake.

Cam appeared in the doorway, impeccably neat as ever, his expression at first quizzical and somewhat annoyed, as if he expected to find boisterous teenage pranksters on the landing in front of the apartment. And then his expression changed to fear, a reaction that Gabriel had never witnessed.

The lead agent, who clearly believed no one would ever question his authority, said, "I need you to step aside, sir."

Seeing the fear in Cam's face and knowing that as a teenager in the Deep South Cam had several times been beaten by local boys in pickup trucks, events that Cam later referred to as his "Matthew Shepard moments," Gabriel lunged forward. The startled men didn't react at first. Even serious drug dealers when confronted by agents with weapons and search warrants tended to become docile. They were startled by a well-dressed doctor who vaulted toward them and pushed the lead agent in the back, making him stagger to the side. The man was momentarily startled and then he was furious, with deadly hatred in his eyes so much like the expression Gabriel had seen in Afghanistan from infantrymen suddenly under attack. "You fucking queer," he shouted as he regained his footing. He reached beneath his jacket and his swift hand emerged with a pistol.

Cam was crying.

Gabriel feinted to his left, and the big man stumbled when he missed Gabriel's head as he swung toward it with the pistol in his hand.

Gabriel laughed at him in the second before two other men, suddenly recovered from the shock of Gabriel's resistance, tackled him. Under their weight, Gabriel fell to the floor. Strong hands flipped him over as other strong hands wrenched his arms behind his back and put plastic handcuffs, tightly, on his wrists. His face was pushed to the floor. Then Gabriel heard Cam screaming, "Leave him alone, leave him alone."

Gabriel also heard Oliver's barking escalate, wildly. He heard, too, one of the men grunt. "Fuckin' dog bit me."

Another voice, authoritative and loud, said, "Shoot the fucker," and a gun with a silencer fired, a thud. Oliver whimpered and wailed, obviously injured. Cam screamed. "Don't, please don't, what did you do? What did you do? Don't hurt him. He's just a dog."

They spent an hour in the apartment, opening every drawer and door, scattering clothes out of Gabriel's and Cam's meticulously ordered closets. Even though Gabriel lay facedown in the hallway, he heard them say repeatedly to Cam, "Where's the damn bracelet? Where did he put it?"

Cam didn't answer. He sobbed continuously. Gabriel's mind was not fixed on the pain in his wrists and arms but on the image of his beloved partner who he was certain was on the floor trying to soothe Oliver, who sustained a constant whimper.

One of the men pulled back Gabriel's long hair and asked, "Where did you fucking put it?"

Gabriel said, vehemently, "Go fuck yourself, Jack."

As the sound of the ransacking subsided and finally stopped, Gabriel heard one of the men speaking on his cell phone. "Not here, no sign of the thing, ma'am." The man paused, listening. "Everywhere, we went through everything." Another pause as the man listened and then said, "He attacked me. I want to bring him in, ma'am." He listened again. "Not a problem, ma'am."

Within seconds of the conversation's end, the handcuffs that had painfully bound up Gabriel were unlocked and he was jerked up to his feet. They left the building without him.

Gabriel ran into the apartment. Cam was on his knees next to Oliver. Always the instinctive surgeon, Gabriel touched every part of the dog's body. There was a long bullet graze on Oliver's left side. Gabriel ran to the bathroom and retrieved the needles and thread he needed to stitch the still-bleeding wound. There was dried blood all over the dog's fur.

When he finished that, Oliver became quiet and looked at him with what Gabriel believed was a grateful gaze.

CHAPTER SEVENTEEN

CHARLIE BRANCATO, GINA Carbone's first deputy commissioner, hadn't slept in thirty-six hours. Although he was considered Gina's male alter ego—he too was raised on Staten Island and had attended John Jay College of Criminal Justice at night while serving as a street cop just as Gina had—he led a different life. He was a party-goer, he loved fun, and he had legions of friends. He was an unabashed womanizer—handsome in the mold of a young Al Pacino, a weaver of stories, a generous man. People loved to be with him for a host of reasons. He had one of the most powerful law enforcement jobs in the country, he appeared to know every detail of the private and public life of the famous woman commissioner of the largest police force in the world, and he seemed closely connected to one of the most popular politicians in the country, Roland Fortune.

Charlie had been up so long because he was out at parties, bars, and after-hours clubs the entire Saturday night and Sunday morning before the first explosions. He had spent time during that long, festive night and morning at parties with Sylvester Stallone, Cheryl Tiegs, and even the party-loving, balding Salman Rushdie. He had intended to end his night and morning with a quick visit to Roland Fortune's birthday party on the roof garden of the Met, but a chance encounter with a young actress had taken him elsewhere.

Charlie knew many journalists, from hard-right, hard-bitten Andrea Peyser at the *Post* to foxy Maureen Dowd at the *Times*.

Journalists cultivated him and he cultivated them. Gina Carbone, somewhat reclusive but attuned to publicity and public relations, valued Charlie because he was able to handle reporters in a way that Gina herself couldn't. She valued him for other reasons as well. He was loyal to her, ruthlessly tough, and a coldly accurate evaluator of people and their motives and objectives. He was also a great cop.

Charlie had seen the byline of Raj Gandhi in the *New York Times* but had never met him or talked to him. He was a foreign correspondent who had recently been reassigned to cover city politics, and Gina had asked Charlie to open up contact with him. "Imagine that," Charlie had said to Gina when they talked about the new reporter in town. "A Hindu covering the streets of New York. You don't see that all the time. We've come a long way from Jimmy Breslin."

"Don't talk to anybody else that way, fella," Gina had said, laughing. "Have you ever heard of political correctness?"

Over the last three hours Charlie's iPhone registered three calls and three text messages from Raj Gandhi. Each of the texts said it was urgent that Charlie call, and the texts and e-mails gave all of Raj's four numbers and his e-mail addresses. Charlie hadn't returned any of those messages, just as he had not yet responded to the dozens of other messages he had from journalists he knew far better than Raj Gandhi.

As he listened to Gina say into her cell phone, "No, leave him alone for now, the last thing I need is to arrest a doctor who people think is a fucking hero," Charlie felt his own cell phone vibrate with the signal of yet another incoming text message. Charlie and the commissioner were in what they called the War Room at One Police Plaza in the drab, Soviet-style building near the East River and Brooklyn Bridge in lower Manhattan. Gina's office and Charlie's adjoining office overlooked New York Harbor and the century-old bridge. Overnight someone had suspended huge, bright American flags from the bridge, that patriotic display that had sprung up just after 9/11.

Charlie read the newest text message twice. He whispered, "The motherfucker."

Gina could do a good street accent, often talking to Charlie as though they were in *Grease*. "You talkin' to me, buddy?"

Charlie was grave. "This guy is on to us."

"Who?"

"Mahatma Gandhi."

"Say again?"

"Gandhi, that new reporter at the *Times*."

"He's on to what?"

"He wants to ask us questions about the eighteen or so men who were picked up yesterday in upper Manhattan and Queens. He claims to have information that they were all picked up in coordinated raids and that they are all in what he says is an 'off-the-books' prison."

Gina Carbone, suddenly and visibly angry, asked, "How does he know that?"

"Fuck if I know. It's in the text message he just sent." He held up the cell phone so that the luminous screen shined in Gina's direction. As he did so, the elegant and miraculous instrument vibrated again with a new text message. Charlie read it and then said, "I'm going to throw this guy in the river."

"What now? We'll talk about the river later."

"You're not going to fucking believe this. It says he also wants to talk to you about Tony Garafalo."

She felt a rush of anger-driven adrenaline. "Check the guy out."

* * *

Rajiv Gandhi had long ago, as a war correspondent in Iraq and Afghanistan, learned to deal with fear. You didn't ignore it because you couldn't; you didn't by an act of the will overcome it because you couldn't; and you didn't deny that you had it because there was no room for denial. At least in Raj Gandhi's case, you told yourself that fear, like all other emotions, shall pass, sometimes in an hour and sometimes in days.

As he drove under the elevated portion of the FDR Drive along the East River, he felt for reasons he couldn't clearly identify, the first stirrings of the body-wide sensation he knew as fear. The steel pillars upholding the elevated highway were a maze. The space was dark and moist-looking, like a basement. Even with only a few cars moving, it was as noisy as a wind tunnel. The parked cars under the FDR looked abandoned as they, in fact, temporarily were because of the lockdown of Manhattan.

He drove slowly, looking for signs of anything unusual at the long-disused warehouses on the piers. "They stuffed these guys in some pier over on the East River in Manhattan," said the foul-mouthed man who had called him early that morning. "Not sure which. Near the old Fulton Fish Market. Maybe they sleep with the fishes already, you know. Maybe the spirit lives on."

After six years with a bare apartment in Beirut that he used only as a jumping-off point for his assignments in Iraq and Afghanistan, Raj had now lived for seven months in New York in a sterile one-room studio apartment in a high-rise apartment building on unglamorous York Avenue. He hadn't developed, and he recognized he would never develop, that discerning ear of long-time New Yorkers who could identify by their accents the boroughs in which people lived. But he did know, when he received a call that registered as an

Unknown number that the man spoke with an accent that had its origins in one of the boroughs, probably Queens.

For Raj, one of the rules of his profession, at least in the old-fashioned way he'd been trained to practice it, was that you did not ignore a tip or a source simply because you didn't like an accent or a messy way of speaking. Even the inarticulate could have crucial information. Content, not style, was important. "Are you the guy who writes for the *Times*?" the man asked.

"I am." Raj's own voice, he knew, would never lose that clipped accent that his youth in Bombay had implanted in him just as permanently as the color of his eyes.

"I've got an unbelievable story for you. Listen up, you'll win the fucking Pulitzer Prize with it."

This began as one of those contacts that was likely to be from a loony, lonely man, the kind of guy who spent large amounts of his time listening to and calling live sports talk radio shows. But patience could have its benefits. "I'm listening," Raj said.

"A bunch of Arabs, probably a dozen or more, were picked up out of their houses yesterday by special details of cops right after the bombs went off. These cops were like Navy SEALs, except they didn't have the flippers." The man laughed at his own joke, a hacking sound. Raj, a reserved person who had learned exquisite manners from his Hindu mother, didn't join the laugh.

Raj asked, "Where did this happen?"

"Queens, mostly. Where the hell do you think the fucking Arabs live? The Upper East Side?"

Raj knew he was dealing with a racist, but he increasingly accepted that this might be a source with at least some information. He asked, "What happened to them?"

"What happened to them was that they were hustled over the East River and locked up in a warehouse on an old pier. Made to disappear. You know the fucking government. They get to do what they want, they get to take away your money, sic the fucking IRS on you, make you disappear." The caller paused, and in that pause, he made the same sucking noise that was probably laughter. "Maybe you haven't been here long enough to know all that kind of shit."

Raj ignored what he recognized was the baiting sarcasm. The man wanted to annoy and provoke him. Raj asked the critical question, "How do you know all this?"

"Good question, Mr. Gandhi. By the way, are you related to the big guy?"

There were millions of Gandhis in India, but he had been asked this question again and again, sometimes from people who should have known better. Raj asked again, "How do you know all this?"

"This is New York, Gandhi. There are seven million souls in the naked city. Thirty-five thousand of them are on the job or have been on the job. Are you following me, Mr. Gandhi?"

There were two things Raj derived from what this angry, sardonic, and bizarre man had just said. He had to be over fifty or have spent time at home watching television reruns because there was a program in the '50s, the *Naked City*, about New York police. That show ended with a solemn voice-over announcing, "There are eight million stories in the naked city. This has been one of them."

And the reference to the "job" let Raj know that the man might have once been in the police department or known cops because that was how they described the institution they worked for, the "job." Raj was a serious student of everything, and since his new assignment to the city bureau of the *Times* he had become a dedicated student of the city and its history by reading and learning about it from books and articles and watching old television shows and movies. He had the time to learn; he wasn't married and never dated. He had lost the habit of developing friendships since he didn't stay in any one place for any real amount of time. He was, he thought, in his own way like the loner now speaking to him. Raj needed to lure the man. "No," he said, "I'm not really following you."

"One thing they don't want you to know is that the people who run the job aren't saints. They want you to believe they're heroes. Everyone's a hero these days. Cancer survivors, people who hide in the basement in fucking Kansas during a tornado, cripples who ride bikes, even female police commissioners. Know what, Mr. Gandhi? A canary told me that there are guys on the job who work for that Italian bitch who do all her dirty work. *Unterschtuppers.* You know what that is, don't you? You need to know Yiddish to get anywhere in New York, you know that, don't you? The *unterschtupper* is the guy who does somebody else's dirty work, usually around the asshole."

Raj waited through the man's odd laugh. And then the man said, "So yesterday morning this what-do-you-call-it elite group fanned out over the city and took down these Arabs and put them into cold storage."

"Where?"

"The canary didn't tell me that."

"Who's the canary?

"If I told you that, I'd have to kill you."

"Are you the canary?"

"Boy, Mr. Gandhi, you are a smart man, that's a good question. Smart, that's why I picked you for this call."

"Can I meet you?"

"Now maybe you're not so smart. No, you can't meet me."

"Can I call you?"

"My God, you're thick. No fuckin' way."

"So what do I do if I need to reach you?"

"I'll keep in touch. I'll know what you're doing."

And then the screen on Raj's cell phone flashed: *Call Ended.*

* * *

As he emerged from under the elevated FDR Drive into sunlight, Raj Gandhi noticed that the esplanade next to the shore of the East River was thronged with walkers, runners, rollerbladers, and bicyclists. There was light traffic on the drive. He wasn't surprised by either the carefree runners or the ordinary traffic even though explosions at one of the world's greatest museums had killed more than one thousand people just twenty-four hours earlier. Through his years in cities under attack and in war, he'd witnessed this almost immediate resurgence of the semblance of normal life even while fighting was underway nearby and often escalating. There had been open markets in Baghdad; men, women, and children on the dust-choked streets of Kabul; and even a soccer match in Aleppo as Assad's warplanes streaked overhead. Often that surge toward the restoration of normal life had collapsed, but he had always seen it and was seeing it now in Manhattan. There were even people fishing, most with their poles leaning on the railing that separated the walkway from the East River as they sat on the nearby benches and on plastic lawn chairs.

He drove slowly on the rutted service road that ran along the side of the FDR. There were only five remaining piers, all abandoned. They were all huge, several stories high and several football fields long. Not one had windows, just vertical aluminum siding. Rusted chain-link fences surrounded all of them. The fences were topped by razor wire and the gates were locked. In the East River steel pilings rose over the surface of the water, blocking access to the loading areas. No one, not even homeless people, was inside the steel fencing. Under each pier were boulders and rocks that the excavators had left in place. In fact, all of the East River had rocky, uninhabitable outcroppings that were small islands, many of them with small towers and flashing beacons to warn river traffic.

Nothing here, Raj thought. He had followed false leads before and this one had taken far less of his time than most. It came with the territory of his work. As he approached Houston Street, he saw an exit leading up to the FDR from the service road. There were no more piers further uptown.

It was when he began the gradual turn toward the exit that he saw the black Ford sedan behind him. He was instantly alert. The Ford had normal license plates, not government or police plates and not the plates with the letter *T* that designated private hired cars or limousines. The Ford also had tinted windows behind which he saw the outlines of the driver and a passenger.

Raj had been followed while driving in foreign countries. Each time the tail was obvious. The Jeeps or Land Rovers were banged up and sometimes rifles were visible, even at times thrust out of open windows. The tailing vehicles sometimes pulled up alongside him or drove so close behind that there was a slight jolt on the rear bumper at red lights or stop signs.

But the black Ford behind him now slowed when he slowed and accelerated when he did, always maintaining the same distance. Raj thought about stopping, leaving his car, and walking over to the Ford to speak to the driver. But he was afraid. He drove rapidly up to the drive. The Ford followed.

Raj felt a slight surge of relief when he merged into the uptown traffic. There was protection in numbers. And there was the spectacular view. In the center of the river, a powerful fountain shot incandescent water at least thirty feet into the daylight. Further upriver, at the southern end of Roosevelt Island, were the skeletal remnants of a nineteenth-century asylum. It was an eerie, medieval structure, and Raj was intrigued by it. Why was it left standing? Along the eastern shore of the river the exterior of the United Nations Building, still looking futuristic almost seventy years after it was built, glinted in the sunlight.

Raj pulled his car over to the narrow shoulder of the elevated drive. He turned on the blinking warning lights, staring in the rearview mirror as the black Ford, moving slowly, passed by. The men in it looked deliberately at him, as if to intimidate him.

CHAPTER EIGHTEEN

ROLAND FORTUNE WAS one of the few people in the world who knew how President Andrew Carter smelled when he was under pressure. In their basketball games in the White House gym, Roland usually played guard to cover the president. He still wore his Los Angeles Lakers shirt. "I never needed to wash it in the two seasons I played for the Lakers," the president joked. "Because I never got off the damn bench."

The president's odor when he was sweating was acrid, distinct, and really unpleasant. Although Andrew Carter was sleek and tall, with carefully combed blond hair streaked with gray, his body was densely covered with darker hair that, when it wetly adhered to his body, emitted a sharp odor that trailed him wherever he moved on the court.

Now as they spoke on a secure speakerphone, Roland heard a tremor in the president's voice. "It's very complex, Roland, to get food into Manhattan."

"It is? Why so? The entire West Side waterfront is open. There are piers at West 42nd Street where the big tour boats are moored along the Hudson. I'm no longshoreman, but the pier where the *Intrepid* is looks huge and very accessible. And the *Queen Mary* regularly comes and goes from the pier at 59th Street."

Harlan Lazarus' brittle voice spoke out in the background: "The quantities of food to feed one million people are beyond the capacity of the piers to handle."

"Is that a reason," Roland asked, "not to get some food and supplies in here? I'm sure the Parisians didn't close down their fabled restaurants after the *attacks* there."

"No, it isn't," Lazarus said, ignoring the remark about Paris. "I'm pointing out some of the reality of this."

"My reality is that the supermarkets, the bodegas, the big drug store chains, the delis, the places where people in Manhattan buy food, paper napkins, baby wipes, beer, cigarettes, condoms, have empty shelves."

The president asked, "Why wasn't this adequately taken into account before?" It wasn't clear whether the president was asking Roland or Harlan Lazarus or someone else this question. Roland refrained from answering.

"It was," Lazarus said. "But we didn't anticipate a series of attacks on Manhattan that would require more than a few hours of quarantine. We envisioned, frankly, a single hit, like 9/11. Even the attacks in Paris were separated by only a few coordinated minutes."

Roland was standing restlessly in his huge City Hall office. Its walls were mahogany. The big windows overlooked the old leafy trees of City Hall Park, whose gates were locked. He said, "That's not an acceptable answer, you know that."

"Let's look at this, Roland," the president said. "What kind of problem, real-world problem, is the food shortage presenting? The food didn't just vanish. It's in people's apartments, don't you think? Are there any reports of people starving in the streets?"

For Roland there was something liberating about the fact that this was not a video conference; it was on speakerphone only. He was annoyed, focused yet again on Harlan Lazarus' presence in the room with Andrew Carter in Washington. He had the sense that Lazarus passed that question along to the president. Roland glanced around the office at the other people he had assembled for the conference. He rolled his eyes to the ceiling. He said, "Hans Richter is here. He oversees much that happens on the streets. His people are out there. They have eyes. And there is less waste being picked up at supermarket sites, because the stores have been swept clean by customers. Is that right, Commissioner Richter?"

"It is."

"Are you saying," Andrew Carter asked, "that the amount of trash waiting on the streets in front of supermarkets indicates something significant?"

Roland made an effort not to show contempt for the questions Andrew Carter, obviously prompted by signals or notes from someone in the Oval Office with him, was asking. Roland said, "Let's be clear, Commissioner Richter, so that President Carter and Mr. Lazarus understand. We don't want to alarm them unnecessarily. Are there any bodies in the streets of people who have died from starvation?"

"Of course not," Hans answered.

"And that's because you followed the plan and dumped them in the East River as soon as you found them, right?"

Hans, who was modest, methodical, and business-like, was startled by the sarcastic question. This was not the well-organized and cordial Roland Fortune with whom he'd spent many hours at highly structured meetings. Hans thought of saying the plans were "to dump the bodies in the Hudson River, not the East River" but instead said nothing. Hans knew he had no sense of humor. He was a nice man who never made anyone laugh or smile.

Roland was exasperated, persistent. "But you heard the president, didn't you? Are there any bodies in the streets dead from starvation?"

"No," Hans said again.

In pain for the last hour, Roland picked up one of the blue pentagon-shaped Vicodin pills on his desk.

* * *

Without appearing to notice, Gina counted that as the third Vicodin he'd taken in the last half hour. She had been told by people on the regular security team assigned to Roland Fortune that he was a drug user, with prescription pills as his drug of choice. She genuinely admired Roland and had no intention of doing anything about his drug use. But now she was concerned that he was entering the cozy, yummy, cottony world of Valium, Xanax, Vicodin, and Percocet. She knew about addictions. Her brother Victor, at one time a heroin user, had in the end become dangerously addicted to prescription pills, and they eventually killed him. She let the cops who served on the mayor's security detail, more loyal by far to her than to the mayor, know that she wanted to be kept informed about the mayor's drug use and that they had to keep it a secret from everyone else.

After Roland swallowed the pill, a look of anticipatory relief spread over his face. He said quietly, "Mr. President, let me tell you what I need. I need some symbol at least that the cavalry is coming to town. So far there's a smattering of Marines on the streets. That's not enough. We have a city where even on ordinary days people call the 911 and 311 emergency lines to ask questions and just to plead and just to complain and moan. This is New York, after all. So please have food delivered by helicopter drop into Central Park if you have to."

"You can't mean that, Roland." The president's tone was skeptical, his words almost a rebuke.

In the background, Lazarus said, "Helicopter? I think the public associates helicopters with the ones on the top of the U.S. Embassy in Saigon as the last Americans were leaving Vietnam."

"That was 1975, Mr. Lazarus. Ninety percent of the people in the city weren't even born then. Nobody knows what the hell you're talking about."

Andrew Carter, by nature a conciliator, said, "Let's not get distracted by the history of 1975 or the Vietnam War."

"Mr. President," Roland said, "I'm a politician, not a military strategist. Why don't you come up here today?"

There was an interlude of dead silence. Roland and the other people in his office looked at each other, exchanging glances as though the speakerphone connection might have been lost.

Then Andrew Carter said, "We've given that some thought, too. After all, Bush was in New York the day after 9/11."

"I was here then," Roland said. "No matter what you thought of him, that was reassuring. I was a new city council member at the time, and I was nearby, and it was a striking image watching him speak through a bullhorn with the towers still smoldering behind him."

A new voice spoke. It was Gloria Reynolds, the head of the Secret Service. "This is different. We knew then that no further attacks were probable. Today we don't know that."

Roland knew that they would have anticipated that he would raise this issue and that they had choreographed this response. They planned to have the authoritative head of the Secret Service rule out a visit on the ground that the president would not be safe. Andrew Carter himself did not want to say that.

"Let me tell you, then, what I'm going to do," Roland said.

He was speaking too loudly. Gina, who knew something about the impact of opiates, also knew that magical thoughts could almost instantly flourish in the mind of a user. Anything and everything seemed possible when an opiate was in the blood.

Suddenly the line went silent, a void with a barely perceptible hum. Roland and Gina glanced at each other. Roland paused for five seconds. "Mr. President?"

No answer. Hans Richter, a master of technical data as well as a master of logistics, touched the laptop computer on the edge of the mayor's desk. His adroit fingers glided over some keys. He said confidently, "No problem on our end. They put us on mute."

"I guess we wait," Roland said.

"This is sick," Gina said. "Are we on our own here?"

"Let's be careful, Commissioner," Roland said. "You never know when they'll open the line again."

"Funny," Gina said, "that didn't seem to bother you a minute ago."

"We can mute our end," Hans said.

Still standing but increasingly relaxed as the soothing web of Vicodin took deeper hold, Roland said, "Hans, I know you love to demonstrate the beauty of the technology, but let's just wait." He smiled.

* * *

As he waited, Roland gazed out of the eastern-facing windows. The mayor's grand office was on the second floor of the three-story building. Barely changed over the years, it had been the office of more than twenty mayors: Theodore Roosevelt, LaGuardia, John Lindsay, and Rudy Giuliani. And Roland Fortune's favorite, Jimmy Walker, flamboyant and racy. Through the tall windows he could see the Brooklyn Bridge, its myriad suspension wires dazzling in the brilliant sunlight. He'd often looked at the bridge. In the daytime on typical days he could see colorful streams of traffic flowing into and away from Manhattan like unfurling ribbons. Today the bridge was empty.

A resonant sound filled the room. The connection was reestablished. The president's voice rang out, "Roland, we need to suspend this. Our embassies in Nairobi, Dar Es Salaam, and Zaire have all just been attacked."

And the connection went dead.

"Who gives a fuck about Dar Es Salaam?" Gina said.

Roland felt the onslaught of fear and confusion. He was, he realized, the leader of a city of millions of people, a place larger than many countries. But what did he really know about a crisis? He'd spent his adult life as a law student, a deputy commissioner when he was in his mid-twenties at the city's Parks and Recreation Department, a member of the squabbling city council in his early thirties, a young congressman, and now the Mayor. He saw himself as a conscientious man with the flair of an actor and the ability to attract hundreds of thousands of votes, and the skills to keep the largest city in America running.

But nothing in his life had prepared him for this. He'd listened to briefings from the Midwestern men and women who appeared to dominate the Homeland Security department. They always struck him as fanatics, the zealots of security, men and women who were building an empire by disseminating fear. All that Roland remembered from those briefings, which they insisted on holding in the secret, antiseptic structure below the basement of the 1970s-style disco on West 14th Street, was the term Code Apache, a silly name that Roland saw as a movie title, like Operation Just Cause, the designation of the invasion of Iraq, as if war were a video game. *Silly shit*, Roland had once remarked to Sarah Hewitt-Gordan, *would be a better name than Code Apache.*

He had to shake himself out of the fear or at least appear to do that. "Talk to me, Gina. The Three Stooges can't hear us. Assume we're on our own. What do we do to stop the killing?"

"We need to take down as many men as possible and interrogate them. It's almost impossible to find weapons or explosives. There are millions of apartments in this city. Any one of them can have an arsenal."

"So, tell me how you find these people."

"We do sweeps and pick up as many Arab street vendors, deli operators, and mosque-goers as we can. We talk to them. Not one of them is coming forward. So we go find them. Any random guy might give us a clue."

Roland gazed at her. "Gina, these people have civil rights."

"They can decide to talk to us or not. We have a right to ask questions. They have a right not to answer. My people don't break legs." Roland did not know that Gina was lying.

"Then we have a problem with racial profiling," he continued.

Gina paused and then said quietly but intently, "We can't really care about that, can we? When this is all over, they can sue us."

"What else? Do you have another plan?"

"We have a very thin network of informants, but so far nothing has surfaced. I can bring in more police assets from other parts of the city. We have hundreds of cruisers stationed outside Manhattan. We also have armored personnel carriers and armored trucks. I can keep them moving around Manhattan. Shock and awe. But nothing will work as effectively as intelligence and information. And nothing will get that as fast as confrontation, as in *I'll beat the shit out of you unless you talk.*"

Roland held a blank piece of paper in his hands and tore it into pieces as small as confetti. "You do what you think is best. And if nothing happens by tomorrow morning, I'm opening up the city."

"Can you do that?" she asked.

It was the Vicodin coursing through his body that spoke, "I can do any fucking thing I want."

So, Gina thought, *can I.*

CHAPTER NINETEEN

Oliver was a heavily muscled dog. Beneath the silken fur his flesh was densely packed. Gabriel wrapped Oliver in a multicolored quilt. Only his head was visible. Although the body was heavy, Gabriel, who had often lifted patients, was strong. Gabriel made his way down the carpeted stairwell and pushed the door open. Suddenly aroused from the long vigil of waiting for him, the reporters scrambled to attention.

He walked among them. "I'm Gabriel Hauser. I have something to tell you."

He paused while the reporters from television stations, newspapers, magazines, and the social media sources suddenly scrambled to attention and activity from their long lethargy of waiting. There were CNN, WNBC, and CBS panel trucks on the street with huge, Martian-like broadcast saucers on their roofs. The reporters with microphones, notepads, and tape recorders were immediately ready to hear the elusive Gabriel Hauser, the Angel of Life, speak publicly for the first time.

The blanket in which Oliver was wrapped was stained with blood. Rather than stand at a distance as if holding a press conference, Gabriel walked among the reporters and cameramen. They formed a tight cluster around him, like football players in a huddle.

"I'm carrying my eight-year-old dog. Armed men from the NYPD, the FBI, and Homeland Security shot him five minutes ago."

Gabriel saw the looks of surprise in the faces around him. He also recognized their excitement. They were the first to hear news that was far beyond anything they had expected.

The first reporter to react was a young woman from CNN whom Gabriel had seen during the few times he watched television. "What were the agents doing in your apartment?"

"Doing? They were ransacking it. And shooting and wounding this loving, innocent dog."

"How do you know they were law enforcement?"

"Law enforcement? That's a strange expression. They were thugs."

Another voice asked, "How do you know they were with the FBI and Homeland Security?"

"Three of them wore windbreakers with those words on them. So I assume they were agents. But they're the kinds of jackets you could buy on the street, just as you can buy baseball caps with logos from the police department, the fire department, Vietnam Veterans."

The same voice asked, "Well, did they say where they were from?"

"No one showed any badges."

Someone at the outer perimeter of the group asked, "What else did they say?"

"That they had a search warrant."

The CNN reporter reclaimed the questioning. She held the microphone within inches of Gabriel's face. Over her left shoulder a camera was trained on him, adjusting to every movement he made. "What did the search warrant say?"

"As far as I know, nothing. They never showed it to me."

"What were they looking for?"

"They ransacked everything, they took nothing."

"How was it that the dog was injured? Was he attacking them?"

"I'm sure they will tell you that. I can hear them claiming they were lawfully in our home, and that we unleashed this vicious beast on them. This is a gentle, sweet animal."

"What," she asked, "do you plan to do?"

"Look for the truth. I want to know why these horrific people invaded our home, trashed our belongings, and shot an innocent animal. And by bringing this to you, I want to prompt you to ask questions. What exactly is the government doing to protect us from the government itself? Who are the terrorists here?"

"But, Dr. Hauser, *you* must have done something that led the agents to get a warrant and search your home."

"Nothing, absolutely nothing. I refuse to let outrageous conduct like this pass without a challenge. No one can shift blame to me. I did not do this."

Still holding Oliver's increasingly heavy, blood-soaked body, Gabriel turned to the five steps that led to the door of the brownstone. Just as he pulled the heavy door shut, he heard the question, "Can you tell us why you were thrown out of the Army?"

* * *

Raj Gandhi watched the handsome, stricken, angry doctor on the screen of one of the big monitors suspended throughout the newsroom at the *Times*. He had been placing calls to every possible source to get more details, any details, about the phantom detention center on the East River. He was still wary of the information the weird caller had given him. But he was also certain that the Ford that had tailed him, which was so much like those eight-cylinder cars in decades-old movies such as *Bullitt* and *The French Connection,* meant something. The tailing scared him; it had also made him angry. He prized the old-fashioned detachment he brought to his work as a journalist, and he wanted to embrace it now. But he understood the meaning of that tough-guy bluster: *This isn't business, it's personal.*

Raj was standing as he watched the flat screen television. He was intrigued by what he saw in Gabriel Hauser. The man was striking. He had that slender muscularity of a professional soccer player. He was intense, he was well-spoken, and he was vengeful.

Raj Gandhi wanted to speak to Gabriel Hauser.

Raj was resourceful. He had not only his own instincts and training as a reporter, he also had the resources of a fading and uncertain but still potent newspaper that, for the most part, was not afraid of letting its reporters loose to do investigative journalism.

Using his computer, Raj learned several things about Gabriel Hauser. He was thirty-eight. He was the son of a failed concert performer, once a briefly rising star for the New York Philharmonic who had committed suicide when Gabriel was twenty-seven. After several years in the Army, Gabriel was dismissed, in the midst of service in Afghanistan and Iraq, under the *don't ask, don't tell* rules which were then still in place and rigidly enforced. He had sent an angry, bitter letter to the editors at the *Times*, which declined to publish it. Like all other letters submitted to the editors, it had been lodged in the infinite ether of the *Times* archival information.

Checking a database that was even more thorough than census data, Raj located Gabriel Hauser living at 17 East 82nd Street. There was no telephone number. Roaming through other data, Raj found that Cameron Kennedy Dewar lived at the same address and in the same apartment. Again, no telephone number or e-mail address. But a ten second Google search revealed Cameron Kennedy Dewar worked at a public relations firm on West 23rd Street, the area around the wedge-shaped Flatiron Building that had attracted PR firms, publishing houses, and literary agents over the last ten years. They had migrated there from the overpriced office space in midtown Manhattan. The only object on the walls of Raj's sparsely furnished, undecorated apartment was a reproduction of Alfred Stieglitz's photograph of the Flatiron Building, in the rain at dusk more than a hundred years earlier. He loved that strange, rain-drenched photograph.

Almost from the day more than six months earlier when his by-line first appeared in the *Times* as a writer covering the city, Raj started receiving calls from PR people representing companies, executives, lawyers, actors, and sports stars, all that vast array of people who wanted favorable coverage for every jerk in the world in the *New York Times*. One of the cardinal rules Raj had learned when he was in journalism school at Columbia was that you never relied on PR people for information.

Raj was familiar with the firm where Cameron Kennedy Dewar worked. Raj also knew that, if he placed a call there asking for Cameron Kennedy Dewar and identifying himself as a reporter for the *Times*, he would get instant attention. This was his conduit to Gabriel Hauser. For any PR agency, a call from a reporter for the *Times* was like a summons from royalty.

"Can I ask you to hold?" a perky young woman who answered the phone said.

Sixty seconds later, an older woman with a crisp corporate style came on the line. "Mr. Gandhi? This is Jessica Brown. So good to hear from you. What can we do to help you?"

"I'm trying to reach Cameron Dewar."

"Cameron's not in the office today. Can I help you?"

"I'd like his cell phone number."

"We haven't heard from him since the attack. His cell may not be working. He lives right next to the museum. Are you sure I can't help you?"

"You can, Miss Brown. I'd like his cell number."

"Are you working on a story?"

Raj Gandhi was always unnervingly polite. "I'm really not sure. I'm just making calls that I need to make. I'd very much appreciate his number."

"It's 917-631-0011." She paused, and in that pause Raj thought about how indifferent this woman was to the fate of someone she knew well. She clearly had no idea whether he was alive or dead, injured or not. She was all business. "Do you want me to repeat that?"

"No, I have it, thank you."

"I hope I can take you to lunch when the dust settles."

Raj, who never went to lunch with anyone, said, "That would be nice, Miss Brown."

* * *

Three hours later Raj sat on a bench near the merry-go-round in the heart of the southern expanse of Central Park. The afternoon was limpid, as clear as the day before. Incredibly, the merry-go-round was operating. Gleeful-sounding kids sat on the big shiny horses while, less than a mile away, smoke still rose from the shattered museum. Most of the plaster horses reared up, forelegs in the air, perpetually ready to gallop. Raj, who had never seen a merry-go-round while growing up in India, was struck by how terrifying the frozen, brightly painted animals looked.

He recognized Gabriel Hauser. Dressed in a blue blazer and white shirt open at the neck, Gabriel walked toward Raj although he'd never seen him before. It wasn't difficult to recognize an emaciated, intelligent-looking Indian man sitting in the area where they had agreed to meet.

Raj stood up. "Dr. Hauser, thanks for coming."

Gabriel, who was at least a head taller than Raj Gandhi, said, "Not a problem."

They sat next to each other. Raj let five seconds pass before he spoke. "I heard what you said on television."

"That's good. I said it because I wanted people to hear it."

Gabriel was a man who had learned to hesitate before trusting anyone. He had never before dealt with journalists. He was still stung by that question he had heard two hours earlier as he walked through the door of the brownstone: *Why were you thrown out of the Army?* He realized that he shouldn't have been taken aback by the question. There were hostile people in the world who were quickly searching Google and Yahoo for and finding negative, private information about him. Gabriel said, "Cam told me about your conversation with him."

"I'm developing a story about the government's reaction to the bombings. More precisely, about violations of people's civil rights."

"So Cam told me. Now I want to hear you tell me."

Raj knew that sometimes he needed to give information before he got it. Often the information he let out was not completely accurate, just as many times information he got in exchange wasn't accurate either. With his usual precise diction, an accent that he knew put some people off, he said, "I have sources who tell me secret arrests are taking place."

Gabriel for the first time managed to get Raj to look into his eyes. He wondered whether the frail-looking man was shy or evasive. Or even a closeted gay man. Gabriel said nothing.

"I have reason to believe there are secret detention centers, black prisons, in Manhattan where these men have been brought."

Between Gabriel and the frail-looking man was a silver commemorative plaque embedded in the bench's green-painted wood. The engraved lettering read: *To J.C. Lover of the park and of life. Gone too soon. C.T.*

Who, Gabriel wondered, *were these people? Did C.T. still grieve?*

"So tell me," Gabriel said, "why you wanted to see me."

"I'm looking into more than the violation of their rights, if, in fact, these arrests and detentions have happened."

"Draw the connection for me."

"Your rights. Someone has tried to terrorize you."

"No one is going to terrorize me, Mr. Gandhi. Do you know who's doing all this?"

"I'm not sure, Dr. Hauser. The mayor? The police commissioner? Rogue agents? Homeland Security? I was hoping you'd have some information."

"Do you?"

There was no trace of bitterness or sarcasm in Gabriel's voice. His eyes were almost blue despite his black and lustrous eyebrows that, set in the perfect symmetry of his face, had attracted so many men and women since Jerome Fletcher first embraced him years ago as he emerged at age fifteen, naked, from the shower in the apartment on West End Avenue.

Raj said, "I have to be honest with you, Dr. Hauser. I have another source who says it was no coincidence that you were near the museum at exactly the same time the bombs went off."

The automated tin-pan-alley music from the merry-go-round switched from the theme song to *Annie* to the theme of *The Sting*.

"Really? And what genius was that? I live on that block. I was walking the dog I love."

"The source tells me you were scheduled to work that morning and that you were uncharacteristically insistent on not doing it."

Gabriel's voice was calm. "Who are we talking about?"

"The source?"

"That word makes him sound like an oracle of truth. Who is he? I need to talk to him. I want to hunt down the people who attacked my partner and my dog this morning. Was he one of them?"

"I wish I could tell you, Dr. Hauser. I promised him anonymity. I can't do my work if I can't keep those promises."

Suddenly a green Army helicopter, its rotors swirling through the sunlight, passed overhead through the tranquil summer sky. The kids and the parents near the merry-go-round looked up excitedly. Gabriel didn't have to look up because he recognized the unique thudding pulsation of the transport helicopters that had brought wounded men to him.

"The source said you developed contacts in the Middle East."

"I did. I treated civilians and soldiers, anyone who was brought to the hospitals. It was the most intimate kind of contact you could ever imagine."

"They say you are bitter."

"Did they say why?"

"Because you were forced out of the military."

Gabriel's voice was still calm, the voice of a man who had many times spoken quietly as he was operating on people who were near death and had often died from their irreparable wounds while he did his work. "Who are these people? I became a jihadist because I was forced out of the Army?"

"There are many disturbing things going on right now, Dr. Hauser. Some of them are happening to you."

Although the last traces of the sound from the Army helicopter were fading, the thuds from the rotors were still almost tangible. The music from the merry-go-round had changed again. It was now a quick, lively version of God Bless America.

Gabriel gazed at Raj's absolutely black eyes. "I know that. But what about you, Mr. Gandhi? You're working on troubling things, aren't you? Do you think that being a reporter for the New York Times gives you some kind of immunity from harm?"

"I'm not worried about myself, I'm looking for facts."

"And so am I."

"Don't you think," Raj asked, "that we can help each other?"

Gabriel paused. A refreshing breeze, creating glittering green in the leaves, swept over them. "Let me have your iPhone."

Without asking anything, Raj passed his phone to Gabriel, who added his number to the contact list on Raj's cell phone. "This is a special number for me. No one else has it. Use it when you want to."

"Do you want mine?"

"I have it. You called me, Mr. Gandhi. As they say in the movies, I've got your number."

CHAPTER TWENTY

ROLAND FORTUNE LIKED people. He loved walking the streets of the city. He often left City Hall to make unexpected appearances in all the boroughs, walking several blocks each time, instantly and always recognizable. He ran almost every weekend in races in Central Park, Prospect Park in Brooklyn, Van Cortlandt Park in the Bronx, and Flushing Meadows in Queens. He attended Mass in churches throughout the city and spoke at Baptist churches in Harlem and Bedford-Stuyvesant. And he was a regular presence at parties in the houses of the rich on the Upper East Side and in Tribeca. He was a man who loved the joy of living each day.

He was also an unrepentant liberal who knew how to practice an old style of politics. The police and fire department unions, overcoming their initial reluctance about a Puerto Rican mayor, embraced him because he cooperated with them on pay and benefits. This was a sea change. Ever since the Giuliani and Bloomberg years, the unions had expected resistance from City Hall. The leaders of the immense civil service populations, men and women in the sanitation department, the schools, all the myriad government agencies praised him as "cooperative, farsighted, inspirational."

So when word had spread that Roland was very disturbed that he didn't know where Sarah's body was located, a group of men and women in the medical examiner's office organized themselves to track down her remains. They found her in a temporary morgue that had been installed at the long-abandoned St. Vincent's Hospital in Greenwich Village. The exterior white walls of the increasingly derelict building were graying under the steady accretion of rain and sunlight, soot and time. But even these decaying buildings on this bright afternoon somehow looked fresh.

Roland was wearing sunglasses as he left the unmarked sedan which took him from City Hall to St. Vincent's in the Village. He had ordered the car and only two security officers in plain clothes to accompany him. They walked near him as he approached the single functioning door, the access to the chilled room where at least seventy-five bodies were stored in the emergency morgue. This morgue was the one to which bodies that had no identification—no licenses, no passports, no wallets, no pocketbooks—were brought. Sarah Hewitt-Gordan was the first of these wrecked bodies that had been identified.

Roland was stunned by what he saw in the room as he entered: three orderly rows of dead bodies stretched out on the concrete floor. They were covered in identical plastic blankets, all blue. Even in the artificial chill, there was the faint but unmistakable odor of dead flesh. Sarah's body, he knew, was one of the sources of that odor.

A huge black man, a nurse in blue hospital scrubs, approached Roland, who asked, "Where is she?"

The nurse didn't speak. He led Roland down the aisle between two of the rows of bodies. Only one of the blue blankets had a sheet of paper attached to it. Her name was on it.

Visibly shaking, Roland Fortune knelt on the concrete floor. After several seconds, he reached toward the blanket. The massive nurse finally spoke, "That ain't a good idea, sir."

Roland looked up. "Is it bad?"

The man nodded. "Big time."

"How do you know it's her?"

"We had a picture."

Roland glanced at his unsteady hands and then completed the movement he had started. He pulled at the upper edge of the blanket, revealing her head.

At first he saw her face in profile. Her eyes were open. There was a scratch on her forehead. The once vibrant skin was now gray.

He leaned closer to her. He gently turned her head so he could have a last look at the face he had loved. He recoiled. "Christ," he screamed.

There was no right side of her face, only a mess of torn flesh and bone.

Roland jumped to his feet. The nurse grabbed the edge of the plastic sheet to cover Sarah's head. At the same time he reached across her body to Roland, who appeared about to fall. He grabbed Roland's left arm to steady him. Still bracing Roland up, he hustled him to the door. He was a powerful man and although Roland, too, was large, the man handled him as if he were a dish towel.

* * *

Roland sat in the back of the car for fifteen minutes. His guards had sensitive instincts. They stood fifteen feet away, waiting. Behind the tinted windows, Roland wailed, a crying that he hadn't experienced since he was a boy, when his father had just walked away from the family and disappeared for good. Roland never saw him again. If he were still alive, Reuben Fortune must have known his son had become one of the most famous people in the country. For some unidentifiable reason, Roland had a sense his father was living. Had Reuben ever returned, Roland would have kissed and embraced him.

Roland needed to reconnect to life. He left the car. Greenwich Village, his favorite part of the city, looked so profoundly quiet and peaceful in the afternoon sunlight: the old-world brownstones, the mature leafy trees that lined both sides of the narrow streets, and the roofs with their water tanks made of curved wood bound in hoops of iron.

He walked downtown on Seventh Avenue South. On any normal Monday afternoon the streets would be alive with people, but this was not a normal Monday. No subway trains were running. The elongated accordion-style city buses were off the streets. Light traffic, mainly empty yellow taxis, raced down the avenue. There would soon come a point when no gasoline would be left at any station in Manhattan, and even that light traffic would then stop.

Roland turned right, his security detail trailing him by several feet. Perry Street stretched out before him. Twenty years earlier, he had been in love with a young woman who lived in a single room studio apartment at 18 Perry Street. He remembered her name. She was Marilyn Botteler, a Kansas girl who sang with a rock band at places like CBGB in the seedy, druggy East Village. But he remembered most the intimacy of the small apartment. It was on the third floor at the back of the building overlooking a small patio with rusty lawn furniture surrounded by frail trees and with debris on the ground. He spent three summer months with her. Where in this vast world was she now? Was she even alive? He had once done a Google search for her. There were no results.

As he passed the steps of the building, wondering how many men and women had lived in that cozy apartment over the last two decades, he was recognized by two men walking hand in hand. They wore tight-fitting shirts, short pants and hiking socks and boots, one of the most recognizable outfits of gay men. They were startled when they recognized him. The taller man said, "It's you."

The instinctive politician, Roland stopped to shake their hands. "It is indeed."

The taller man said, "This is really surprising." Smiling, he waited several seconds before asking, "Why are you here?"

"To see with my own eyes how people are doing. How are you?"

"Enjoying the day. It's like the days after 9/11. We don't have to go to work, it's like a weekday holiday. One of the fringe benefits of disaster."

Roland was struck by the callousness of what the man said, and by the honesty. He was used to people filtering what they told him, often trying to anticipate what they believed he wanted to hear. But this man frankly was saying something Roland never expected to hear: his dominant selfish thought about the bombings and the deaths of a thousand men, women, and children was that he'd been granted a day and possibly more off work. Roland didn't know what to say, but there was no need to respond because other people were recognizing and approaching him. He continued to walk, surrounded by a small crowd. He felt revived. The presence of other people energized him.

For him the most familiar landmark in the West Village was the cigar store, Village Cigars, at the intersection of Seventh Avenue South and Christopher Street. The store and its vivid red-and-white sign had been there since the time he first saw the Village, when he was seventeen and on his first exploratory trip into the lower parts of Manhattan from the Bronx. He had come out of the No. 1 subway train at the intersection of Seventh Avenue South and Sheridan Square. The Village, as intimate and companionable then as it was now, was another country for him, so different from the housing project where he was raised. In all the years since that first sighting, he had seen that sign hundreds of times, in rainy weather, snow, fog, and crystalline days such as this day.

Before he could reach the store, three police cruisers and two unmarked cars arrived. They had come for him. His two security people had contacted their bosses, and word that the Mayor of New York City was walking essentially unguarded through the streets of the Village had reached Gina Carbone. "Who the hell are these bozos to leave him out there?" she had asked. "Get over there and pick him up. All I need today is a dead mayor."

Reacting like a teenage truant, Roland said to Rocco Barbiglia, the lieutenant who had first told Gina about the attack as she had lunch with her family on Staten Island, "So she found me out?"

"Hey, Mr. Mayor, she's going to send you to the principal's office."

CHAPTER TWENTY-ONE

GABRIEL HAUSER LOVED his work. The seventy-hour weeks never fatigued him. In fact, they gave him a purpose and energy. He had reached the stage in his career when he could have left the demands of the emergency room, where the pace was dictated by the randomness of stabbings, shootings, accidents, heart attacks, and drug overdoses, for a private practice with its regular hours, predictability, and bigger income. But he had learned his trade in war zones. He'd experienced the miracle of repairing shattered bodies and restoring life. And he accepted the fact that often people were brought to him so damaged that the ingenuity of his hands and the creativity of his mind could not prevent their deaths.

Whenever he walked into the hospital, Gabriel felt a sense of relief, comfort, and the return to the familiar. He had the same reaction when he entered the apartment where he lived with Cam, the reassurance that he was in the place where he was meant to be. The doctors' entrance, through which he passed simply by waving a plastic card over an electronic eye, opened into a gleaming hallway.

The changing room had the look and feel and atmosphere of a locker room in a men's gym. There were rows of steel lockers, a sauna, a steam room, and shower stalls. As in a locker room at an old gym, the air was always moist.

When he reached his own locker, he was immediately taken aback by something totally unexpected: the combination lock to his locker was missing. He pulled the door open. The locker was empty.

Gabriel heard Vincent Brown speak behind him. "Dr. Hauser, we had quite a scene this morning. Too bad you weren't here for it."

Gabriel turned. Brown was in his starched scrubs. He was the senior doctor in the emergency room and, like a commanding officer in the Army, his uniform always looked "strack"—the Army expression for neat and stiff.

"What happened?"

"Mama Bear, Papa Bear, and Baby Bear came to take away your stuff."

"Do you think, Vincent, that you can stop for once with the sarcastic shit? What's going on?"

Vincent Brown approached him. He was shorter than Gabriel. He had a neat mustache and the haughty look of a minaret. He was angry. "What the hell are you up to, Hauser?"

"Up to? I came here to work." Gabriel, too, was angry. Suddenly he had the sense that he might hit Brown or that Brown might hit him. It was that infusion of street adrenaline.

"There were cops all over this place. They smashed your locker, they took your clothes. They showed me a picture of Patient X52."

"So what?"

"So what? They asked whether you treated him. I said 'yes'. They asked for how long. 'Thirty minutes.'"

"Thirty minutes? That's bullshit."

"They asked whether I saw you talk to him. 'Yes'. How long? 'The full thirty minutes,' I said."

"I was with him for three minutes, you know that. What are you doing to me?"

"And they wanted to know whether you took anything from him. 'Probably,' I said, 'possibly.'"

"That's a lie, and you know it."

"Or whether you gave him anything. I said something went back and forth between the two of you."

"You weren't even on the floor then."

"They asked to take a look at your treatment notes on Patient X52. You didn't make any."

"Nobody made notes. This place was chaotic."

"They asked if you knew that Patient X52 was really named Silas Nasar?"

"Silas who?"

"Certainly you did. That's the name written on the discharge papers you signed."

"That's crazy. I never signed discharge papers."

"You want to know what else?" Brown was trembling, the shaking that rage created. And Gabriel was trembling, too; it was the same rage. Brown said, "They took your personnel records."

"Don't tell me you let them do that?"

"Of course I did."

"Those are private, really private."

"So what?"

"Did they have a search warrant?"

"Search warrant?"

"They can't just take my records."

"Why not? What are you now? An ACLU lawyer and not just the Angel of Life?"

Gabriel stepped backwards, wanting to put enough distance between Brown and himself so that he didn't follow through on the urge to punch or push him.

"Tell me, Brown, what is it about me that you hate?"

"Just about everything."

"Why are you lying? Why did you tell a reporter that I refused to work on Sunday?"

"Why was the guy with the birthmark the guy you ran to first?

Silas Nasar? The cops wanted to know that. Why was Silas Nasar so special to you?"

"What bullshit is that? He was the first hurt person I saw. Everyone else was dead."

Brown, too, stepped back, widening the gap between them. He now had the familiar sardonic look. "I'm e-mailing the board of the hospital to ask for an immediate suspension of your privileges. I want you out of my hospital. Angel of Life. What unmitigated crap."

CHAPTER TWENTY-TWO

WHEN GINA CARBONE arrived at the gritty corner of East 125th Street and Lexington Avenue, she saw that her orders had been carried out, as they always were. She had personally given the order one hour earlier, at three in the afternoon, to cordon off entirely a ten-block area from East 125th Street to East 135th Street and from Lexington to Second Avenues. That area was now entirely quarantined—no one was allowed to move into it and no one could leave it.

And that heady rush of anticipation came from the view, which she had last seen during the night before the invasion of Kuwait and Iraq in 1991, of hundreds of armed men and women massed quietly in green uniforms, helmets and body armor, and the lethal mobile equipment of warfare. As a soldier in the strange, starlit desert of Saudi Arabia, she had been awestruck and excited by the vision of an immense Army concentrated and ready to move, only awaiting orders. And now she was the person who would issue the orders.

Billy O'Connell, the smartest of her deputy commissioners, said, "They're in Building 5 in Carver Towers."

The George Washington Carver Towers were a bleak brick public housing project built in the 1940s or 1950s. Gina knew about the Carver Towers because they were constructed over the blocks where her father had been raised when East Harlem, in the 1930s and 1940s, was still an Italian neighborhood.

"What floor?" she asked.

"Parts of the fifth and sixth floor on the southwest side."

"Do we still think there are six of them?"

"Not completely sure. Maybe more."

"And what about the hostages?"

O'Connell said, "There may not be any. Our people are saying that they may be straw hostages. Fakes, members of the crew pretending to be hostages."

"In the Army," Gina said, "we used to complain about pain-in-the-ass civilians getting in the way."

Billy O'Connell was cautious and quiet-spoken as usual. "Like I said, Commissioner, there could be hostages or not."

"We'll find out soon enough. As soon as Reilly says it's a go, we're going."

"Are you sure? It could be just a street gang caught up in something they can't understand."

"Really, Billy? I've got enough information to see it otherwise. A street gang would just walk out the front door when they saw armed vehicles and hundreds of my people dressed up like ninja warriors. Gang guys are punks, not heroes."

"It's your call, Commissioner."

"That's right, Billy, it is."

* * *

Three minutes later, Tom Reilly, an ex-Marine with three tours of duty in Iraq and Afghanistan and now the leader of a squad of twenty heavily armed and well-trained men, and one combat-trained woman, called Gina Carbone. He said, "The cat's on the roof." It was their code to signal that his crew was ready.

"Go," she answered.

Almost immediately there was a deafening succession of detona-
tions from stun grenades designed to be loud enough to disorient
anyone within fifty yards of the explosions. During the concussions,
six men and one woman in uniform raced across the housing project's grassless, cheerless lawns. As they smashed through the service
door on the ground floor of Building 5, they heard a three-second
burst of shots from an M-16 several flights above them in the urine-
stained and urine-smelling stairwell. On a receiver in his left ear as
small as a hearing aid, Ike Tapscott heard Hank Carbornaro, the
head of the squad of seven descending from the roof of the building, ask, "That you?"

"No," Hank answered. "Motherfuckers are firing up the stairwell."

A grenade bounced from side to side down the center of the
stairwell, exploding only three flights above Harry Stonecipher, the
point man of Ike Tapscott's squad. As Stonecipher wailed through
his excruciating pain, another man shouted, "I see the fucker who
tossed the grenade!"

No one in Tapscott's squad would shoot in the stairwell since
an upward rising or downward fired bullet could strike one of his
people or Carbonaro's or any of the tenants who might be in the
stairwell. As they had been trained to do, the disciplined members
of his squad continued to run up the stairs. At the landing on the
fourth floor Stonecipher lay on his back, his legs and arms sprawled
in a pattern that only a corpse could make.

And then there was silence in the stairwell. They were at the
door that led to the east entrance of the fifth floor. Carbonaro's
crew was now behind the door at the west entrance at the other
end of the grimy hallway. There were sixteen apartments lining the
cinder block walls of the fifth floor. Tapscott, glancing through the
small porthole window in the metal door, saw that the hallway was

cluttered with bicycles, baby carriages, and even a barbecue grill. The tenants used the hallway as a storage room.

Only Tapscott had been in close combat before. He glanced at the six remaining members of his crew. He saw in their faces the terror he had seen so often in Iraq and Afghanistan. Their green uniforms were soaked with sweat.

Tapscott waited for Reilly's voice to speak in his earbud. The helicopter aloft around the tower had devices that could pinpoint the location of objects such as rifles and canisters that contained explosives. Tapscott knew that no technology that was supposed to work in this kind of chaos was perfect.

Reilly's voice, small and intense, suddenly materialized in his ear. "Apartment 5G. To your left, seven doors down from where you are. There's a dried-up Christmas wreath on the door. At least six people inside. It's a very hot spot. The experts in the helicopter say they're all hot. The place is filled with men with assault rifles, grenades, all kinds of shit like that."

Tapscott flung the door open. *"Move, move!"* Crouching, he ran toward the door with the dried-out wreath. He vaulted like an Olympic steeplechase runner through the clutter of tricycles, baby carriages, and shopping carts.

He halted at the far side of the door to Apartment 5G, waiting for the other crew members. In that instant, in the din of shouting men, clattering objects, and the roar of blood in his own head, he saw two men leap into the hallway from an apartment five doors beyond Apartment 5G. In a frozen instant, he recognized that the men were identical to the Iraqi and Afghan fighters he had seen over the last seven years, except that they were dressed in civilian clothes. They had assault rifles.

In the first burst of fire, Ike Tapscott was shot in the face. His head disintegrated.

CHAPTER TWENTY-THREE

GABRIEL HAUSER IMMEDIATELY recognized, as only someone who had been in a war zone could know, that the intense *pop pop pop* sounds were from the exchange of rifle fire, not the repercussions of firecrackers. Several times in Afghanistan and Iraq he had been less than a hundred yards from fully engaged combat. Although the clatter of rifle fire was harrowing each time he heard it, it also had an odd resonance, as though it couldn't be serious, it had to be a game that boys were playing, not a situation that could maim or kill. Just play-acting—nobody was going to get hurt. It always took seconds for that sense of unreality to wear off and for the fear of dying to overwhelm him, as it always had.

As a doctor, Gabriel had the instinct to run to people who might be injured. It was the reason he went to medical school and enlisted as a second lieutenant in the Army just as the Afghan war began. He wanted to help, not to harm, to restore people to life, not see them die. He first heard the unmistakable noise of gunfire as he was walking downtown on Fifth Avenue under the mature, rustling branches and leaves overhanging the tall stone wall that bordered the park. The bright air was just as it was on any other glorious, life-giving day in June. He turned and ran east in the direction of the dangerous clamor.

Ever since that time more than two decades earlier when the now-dead Jerome Fletcher had led him in his first runs on the long

paths in Riverside Park, and then had waited in all his energetic
vitality for the fifteen-year-old Gabriel to emerge from the shower,
Gabriel had been an ardent, fluid runner. He had learned the terrain of the city through long runs everywhere in Manhattan when
he was a resident at Mount Sinai working fourteen hours a day,
seven days in a row followed by four days off. In those four-day
intervals, he spent serene and dedicated hours running in Central
Park and Riverside Park, along the concrete waterside walkways on
the borders of the Hudson River and the East River, and from the
windswept Battery at the southern tip of Manhattan about which
Melville wrote in the first chapter of *Moby Dick* to the heights of
the George Washington Bridge on the West Side and the Triboro
Bridge on the east.

Gabriel also learned the internal streets of the island: the shining
old cobblestones on Greene Street and Mercer Street in Soho on
which the worn stones glowed in sunlight or glinted in the rain;
the intimate, exciting length of Christopher Street in the West
Village; and the sweeping empty corners of far West 14th Street as
it opened out to the Hudson River.

But he rarely ran on the grid of streets in East Harlem even
though the western edge of it started on Madison Avenue just behind Mount Sinai. He knew there were housing projects spread
through the area and that there were some old blocks with rundown brownstones in parts of East Harlem that were once Italian
neighborhoods and had later become crack houses.

The closest he ever came to this section of the city was in the four
New York City marathons he had run. A three-mile stretch of the
course was on First Avenue from 96th Street to 124th Street where
the avenue veered onto a ramp that led up to the old Willis Avenue
Bridge and then into the South Bronx. Block after block on First
Avenue was lined with old tenements where the ground floors were

occupied by thrift shops, bodegas, bars, and even places that fixed flat tires on the sidewalks. There were one or two storefront evangelical churches with Spanish names. To the left some blocks were occupied by grim, red-brick housing projects named for African American men, most of them scientists, who had been famous in the late nineteenth and early twentieth centuries but were now forgotten, Booker T. Washington, George Washington Carver. On this stretch of the autumn marathon there were no cheering crowds, unlike the thousands of ecstatic, applauding crowds in Brooklyn and the frenzied people at the long turn from the arduous two mile route of the 59th Street Bridge arching from Queens over the East River into Manhattan.

On largely deserted upper First Avenue, grinning children bolted into the stream of thousands of runners, all of them by now silent and beaten up by the eighteen miles they had already covered. The kids wanted to high five as many runners as they could touch. Most of the determined, increasingly exhausted runners pressed straight ahead, no longer fueled by the thousands of onlookers. But not Gabriel: he slapped each hand that reached out to him.

Now on this limpid Monday afternoon, Gabriel trotted uptown on Madison Avenue from 86th Street. He passed the small Parisian-style stores—the shops with French names carrying expensive baby clothes, the old-fashioned pharmacy at 90th Street called simply the 90th Street Pharmacy with its odor of medicinal compounds and ladies' powder, and, at 93rd Street, the cozy, companionable Corner Bookstore with its bright red façade and windows behind which new books were arrayed as deliciously as pastries. Above 96th Street, the avenue changed into the same type of unappealing stores that lined the street level on First Avenue.

It was the acrid smell of cordite, the odor of igniting powder that was at the core of every gunshot, grenade, and explosive device, including roadside bombs and fireworks, ever made, that first arrested his attention and led him toward the blocks between 125th and 129th Streets. Some of the wounded men he had treated in Iraq and Afghanistan still exuded cordite's odor when the injuries were closely inflicted.

Intensely flashing emergency lights on cars, police vans, and ambulances rotated everywhere. Gabriel saw at least five military armored trucks, each of them mounted by a bulky soldier in protective gear next to a machine gun. There were soldiers in the bleak inner spaces among the project's towers. Even windows on the high floors had iron mesh, as if the tenants on the fifteenth floor needed protection from outside break-ins. On the ground floor of one of the buildings was a fluorescent-lit community center. Its windows were smashed.

Gabriel, dressed in his ordinary street clothes, a blue sports jacket, white button-down Brooks Brothers shirt, green chinos, brown loafers and no socks, realized that his next step was absurd. He approached a bored cop, a man who clearly was not one of the police warriors, and said, "I'm an emergency room doctor." As if to validate himself he took his stethoscope out of the inside pocket of his jacket and held it out like a talisman. "Can you tell someone I can help if I'm needed?"

The cop's name was Ballestros, brightly engraved on his plastic name tag. "I don't think they need you. Everything that was going to happen here happened."

It was not a rude or dismissive statement. The man had the relaxed attitude of a cop assigned to a street fair and accumulating overtime.

"Thanks, Officer," Gabriel said. "How many people were hurt?"

"Don't know."

Suddenly a convoy of vehicles emerged from inside the cordoned area. They were mainly black SUVs with heavily tinted windows. The wailing of their sirens displaced all other sound.

"Important people?" Gabriel asked, nodding toward the convoy.

"They think so."

* * *

Gina Carbone was in the back seat of the third vehicle. She gripped the handle embedded in front of her as the SUV made a sweeping turn onto 125th Street. Almost instinctively, her long-ago training as a patrol cop still caused her to look at faces in a crowd. As clearly and distinctly as if she were staring at a photograph rather than scanning a chaotic crowd, she saw and recognized the Angel of Life, Gabriel Hauser.

"Can you believe it?" she said to Rocco Barbiglia.

Rocco—as good-looking as a young Robert DeNiro—glanced in the direction toward which Gina pointed. "What's up, Chief?"

"Over there, look. The doctor who treated the guy with the big birthmark at the museum."

"Right, I see him, Chief. The guy gets around."

Gina said, "He's Zelig, the man who shows up everywhere. He's been talking to the cop next to him. Rocco, find out who the cop is and have him tell us what the Angel of Life had to say."

Gina knew the ambulance that carried a person she described as "Gift No. 1" would not arrive at Pier 37 for another hour. She had given instructions for the ambulance to drive slowly through the West Village and the West Side Highway below 14th Street as though on an ordinary cruise. That was a tactic, she knew, that would allow the ambulance to elude reporters or anyone else who might have seen it leave the George Washington Carver projects.

The ambulance was not going to any hospital. Silas Nasar was strapped and handcuffed to a gurney. Rifles were pointed at him.

Since she had some time before she, too, would arrive at Pier 37, she told her driver to stop at the service entrance to the Regency Hotel on 61st Street. Accompanied by two guards dressed as hotel porters, she took the huge service elevator to the sixth floor. The elevator had the faint but distinct scent of the garbage which had been accumulating in the hotel's basement during the long quarantine of Manhattan.

When she entered the room, Tony Garafalo was reading a book. One of the things that attracted her to him was that he was a complex, unpredictable man, so much more interesting than the conventional people who surrounded her in her daily life. During his years in the legendary Supermax federal prison in Florence, Colorado, the most secure of all the prisons in the federal system, the place where the Unabomber, Arab terrorists, John Gotti, and Mexican drug lords were imprisoned, he had developed a passion for reading the classic books: Thackeray, Tolstoy, Conrad, even Jane Austen. As she approached him, he put down the Modern Library edition of Dostoyevsky's *The Brothers Karamazov*.

"Hey, big guy," she said, "pretty soon you can start teaching a course on the Great Fucking Books at Harvard."

"Hey, doll. There's only one course about fucking I want to teach."

"I'm all ears, teacher."

Tony led her to the elegant bathroom, all marble and glowing brass. Naked, she stood under the shower, her hair soon streaming black and straight, and Tony, muscular and powerful, stood behind her. She pressed her glorious ass into his groin. He kissed her hair and shoulders and the length of her spine. When he reached the firm cleavage of her ass, he gently turned her. He was on his knees. Her vagina was in front of his face. He pressed his tongue into her, the water flowing over his mouth. As his tongue caressed her clitoris from every angle, she moaned, "Tony, Tony." Finally she said, "Fuck me."

He stood. They were face to face, chest to chest under the clean flowing water. He entered her. She placed her hands on his shoulders. She was ecstatic. So was he.

CHAPTER TWENTY-FOUR

"Do you have any idea, Gina, how unacceptable that is?" Roland Fortune asked. "How bad, bad?"

"It's what it is," she said.

"It's a disaster."

"We knew there were risks."

"Seven of our twelve people? Risks? Seven of our people dead? Every fucking guy in the apartment? That gives a whole new meaning to risks. It's more like a suicide video game."

Roland raised the right hand he had held like a visor over his eyes. Outside, the leafy trees in City Hall Park were suffused with the green, comforting glow of afternoon sunlight.

"When you act, there are consequences."

Roland resisted the impulse to say *Tell me something else I don't know.* Instead he said, "Have the families been told yet?"

"Of course not."

"Has Lazarus been told?"

"No, not yet."

"So who knows, right at this moment, in real time?"

"You. Two or three of my top people."

"What did you find in the apartment? Beyond dead bodies, I mean."

"Weapons, ammunition."

"What about bombs?"

"None."

"Bomb-making materials?"

"Nothing so far."

"Computers?"

"Nothing."

"Nothing? Three-year-olds have computers."

"We're still searching."

"Still? How big is the place?"

"One bedroom."

"It's not the Vatican. Do you really expect to find something?"

"I don't expect anything, Mr. Mayor." That abrasive bluntness of Gina which Roland had admired for so long emerged at the edge of her tone. "Whatever is there is there. Whatever isn't there isn't there."

"Gina, we had a Defense Secretary once who spoke in enigmas. Remember? Rumsfeld? All that amusing crap about known unknowns. Known knowns."

It was the Gina Carbone who never tried to be charming who spoke. "I don't expect to find anything buried in the walls. What we have now, and what we know now, is likely to be all there is. Let me say it again: seven of our people dead, all nine of the Arabs dead. Ten assault rifles. Six pistols. Enough ammunition for those weapons, nothing like an arsenal. No grenades, no homemade bombs, no pressure cookers, no books, no computers."

"How about cell phones?"

"Three cell phones. Those are in the hands of our technical people. Here is a known unknown: I don't know what is in them."

How many hours ago, Roland thought, did he wake in a sun-drenched room in Gracie Mansion beside the still-sleeping, sweet-breathing, vibrantly alive Sarah Hewitt-Gordan? Sounding subdued, he said, "All right, Gina, keep me posted. Call at least every ten minutes, more if necessary."

Gina said nothing about Silas Nasar, Gift No. 1, who, unhurt, even in the cauldron of gunfire and explosions in the apartment at the Carver Towers, was still being driven around the city in a quiet ambulance before he would be delivered to Pier 37.

* * *

The images on the immense high-definition television screen were somehow familiar, like images from Baghdad, Kabul, Damascus, Aleppo, anyplace where chaos was unfolding. Armored vehicles all over the streets, men and women in uniforms, the blackened side of a heavily damaged building, thousands of spinning emergency lights, ambulances. Roland said to the men, Irv Rothstein and Hans Richter, who were with him in his office, "Enough, turn it off, this isn't telling me anything that hundreds of millions of people watching CNN and Fox don't already know. This makes the Paris assaults look like a holiday."

Seated in a wooden chair in front of Roland Fortune's desk, Hans Richter removed the white earbud from his left ear just as the scene on the television screen dissolved into a pinpoint of evanescent light. He said, "The president is on the line now."

Roland nodded, held up a silencing hand and instantly the room resonated with an electronic hum. There was no video this time, at Roland's direction. The eerie electronic resonance lasted for at least ten seconds. It ended when Andrew Carter said, "Let's have a head count. Mr. Mayor, who is with you?"

There were no gracious preliminaries this time, no greetings.

Roland was no more interested in introductory pleasantries than Andrew Carter was. "Two deputy mayors, Rothstein and Richter."

"And what about the police commissioner? Capone?" Carter asked.

"Carbone," Roland said. "She's in the field."

"Don't you think it's important to have her in on this?"

"No."

"I would have wanted her here. Can we get her?"

"No."

"Would she be available if I need her?"

"Not now." Roland's voice was strong. All his instincts told him that this sudden conference was designed by Andrew Carter and Harlan Lazarus as a score-settling, blame-allocating exercise. From the time when he was twelve and a potent street fighter, Roland had learned that anyone who confronts you has to be kept off-balance. "And who's with you?"

"Judge Lazarus. General Jones. Ms. Bates. Director de Carlo."

Roland sensed that Andrew Carter didn't want to give a complete roster. "And who else, Mr. President?"

"My Chief Counsel, Loretta Andreano. Loretta, say hello to the mayor."

Loretta's seductive voice rang out. "Roland, I'm so sorry about your loss." Clearly she meant Sarah Hewitt-Gordan.

Roland and Loretta Andreano seven years earlier, when he was starting his first term in Congress and she was newly minted as the chief lawyer for the New York Governor, had a happy three-week affair. It ended when *Page Six*, the gossip page of the *New York Post*, carried a twenty-word entry that Roland Fortune had been sighted holding hands with Madonna at two in the morning at Tartine on West 11th Street. A cool and graceful woman, Loretta had simply said at the time, "Lucky you, enjoy yourself. And go fuck off." Roland wondered briefly how many people involved now in this call knew that there had once been an intimate connection between him and the chief counsel to the president. He said, "There have been many losses to many people in the last day, Loretta. I hope your family has been safe."

Andrew Carter said, "And I also have Beau Broadbent here."

Roland saw Irv Rothstein roll his eyes upward. Beau Broadbent, who was the president's press secretary, had worked for two years as a national reporter for the *Times* when Irv was there. "The glibbest Southern boy Robert E. Lee ever fathered," Irv once told Roland about Edward Beauregard Broadbent. "Always be careful with him," Irv had said. "They invented buses so that Beau Broadbent could throw people under them."

"Is that it?" Roland asked.

"On our end? Yes, sure."

"And are you recording this?"

"Of course. Are you?"

"No, of course not." It was a lie.

Roland decided to wait. There was a faint electronic hum in the silence. Andrew Carter spoke. "What happened?"

"Seven of our people are dead. There are ten or so dead suspects in the apartment."

"Any prisoners?"

"No."

"It would have been nice to have a survivor, don't you think? Like that Tsarnaev brother from the Boston Marathon bombing."

"These people weren't interested in survival."

Harlan Lazarus spoke, "Who were they?"

"Is that Mr. Lazarus?" Roland asked.

The president said, "Yes, that's Judge Lazarus."

"We don't know yet who they were." And then he added, "It's always good to know, Mr. Lazarus, that you're in the middle of everything when we need you."

"Who did you think they were when you decided to mount this attack?" the president asked.

"You know the answer to that. We had information, obviously

accurate, that there were as many as ten men with heavy weaponry in an apartment in a public housing complex."

"Judge Lazarus tells me you decided to handle this as a local police issue."

"Andrew, no one ever said that to Mr. Lazarus. The commissioner explained to Mr. Lazarus' assistants, since she wasn't able to reach Mr. Lazarus himself, that we had highly reliable informants' tips and surveillance that there was a concentration of unknown force in a public housing project."

"The judge tells me he offered further intelligence assistance before any steps were taken," Andrew Carter said. "Isn't that right, Judge?"

"That's correct," Harlan Lazarus said. It was a piping, shrill voice.

"You know what?" Roland asked. "I don't care. And Harlan Lazarus doesn't care, either. I'm just a simple country mayor, but for years very odd people from Homeland Security, the CIA, the FBI, the Girl Scouts of America, and the Stepford Wives have been telling me how seamlessly coordinated all these anti-terror agencies are. Out of many, one. *E pluribus unum.* All that pablum. And what do I see when the rubber meets the road, the shit hits the fan? The echo chamber. The faint, distracting, eerie moan of a thousand people looking at each other and murmuring, *What the fuck do we do now?* The only voices that speak to me are my own people saying they know there are bad guys with assault weapons suddenly appearing in a public housing project. What better place to be in Manhattan if you have guns and a lust to maim and kill than a housing project in Manhattan? They are not places where people who see something really want to say something. The George Zimmerman types, the neighborhood watch dogs, in other words, the people who live in those projects get fed to the dogs in places like the George Washington Carver Houses..."

"Mr. Mayor," Andrew Carter said. "Roland?"

"Let me finish. So when I have Gina Carbone, a woman I trust, a person I can see, touch, and smell, tell me there are as many as ten guys with powerful weapons who will likely soon disperse and do some dirty work, do I wait to get more guidance from Harlan Lazarus? Maybe there are better people in the world than I am, but the only thing I know to do is say yes to the people I trust."

"I'm not following that, Mr. Mayor," Lazarus said. "We have multiple resources there."

"Really? So seamless as to be invisible? So transparent because it has no substance?"

Neither Carter nor Lazarus responded immediately. In the faintly resonating interlude of silence, Roland envisioned the president glancing around the Oval Office in which he sat, an expression of bewilderment or scorn on his face. Then Carter said, "Cooperation is a two-way street, Mr. Mayor. We weren't given an opportunity over the last two hours to give intelligence and tactical support."

"And how do you know that?"

"The judge and his people told me so."

"Is that so? We better check the timeline. At one today, the commissioner learns there are several men with heavy weapons in an apartment in a public housing project. Arabs. Arabs don't live in public housing projects. Ten minutes later she reports that information to me. I ask her what the source of that information is. An informant, she says, corroborated by eye and ear confirmation from a small team of her anti-terrorist unit. I ask if the Feds are involved. She answers they aren't. I instruct her to contact Harlan Lazarus. When I speak with her fifteen minutes later, I approve the cordoning off of the complex. In that conversation, I ask about her conversation with Harlan Lazarus. No response from him. He hadn't called her back."

Andrew Carter said, "I'm looking at him right now." There was a murmur of voices, of people speaking almost inaudibly. "There is no record of that on our end."

"There is no record of it, Mr. President? Or it didn't happen? Those are two different concepts. No record of an event isn't the equivalent of no event."

Another pause. Andrew Carter said, "It did not happen. Your commissioner didn't call the judge. She's lying."

"I'm not going to have a debate, Andrew. At three p.m., the commissioner let me know that the men in the building may have hostages. I gave her permission to use her judgment in terms of bringing the situation to an end."

"Why do you think they were terrorists? How were they connected to the other attacks?"

"I never said that, Mr. President. Our information is that there were as many as ten men in an apartment or cluster of apartments on a floor in a project. No one in the project had seen them before, according to the reports we had. It is also a project that has been relatively peaceful for the last three years, as far as we know, free of gangs because of Gina Carbone." Roland stopped for a moment. "It could not have been a complete coincidence that these men surfaced just as these attacks are taking place."

"Coincidence? We could have helped you sort that out if we'd been consulted."

"I'm not buying into that version of the story, Andrew. We acted because these men, whoever they were and wherever they came from, were an unacceptable danger. And a danger in my city, not yours."

There was a twenty-second suspension of the conference. Roland was determined not to speak the next words. Andrew Carter did. "You don't have a rosy outcome here."

"Don't worry, Mr. President, I'm responsible for the outcome, not you, and certainly not Mr. Lazarus. What was it that JFK said? Victory has a thousand fathers and defeat is an orphan."

"What is it that you plan to do?"

"In forty-five minutes I'm holding a press conference to tell the world what we know."

"Don't you think you have to be careful?"

"Is there anything I've done that has not been careful, Andrew?"

Lazarus' voice rose up. "Isn't that what we've been discussing here. The absence of carefulness." It was not a question.

"Andrew, my primary obligation is to the people of this city. And what that means today, in this moment, is to keep them safe. And to do that I can only use the resources Commissioner Carbone has."

"And we've done everything we can to help you with that. We've activated an Army reserve division which I'm told is already in Manhattan."

"And guess what? Hundreds of them are gathered around Times Square, attracted by the bright lights, big city. We have zero information that there's any threat in Times Square. Do you?"

Another pause, this one filled by an old-fashioned audio screech like the sudden roar of a 1960s loudspeaker system.

"Your press conference is problematic, Roland. What will you say about the role of Homeland Security?"

"Don't worry, I won't describe this as a joint operation. I will thank Homeland Security for its continued assistance and cooperation."

"I want one or two of our people to be there standing behind you."

"Not Lazarus."

"The judge has no intention of being there."

"Now that's cooperation I can genuinely appreciate."

CHAPTER TWENTY-FIVE

RAJ GANDHI, WHO had just spent several years in Lebanon, Iraq and Afghanistan, had what he called on-the-job-training in the petty corruption, greed, arrogance, and blind egotism of politicians. When he started as a journalist fresh out of graduate school a decade earlier, he had Plato's idealized view of politicians as men who exercised their creative powers for the common good. But what he had seen on a daily basis during nine years overseas were powerful elected and unelected men who lied, diverted immense amounts of money to themselves and their families and clans, and never hesitated to order murders. They weren't statesmen. They were harlots who made no effort to conceal what they were doing.

When he returned to New York, he made a deliberate decision to give politicians in the United States the benefit of the doubt. He saw his role as a journalist in an old-fashioned way, and for him objectivity was an important goal. But nothing he had seen during the months he'd already spent in New York justified the giving of the benefit of the doubt. He wanted to resist the pull of gravity in the direction of viewing local politicians as New York versions of the ruling men in Iraq, Afghanistan, and Lebanon, but it was difficult not to see the men and women who were city council members and their staffs, local New York state assemblymen, and borough presidents as mirror images of the men in the clans that surrounded the presidents in Afghanistan and Iraq.

Yet, Roland Fortune had consistently impressed him. Raj had attended only two of his press conferences, and each time the mayor was relaxed, responding to the questions he was asked instead of delivering a speech about the issues he wanted to discuss, and he was respectful. And often funny in the understated way Raj, never a backslapper, preferred. The only thing about Roland Fortune that had aroused Raj Gandhi's critical instincts was that when the mayor called on him at a press conference he used Raj's first name. Roland had taken the time to know the new faces in the press corps at City Hall, obviously for the purpose of stroking their egos. Raj decided not to let his ego be stroked or to hold this against Roland Fortune.

Raj Gandhi was one of six *Times* reporters who watched the elevated television screen in the newsroom as Roland Fortune made a statement and then answered questions at the press conference about the battle at the George Washington Carver projects. His delivery was deliberate, sober, informative, even modest. He described the murdered police as antiterrorism officers and never once used the constantly repeated word *hero*. As the anonymous caller had said, since 9/11, every fireman was a hero, every cancer survivor was a hero, all soldiers were heroes, every first responder was a saint. Strangely the weird caller in the mocking way he spoke had confirmed what Raj had privately thought for a long time. Raj cringed at the use of the word hero, and admired Roland Fortune for not invoking it.

He listened as the mayor lucidly and calmly said as the conference was coming to an end, "The simple truth is that we do not yet precisely know who is responsible for these despicable acts against the people of New York, indeed, against the entire country. There could be more than one group. Or there could be elements of one centrally controlled group. And we don't know whether the men who are doing these things are Muslim, anarchists, fringe right-wingers or far-out leftists. And I will not speculate."

An unseen reporter said, "There are rumors that the slain men in the apartment were all dark skinned."

"I don't want to comment on that. Their skin color won't tell us who they were, what organization they had, or whose orders they were carrying out. Certainly I authorized the action that was taken because I had crystal-clear evidence that a group of six to ten men had seized control of a floor in a public housing project. That they were heavily armed. That the floor might have been only a staging area from which they would soon disperse and mount other operations. That we had one last clear chance to stop them. That they refused to negotiate. That they may have had one or more hostages."

"Who made the decision to go in?"

"I did, with the assistance of Commissioner Carbone."

"Aren't you concerned that they are all dead?"

"It was not our objective to kill any one or all of them. It was our objective to stop them. But this was combat in very close spaces. Our team's highest priority once they were engaged was to protect themselves. I've never been in combat, nor have any of you. I won't second-guess any of our people. All or almost all of them were infantry veterans of multiple tours of duty in Iraq and Afghanistan. They sustained terrible losses within seconds. Obviously they had to do whatever they thought was necessary to avoid more losses."

Then a voice behind Roland Fortune, the voice of the Brooklyn-accented Irv Rothstein, firmly intoned, "That's what we have for now, ladies and gentlemen."

And Roland Fortune, cool, formidable, and extraordinarily handsome, turned away from the podium, and like an actor at the end of a scene, slipped through a door behind the stage.

* * *

Raj Gandhi's cell phone vibrated in the left pocket of his pants. He had several seconds of trouble extracting it. When he finally had the phone in his hand, he touched the icon that resembled a telephone receiver.

"Hey, man, did you ever hear such bullshit?" It was, unmistakably, the voice with the Queens accent.

"What?"

"*That* bullshit."

Always polite and formal, Raj said, "I am not sure what it is you're referring to."

"Our slick mayor."

"Tell me, please," Raj said, "what is it that I missed?"

"Come on." He paused. "I guess I shouldn't be surprised. You miss a lot."

"I'm sorry about that."

"Don't apologize. Just do your job."

Raj didn't answer. More bantering with this strange man, he felt, was a waste. He had called for a reason, and Raj felt that if he said as little as possible this man would reach the point of his calling. The man was a talker.

"I keep on looking at the *Times'* fucking website for the story I led you to. All of your other reporters are writing obvious stuff. Garbage on the streets, uneasy populations, scared-to-shit Upper East Siders. Like, this is news to me, right?"

"Do you want to tell me something?"

"That's what I've been doing. And you've done diddly-squat with it. I gave you this big story. You know, Mr. Gandhi, I could've given it to somebody else. Somebody who's more industrious. Like, more daring, one of those guys from the *New York Post*."

"I drove up and down the FDR Drive. I saw all the abandoned piers below Houston Street." Raj had only recently learned that the street was called *Howston*, not *Hewston*. He had been embarrassed when he pronounced the word to sound like the city in Texas. "And they were all just abandoned piers."

"Sure they were, Raj, sure they were. That's what they're supposed to look like to ordinary pain-in-the-ass civilians driving on the FDR. But you needed to get out and walk around. Look what Woodward and Bernstein did: they used shoe leather, they walked around. That's how they got that Watergate shit. Now all you great reporters do is sit on your asses and Google for info."

Scorned and demeaned and repeatedly insulted as an overtly bright Indian teenager living in tough neighborhoods in Bombay, Raj had learned not to respond when someone provoked him. *Patience*, he thought, *just listen.*

"I'm willing to give you a second chance."

"Thank you." He used what he thought of as his Gunga Din voice. He intentionally sounded compliant, appreciative.

"Did you hear the Soldier of Fortune talk about all the dead guys in the apartment?"

"Yes, sir."

"Well, they weren't all dead. One got only a little boo-boo on his arm. They dressed the fucker in one of their uniforms after they had him clean himself up. He was such a brave martyr that he'd shit all over himself."

Raj didn't respond. He breathed slowly. This had the feel of extraordinary news or extravagant invention. The man laughed in that odd way, the loner's laugh, not the kind of laughter people learned from laughing together. "Are you there, Mr. Gandhi-baby?"

"I'm here."

"So they marched him out of the building, holding on to him like he was one of them but only a little shaken up. They put him in an ambulance. It was all playacting."

Quietly Raj said, "How do you know this?"

"I don't answer questions, Mr. Gandhi. I'm not in this to get famous."

"Who are you?"

"I'm your friend. I'm trying here to give you insights into the war on terror."

"Where is this man now?"

"Tell me this, Mr. Gandhi: Where you grew up, did they have little books with dots? The kind where you draw a line between the dots, and, before you know it, you have a picture of a duck, or a house, or a bridge or Jesus H. Christ?"

"Can you give me your e-mail address?"

"I'm not an e-mail kind of guy."

"Who else knows about this?"

"You leave me in a constant state of worry, Mr. Gandhi. Who else do you think knows about this? Do you think the police commissioner might know? Do you think the Soldier of Fortune might know? Hey, try to find Tony Garafalo. He just got his brains fucked out by his girlfriend at their love nest at the Regency. She needed a break. War is a bitch on the nerves. Maybe the commissioner gave up this info when she was taking her break in what Sinatra called the afterglow of lovemaking."

"I know you want me to believe you. And I want to believe you. But you make that hard to do sometimes."

"Hey, I'm sorry if I offended you. It's not a nice way to talk about our public servants, I know."

"Where are you getting this information?"

"What did I tell you before? Remember? If I told you I'd have to kill you."

Raj heard that loony loner's laugh, and then the sound of the call ending. He tried to redial the number. It was blocked.

CHAPTER TWENTY-SIX

MOHAMMAD HUSSEIN WAS a slender man. From the very beginning, from the moment Gabriel Hauser first saw him enter the grim ward where amputees were briefly held before their flights to Germany and then on to a lifetime of permanent disability in the United States, Gabriel's attention was arrested by Mohammad's striking face, absolutely black hair. His eyes were not just brown, but virtually black, his nose straight and narrow, his lips full, and he had a cleft chin like Cary Grant. Gabriel was too accomplished as a doctor to stop the painful conversation he was having with a bitter soldier whose right arm below the elbow was severed, but he sensed the presence of the new male nurse in the ward.

Gabriel had not had a lover in the almost two years he spent in Iraq and Afghanistan. Once, for three days, he had taken a leave in Amsterdam and had so much sex that he was alarmed, even disturbed with the intensity. He had come of age long after the years of bathhouses, the gay clubs around Sheridan Square in Greenwich Village, all of which had closed when AIDS became rampant, the modern Black Death, in the early to mid-1980s. He had in fact been put off by accounts he had read and stories he had heard from older gay men about the reckless, endless orgies of the late 1970s. He imagined that Jerome Fletcher had taken part in them in the era before AIDS, the era, as Gabriel sometimes thought, before Jerome made the transition from sex with multiple anonymous men to intercourse with boys. Gabriel still wanted to believe that Jerome had loved him, alone, during the three years their lives overlapped, but he knew that wasn't so. The horrific trial of Dayvon Williams, the black prostitute who had strangled Jerome with an electrical cord before stabbing him repeatedly in the face at the now-closed motel in the South Bronx, had in three days of testimony disclosed Jerome's long-standing insatiable taste for boys under the age of eighteen. Gabriel's three crazy days in Amsterdam had evoked the question, *Who am I really?*

Gabriel found time and opportunity over the next two weeks to come into contact with Mohammad. Three days after they met, Mohammad accepted Gabriel's invitation to have tea at a dusty, beaten up café not far from the cinder-block hospital in Kabul. Gabriel soon learned that Mohammad was married and had three children. On his iPhone there were pictures of his wife, their two daughters, and their son, a miniature version of Mohammad. In the vivid color pictures of her, Mohammad's wife was smiling, ravishing. She looked like a model, not hooded and dour like the typical, silent women of Afghanistan.

Although Gabriel smiled at the sequence of family portraits, he was disappointed. He had hoped that Mohammad, gentle, intelligent, attentive, and so fundamentally different from the thousands of menacing and taciturn Iraqi and Afghan men Gabriel had encountered for two years, was attracted to him. But Mohammad's marriage to a vibrant woman undermined Gabriel's hopes, expectations, and desires.

But then Gabriel learned that it had been many months since Mohammad had seen his wife and children, who lived with his parents in Helmand province. Mohammad, who learned to speak English extremely well from a man who had worked with CIA advisers during the ten years of the futile Soviet invasion, had been recruited by the Army to train and work with American soldiers. He had been essentially unemployed since the 2001 invasion and the opportunity to work with the U.S. Army carried rich rewards. He was given a new skill, nursing, and a salary far richer than anything he had ever earned.

Gabriel lived in a building not far from the hospital. Constructed with cinder blocks in two months, the building was integrated, meaning that Army officers had most of the apartments, but Afghan civilians who worked for the Army as medical personnel, security guards, and translators also lived there. Gabriel's place was neat and Spartan. He actually liked its feel of austerity and orderliness.

It took an enormous amount of planning and tension for Gabriel to pull together the nerve to invite Mohammad to the apartment for the first time. Once they were there, Gabriel served tea and cookies. He didn't drink booze by choice and Mohammad didn't drink it because of the rules of custom and religion. They faced each other over a glass coffee table, Gabriel on a hard white sofa and Mohammad in an ersatz Eames-style chair. In the background, the civilized voices of the NPR anchors spoke about the civil war in Syria and a new movie by Woody Allen.

Mohammad was a reader. Like almost every other Afghan associated with Americans, he owned a cell phone and an iPad. It often struck Gabriel as he walked in the streets of Kabul that people who had little or no food did have cell phones. Mohammad had a subscription to the *New York Times* and the *Guardian* on his iPad.

Their conversations were always easy, wide-ranging, and unrestrained except for one area, Gabriel's love for men. Mohammad rarely mentioned his wife and never talked about sex. For his part, Gabriel found it difficult to shift his attention away from the slender man's handsome face, the elegant gestures of his hands, and lucidity of his intelligent eyes. It didn't escape Gabriel's notice that in all the hours they spent together at the hospital, he never once saw Mohammad give even a furtive, much less leering, look at any of the female doctors and nurses.

On a hot Thursday night after Mohammad had left his apartment, Gabriel Hauser made a decision: the next evening when they were drinking tea in his apartment he would reach out for Mohammad's slender, almost hairless hand and say simply, "I'm in love with you." He was prepared to lose this alluring, gratifying friendship, and to risk a horrified reaction, or to provoke a beating, on the frail hope that this man might kiss him and slip out of his clothes to reveal a body that Gabriel was certain was sleek and sylph-like.

But that moment never came. It was on that Friday morning that the unctuous colonel asked, "Can I have a few words with you, Major Hauser?" and told him he was being removed from Afghanistan that night, sent to Germany, and dishonorably dis-charged from the Army. Three hours before reporting to Bagram Air Base for his flight out of the country, he met Mohammad in the shabby café that had become the place where they regularly took their breaks together. He told Mohammad he was being ex-iled from the country immediately. "Do you want to know why?" he asked Mohammad.

"I know why, Gabriel."

Mohammad walked through the stifling, dusty Afghan evening to Gabriel's apartment building. Gabriel's duffel bag and soft suit-cases were already in the lobby of the building, and the locks to the apartment door had already been changed. In the dark in the last twenty yards of their walk Mohammad's soft right hand sought out and clasped Gabriel's hand. Gabriel was overwhelmed by love for this man. And by hatred for the Army.

* * *

Cam was visibly distressed. When he was angry or disturbed, he repeatedly moved small objects from place to place. There were clean
coffee mugs on the small dining table, and Cam was shifting them
as if they were inverted cups in a shell game.

Even as he registered that Cam was upset and distracted, Gabriel
kissed him on the shoulder as soon he entered the apartment. Cam
had taken the responsibility for bringing the wounded Oliver to the
office of their friend John Higgins, a gay veterinarian whose cozy
animal hospital on East 84th Street was the most popular veterinary
hospital on the East Side. John loved Oliver. The wonderful dog re-
ciprocated that love. Even though Oliver knew that the brownstone
where John lived and worked was the place where he was poked and
pinched and sometimes put in the kennel for a weekend, he always
bounded happily up the steps and barked joyously when he saw Dr.
Higgins in his immaculate white coat.

"John almost vomited when I unwrapped Oliver's blanket. He
was upset; he asked what happened."

"'The fucking police,' I told him. 'Gabriel stitched up his wounds,
but we need you to take a look at him and treat him here'. John said
he would, and I left Oliver there."

Always sensitive to Cam's moods, Gabriel sensed that Cam's obvious irritation was tied to something other than, or in addition to,
the injuries to Oliver. "You're upset, baby, aren't you?"

Gabriel was right. Every muscle of Cam's long and elegant body
seemed to tense up. Cam began speaking rapidly, as if in the mid-
stream of his thoughts. "After I left Oliver at John's two men started
walking beside me. They said they were agents from the NSA. They
offered to show me their badges. I told them I didn't have any spare
change today."

"I'm so sorry I got you into this."

"No bother, Gabriel. I'm in it, hook, line, and sinker. I couldn't shake them off. They were like seasoned panhandlers. They just continued walking with me, one to my left and the other to my right."

Gabriel leaned against the refrigerator in the sleek, sun-filled kitchen. It pained him to see Cam's nervous agitation and distress. Gabriel said again, "I'm sorry."

"But listen, Gabriel. They told me things that truly scare me. About you."

Internally Gabriel flushed. It was a powerful emotion of fear, concern, and inchoate shame. *What now?* he wondered.

"They handed me pages of e-mails between you and a man in Afghanistan named Mohammad Hussein. Lots of them read like love letters."

"Cam, I told you I had a dear friend there. I even told you his name. Don't you remember?"

"I don't intrude on your e-mails, Gabriel. I assumed you sent notes like postcards to him from time to time."

"He was the only friend I had for two years." Gabriel, still so physically anxious that he detected the quaver in his own voice, said, "He has a wife and kids."

"Bullshit. You were betraying me, Gabriel. For six months you were telling him everything you were doing to get permission for *him*, not him and his family, to come here. You described your letters to the State Department, to the Secretary of the Army, telling them about all the heroic work Mohammad did for injured soldiers, the hours he spent just sitting with them. Christ, you even compared him to Walt Whitman spending two years in Union Army hospitals during the Civil War playing guardian angel to wounded soldiers. As if the people you sent these letters to even knew who Walt Whitman was. A gay poet trying to comfort wounded soldiers and falling in love with some of them."

"I thought he was in danger in Afghanistan. I think he still is.

After all, he's devoted his life to working with Americans. He's a marked man."

"And what were you going to do if you got him here?"

"Set him up as an aide or a nurse in a hospital."

"I don't think so. I saw pictures of him. He is very attractive. Very. I read the e-mails. They weren't about travel arrangements or finding work for him."

"Come on, Cam, please, I love you. And besides, he lost interest. I haven't heard from him in a month."

"I know. Your e-mails to him have been heartsick. He hasn't gotten back to you in a month, no matter how much you plead."

"That's not true."

"Don't jive me, Gabriel. I've read them. I've got them here." He gestured to a neat stack of papers on which the e-mails had been printed.

"I'm sorry, Cam. It was one of those runaway emotional attachments. There was never a chance that he'd be allowed to come here. I'm not the only person in the world who loses control over what he writes in e-mails and text messages."

"Do you want to know why you haven't heard from him?"

Something in the wounded, angry tone with which Cam now spoke made Gabriel even more anxious. He asked, "Why? What's wrong? Has he been hurt?"

"No, Gabriel. He's been arrested. The guys who walked with me and gave me these e-mails said he was part of a plot to blow up a hospital. He was a plant of ISIS or Al-Qaeda. He cultivated you because he thought while you were there you would lead him to a hospital or ward where high-ranking officers were treated. After all, you were a major. When they booted you out of Afghanistan, your lover thought that you might be able to bring him here. These guys from the NSA said your boyfriend from Afghanistan would become a 'sleeper,' a plotter for ISIS. That's why he begged you to help him. What a perfect cover, if you think about it."

"None of that's true."

"This is why these people are so interested in you, Gabriel. You need to hear this. Your friend Mohammad has told them you knew about these bombings before they happened."

"That's off the wall, Cam. Totally beyond crazy. They're making it up."

"They told me he sent you regular letters, by mail, introducing you to his 'family' here. I saw the letters. They were picked up by the government from Nasar's home just after the first bombings at the Met. One of them is about Silas Nasar. A man with a big birthmark on his face."

"I never met that man."

"Really? You met him at the museum. They know you treated him on the steps of the museum and then at the hospital. Even exchanged what looked like a big bracelet with him. Muslim men don't wear bracelets. The NSA guys think it was a communications device."

"That's a fantasy. Why would he be there and let himself get caught in an explosion?"

"Because he was overseeing the last-minute preparations, they said, and the first food wagon had a faulty timing mechanism. It worked, but too soon. And Silas got caught in it."

"You know this is crazy, Cam. Why would I do these things? I just want to lead a quiet life, treating patients, doing whatever good I can do. And loving you."

"They know about all the angry protests and objections and appeals you filed after you were discharged. Your letters to the *Times* and other papers that were never printed. They think you're angry and sick and deluded. They told me I should persuade you to talk with them right away. If you help them, they say, you can help your-self. You might get a lighter jail sentence, they said, if you cooperate right away."

Gabriel knew that his hands and lips were shaking and that Cam could see that. Cam moved to him and hugged him. "This is all so sick, Gabriel. I want our life back. Look at what we've lost."

CHAPTER TWENTY-SEVEN

SHE WAS LARGER and older than most of the women runners who even on this day, three hours after the assault in the George Washington Carver Houses, flowed uptown and downtown on the narrow esplanade along the shoreline of the East River as if this were a holiday on a lucid day in early summer. Gina had changed into running clothes in the back of an unmarked van parked near the seaport piers that had long ago replaced the seedy, mob-dominated Fulton Fish Market and that now had the feel of a suburban shopping mall. She slipped into the crowds of young runners. Moving gracefully, she made her way uptown to Pier 37.

The narrowest possible slit was open in the rusty, rundown chain-link fence that ringed the front of Pier 37. Unobtrusively she veered out of the stream of other runners, the innumerable slim blond girls in running shorts and tops and baseball caps out of which their ponytails hung, the tall young men, even a team of Sikh runners with their turbans in place, and slid through the slit in the fence. She was followed by the three muscular men, also in running gear, all carrying weapons in pouches in Nike belts—her bodyguards.

Raj Gandhi stood directly in front of the pier. He had been stung by the odd caller's criticism that he hadn't done enough shoe leather work. After Raj had reserved one of the plain unmarked Fords owned by the *Times*, he drove crosstown and parked the car near a cluster of several abandoned piers south of Houston Street.

The numbers assigned to the piers were random, inexplicable. Pier 63 was followed by Pier 71 and then Pier 37. All of them were massive, abandoned for decades, relics of the 1940s and the 1950s. Like prison camps, they were surrounded by chain-link fences, some with razor wire on top.

Before he saw Gina Carbone slip like a phantom through a gap in the fence, Raj was baffled as to why he had acted on the eccentric direction of a man who could be, and probably was, deranged. Raj felt if he had been a savvy New Yorker rather than a newcomer and outsider he would have seen through the caller to the crank and recognized that it was just a guy who entertained himself with the fun of sending a *New York Times* reporter on a pointless frolic.

But Raj had the reporter's imperious urge to act, the sense that he and he alone was learning something remarkable. And suddenly he was rewarded by the sight of the raven-haired and disguised police commissioner of the largest city in America, a woman who was the leading general of a police force bigger than the armies of most countries, slipping through a slit in the fence and jogging in runner's gear toward a derelict warehouse. He used his iPhone to create a video of the scene.

Raj was a small man. He was also frail. When he had been taunted at Oxford for his accent, his clothes, and his diminutive parents the two times they visited their scholarship-endowed son, he stood still, shaking with fear, and took whatever abuse, punch or push was inflicted on him. During his years as a young journalist in Lebanon, Syria, and Iraq, he always cringed at the sound of gunfire or explosions. There was a time in Iraq when he was essentially confined to the fortress known as the Green Zone, living in such anxious fear that he used Valium and Xanax so often that he was afraid he would become addicted. He never drank alcohol.

But now he walked deliberately and steadily to the slit in the chain-link fence through which Gina Carbone and her guards had passed, as if into another world because they had disappeared quickly into one of the warehouse doors. There had been reporters in Iraq who thought of themselves as swashbucklers and who in fact acted that way. Although Raj was not one of them, he felt energized and fearless as he approached the same gap, the only non-runner on the chipped concrete pathway in front of the fence.

His sleeve caught on the exposed point of one of the torn links of the fence. That tug, that slight tear in the fabric of his shirt, also ripped his courage away. He jerked back from the fence as if it were a lick of fire. Once inside the perimeter of the fence, alone on the rutted pavement, he had a sense that he was vulnerable and exposed to danger. And then he had what he knew was an absurd thought: *I'm invulnerable, I'm a reporter for the New York Times.* As a student at Oxford he was obsessed with Shakespeare's plays. Now he focused on the line in *The Tempest* where a powerful, invulnerable spirit says of his companions, *My ministers are alike invulnerable.*

Trembling, expecting to be hurt by someone or something, Raj stood in front of the big roll-up door. He tugged on the rusted chain that controlled the door. The chain rattled. Rust covered the palms of his hands. He hit the door with his fists, a feeble gesture. He shouted as loudly as he could, "Anybody home? Anybody home?"

He had the cell number of Commissioner Carbone's gregarious press secretary, Charlie Brancato. He touched the screen of his cell phone and as he waited for the call to connect, he continued to stare at the massive front of the pier.

Like any good press secretary, Charlie had Raj Gandhi's name and address in the memory index of his phone. When he saw Raj's name on the screen of his iPhone, he took the call. "Mr. Gandhi, what can I do for you?"

"I'm interested in speaking to the commissioner."

"I don't know where she is."

"I do."

"You do? How can that be? Her movements and whereabouts are classified for security reasons."

"She's inside Pier 37 on the East River. Just a few feet from where I am."

"I don't think so."

"I need to speak to her. She's twenty yards from me at the most."

After a pause in which Charlie seemed to inhale on a cigarette, he said, "Maybe I can pass your questions along to her?"

"This is urgent. Tell her I need to hear from her in fifteen minutes. First, I have information that there is a dark prison inside Pier 37. I need to know whether men were secretly picked up. Extrajudicial arrests."

"Say that again, Mr. Gandhi."

"Extrajudicial arrests."

"Meaning?"

"They were hijacked from their homes in Queens and Washington Heights and not taken to jail or before a judge. They're hidden."

"That's off the wall, Mr. Gandhi. Who's telling you this shit?"

"I also want her comment on the fact that there was a survivor among the men who were attacked at the Carver projects."

"Mr. Gandhi, I'm going to contact Sandy Ellenbogen. These questions are completely out of line. You're out of your freaking gourd. Unmoored from reality."

Sandy Ellenbogen was the new managing editor of the *Times*. Raj had met him only once. Like other reporters at the paper, Raj had reservations about him. Sandy Ellenbogen was in his thirties, the youngest person ever to hold the exalted job of managing editor. Not long before his appointment, he had served as the editor of the *Style* section and credited with jazzing up the stories so that many of them became the most e-mailed articles of the entire paper every Sunday. Raj said, "That's your prerogative."

"The days of the Pentagon Papers are long gone, Mr. Gandhi. And Edward Snowden is going to rot in Moscow. You're playing a losing game. Dangerous game, Mr. Gandhi."

CHAPTER TWENTY-EIGHT

"Chaos, pure unadulterated chaos."

If sober, methodical and detail-oriented Hans Richter described what he was seeing at the complex roadways that converged on the entryways leading up to the Triboro Bridge out of Manhattan as *chaos*, Roland Fortune accepted that. He had never known Hans to exaggerate or minimize anything. He was always calm, laconic, and accurate. That was rare in the world through which Roland moved. As he stood on the flagstone terrace of Gracie Mansion overlooking the East River and gazed at the arc of the bridge, its rows of lights beginning to glimmer in the oncoming slow summer dusk, he could see distant signs of that chaos. He saw wild concentrations of swirling police lights. Helicopters were suspended over the bridge. One of them even flew under it.

Roland asked, "What do you see?"

He didn't want to hear the answer. He was alone for the first time since dawn, his body pulsated with pain, and his exhausted mind dwelled on the image of Sarah's face and destroyed head on the concrete floor. He wanted to call her father, wanted to take more Vicodin, wanted most of all to sleep for hours and wake to the normal world of the city on the day before it was mutilated.

But efficient Hans Richter, of course, answered his question. "Traffic is backed up from the ramps and all the way back to Lexington Avenue along 125th Street. Horns honking. Hundreds of people out of their cars. Trash cans on fire. There's a cordon of soldiers with rifles at each ramp to the bridge. There are guys screaming at them."

"Soldiers?"

"Yes."

"Not our cops?"

"Army soldiers, no cops."

"I see emergency vehicle lights from here."

"All Army."

"When did they replace our people?"

"Not sure. They were here when I got here an hour ago."

"Where are our people?"

"Nowhere in sight."

A cool wind blew over the darkening terrace, as if miraculously created atop the glimmering waters of the East River to soothe him. He sat on a wrought-iron chair. "Hans, this stupid Code Apache plan: How long would it take to open the city?"

"You mean lift the lockdown?"

While he couldn't be certain of it, Roland believed his calls were being monitored and recorded by Homeland Security. He hoped they were. "You know what, Hans? I hate the word lockdown. Every time somebody makes a loud noise in the mall, or some obvious crank calls a school, everything goes into lockdown. Lockdown this, lockdown that. When these clowns from Homeland Security started having these bullshit confidential meetings with me about attacks and responses and talked about lockdowns, I rolled my eyes. This is Manhattan. Only some jerk from Kansas could imagine that you could close off this island. These plans were made by comic book action figures."

Roland rubbed his eyes, still detecting that uncomfortable sensation that a film of grit covered his corneas. He waited for Richter to speak. Finally Hans said, "Who can lift it?"

"I can," Roland said.

"I'm not sure of that."

Roland wasn't certain either but was convinced there were things he could do, such as a press conference or a speech, to force it to happen. "Hans, get back to me as soon as you can with a plan for what needs to be done to get services, like trash pickup, street cleaning, back up and in place."

"I'll get it done right away," Hans said.

And Roland knew he would.

*　*　*

Irv Rothstein rapped with the edge of a coin on the glass of one of the tall French doors that opened onto the terrace. Roland genuinely liked Irv, a gregarious man in his late fifties who had the style of an earlier generation that led him to quick jokes as continuously as Walter Matthau and Rodney Dangerfield. But Roland held a hand up to wave him off. Roland knew that Irv had something important to tell him because, even in ordinary times, Irv was careful not to waste Roland's attention on distracting or trivial issues. Roland had to make finally the call he'd put off for more than a day.

Although it was the middle of the night in England, John Hewitt-Gordan picked up his cell phone on the first ring. His voice was as clear as if he were answering a roll call in the British army. "Roland, thank you for calling."

"I wanted to call you earlier, I'm sorry."

"Don't apologize. I know you're busy. I am listening to everything."

"John, I found Sarah."

"Very well."

Roland had spent enough time with Sarah, John, and other British people to know that "very well" meant "oh." It was just a remark, a punctuation, an invitation for Roland to say more. "I saw her, John. She died instantly."

John said, "That is often said to be a solace. But, Roland, I've never been certain of that. In my many years in the service I was never in combat so I can't say that I've had experience with sudden death in combat. But it has to be, don't you think, that there is an instant, however brief, when a person has that moment when the thought, the reaction, the imprint on the mind is *I die now*."

Roland knew John Hewitt-Gordan was cerebral, a tactician, a retired high-ranking officer who had commanded several support and intelligence divisions, including the British recapture of the Falkland Islands. Sarah, too, had some of these qualities. One of the senior partners at Goldman Sachs had told Roland that the key to her success was her ability to visualize big strategies, not her skills with numbers.

Roland knew that John's use of sentences sometimes masked his anxieties or fenced away subjects he wanted to evade. Roland said, "I don't have the answer to that, John. I was never in a war. I never saw people die in front of me until now. I was there. I can tell you that it was sudden, overwhelming."

"How are you, Roland? The first news reports were that you were gone, too. Now the reports are that you were injured."

"Thanks for asking. Just a scratch." At that moment, as the deliciously smothering effects of the last Vicodin receded, he felt that pulse of acute pain that came with each surge of blood in his system. What he had on his shoulder and back was in fact a deep gash. It was becoming infected.

"What," John asked, "is happening to her now?"

Roland was disoriented by the question. All he knew at that moment was that Sarah was on a floor in a cool former auditorium in an abandoned hospital in the West Village. There were at least one hundred other bodies there, assembled in straight rows under identical blue sheets, like the orderliness of military cemeteries. "The simple truth, John, is that I don't know. I just don't know."

"Understood, Roland. Your only concern now is with the living."

This man, Roland thought, has that high-minded style of a colonial general in India in the 1800s. Roland admired that. He said. "I have a suggestion, John. The airport in Boston is now operating. Why don't you fly there and then drive to Connecticut or New Jersey?"

John chuckled, "The gates of Carthage." That literate British humor.

But Roland's complete attention was arrested by that. For the last two days the words *Carthago delenda est* had been fixed in his mind, *Carthage must be destroyed*, like a phrase of music, Cato the Elder's words about the Roman army's destruction of Carthage on the shores of North Africa. *Carthage has been destroyed* evolved in his mind to *New York delenda est.*

Roland said, "I expect the lockdown to be lifted gradually in the next twenty-four hours. As soon as I can, I will have one of my helicopters pick you up and bring you here when you reach Connecticut or Westchester County. We'll go to the morgue together and we can figure out a way to give her to you." He paused. "To take her home."

"That would be very consoling, Roland. But wouldn't that lay you open to criticism? Certainly the media will pick it up. Preferential treatment, that type of issue."

"I'm at a point where that doesn't matter to me. I'm surrounded by death and killing, John."

"You're a brave man, Roland. Very few people act well under catastrophic circumstances. Wasn't it Hemingway who defined courage as grace under pressure?"

For a moment Roland wanted to tell his lover's father that he was consumed and totally preoccupied by dread, fear, and uncertainty, not courage or grace. He was angry. He was in pain. And he was

worried about his own mortality. He was aware of his vulnerabil-
ity. Somehow he had survived three deadly explosions, any one of
which could have killed him. It could have been that one of them,
the first as his birthday party unfolded, was calculated to do just
that. He had never in his life had to deal with deadly, anonymous
people who had the will and the ability to kill. And Gina Carbone
and others had treated him as if he were a target, and he believed
he was.

He said, "Thanks for the kind words, John. Let me know when
and where you arrive."

CHAPTER TWENTY-NINE

GINA CARBONE DIDN'T change out of her running clothes. Almost at a jog, she passed through the security checkpoints inside Pier 37. Rocco Barbiglia led her to the far eastern corner of the pier to what was called the Supermax wing of the pier, isolated and austere.

Silas Nasar sat in an aluminum chair. There was no other furniture in the cell. He was naked. The birthmark on the left side of his face—shaped like a seahorse—was even more distinct than in the pictures she had seen of him.

"Mr. Nasar," she said, "we've been waiting for you."

His eyes, profoundly black, were alert. He was fully conscious, almost brazen, defiant. She was surprised and impressed to see this. His left arm was wrapped from shoulder to wrist in tight, blood-stained bandages. There was, as she had been told there would be, an untreated gash across his hairy chest inflicted as he was dragged across the glass-strewn floor in the smashed apartment from one of the rooms at the Carver Towers.

"Who were the people in the apartment with you?"

No answer.

"I don't have time, Mr. Nasar. I don't have time to wait for you. You are going to talk to me."

He stared at her. She recognized instantly that he was a special man. He was seriously wounded. He was naked. Just hours earlier he had been in a room of unimaginable chaos: thunderous noise from guns and rifles and grenades; the stench of cordite; and the sight of dead bodies, blood and torn flesh, some of it smeared on and clinging to the walls and ceiling. He had been dragged from that room. He had been blindfolded. He had been bound up for two hours in a slow-moving ambulance. He was now in an unknown place with strange people capable of torturing him and killing him. He was face to face with an unusually beautiful woman who was plainly in total command of the men who had seized and held him.

Gina said, "Many, many men, women, and children have died in the last day, Mr. Nasar. Hundreds of children. I know you have children. You're a good family man, sir."

Gina was unsettled by the impassive silence and solidity of the man. Roger Davidson, the former Secret Service officer who was one of the chief architects of this off-the-books program and this dark, undocumented prison just half a mile from the United Nations building, stood behind her. He had the reputation of a stone cold killer. She resisted the impulse to cede the field and have him take over the unnerving contest with Silas Nasar.

"You're a seriously religious man, Mr. Nasar. We've known about you for a long time. We're surprised that you let yourself become involved in all this carnage. It's not in your character."

Davidson stirred behind her. He was an impatient and explosive man. She held up her right hand, signaling him to remain quiet.

"I need you to tell me where your other people are, Mr. Nasar. You know where they are. You are the electronics expert, you know in real time where these men are. You even have that information in the bracelet you gave to your doctor friend. And I want to hear from you everything you know about the doctor, too. No secrets, no holding back."

No answer.

"If you don't talk to me and tell me what you know, let me tell you what's going to happen. We are going to arrest your wife, your children, your son-in-law. I know they moved the day before the bombing. Do you think we're stupid? We know where they are."

He listened but didn't respond in any way. *Bulletproof*, she thought, *this man is bulletproof.*

"Do you know where you are? No one else does. You belong to me. I have the power to let you live and to let you die."

After ten seconds of utter silence, Gina said, "Do you see the men behind me? They have spent years in Iraq and Afghanistan. They do things that I don't know how to do. That I don't even want to think about. We're the only people who know you're here. In a way, you're already dead. We left your body in the apartment with your friends. Do you understand?"

When Davidson stirred again, she didn't raise her hand to quiet him. "Commissioner," he said, "we can help you."

If Silas Nasar flinched at all, if he had any kind of reaction, Gina Carbone didn't see it. "You're not a very smart man, Mr. Nasar."

Roger Davidson nodded politely at her as she left the cell. Terrible things, she knew, were about to happen here.

* * *

The Olympic Tower, at 51ˢᵗ Street and Fifth Avenue, was all black. It was built in the late 1970s directly across from St. Patrick's Cathedral. The construction was financed by Greek shipping magnates, rivals of Aristotle Onassis, hence the name Olympic Tower. Greeks, in fact, had lived on its top floors until the early 1990s when the rich from Saudi Arabia, Bahrain, and Kuwait began to supplant them, but the building still retained the Olympic name.

Within minutes after Roger Davidson reported to the commissioner, and that was only half an hour after she had left Pier 37, that nine men in black combat uniforms, body armor, and weapons entered the towering granite lobby. Ambient sound filled the lobby from the waterfall that shimmered perpetually down the surface of a three-story wall.

There were two elevator banks. One was for the commercial tenants on the first ten floors, which were law firms, public relations companies, a charitable foundation. The other elevator bank was for the private apartments on the upper forty-one floors, each of them larger and more opulent as they ascended: the two apartments on the two highest floors had Olympic-size swimming pools.

One of the armed men shouted at the doormen: "On the ground, on the ground." The nine men moving rapidly through the lobby all wore jackets on which the words *NYPD Counterterrorism Unit* were stitched in big letters. Like most of the people who lived in the building, the two doormen were Saudis. They were stunned by what they saw and fell first to their knees and then to the floor, as if praying.

The team divided into two squads. Roger Davidson, who was steeped in the rare ability to command with the absolute certainty that his orders would be obeyed, signaled the first squad into one of the elevators. When that elevator reached the eleventh floor, Davidson led his squad, three large men and Cynthia Chambliss, a slender and gorgeous black woman with a knowledge of weapons almost as skillful as his own, into the elevator. They rose in total silence to the fifty-first floor.

As soon as Davidson emerged from the elevator, he knew the information he had was accurate. Despite what all the politicians and television experts said, torture, especially extreme torture of men like Silas Nasar, in his experience, was a fast and efficient way of extracting very reliable information.

The wide church-like double doors to the top-floor apartment, once owned by Adnan Khashoggi, the arms dealer who in the 1980s had helped to manage the Iran-Contra exchange of weapons for cash, were already blasted open. Just as he had been told by the now broken-armed Silas Nasar in the total privacy of the Supermax cell, an orderly row of six RPG launchers stood at the floor-to-ceiling windows overlooking the world famous cathedral. The RPGs were locked and loaded, that expression Davidson had first heard at the transformative moment when, at the Marine base at Quantico, he had for the first time pushed a full magazine into an M-16 and disengaged the safety switch. The RPGs were, as he had known for the last forty-five minutes, smuggled into the apartment piece by piece over the last three weeks by men posing as guests of the current owner, Ahmed Khalife, and as electricians, a pool cleaner, cooks. The doormen now kneeling in the lobby had played to perfection the roles of the "hear-no-evil-see-no-evil-speak-no-evil" cartoon characters.

Precisely cut holes had been excised from the row of floor-to-ceiling windows overlooking the immense roof of the cathedral. On the floor three black-haired men in business suits were already bound up in plastic sheathing from their upper chests to their feet. One moaned just as Davidson had been told to expect. The others were quiet.

"How close were we?" he asked Jorge Ortega, the squad leader.

"Close, sir. Motherfuckers had just engaged the rocket grenades."

"Any resistance?"

"They're pussies. Nothing. They were all crying, 'Please don't hurt me, please.' One of them is still crying like a baby."

Davidson raised his hand to silence the room. In that hand was his secure cell phone. Almost instantly he heard Gina Carbone's strong voice: "What's the story?" she asked

Roger Davidson respected her. She was steady, calm, no nonsense. She wanted the scene described in the way it happened.

"The story is good, Commissioner. We stopped them in their tracks. The RPGs were fully engaged and set to go. They would have blown St. Patrick's to kingdom come. The room is secure. Three arrests here. The two doormen are under arrest, too. They must have known who was bringing the elements of the weapons up here."

"What fucking condition are the three of them in? Don't tell me they're wasted. I have enough dead Arabs on my hands already."

"They're all alive. Not a scratch on them. One of them seems to be suffering a damn emotional issue. He's crying like a baby and wants his mama. I'm going to give him a hug soon and tell him everything will be just fine."

"Don't," Gina said, "let anything happen to them. I want them clean, presentable, and charming. The Kingston Trio. Don't bring them to the river. I want them at Central Booking downtown just like anybody else who's been arrested. I'm making arrangements with a judge to get them charged and with cameras in the courtroom. I also want the weapons down here so that I can show them to the press. Get pictures of the RPGs pointed at the cathedral. The mayor will have a press conference. I'll be there. Nobody sees your face anywhere."

"What face?" Davidson asked. "I'm not even sure what my name is any more."

Gina spoke evenly. "You did a great job getting this stuff out of Mr. Nasar. He had a reputation for stamina."

"Really? I didn't see that once I got to know him a little better. He found his voice, so to speak."

"And one other thing."

"Yes, ma'am?"

"That Indian reporter."

"Is he bothering you?"

"I don't think his presence is very helpful."

CHAPTER THIRTY

GABRIEL HAUSER WAS immediately overwhelmed by the utter silence in the apartment. Over the last several years there'd always been movement and excitement. The familiar, welcoming sounds as Oliver ran to him, his toenails clicking on the floorboards. Cam—whom Gabriel always called from the hospital as his shift was ending—making sandwiches or soup in the kitchen with the radio on NPR regardless of the time.

Calling Cam's name softly, Gabriel walked through the apartment they loved. He even opened closet doors. For what he realized was a moment of lunacy, he was afraid Cam was dead.

In the small kitchen, the only room in which the lights were on, everything was as usual, clean and orderly. The only objects on the counter around the sink were a gleaming toaster, a blender, and a coffee grinder, all in brushed, burnished metal. On the kitchen table was a slender vase with new flowers.

And then Gabriel noticed in a corner on the floor a neat stack of white paper. Gabriel instinctively knew what the papers were: they were printed copies of the e-mails he had exchanged with Mohammad Hussein. Gabriel carefully, and nervously, raised the neatly compiled papers and carried them to the living room. He sat on the sofa in front of the coffee table.

The e-mails were in chronological order, for the most part in chains of one e-mail responding to the preceding on consecutive pages. For Gabriel it was like reading a diary he had cowritten with Mohammad. It was Mohammad who sent the first. It read: "Doctor, what happened to the soldier with the burns on his chest? You were wonderful with him."

Gabriel remembered the inner thrill he experienced when he first saw the e-mail. This beautiful, intelligent man had made the initial overture. It was only when he saw his response to that first e-mail that he recalled the soldier, Rodney Jones. His answering e-mail, sent on the chunky cell phone less than five minutes after Mohammad's e-mail arrived, said that Rodney Jones had been air-lifted to Germany for treatment. "I think he'll recover," Gabriel wrote. Nothing else on Rodney Jones. And then, as Gabriel was now surprised and almost embarrassed to see, his very first e-mail had been a flirt. "Would like to see you."

It took four days for Mohammad to answer. In those four days Gabriel was in turmoil. Had his e-mail been too blatant? Afghanistan was not Christopher Street in Greenwich Village, still that epicenter of gay life. Moreover, Gabriel didn't truly know who Mohammad was, other than a man in hospital service who had just one day appeared at the hospital at the Bagram Air Base. As he now read it, he remembered how elated he was with Mohammad's next e-mail. "How about Tuesday at three at the Red Rose on Zafir Street? Do you know it? Let me know?"

Gabriel let him know in ten seconds that the answer was *yes*. And so it had started, as Gabriel was reminded when he read through the several hundred e-mails, some as brief as three words, that he was rapidly falling in love. He could see now that anyone reading these e-mails, even though some were terse and appeared coded, could trace the evolution of the relationship and how it continued even after Mohammad first mentioned his wife and children. The disclosure that Mohammad had a family didn't give Gabriel any pause. He ignored it. He had had affairs with married family men in the past.

And then as he read the e-mails, Gabriel came to their abrupt stop. That's when the pudgy colonel had informed him that his longing notes to Tom Lathem—his fellow intern and lover at Mount Sinai long before he met Cam—had been discovered. Gabriel had been taken out of Afghanistan immediately and his military e-mail account suspended. During the two weeks it took to process his discharge at Fort Leonard Wood in Missouri, he did not have access to his personal e-mail. When he did retrieve his personal e-mail, it was easy for him to remember Mohammad's e-mail address.

Weeks later, it was Mohammad who first wrote about wanting to leave Afghanistan for the United States. He was worried, he said, for his safety. Too many of his neighbors knew that he had friends who were American officers. Those watchful, suspicious neighbors believed he was a translator for United States soldiers, or a nurse who treated only wounded American soldiers and contractors, or an informant.

Gabriel also saw, to his embarrassment, that his own e-mails to Mohammad were self-aggrandizing. There were suggestions that he had the power to bring him and his family to the United States. Gabriel knew he had no such power. Any semblance had been stripped from him with the patches that gave his major's rank, that ancient status between captain and lieutenant colonel. Some of the e-mails included as attachments the futile letters Gabriel, in fact, wrote to the secretary of defense, the president, and the two senators from New York. In college Gabriel had read Saul Bellow's *Herzog*, in which Moses Herzog, the lead character, obsessively wrote eloquent and pointless letters to the famous living and dead. Herzog's letters were pointless. So, Gabriel knew, were his.

Gabriel could see in Mohammad's final e-mails a more strident, pleading tone for help in getting out of Afghanistan. Some of the e-mails attached pictures of his attractive wife and children. He even wrote that he would leave them behind.

Suddenly Gabriel discovered e-mails that were addressed to him by Mohammad and had date and time stamps. But Gabriel was certain he had never seen them before. There was a chain of e-mails from Mohammad that asked Gabriel if he could find several men. Gabriel recognized only one of the eight names. Silas Nasar. There were e-mails from Gabriel to Mohammad in which Gabriel asked for information about Silas Nasar, a name he had never seen or heard and other men with Arabic names whom Gabriel had met in Afghanistan and who were friends of Mohammad and Silas, who, Mohammad wrote, were now living in all the boroughs of New York City except Manhattan.

Gabriel had never seen Mohammad's last chain of e-mails. And he had never seen, and certainly had never written, the e-mails that bore his address: *drhauser@aol.com.*

And then Mohammad's e-mails vanished two months earlier. Gabriel's last, pleading, almost hysterical e-mails to Mohammad asked, *Where are you? Can you call? I'm worried.* It was, he recognized, the same sense of bewildered loss he'd experienced years earlier when Jerome Fletcher, just weeks before he was stabbed to death, had simply stopped communicating with him.

When he finished his hours of reading, Gabriel restacked the papers neatly on the coffee table and fell back more deeply into the sofa. He realized that anyone reading all these e-mails would know that he had been in love and, while living with Cam, he had operated in secrecy to bring Mohammad Hussein to the United States so that they could be together. For the first time, the collective weight of these e-mails led Gabriel, too, to acknowledge to himself the depth of this attachment to Mohammad, this now-obvious love for him.

* * *

He desperately needed to find Cam. There was no doubt that he also loved Cam and needed to explain, if he could, the emotional betrayal the e-mails laid bare. Using his iPhone's contact list, he called the ten or so friends they knew most well. He reached five of them, three women and two men, and they didn't know where Cam was and hadn't heard from him. He left urgent voice mail messages for the others. He called Cam's office. A recording said the office was closed for the day but that the caller could leave a message in the firm's general voice mail box.

Cam Dewar was a man who always made himself available. He was in public relations. He had an iPhone, a Galaxy, and an iPad with him at all times. During the course of each day he sent a steady stream of text messages to Gabriel. They were love notes, reminders of things to do or places to go, gentle jokes. Gabriel had not received a text message from Cam in four hours.

Cam was lost in the world, Gabriel thought. His mind raced through the possible wreckage. Cam could be dead, he could have been arrested, he could have decided to sleep in the park along with the thousands of stranded out-of-towners. No matter what else, Cam was certainly hurt in his heart, at that deep emotional level of love betrayed.

Raj Gandhi answered on the first pulse of his cell phone. "Dr. Hauser?" he asked.

"Where are you?"

"Where am I? In my newsroom." He waited. "How can I help you?"

"I need to see you."

"When?"

"Now."

"Why?"

"Silas Nasar."

"I know that name."

"I know the name, Mr. Gandhi, and I know that person, too."

CHAPTER THIRTY-ONE

GINA CARBONE WAS standing at Roland Fortune's left side. Three senior officers, in full dress uniforms, were at his right. In front of them was a table with weapons, such as grenade launchers and M-16s and other assault weapons that Roland had never seen or smelled before. They had the distinct odor of grease and cordite. On a video screen behind them were oversize images in high definition of the three men arrested in the Olympic Tower. Unlike the secret prisoners at Pier 37, these men were now, as Gina had intended, public figures.

Roland Fortune spoke to a press room with at least thirty reporters seated on folding chairs. "I'm pleased to announce that, just two hours ago, elements of the New York City Police Department's counterterrorism unit thwarted at its final stages an attack by rocket launchers and high explosives on one of the most sacred places on the planet, St. Patrick's Cathedral in the heart of Manhattan. This impending assault was not, we believe, a random plot by rogue opportunists. Our best assessment is that the individuals who were on the brink of destroying the cathedral are linked to the despicable assaults on the Metropolitan Museum of Art, the 9/11 Memorial, the brutal assassinations of our brave police, the bombing of the historic intersection of Wall and Broad Streets, and the war at the George Washington Carver Houses."

Briefly turning to the video screen behind him—incongruously, the men were dressed in Western clothes, including one who looked like the young Omar Sharif in a well-tailored blue blazer—Roland said, "The men pictured here were all arraigned before a New York State judge fifteen minutes ago. They are Amir Butt, Ravi Al-Haq, and Alan Richards. All of them are United States citizens. Butt and Al-Haq are native-born citizens, Butt was born and raised in Chicago, Al-Haq in Providence, Rhode Island. Richards, whose real name we might not know, was born in Saudi Arabia but is a naturalized U.S. citizen."

Roland resisted the temptation to drink water. He thought doing so would show a lack of resolve, a sense of anxiety, weakness, or fatigue. "Our best information is that a common link joins them to the earlier attacks. They have each spent two to three months in Sudan and ISIS-controlled areas of Syria, although at different times. Al-Haq, we believe, is an accountant. Butt has worked as a manager of a car and limousine service. Richards has said he is a New York lawyer, a claim we need to verify since there are five law-yers in New York named Alan Richards."

Although Irv Rothstein had told the reporters in the room that they should not ask questions until after Roland had finished, three people started urgently waving upraised hands. Roland ignored the hands. "Al-Haq, Butt, and Richards have been removed from New York. They are now in separate, secure facilities. They have each been charged with attempted murder and conspiracy for mass destruction."

Irv Rothstein gave Roland an almost imperceptible signal to wind up the prepared part of his statement. "From the outset of these awful events, Commissioner Carbone and I have committed ourselves to truth telling in describing only what we know. And truth about what we don't know. We do know, as a result of the events two hours ago at St. Patrick's, and the events earlier today at the George Washington Carver Houses, that we are closing in on the people responsible for these vicious acts. And, more important, that we are shutting these people down and preventing further devastating attacks. The fact is that we are now on the hunt. We are the hunter, not the victim."

Gina Carbone knew that Roland's prepared statement was over. She shifted slightly in the direction of the microphones into which the mayor had spoken. They had done many joint press conferences in the last few years. They worked very well as a team. Gina said, "We will take questions. But as you'll all understand, there are probably going to be many questions we will not be able to answer for security and law enforcement reasons. But Mayor Fortune and I will do our best to give you all the facts that we can."

They had decided that Roland would select the reporters who wanted to ask questions. He started by pointing at Beth Connor of CNN, a competent reporter who had interviewed him several times. She was not friendly or unfriendly; she was straightforward. "How was this plot to destroy St. Patrick's uncovered?"

Gina took the initiative. "We can't comment on that specifically. But suffice it to say that we have, among many other sources, confidential informants. Some of them are useful. Others not."

"Was this informant under arrest?" Connor asked.

"I can't comment on that," Gina said.

"Is that informant being protected?"

"I can't comment on that either," Gina said.

Other hands waved like small flags in the wind. Roland pointed to Jack Kramer of WNBC seated in one of the folding chairs in the middle of the press room. "How many people have been arrested since the bombing at the Met?" Kramer asked.

Gina lied. "Forty-five." This answer did not include the eighteen men on Pier 37. Or Silas Nasar.

"How many more arrests will there be?" Kramer asked.

"As many," Gina said, "as are needed. We will arrest them all or we will disable them all."

Roland nodded at Jackie Lin of NPR. She asked, "Why were no prisoners taken at the George Washington Carver projects?"

Gina answered, "It was in reality a combat situation. There were ten terrorists on the fifth floor in the Carver Towers. Our information was that they were about to mount a major operation. We had to act decisively. Our counterterrorism officers were all combat veterans from Desert Storm, Iraq, and Afghanistan. They confronted men who obviously had also been in combat, somewhere in the world. As Mayor Fortune mentioned just a few hours ago, if you have been in combat yourself, you understand that your overriding task is to defend yourself and the other members of your team. And to carry out your mission."

"Was it the mission to kill every person in that apartment?" Jackie Lin asked.

"No." Gina's voice and tone never varied. She was cool and powerful and attractive. The question was, Roland recognized, meant to provoke her. Gina said, "The mission was to prevent these terrorists from inflicting damage on the people of this city. It's important to remember that the men in that apartment elected to be there. Our information is that they had rented the apartment three months ago and gradually built up an arsenal. And, as we can tell in the inventory of the weapons seized there, they had reached a point of complete readiness to mount other assaults. These were professional killers who were themselves prepared to die."

Roland now recognized that the clamor of questions had reached the point that always caused concern to Irv Rothstein. Irv had often urged Roland to exert control by pointing to reporters Roland knew were friendly or noncombative. But now it was at the stage when the quickest or loudest or most distinctive voice took over the event. Despite Irv's seasoned advice, Roland, always surefooted, often let these more active and intense conferences take their own course. He enjoyed the give and take. Since he'd had many press conferences with Gina over the last three years, most often after gang killings in which innocent children were bystander victims or the murders of cops, Roland had complete confidence that she, too, was a master of the freewheeling news conference.

A woman's voice rang out from the near center of the active crowd, "Were the dead in that apartment part of the group that bombed the Met and the memorial?"

"Obviously there's every indication they were," Gina said. "It's clear that these were organized cadres."

The same voice: "Was it an ISIS affiliate?"

"It's natural to think that, but at this stage we don't know."

"Can you explain the chaos at the approaches to the Triboro Bridge?"

"First," Roland intervened, "let me say it shouldn't be characterized as chaos. Even in extraordinarily troubled times like this, it's important to keep perspective and not get swept away in overcharged words. Yes, there are several hundred cars that, as their drivers must have known, would not be permitted to leave the city. At least not yet. But almost one million men, women, and children live in Manhattan. There have been no organized disturbances. We have seen cooperation, steadiness, and the legendary resolve of those who live in this great city. The fact that one or two hundred motorists are expressing frustration only underscores the discipline and resolution of hundreds of thousands of others. In the final analysis, the issue at the Triboro Bridge is a traffic problem, and not a significant one."

The next sharp voice, this one from the rear of the crowd:

"Mayor, Manhattan has been locked down for more than thirty hours. When do you plan to end the lockdown?"

"The easy answer," Roland said, "is when the conditions warrant it. But the real answer is that the end of the lockdown is in sight. It was never intended that the lockdown be open-ended. Its purpose was to contain and confine. It may have outlasted its purpose. That's under evaluation."

A voice with a strident, skeptical tone sounded through the others, distinctly audible to Roland, everyone else in the room, and the audience around the world: "There are reports of confrontation and nasty words between members of your police department and Army soldiers attached to the 101st Airborne Division on the bridge."

Roland said, "We have no such reports. The coordination among federal, state, and city agencies has been remarkable."

Another voice, a baritone, recognizable as one of NPR's radio broadcasters but impossible for Roland to name because of the anonymity of radio: "Do you have a timetable for President Carter's arrival?"

"Certainly the president is the best source of that information. I don't have it. I can tell you that he is in touch with me continuously. Everything I do, everything we do, is with his knowledge and approval and with the coordination and support of the exceptional professionals who serve him."

"There are reliable reports," the NPR reporter said, "that the president's security people view Manhattan now as a city in chaos and under siege, a kind of Baghdad or Kabul on the Hudson, and that the reason the president is not here rests on profound concerns about his safety."

"Again I believe it's crucial not to exaggerate. New York is not Kabul or Baghdad or Damascus. There are not terrorist armies on the outskirts about to invade. There have been terrible events committed by cadres of sick people. Those people are now, through the heroic efforts of Commissioner Carbone, either dead or captured or in disarray."

The same voice continued, "But what about the president's arrival? What do you expect if he arrives?"

"Commissioner Carbone, in conjunction with the Department of Homeland Security, the Secret Service, and the other top-notch federal agencies involved with us, can protect the president."

"When is he arriving?"

Gina leaned toward the microphone: "For security reasons, we can't make a comment on that."

And then slender, soft-spoken Raj Gandhi spoke up. "Who is Silas Nasar?"

"We have no idea who that is," Gina Carbone answered.

"Where is he? Is he in detention?" Raj asked.

"That, too," Gina said, "is not something we can answer. It's difficult to detain a person we don't know."

In reality, Gina Carbone wanted to find some way to confine, silence, or eliminate Raj Gandhi. None of that, she knew, was easy to do to a reporter for the *New York Times*.

Irv Rothstein then stepped directly in front of the microphone. "That, ladies and gentlemen, is all the time we have for now. Thank you for your attention."

CHAPTER THIRTY-TWO

RAJ GANDHI MET Gabriel Hauser on the stone bench at the front
of the Church of the Heavenly Rest at the corner of 90th Street and
Fifth Avenue. Directly across the avenue, at the Engineers' Gate to
Central Park, dozens of runners moved north and south on the internal roadway that encircled the park for six miles. Bicyclists on
five-thousand-dollar sleek machines and wearing colorful skintight
clothes raced by. Just beyond the runners and bikers the leaves of an
immense ancient tree shimmered in the clear light. And the acres of
water in the reservoir glowed so much that the air above it seemed
to have an incandescent brightness. A cluster of three fountains embedded in the reservoir sprayed tall columns of white water above
the reservoir's surface, just as they did on normal days.

Raj removed his iPhone from the rumpled seersucker jacket he
always wore. "Dr. Hauser, are you sure I can record this?"

"I said so twice, haven't I?"

Raj pressed the icon that converted the miraculous object to a
voice and video recorder. "Let me start," Raj said, "by telling you
that I believe Silas Nasar was one of the masterminds, one of the key
planners, of these attacks."

Gabriel gave Raj a charming smile, saying something that Raj had
never heard from anyone who had given him permission to record
an interview. Reaching into the pocket of his well-tailored slacks,
Gabriel brought out his own iPhone and held it aloft alongside

Raj's identical iPhone. "Not that I don't trust you," Gabriel said, still smiling. "But I've read about the famous eighteen-minute gap in the Nixon Watergate tapes."

Although surprised, Raj remained impassive.

Gabriel started, "Not Silas Nasar. His real name is Hakim Khomani."

"How do you know that?"

"I had a close friend in Afghanistan. When I left the country, we continued to e-mail one another. He was, and I hope still is, a friend."

"Who is he?"

"A nurse. He worked with me at the central hospital in Kabul. I was hustled out of Kabul quickly. I didn't even have a chance to say goodbye. I did have his e-mail address. *Caregiver7@aol.com.*"

Gabriel, a man who was trained to observe people as a whole person so that he could detect and diagnose conditions such as fear, deceit, illness, or comfort that other people might not see, for the first time looked at Raj Gandhi as he might look at a patient. Raj had slightly jaundiced eyes, thin hair, fingernails that were almost transparent, cheeks that were in the early stages of waste. He was either an incipient diabetic or a man who didn't yet know he was HIV-positive. He was also, Gabriel saw, shy and sincere. Reliable, a truth teller. And doomed.

"How do you know Khomani?"

"My friend in Afghanistan—we were lovers, Mr. Gandhi, as well as friends—told me he had relatives in the U.S. who had been able to come here during the Russian invasion in the '80s. Khomani, my friend's cousin, had a degree from MIT in electrical engineering. So when that war was under way, and Khomani told the American embassy he wanted to come here, he had easy access. Clans, blood relationships, those kinds of ties are important among Afghans.

The cousins stayed in touch. First by phone, expensive land lines at the time, by letters, and then by e-mails and text messages. They were both science types, well-educated, interested in technology, very early users of the Internet."

The simple marble bench in front of the elegant church, which was like a cathedral on a small scale and one of the most beautiful buildings on the Upper East Side, was a popular resting place for people who had finished long runs in Central Park and for tourists to sit. Raj and Gabriel stopped speaking when a young woman runner, sweating, wearing a baseball cap from the back of which her braided blond hair extended to her shoulders, sat on the bench next to them. She took a slender cell phone from a pouch on her waistband. "Chumley's," they overheard her say, "just reopened. Let me shower and change. See you there in two hours."

Gabriel knew Chumley's was a bar on Second Avenue at 80th Street. When she said, "*Ciao*," Gabriel for the first time smiled at Raj Gandhi. When she stood up, moving effortlessly, she said to them, "Have a nice day." And on her perfect legs she began running east on 90th Street.

Gabriel, noticing that Raj had not looked at this exquisitely built young woman, said, "Life goes on." Raj smiled. Gabriel had never met a gay Indian.

"Did you," Raj asked, "meet Silas Nasar? Or Khomani?"

"I didn't, but I planned to."

"Why?"

"I cared very much about Mohammad, my Afghan friend. He wrote that Khomani had married, and now lived under the name Silas Nasar. He had e-mailed pictures of Khomani's wife and their two sons. The wife was an Afghan beauty, as I could see from the pictures. But the younger son had cerebral palsy. He was three. From the pictures, I could see, Mr. Gandhi, that his condition was terrible. I felt that Mohammad, who was a very compassionate man with children of his own, wanted to know more about his cousin and his family."

"Mohammad was married?" For the first time Raj, impassive and matter of fact, looked surprised.

"Yes. Haven't you ever heard of such a thing before? It was once known as closeted gay men."

"Of course."

"Do you have children?" Gabriel asked.

"No, I work. I'm one of those people married to my work. No children, either."

Gabriel's tone became more intense. He cultivated a quiet, comforting demeanor, that doctor's style of reassurance. "You told me that you had crucial news for me. Your words, Mr. Gandhi. I've said a lot. I'm a doctor. I've learned to listen. Where is Cameron?"

"Cameron Dewar is missing because he was arrested."

"Say that again."

"Arrested."

"Where is he?"

"The Secret Service has him."

"Why?"

"Why, Dr. Hauser? Because he knows *you*."

"Where is he?"

"I don't know."

Gabriel was for a moment angry with this evasive, overly well-mannered, fragile-looking man. "How do you know he was arrested?"

"The source I mentioned."

"Who the fuck is this source? I want to talk to him."

"I truly don't know who he is."

"First you tell me you can't tell me who he is. Now you tell me you don't know who he is." Gabriel caught himself. His anger at various times during the last two days was, he believed, far too intense and unpredictable. His work as a doctor had taught him that quiet persistence drew out more of the truth and more information from patients. "What else did this man say? Or is the source a woman?"

"It's a man. Quite sarcastic, unpleasant to deal with. But so far everything he's told me has been accurate. He is what we call in our business a reliable source."

"What else did he say about Cam?"

"He's in a secret place. He's being asked questions about who *you* know, who *you* have conversations with, what *you* hear, what *you* write, to whom *you* write."

"What are they doing to him?"

"So far just talking to him. And he is talking to them. How the two of you met? When did the two of you become sexually active? Do you have HIV? What have you told him about the Army? Has he read the letters you wrote to the president, congressmen, the secretary of defense, even the editor at the *Times* when you were objecting to *Don't ask, don't tell*. They seem to have copies of every letter you wrote."

"Of course they do," Gabriel said. "I sent them. I wanted them to be read. I kept copies. They were all in a Barneys shoebox in our apartment. I don't think Cam ever looked at them until a few hours ago."

Raj paused. He, too, was patient. Like Gabriel he knew that patience, not anger, not threats, not shouting, extracted information. Raj said, "Most of all, though, they want to know about you and Silas Nasar, the cousin."

"Silas Nasar? They already know about Silas Nasar."

"They also believe," Raj said, "that you met him and knew him before the bombings."

"Knew him? No, I never saw him. But we spoke. Several times. We exchanged e-mails and texts. He sounded so much like his cousin. They were raised together. I knew he was going to be on the steps of the museum on Sunday. He told me he resembled his cousin. He even sent me by text a not particularly clear picture of himself. I knew we would recognize each other. The picture did make me believe they were related."

"They believe," Raj said, "that you had already met him and knew him. How often did you talk to Silas?"

"Not really sure. He was very easy to talk to. He had lots of opinions, as did his cousin. But Mohammad was more difficult to speak with, although his English was completely understandable. But the language was a Sunni dialect. Silas was almost, you would think, a native English speaker."

Everything about the elegant Church of the Heavenly Rest was symmetrical. The two identical low spires, the carved facades that were mirror images of one another, the twin huge medieval doors whose gold hinges were identical. And that remarkable name, almost symmetrical itself: the Church of the Heavenly Rest which, as Gabriel had thought since he was a boy, had a distinctive name so unlike any other church he'd ever heard of except possibly the immense, poorly maintained, and never completed Cathedral of Saint John the Divine near the Columbia campus on upper Amsterdam Avenue. That cathedral stood at the edge of the then still dangerous Morningside Park, dense as a jungle, boulder-strewn, an ideal haven for thieves and muggers.

The Church of the Heavenly Rest was so symmetrical, so balanced, that there was a marble bench on the other side of the ornate wooden doors. And there were large concrete planters next to each bench that bore slender yew trees newly planted because the previous harsh winter destroyed the earlier, more mature ones. A banner imprinted with the single immense word *Rejoice* was suspended over the doors. It rustled in the mild summer breeze.

Minute recording devices had been implanted in the tender flesh of the new trees in the planters as soon as Gina Carbone had learned that the two men had arranged to meet on one of the church's smooth granite benches. Across the avenue just inside the entrance to the Engineers' Gate, a thickset man who had the heft and dimensions of a college football player and a skinny woman, both in runner's clothes, listened on earbuds to every word that Gabriel Hauser and Raj Gandhi spoke. So, too, did Gina Carbone.

The man posing as a runner asked into a small microphone that was a part of the earbud, "What do you want us to do?"

* * *

Naked, Tony Garafalo stretched out on the sheets on the bed near the desk at which Gina was seated. She was naked, too, except for a thick Regency Hotel towel draped around her waist.

Tony was staring at the profile of her remarkably shapely, youthful breasts.

Gina said, "Remember, you're runners. Keep moving. These two guys are smart. They'll notice you if you're just standing around." Gina was one of those rare people who knew the arts of command. "Get your asses moving. You have the drop on them for five hundred yards. Your equipment will pick up everything they say even when they can't see you."

Then Gina heard Gabriel Hauser's increasingly edgy, aggravated voice. "Mr. Gandhi, when I called you because I couldn't find Cam you said you could help. So far you know only something I had already suspected. That the bastards have arrested Cam. You haven't told me how much danger he is in, where he is, how I can get him back."

"I believe I know where he is."

"Where?"

"There's a dark prison in an old pier on the East River. In it are about two dozen Islamic men who were secretly arrested within minutes or hours after the first explosions yesterday."

"I'm going down there. I have a bike in the basement of my building. Where is it?"

"A derelict pier just below Houston Street. I've tried to get in a few times. Haven't succeeded. Pier 37."

Two casually dressed men, both Sunni Muslims, stood at the iron fence surrounding the Cooper-Hewitt Museum just across 90th Street on the east side of Fifth Avenue. Behind the ornate fence the museum itself was shrouded, as it had been for two years, by gauzy, translucent veils that protected the museum and passersby from construction debris during the long course of the museum's reconstruction. Using slender, essentially invisible equipment that Silas Nasar had given them, they, too, listened to the conversation between Raj Gandhi and Gabriel Hauser. They could have been the tourists they appeared to be.

"Mr. Gandhi, I have no confidence in reporters, their newspapers, CNN, the *New York Times*. I made every effort I could when I was hustled and bundled out of my hospital in Afghanistan, where I loved my work as a doctor, and then out of the Army, where I planned to stay for years. No one, no one, in your business paid any attention to me. I felt like a leper."

Quietly Raj said, "I'm sorry. But now *Don't ask, don't tell* has been eliminated."

"Too late, not to mention the twenty years it was in effect and all the years and years before that when openly gay people could not serve. I'm one of thousands and thousands of people with what the Army still calls less-than-honorable discharges."

"You can ask to have that changed."

"I'm not interested in *asking*. I have a thing about *asking* the Army or the government for anything."

"That must be painful."

Gabriel leaned closer to Raj. "Why haven't *you* done anything, Mr. Gandhi? It's been many, many hours since you learned important things, things that need to be exposed. But here you are, on a bench, talking to me about what you know." Gabriel paused, continuing to gaze at Raj's delicate face. "What are *you* going to do?"

"I work for a paper with an opaque hierarchy. Layers of editors. Their watchword is verification, corroboration."

"You have your source."

"I don't know who he is."

"You have me. You know my life partner has disappeared and is under arrest. I see stories from the *Times* on my cell phone about our courageous mayor, the extraordinarily brave police commissioner, garbage on the streets, the count of the dead, lists of names of the dead. But I don't see anything about the underside of all this."

Raj Gandhi spoke slowly. "You're wrong, Dr. Hauser. I have a blog and access to YouTube. I have the secret caller on tape. I have a video I took of Gina Carbone slipping into Pier 37. I even have a video of her going in and out of the Regency. And I have a source on the service staff at the Regency who tells me that Gina Carbone has a different kind of captive at the Regency, a lover. I even have his name. Tony Garafalo. And like the rest of the world I have Google. It took me ten minutes of a Google search to find out that this Tony Garafalo served at least eight years in a federal prison, the worst one, in fact, the Supermax facility in Florence, Colorado, where the Unabomber and the shoe-bomber are held, where John Gotti was once a prisoner. Mr. Garafalo was an associate of the Gambino family. And that Garafalo was convicted of using force to silence witnesses who were about to testify about the Gambino family."

"And the people you work for have no interest in that?"

"Not yet."

"When will *yet* come? After Cam is dead? After the pier is empty? After I'm arrested?" Gabriel stood up. "You're wasting my time, Mr. Gandhi."

"Don't leave." Gandhi's delicate voice was as loud, as definitive as it could be. "In two hours I am putting everything I know, corroborated or not, on my blog. On YouTube, on Snapchat, on Twitter, on all those instantaneous social media devices. The pier and its dark prison. The movements of the police commissioner. You, your injured dog, your lover. Even this interview."

"I don't believe you, Mr. Gandhi. You don't have the inner strength to do that. It's not in your DNA. The *Times* will fire you. You're the only Indian there. You have all that prestige, that loyalty. You're Gunga Din, loyal to the British, to the powers that be."

"Are you a racist, Dr. Hauser?"

"Far from it. I'm a realist."

Gabriel Hauser turned off his cell phone. "I'll take care of this myself," he said. He stood and disappeared around the corner on East 90th Street. His beloved apartment was only eight blocks away. He cried all the way to the home he loved.

CHAPTER THIRTY-THREE

RAJ GANDHI'S WALK east from Fifth Avenue and the Church of the Heavenly Rest took him, once he crossed Lexington Avenue, through the dreary streets filled with decaying brownstones in which multiple small apartments, some of them only the size of a small living room, had been partitioned with thin walls. Garbage cans and wooden bins, most of them overflowing with the ordinary debris of human life, stood next to each fluorescent lobby.

Now, so many hours after the bombings and the lockdown started, there were mountain ranges of huge black plastic bags on the curbstones. In the gathering dark Raj Gandhi saw rats on the sidewalks. They reminded him not only of his early years in his native Mumbai but the fictional rats that suddenly proliferated at the start of Camus's novel *The Plague*. Oran in that novel had been quarantined, a whole population confined by the presence and fear of a disease that was a modern Black Death. The noblest characters in the book, doctors and journalists, had died as the epidemic progressed and before it came to its natural, miraculous end. Raj had read the novel often. He felt he was now living it.

His own building was constructed ten years ago. It looked to him as if a refugee Soviet-era architect had designed it. At thirty-three stories, it was one of dozens of anonymous new apartment buildings lining cheerless York Avenue. It had a comfortable lobby and friendly uniformed doormen who knew his name.

His own apartment, a studio, was on a high floor with a view of the East River. For a curtain on the single large window he had tacked up a burlap fabric which he never opened and so never looked at the majestic expanse of the river and its legendary bridges. The apartment was replete with gadgets, laptop computers, iPads, a variety of cell phones, four television sets that had access to every available news and cable station, CNN, Fox, Al Jazeera, even the Weather Channel. He spent almost all of his income on these technological marvels. He had a pull-out sofa on which he slept, as uncomfortable as a plank, and three small tables he had assembled from IKEA for his equipment. There were three folding wooden chairs. No carpets.

As soon as he unlocked the door to the apartment, the voice he heard was shockingly familiar. "Jesus, Gandhi, you live like a college freshman at a bad school. Look at all of this crap."

Fear seized Raj. "How did you get in here?"

"Don't worry. This isn't exactly a first-class building. And a quadriplegic with a blindfold could open your door."

As Raj saw in the glare from the two unshaded lights, the man in the wooden chair was exceptionally good-looking, obviously Italian. He was large, not at all fat, but tall and muscular. His powerful appearance was for Raj entirely different from the voice he had heard in the calls from the unknown source. The man Raj had envisioned from the sound of the voice was scrawny, bald, furtive.

Still seated, the man said, "I thought it was time we should meet. I'm losing my patience." No accent. A clear voice Raj couldn't place, easily the voice of a man who was literate and persuasive. But this man was obviously a great mimic, able to sound like a crank from Queens or Brooklyn whenever he wanted to.

"What do you want?" Raj asked. His own voice, as he recognized, had a tremor.

Standing, the man gestured at all the technological devices on the desks. "I've seen your blogs and Twitter feeds, Mr. Gandhi. You have an impressive audience. Hundreds of thousands of followers. More than your namesake, the great Mahatma. And you work for people at that godawful newspaper of yours who will not let you write the information I give you. It's time for you, Mr. Gandhi, to get the word I've been giving you out to the world all on your own. I decided to help you write it."

"I'm not sure," Raj said. "Who are you? What's your name?"

"Linda Lovelace. Deep Throat."

Raj recognized the names, but had never seen Lovelace's movies. He had never in fact despite all the gadgetry even glanced at porn. He said, "I still haven't quite finished my work."

"You have. Let's get on the computer. We'll write it together."

Raj sat at the table with the laptop computer at which he ordinarily wrote his blog and Twitter feeds. Almost daily he used his blog to summarize or elaborate on his stories as they had appeared in the *Times*. Some of those blogs were written in his native language, Hindi. Far more were in English.

The well-dressed man pulled one of the folding chairs next to Raj.

"Let's start, Mr. Gandhi. Listen to me and start typing. Write this down: *In the midst of violence on the streets, officials in the government, particularly members of an elite, highly secretive unit of the New York Police Department, have unleashed a campaign involving secret arrests, kidnappings, torture and assassinations of dozens of men, some of them United States citizens, all of them of Middle East and African descent.*"

Raj rapidly typed those words. Whoever this man was, his voice, the way he was able to put together words, phrases, and sentences, were so different from the crude, mocking voice Raj had heard on those strange phone calls.

As if sensing Raj's surprise, the man reverted to the accented tone of the caller. "Listen carefully, Mr. Gandhi. Here are your next sentences. *Sources who have spoken on condition of anonymity because of fears of reprisals have disclosed that, within minutes of the devastating explosions that began with the murders of more than a thousand people at New York's Metropolitan Museum of Art two days ago, the secretive unit made a sweep of almost two dozen men who were taken to a dark prison on an abandoned New York pier on the East River.*"

The man paused and had Raj scroll through the words that he had merely transcribed. "You're a good typist, Mr. Gandhi. At least there's something you can do right." It was again the sardonic, sarcastic voice of the man on the cell phone.

And then the voice changed again, surprisingly literate, sounding like a broadcaster, the voice of someone who had done a great deal of reading.

He dictated, *Sources reveal that the unit was conceived and implemented by Gina Carbone, the first female commissioner of the police department and a veteran of the Gulf War of the early 1990s. It is known as the Black Unit and consists almost entirely of former CIA and NSA officers who for several years have been nominally assigned to the NYPD with innocuous titles such as 'community liaison representatives.' They are, according to the sources, primarily men and two women responsible for extraordinary renditions, torture, and murder in the Iraq and Afghan conflicts. Commissioner Carbone recruited them for their unique talents. Some are veterans of discredited mercenary organizations such as Blackwater.*

During a pause, Raj looked at the muscular man in the chair beside him. "How do I know you haven't made this all up?"

So quickly that the movement of his hand was almost invisible, the man punched Raj's left cheek. The pain was immediate, intense, and excruciating. Raj's dark skin almost instantly turned purple, a bruise.

"Don't you wiseass with me, you fucking dothead." Once again it was the tone of the loony caller.

His fingers trembling over the keyboard, Raj wrote as he listened. *Commissioner Carbone has not divulged the existence of this death cadre to anyone except its ten to twenty members. Publicly she is credited with coordinating the assault several hours ago on the George Washington Carver Towers in East Harlem where, it is believed, as many as several members, one of them a woman, of actual and known members of the Counterterrorism Unit of the NYPD were killed in intense, close, virtually hand-to-hand combat with men said to be ISIS or Boko Haram veterans, all of whom, with what is believed to be one exception, were killed. Thirteen members of the NYPD counterterrorism unit that conducted the assault survived.*

Staring at the bright screen, his virtually black eye sockets sunk deeply into his face despite the screen's otherworldly glow, still afraid, Raj asked, "How do you know these things? This is my blog. I'm expected to write the truth."

"You're a Hindu, right, Mr. Gandhi?"

"No. I was born into a Hindu family. But no, I'm not."

"Did you ever read our Bible?"

"No."

"If you had, you'd know that Jesus was always being asked, *What is truth?* And he always answered, *What I tell you is truth.*"

Raj had no reaction other than to stare at the screen, even more afraid.

"What I tell you, Mr. Gandhi, is the truth. Don't worry. Your readers will believe you."

Raj glanced at him. Despite his bruise and his pain, he wanted to remember the face.

"You can stare at me as long as you want. But we're not finished. And you'll never remember me, anyhow."

Raj turned again to the keyboard. Listening in the barren room, he wrote what was said to him. *Sources have also said that one man was taken alive from the shattered apartment at the Carver Houses. Known to the secret squad and Commissioner Carbone as Silas Nasar, but also utilizing the name Hakim Khomani, the survivor is said to be a naturalized U.S. citizen with a degree from MIT and a specialist in the use of highly sophisticated communications devices. It is believed, the sources have disclosed, that he is one of the people who conceived and implemented the initial attacks at the Metropolitan Museum of Art.*

Raj said, "I know that name. Those names: Silas Nasar and Hakim Khomani."

"That's no surprise to me, Mr. Gandhi. I know what you know. Now listen again. *Dr. Gabriel Hauser, hailed over the last thirty hours as the Angel of Life, is and for some time has been a 'special friend' of Silas Nasar. It is not clear to Commissioner Carbone or her elite group whether the* Angel of Life *knew of the plans for the initial attacks, but his presence at the scene of the first explosion was, according to the sources, no random coincidence. He and Silas Nasar had prearranged their encounter.*"

Raj Gandhi, still afraid of another hit from this man who was completely unlike anyone he'd ever known, stopped typing and glanced over his shoulder. This time the man simply reached into one of the inner pockets of his well-tailored blue jacket, pulled out his cell phone, and put it on the table next to Raj.

For ten minutes, his expression utterly impassive, Raj watched on the stranger's own cell phone the interview he had just conducted with Gabriel Hauser on the bench at the Church of the Heavenly Rest.

"How did you get this?" Raj asked.

"It doesn't fucking matter, Mr. Gandhi. It just doesn't matter."

Raj said nothing.

"Now, Mr. Gandhi, let's make believe I'm your editor. Print out a copy of what you just wrote."

"I didn't write anything. You did."

For a furtive moment Raj glanced at an object he kept on the table, a letter opener shaped like a dagger. It was a relic from another era. Raj lived completely in the modern cyber world. He never received ordinary snail mail, he had no use for a letter opener. But he kept this like a sacred object because his father, a civil servant in the city then known as Bombay, had given it to him as a present when the intellectually gifted but shy and awkward Raj left for Oxford at the age of sixteen.

When he was in Lebanon, Iraq, and Afghanistan, Raj knew that from time to time journalists and photographers were kidnapped. While he was in those distant countries, he had thought about strategies for evading a kidnapping. His main strategy was running. As a kid, barefooted, he had loved to run. He was fleet, light, evasive. But here there was nowhere to run. His speed didn't matter in this small room.

But the letter opener, for just a second, offered another strategy to Raj. He made the mistake of twice glancing at it. Raj had no way of knowing that he was in this tight and cluttered room with a man who since he was twelve had learned all the dirty arts of hurting others and protecting himself.

Deftly, Tony Garafalo picked up the nineteenth-century, ornate letter opener. He threw it to a far corner of the room. "I'm a mind reader, Mr. Gandhi. I didn't like what was on your mind."

Again not speaking, Raj turned to the computer, like a secretary waiting for instructions.

The instructions came. "I want you," Tony Garafalo said, "to post this interview on your blog with what you've just typed up. And I also want you to post the scene you taped on your cell phone of Gina Carbone running through the fence and into Pier 37."

Raj said, "Why do you want to do that? She's your lover."

"My, my, Mr. Gandhi." It was the voice of the odd caller. The man, Raj thought, was Janus-like. He had two attached faces staring in opposite directions. "See, I was right about you all along. You do good work as an investigator. Sure, she is one of my girlfriends. But there is something you don't know. She was one of the undercover cops eight years ago who worked on the crew that put me in prison. We grew up in the same neighborhood on Staten Island. My family knew hers. You know what? She should have given me a heads-up, not have helped to take me down. I learned a lot about payback, and she has a side of her that's reckless. I got to know her again when I came out of prison, at a family get-together not long after she became the top cop. And she got to like me again. And she loves a good fuck. And so do I. Now I'm giving her the fuck of her life."

More than anything else he had ever wanted, Raj Gandhi wanted this man to leave his apartment. He fed the scenes in his cell phone into the computer that contained his blog. The process took only seconds.

"Now," Tony Garafalo said, "send it out into the wide, wide world."

On his own cell phone he quickly found Raj's blog. As Raj continued to sit in absolute silence, Tony Garafalo read on his cell phone the script he had dictated and watched the scenes of Gina Carbone and Gabriel Hauser.

"Mr. Gandhi, it says here that you have 253,673 followers. You're already a celebrity." It was the voice of the caller. "Now you're going to be even more famous. I'm telling you, Mr. Gandhi, I see a fucking Pulitzer Prize for you. And when you give your acceptance speech, you'll give me credit, won't you?"

Raj simply continued to stare at the screen. He sensed that Tony Garafalo was moving toward the door.

"Mr. Gandhi, I want you to look at me and say thank you."

When Raj turned to look, he saw that the handsome, well-dressed man held a pistol. The single shot entered the center of Raj's forehead. It was a clean, red, small hole.

"The dothead," Tony Garafalo said aloud just before he opened the door. *Now he really is a dothead.*

CHAPTER THIRTY-FOUR

It was three in the morning when Roland Fortune, wearing only his underwear, looked at the Raj Gandhi blog that, as the reporters on CNN said, had "gone viral."

Irv Rothstein and Hans Richter stood behind him in his bedroom at Gracie Mansion, the bedroom in which Sarah Hewitt-Gordan had slept with him, and made love to him, almost every night for the last year.

"Why," Roland asked, "should I believe any of this? Why didn't the *Times* publish this? If it was reliable, you'd think this guy's newspaper would have it on its Internet site and on the front page."

Irv said, "I spoke to this guy's editors at the *Times*. They said he was following leads to this but they weren't satisfied there was any adequate support, at least not yet."

"And what does this guy Gandhi have to say? This was posted five hours ago."

"Mr. Gandhi," Hans said, "is dead."

"What?"

"Gina sent cops to his apartment three hours ago," Hans Richter said. "The door was closed but unlocked. There was a single gunshot wound in the middle of his forehead."

Roland stood up. He was shivering. He draped his bathrobe over his shoulders. On the nightstand below the warm glow of a table lamp was the brown bottle that contained his replenished Vicodin. He opened the cap and picked up a glass of water. As he was shaking two of the pills into his palm, Irv said, "Do you really need those?"

"Who the fuck are you to tell me what I need and don't need?" Roland shouted.

"It took us four fucking hours, Mr. Mayor, to wake you up so that you could look at this blog," said Irv, also shouting. "Four fucking hours. You must have had five of those before you went to sleep."

Roland, raising the palm of his hand to his mouth, drank water. "Now that's two more."

Irv said, "Hans, why don't you tell Mr. Mayor what's happened while he's been in Wonderland, beyond the Looking Glass?"

"Harlan Lazarus, the once-upon-a-time judge himself as he reminds everyone, got a federal judge to sign a search warrant four hours ago, not long after this blog was posted, to have the FBI and Secret Service go into Pier 37."

"And?" Roland asked.

"They found a completely modern operation setup, with prison cells."

"And?"

"No one was there. All the cells were empty. They examined the cells for fingerprints and DNA. When they checked the federal data banks, they found no matches for anyone."

"What is this place?"

"Gina used money from the police budget to have this facility constructed over the last three years."

"She never told me about this."

"That's interesting," Irv, now calmer but still intense, said. "She claims you authorized it. That you both thought it was useful to have a secure facility if there was a terrorist attack."

"That never happened. She never discussed that with me." Roland paused. "What did she say about the blog?"

Hans answered, "That it was all a fantasy. The place was never used. She says everyone who has been arrested so far is accounted for and is now being held in Central Booking downtown or in a heavily guarded wing on Rikers Island. No secret prisoners. Everything by the book. Everything is transparent, she says."

"Where is she now?" Roland asked.

Irv answered. "She just finished a press conference. Here's another thing you don't know because you were in the land of dreams. Three hours ago she led a military-style operation on the lower East Side. She wiped out a group of Arabs who had been living in apartments for the last few months around Tompkins Square Park. Seventeen of them were killed. Four arrested. The television films make it look like a major battle in Baghdad, Syria, places like that."

"Why didn't I know about this?"

"Are you kidding, Mr. Mayor?" Irv asked. "This happened three hours ago. Every time we woke you up, you dropped back to sleep." Irv picked up the pharmacy bottle that held the Vicodin. "Dr. Sleep. Eventually, you know, Dr. Death comes with enough of these magical little pills. What were we supposed to do? Take you out in front of the cameras in your underwear?"

"Where is Gina now?"

"She's at the Regency, resting with her boyfriend."

"The Mafia guy?"

Irv said, "The once Mafia guy, if there is such a thing. Mr. Garafalo is supposedly now a reformed member of the human family. He's a sales manager at that beautiful Mercedes dealership in Queens. Don't you remember? You said two years ago that it was nobody's business what lovers a grown woman decided to have. That male police commissioners all had girlfriends. Power is an aphrodisiac, you said, and that was as true, you said, for women as for men."

"That's right. It's her business. One of my male commissioners has several boyfriends."

"And," Irv said, "Mr. Garafalo is married to a nice Italian girl and they have a nice house in Bay Ridge."

Roland, now fully awake as if his screaming had rejuvenated him, said, "What else has happened while I was sleeping, apparently deep in the cave of Morpheus?"

"Andrew Carter's people have been trying to reach you. And your buddy Harlan Lazarus landed by helicopter fifteen minutes ago at Pier 40 on the Hudson River and wants you to go see him."

"*Me* go to see *him*? Pigs will fly before that happens. He knows where I live if he wants to see me."

Inside the shower stall were the bottles of fragrant soap and shampoos and other jars that Sarah Hewitt-Gordan had last used just two days earlier. At the sight of the liquids that gave her the scent that he always found so alluring, Roland felt completely alone in the world, realizing that her death meant something essentially simple: *He would never see her again.* He had never lost anyone so close to him. When he suddenly recognized that he was about to cry, he turned the flow of shower water as high as it could run and stood directly under the powerful, noisy stream, and cried. There was no way, he believed, that the two men standing near the big bathroom's entrance could hear him. His tears were swept away by the cascading shower water. Eventually he turned off the water only when he believed that his urgent, unexpected, convulsive need to cry had passed. When Roland stepped out of the shower he draped a towel over his head and rubbed his abundant black hair and his eyes, convinced that, if these two men on whom he so much relied saw the redness of his eyes, they would think it was caused only by soap and shampoo.

Glancing into the steamy mirror as he prepared to shave, he said, "Irv, I'm sorry I yelled at you."

Irv said, "Not to worry, Roland. My wife does it all the time, especially when I wake her at three in the morning for a fuck. She gave up the 'I've-got-a-headache' routine years ago. Now she just yells and tells me to go fuck myself."

* * *

An hour later, as they sat in Gracie Mansion's gleaming kitchen, Gina Carbone looked radiant, confident, and utterly at ease. She sipped coffee and with a small sharp knife slit in half the two hard-boiled eggs that Juanita, the full-time cook from Guatemala who lived in a neat little apartment on the second floor of the mansion, had prepared for the commissioner of the New York City Police Department and the movie-star mayor. The commissioner and the mayor often had predawn meetings. Juanita, heavy and matronly, loved the always polite mayor and was in awe of the vivid police commissioner.

"I had room in the department budget to renovate and modernize that pier, Roland. I had no reason to ask you if I could authorize a space that I thought might be useful if there was unrest in the city. And you've always told me I had a free hand to make New York the safest city in the world."

"My concern," Roland Fortune said, "is not that you had an off-the-books, unpublicized facility built, Gina. My concern is that a *New York Times* reporter told the world that you had made secret arrests."

"Nobody did that, Roland. There's never been a single person locked up there. Your friend and mine, Judge Harlan Lazarus, had his agents go through it. No one except people on my staff was ever there. And the *New York Times* didn't report any of this. This Mr. Gandhi was off on a frolic of his own. Just two hours ago the *Times* posted a statement on its website saying its editors were aware that he was investigating the pier, the arrests and *me*, but that Gandhi never gave his editors enough information to corroborate anything."

Roland picked up his cell phone. It had been facedown on the table next to his coffee cup. "Gina, I have a text message from Harlan Lazarus that came to me about an hour ago. He wants you to resign."

"So what?" She was, as always, direct, all business. "Do *you* want me to resign? Do *you*?"

"I need to know the truth."

"The truth, Roland, is that I'm the only person who has fought this battle. Harlan Lazarus hasn't. Andrew Carter hasn't. I'm the one who has been in the ring. I'm the one who has stopped cadres of fanatics from carrying out more attacks. I'm the one who has made arrests of dangerous people. I'm the one who has developed the information and sources that prevented three goons from blowing up St. Patrick's." Gina took a sip of hot coffee. "And, Roland, I'm the one who has given you the credit for masterminding this war. Harlan Lazarus wants *me* to resign? That's rich."

"And what have you been doing with Gabriel Hauser?"

"Roland, what's the matter with you? I've got a police force with 40,000 people. Seven, just seven, have taken an interest in an outspoken, discredited, holier-than-thou queer who has been in the wrong places at all the wrong times, a guy with an axe to grind that would make Harry Reems seem like an altar boy. Why wouldn't I have seven people treat him as what we in the business of law enforcement like to call a PIN—a person of interest? I'm sorry his dog got hurt. He has shown up in too many of the wrong places at the wrong times."

"Where is this doctor now?"

"Among the missing. We started looking for him as soon as the blog went out. His apartment is empty. Nobody's there."

"What about his boyfriend?"

"If you think we have him, we don't. That's bullshit, too. We have had our people talk to him. He's a spurned lover. He knows nothing except what is in those e-mails, those love notes, between Gabriel Hauser and the man he loved and had to leave behind in Afghanistan. And that man, the CIA has told us, is a dedicated jihadist. And that man, Dr. Hauser's lover boy, wanted the doctor to meet Silas Nasar."

"And who, Gina, is Silas Nasar?"

"We wish we knew."

"The *Times* reporter said you had him."

"Wish I did. We think he's the cousin of Gabriel Hauser's love interest in Afghanistan."

Roland's cell phone vibrated with another incoming text message. It was from Harlan Lazarus. *You must announce that Capone has resigned. Imperative.*

Gina ate a segment of the boiled egg. "Do you want to tell me what that is?"

"More from Lazarus. He still thinks your name is *Capone*. And he still wants you to resign. Now."

"So tell him *Capone* will resign. After all, Capone has been dead for seventy-five years."

Roland stared at her. Somehow she was different now from the competent, straightforward woman he had known for three years. He was, he now realized, afraid of her for there was another dimension to her. She was not the hard-working and intuitively smart girl from the outer boroughs in whom he had had so much confidence.

When the next incoming text message made his cell phone vibrate, and as he reached to pick it up, Gina said, "I'll bet it's Lazarus again. This is the era of the serial texter."

Roland read the text, leaned across the kitchen table, and held his phone in front of her. The message read: *This order is from the president.*

As Roland retrieved the cell phone, he was surprised to hear Gina say in Spanish, "Juanita, leave the kitchen. Mr. Mayor and I need to talk." Roland was surprised because he had no idea she could speak Spanish with such apparently effortless fluency or that she would give an order to a member of his personal staff.

Juanita left.

"Talk to me, Mr. Mayor, what do you plan to do about this?"

"No," Roland said, "you're the strategic thinker. What is your plan? What, for example, just as starters, do you plan to do about the questions every pain-in-the-ass reporter will ask you about the last blog of a dead reporter?"

"I already answered that. Haven't you seen the press conference I did at one this morning after what's being called the Battle of Tompkins Square?"

"No, I was sleeping."

"I know that. I tried to get you involved. Hasn't Irv shown you reruns?"

"Not yet." Roland waited. "And so enlighten me, Gina. What did you say about the blog?"

"That of course my department had multiple complex facilities for dealing with unprecedented acts of hostility. That we had people trained in the arts of counterinsurgency. That we had confidential informants and invisible as well as visible resources for protecting a city with more than seven million people."

"And what did you say when they asked you about secret arrests, dark prisons, torture?"

"That Mr. Gandhi had brought the concerns he had to our attention and that they were unfounded. Those things never happened. That even the editors of the *Times* had distanced themselves from him and his concerns."

"You don't think that will stop the questions, do you? You're living in dreamland, Gina, if you think that will satisfy anybody." He stared at her, trying not to appear as unsettled as he now was. "And you know what, Gina? I still have questions and doubts. There was a great deal of difficult, disturbing information in Gandhi's report." He sliced the hard-boiled egg. "And much of it was about you."

Gina Carbone placed her own cell phone on the table. "Now listen carefully to me, Mr. Mayor. Only *you* can fire me. Not our invisible president who is still missing in action, a candy ass who still hasn't found the time to come to our city. And that scarecrow Lazarus can't fire me. Only you can."

"Commissioner, you can resign."

"That's not going to happen. It's not in my nature."

"Who," Roland asked, "is Tony Garafalo?"

Ignoring the question, Gina spun her iPhone on the table. "Do you want to know why you're not going to fire me and why I'm not going to resign?"

Roland stared at her, waiting. His right hand trembled.

"Because," Gina said, "you're a drug addict, a pillhead, what's called on the street a *garbagehead*."

"What the hell are you talking about? I have a damaged shoulder. The doctors gave me Vicodin to deal with it."

"Listen to me real carefully, Roland. That's the first and only prescription from an actual doctor you've had in years. From the start your security detail has had officers who are totally devoted to me. In this tiny magic phone and on my office computer I have confidential reports and dozens of pictures of well-dressed men and women, otherwise known as classy drug dealers, going to your office and coming here to deliver Vicodin, Xanax, Percocet, Oxycodone, every scheduled drug known to modern chemists, and in those pictures you're handing over cash for these yummy pills."

After staring at her for twenty seconds, Roland said, "Let me tell you something, Gina. I am the mayor of the largest city in this country. I take that responsibility seriously. I didn't get here by being just a pretty boy, or the son of famous parents, or by winning the lottery. I got here, believe it or not, by hard work and by caring about people. I came up off the streets. I've been threatened by people before. When I was a kid my father taught me that if a bigger kid pushed me around I should go find a baseball bat and swing hard at the other kid's head."

She was as steady as ever. "Roland, I've got the bat. It's in this phone. I know how to swing at heads, too. We're not that different. In fact, we're brother and sister."

"Let me ask you something. Who are you? We have a city out there that's under siege. Thousands of people are dead. No one, no one, seems to have an exit strategy. Do you really think that by threatening me with being a garbagehead I'm going to make decisions, or not make them, that I think are in the best interests of the city? It's not a good idea to threaten me."

The commissioner of the New York City Police Department stood up. "You know what, Mr. Mayor. I've got my responsibilities, too. It's not good for the city to be run by a drug addict."

CHAPTER THIRTY-FIVE

GABRIEL HAUSER, as soon as he changed into fresh clothes in the quiet apartment, walked four miles down Fifth Avenue, all the way to the enormous nineteenth-century arch that dominated Washington Square Park. During most of the walk he was in the middle of the grand avenue. Thousands of people crowded the sidewalks and the avenue itself. There were no barricades. It was like one of those street fairs that sometimes closed long segments of other avenues, but never the jewel of Fifth Avenue.

Gabriel turned left instead of entering the park that he always associated with the early Henry James novel, *Washington Square*, which he'd read in his last year in high school. He headed to the East Village. At the corner of Kenmare and Mott Street, in the old, largely abandoned St. Vincent's Church, was the homeless shelter where, for three years, he had volunteered once each week to treat the street people, an ever-shifting population of suspicious, sometimes bizarre, men and women, often with stunned, always silent children, who drifted in and out of the fetid shelter. It had sixty beds, no partitions, and two toilets that smelled like Army latrines. At one far end of the gymnasium-sized room was a door that led to a smaller room where, three times each day, groups of people from Alcoholics Anonymous and Narcotics Anonymous gathered for their meetings.

One of the full-time staff members, a recovering alcoholic and drug addict who had tattoos even on his face, shouted, "Listen up. The doctor's here. Anyone want him to take a look-see?"

Five hands went up, all from black and Puerto Rican mothers with small children. Gabriel spent ten or so minutes with each of the kids. Not one had even an elevated temperature. All of the mothers bore that shell-shocked look of the displaced Iraqi and Afghan women he had often seen in tent camps. Not all of these women in the church basement, he realized as he spoke to them either in English or his sufficiently effective Spanish, had any idea or cared that bombings and battles had been raging for days on the streets of the city in which they lived. The poor lived entirely in their own heads. Nothing and no one else concerned them.

Gabriel was here to hide. On his long walk downtown to the shelter he had looked at his cell phone and saw Raj Gandhi's blog, together with the entire video of his meeting on the bench of the church. And then an automatic e-mail from NPR entered his phone, carrying the news that Raj had been murdered, shot one time in the center of his forehead. Fear had given a special urgency to Gabriel's original plan to treat the homeless, a job that normally took hours, but this time, on this day, it had taken far less than even an hour.

Still frightened and confused, not wanting to leave the homeless shelter, Gabriel walked into the big kitchen adjacent to the basement with its dozens of neatly arranged rows of cots. The kitchen, at least forty years old, was immaculately clean. Gabriel had arrived during the long interval between meals, and there were no cooks, food servers, or other volunteers there.

Everything in the kitchen, the countertops, the sinks, the industrial-size stoves, was made of gray steel and the surface of the stove was black iron. All that steel and iron had been cleaned hundreds of thousands of times with steel wool pads and ammonia. It shined with a scoured luminosity.

And the pots, pans, and kettles, all carefully put away, many of them dented, were polished and clean as well. The old linoleum floor glowed. Obviously it had just been swept and washed with a mop soaked in ammonia and water. Gabriel felt an urgent need not only to remain in this anonymous but familiar place but to work with his hands. As he looked at the entire basement from the vantage point of the kitchen, he saw that at least half the cots were abandoned, unused. He'd learned that the transient men, women, and children who came and went from this place never made the beds in which they had slept or just rested for a few hours. So each unused bed was covered with crumpled, off-white sheets, wrinkled wool blankets, and pillows with half-removed pillowcases. Worn, dirty towels were dropped everywhere.

Gabriel went to the row of steel green army-style lockers in which newly washed and freshly pressed sheets and blankets were stored. He was a methodical man. From the lockers he collected two sheets, a blanket, a pillowcase, and a towel. He carried them to the first cot in the nearest row of cots. He put the fresh bedding on the floor next to the first cot and stripped away from that cot the soiled sheets, blankets, and towels.

Whoever had last used the cot was foul. There were stains of shit and urine on the sheets. He piled the filthy sheets, blankets, and towels on the other side of the bed. With a practiced hand he swept bits of debris off the bare, exposed mattress and then carefully spread the clean, fitted sheet on the mattress. Once he had created a smooth surface, he carefully draped the top sheet and the green wool blanket over the bed, turning down the upper edges of the top sheet and the blanket. He then stripped the stained pillowcase off the pillow, shook the exposed pillow which had indelible sweat stains, and then slipped the fresh pillowcase over it. He placed the pillow in the center of the cot. The cot's simple orderliness was a marvel. It had taken him fifteen minutes to create this.

Always adept at math, Gabriel calculated he would use six hours to remake each of the unoccupied beds. He could even extend the time by helping to prepare suppers, serve the food, and eat the same food. His plan was to spend the night in one of the cots if the shelter was not completely filled. It almost never was. The fact that the city would likely remain locked down for the rest of this night made no difference since stranded out-of-towners would never spend the night and sleep among street people in a homeless shelter.

But Gabriel Hauser didn't spend the night in the basement shelter. At seven, as he was scrubbing the last of the dishes in the hot, soapy water—there was no automatic dishwasher—six men, two in suits and the rest in combat gear, entered the basement. He knew instantly why they were here, even though he had never seen any of them before. Gabriel's hands were soapy. He shook his hands vigorously but didn't bother reaching for the already soaked dish towel to dry them as the lead man, in a suit, approached him. He carried handcuffs. "Put your wrists together behind you," the man said.

Gabriel did that. They were plastic handcuffs. They were pulled so tightly he worried about the circulation to his hands. But he said nothing. Everyone, all the homeless people he had fed and cared for and whose beds he had cleaned, was absolutely quiet. Whatever was happening to the doctor was none of their business.

* * *

The Holland Tunnel, unlike the Lincoln Tunnel two miles further uptown, could only be reached by following the maze of streets in old downtown Manhattan. Despite all the new buildings in that area, including the new triangular tower, the tallest building in the world constructed on the site of what had been in Gabriel's eyes the two ugliest buildings he had ever seen, the World Trade Center

Towers, the access to the Holland Tunnel still was a crazy complex of streets such as Vesey, Carlton, and Canal Streets that he had always avoided.

Still in the blood-constricting handcuffs and still silent despite the questions he heard from the three other men in the unmarked, over-powered Chevy Impala, Gabriel didn't see any other vehicle as they approached the mouth of the brightly illuminated tunnel. He did see dozens of Army soldiers, dressed in the same desert-gray uniforms he had worn in the Army, on the sidewalks. The barriers that blocked access to the tunnel were moved to the side as the Impala, at a steady ten-mile-per-hour speed, approached. This trip, he knew, had been prearranged. How, he wondered, had the men who entered the homeless shelter known he was there?

And then the answer, the painful answer, came to him. Cam had told them.

CHAPTER THIRTY-SIX

HARLAN LAZARUS WAS furious. When he had arrived at PS 6 thirty minutes earlier, he had expected Roland Fortune to be waiting. Lazarus had sent two text messages to the mayor, messages which closed with the words "Judge Lazarus," directing Roland to be there. As soon as he walked through the bright red school doors, he asked, "Where is Fortune?" The answer in a crisp voice from one of Lazarus' staff members was, "No sign of him, Judge."

"I told him to be here."

"He isn't."

"Have someone call that guy Rothstein, the joker, who's always with Fortune. And tell him that I'm going to call the president in fifteen minutes unless Mr. Fortune is here or it's confirmed that he's on his way."

Lazarus stood at a window in a first-grade classroom that faced east. Directly across Madison Avenue was the quaint Crawford-Doyle Book Store, closed; the coffee shop at the corner of Madison and 82nd Street, which Lazarus had been told was a favorite place for tourists, was also closed. The explosions more than three days ago had been so powerful that the windows of the Nectar Coffee Shop were all shattered.

The final death toll—final unless more bodies were found in the debris inside the museum—was 1,766 people, at least 300 of them from foreign countries. Lazarus, although he now commanded what was in effect a force of more than 100,000 agents, had never been in the military or a war. As he looked down 82nd Street toward Fifth Avenue, beyond which he could see a narrow segment of the broken stone façade of the museum, he detected an odor he didn't recognize. He said to the armed guard who stood next to him, "What's that smell?" There was a joke in his department that he was so security conscious, so concerned about his own safety, that he slept every night with fully armed guards on either side of him.

The guard, who wore full combat gear, including a helmet, was a veteran of three tours of duty in Iraq. He hesitated before he answered. Although he'd spent hundreds of hours with Harlan Lazarus, Lazarus had never said a word to him. "That's the smell of rotting flesh," the guard finally said.

Al Ritter, Lazarus' chief deputy, walked into the classroom. "He refuses to come over."

"Refuses?"

"Rothstein says that Fortune is calling a press conference in an hour to announce that the lockdown of Manhattan will be lifted in three hours."

Lazarus reached for the special cell phone he carried in a holster attached to his belt. There were only four numbers on that phone. One was President Carter.

Ritter said, "There is something else I need to tell you, Judge, something we just learned. It concerns Raj Gandhi."

"And who is that?"

"The reporter for the *Times* who posted the blog about the police commissioner."

"You mean the dead reporter? Gandhi?"

"That's right," Ritter said.

"So what is it?"

"We've just arrested the killer."

"I'm just about to call the president of the United States, Al. Why do I need to know about this?"

"Because the man we've arrested is a mobster, an ex-con, named Tony Garafalo."

"How the hell did an Indian reporter get killed by a mobster?"

"He's a special mobster. He's the lover of Commissioner Carbone. In fact, they're so close that she's been keeping him at the Regency Hotel since Sunday. Apparently she can't function without whatever it is that he's been giving to her for the last year or so."

"Human nature," Lazarus said, "is a marvelous thing." He laughed. It was probably the second time in the three years in which Ritter had worked with him that he heard Lazarus laugh.

"There's more," Ritter said. "Our people found out that Mr. Garafalo had been feeding his pillow talk with Commissioner Carbone to Mr. Gandhi. Apparently the commissioner becomes talkative when Mr. Garafalo does whatever he does to her."

"How do you know that?"

"Mr. Gandhi was a techie-kind of guy. He recorded every conversation he had on his cell phone."

"That," Lazarus said, "can be a dangerous habit."

"It was. Gandhi was getting calls from a guy who imitated a crank from Queens or Brooklyn. Garafalo is the ventriloquist. Of course he never gave his name or said where he was getting his information. The commissioner must have whispered sweet nothings into Tony's ears about the state-of-the-art dark prison on Pier 37 and her special anti-terror unit. Garafalo knew about the arrests of Arabs on the hit list Carbone's people created."

"And this Italian guy told a reporter for the *Times* about this? Will wonders never cease? Why?"

"Tony and Gina—sounds like the cast of *Grease*, doesn't it—grew up together. Their families are part of the immense, closed-off Italian American tribe on Staten Island. Our intelligence people have quickly figured out that Garafalo, whose male relatives were always soldiers in the Gambino family, was upset, and that may not be the right word, when he found out during his trial that the then newly minted detective Gina Carbone was part of the large team that investigated him in the '90s. He went to jail for seven or eight years for threatening people called to a special grand jury. When he came out, it so happened he met Gina at one of those big Italian barbecues. He had gone straight, he told her. He had taken a job at a Mercedes dealership. He is one extraordinarily handsome man. Carbone was attracted to him. She's brave, she's reckless. She's also a devout Catholic. She believes sinners can be redeemed."

Lazarus' arms were folded. "And Mr. Garafalo holds grudges?"

"Big time," Ritter said. "He was looking for a time and place and the right circumstances to hurt her."

"And where," Lazarus asked, "is the commissioner now?"

"We're not sure. Until an hour or two ago she was with the mayor, at breakfast."

"I want her arrested, too," Lazarus said.

CHAPTER THIRTY-SEVEN

CARL SCHURZ PARK was a gem which few people even in Manhattan knew. Gracie Mansion was at the northern end of the jewel-like grounds. The park was only the depth of a city block. It ran from Gracie Mansion to the far end of East 83rd Street. Quiet East End Avenue was its western border. To the east was the river and an esplanade that overlooked vistas of the river itself and in the distance the Triboro Bridge, the shoreline of Queens, Roosevelt Island and, to the south, the 59th Street Bridge. The park had graceful stone paths, ancient trees, alcoves with benches, flower beds, a small playground and two popular fenced dog runs, one for the big dogs and the other for the small dogs. There were sloping lawns where young men and women sunbathed.

Roland Fortune, who took pride in knowing every street, park, and neighborhood in Manhattan, arranged for his press conference at the heart of the park. It was a stone and granite area next to the esplanade where two large staircases divided to lead to a gorgeous walkway that formed the main entrance to Carl Schurz Park at East 86th Street and East End Avenue.

It was another glorious morning in the stricken city, slightly cooler than the three previous days. Through Irv Rothstein's marvel of contacts with the press and Hans Richter's magician-like tactical abilities, clusters of microphones and wires had been assembled in an hour at the heart of the park so that Roland could stand with a background of flowers, trees, and the nineteenth-century stone walkways behind him. A city in which thousands of deaths had just taken place was made to appear like the most famous European capitals, the work of master landscape architects of the late nineteenth-century.

It took fewer than three minutes for Roland, wearing a blue blazer, slacks, and a fresh white shirt, to walk from Gracie Mansion's terrace to the press conference. The benign light from the early morning sun over the East River gave his whole presence a kind of relaxed radiance. Gina Carbone walked with him.

Roland began, "Good morning, ladies and gentlemen. Consistent with my promises since the start of this crisis, I have current information for you. The first and most important is that I have issued ten minutes ago an order lifting the lockdown of Manhattan."

A small group of early morning walkers, for the most part people with their dogs, had gathered at the unexpected sight of reporters and the mayor of New York City suddenly materializing in their beloved park. There was applause.

Roland briefly acknowledged the applause. "The lifting of the lockdown will take place gradually and in an orderly fashion over the next several hours, beginning now. Commissioner Gina Carbone is here with me. Let's be clear: her skill, ingenuity, and command abilities have made the lifting of the lockdown possible. Manhattan is safe enough to be reintegrated with the world."

Gina, who looked almost as radiant as Roland in the fresh sunlight, nodded and smiled slightly.

"This is not to say," Roland continued, "that the danger has passed. Over the last two days, the remarkable members of the New York City Police Department have engaged in war-like battles, all of which they have won, and they have thwarted attacks on landmarks of national, indeed international, importance, such as St. Patrick's Cathedral. The commissioner, with the assistance of the U.S. Department of Homeland Security, has ongoing efforts in place to trap and neutralize terrorists who may—and I stress *may* —still have cells in Manhattan or elsewhere in the city with more plans for assaults and mayhem. But we believe the major sources of danger have been eliminated or neutralized."

A reporter's voice rang out. "Commissioner Carbone, what can you tell us about Tony Garafalo?"

Roland said, "We are not here to comment on anything other than essential information. We're not going to be distracted by trivia. The people of Manhattan are interested in one thing only, and that is their safety and the restoration of order, reconstruction, and the return to the wonderful vibrancy of this stricken paradise known as Manhattan. Even as we speak, the barriers at every bridge and tunnel are being taken down, although there will continue to be checkpoints at both ends of each tunnel and bridge to be sure that those who have done damage will be caught. There are no places where the evil can hide or to which they can escape."

Roland paused and extended his right arm. "You see around us here one of the gems of this city, Carl Schurz Park. There are thousands of miraculous places in this city. Several of them have been defaced and desecrated by the cowards who carried out these attacks. Every place that has been damaged will be restored. While we can never rule it out, Commissioner Carbone and I are confident that the people responsible have been arrested or are dead or that we know who they are and where they are. And, to them, we say, *We are coming for you. There's no place to hide.*"

Another reporter's voice: "Commissioner, can you tell us when the dark prison on Pier 37 was built?"

Roland said, "When I had the incredible good fortune to appoint Gina Carbone the NYPD Commissioner, my first and only instructions to her were that she had my complete support in achieving a single objective: protecting the people of New York City from anyone and everyone who would harm them. She was herself a warrior with years of experience in major combat operations in the first Gulf War combined with years of experience in the day-to-day operations of protecting the people of this city. Under her command, the rates for crimes ranging from fare-jumping to murder have fallen to levels much lower than those of cities with fewer than 200,000 people. We have more than seven million people who live here in the safety of ordinary times."

"Did you," another voice asked, "know about the dark prison on Pier 37?"

"In the final analysis, the responsibility for protecting the people of this city rests with me. I gave Commissioner Carbone the task of protecting the city as she in her experienced professional judgment saw fit to do."

"What did you know," the same voice asked, "about Pier 37 and when did you know it?"

"I knew there were secure facilities established all through the five boroughs of New York City, Queens, the Bronx, Staten Island, Brooklyn, and Manhattan, that were designed by the commissioner to give her and her force of almost 40,000 officers the ability to deal with the dangerous unpredictabilities of the world in which we all live. As I now understand it, Pier 37, an abandoned warehouse on the East River waterfront from the era of the classic *On the Waterfront* film, was reconfigured to serve emergency purposes. I have never set foot on Pier 37. If it was reconfigured by the commissioner, she did that under the general mandate I gave her. She, in other words, had my complete approval."

"What about the secret arrests and torture reported on the Gandhi blog?"

"I'm assured there were no secret arrests. Everyone—and there are hundreds of people—who has been arrested has undergone the usual processing even in these extraordinary times and either has been or will be brought before a judge for arraignment. Those judges will, as always, ask for pleas of guilty or not guilty and will apply the usual standards that apply to bail decisions on whether to let an accused go free to await trial or to detain him or her. The issue for the judge at that stage always is twofold: Is the person a danger to the community? Is that person a risk of flight? If he or she is one or the other, he or she will be detained. And all of this is a matter of public record."

"What about torture?"

Just as Gina had instructed him, Roland answered, "There has been no torture. Certainly there has been questioning of detained people. And some leads have proven useful. They were voluntarily given, not forced."

And then another voice: "We understand just now that the FBI has arrested Antonio Garafalo, a close friend of the commissioner, for the murder of Raj Gandhi, an investigative reporter for the *New York Times*."

Roland Fortune was a consummate actor. He made believe the question hadn't been asked and he made other people believe the same thing. "Even as we speak, delivery trucks containing all the myriads of essential products on which the people of Manhattan rely—food, water, flowers, and, yes, even beer—are arrayed in Queens, Brooklyn, and the Bronx and have been cleared for entry into Manhattan. Our stores will soon be replenished. The pulse of this vibrant city will soon return to normal. Any threats will be stifled. The only changes Manhattanites will see that will make the city different from the tranquil world of four days ago will be the welcome presence on every street corner of soldiers, police, and military equipment."

Roland raised his left arm, an embracing gesture. "Manhattan will soon be what it always has been. The streets will be alive with all of our vibrant residents. The subways will reverberate under us, like the flow of blood through healthy, vigorous bodies. Tourists from every nation will fill our streets. Yes, we will have all the noise, the excitement, and all the quiet places of refuge, the museums, the parks, the book stores, the irreplaceable diners, that provide the texture of this greatest of all cities."

As had so often happened in his flawless and charmed career, Roland Fortune smiled at the reporters gathered in front of him, a motley group of some well-dressed men and women who could have passed for bankers to scruffy people who seemed to have been transported in time from Berkeley in 1968, and said, "Thank you all for coming. Relax, resume your lives."

CHAPTER THIRTY-EIGHT

THE PRIVATE CORPORATE jet seated just twelve passengers. The aircraft bore no external markings or seals except for the name of the manufacturer Bombardier, the Canadian company selected by the Secret Service for the rapidly assembled flight on the theory that its most important passenger would fly only on a North American-constructed corporate jet. There was not a single symbol of American power or prestige or presence on the jet's gleaming surfaces.

President Andrew Carter, as he glanced from the window, was struck again by how the New Jersey Meadowlands, whether he saw them from the ground or the air, were one of the most desolate areas in America. As the jet gradually slowed for its descent into the small Teterboro airport in northern New Jersey, it was less than two thousand feet above the expanse of Meadowlands that always made him think of the title to the Eliot poem *The Waste Land*. Still-polluted rivers and streams ran through the reeds. There were ragged open areas where car and truck dumps were fully exposed, rusting. Unadorned and anonymous warehouses whose flat roofs were at least two acres large were scattered among the reeds and filthy swamplands. Even the new professional football and basketball stadiums, fed by long ribbons of new highways, looked from above like Lego toys, a failed effort to create a Disneyland in a wasteland.

As the jet banked just slightly, that most spectacular of all man-made views in the world came suddenly into sight: the island of Manhattan. Carter scanned the city skyline beginning at lower Manhattan. The new World Trade Center tower, a triangular, multi-sided building that glinted like a sword and was topped by an immense antenna, dominated the downtown collection of tall office buildings. Then, slightly farther to the north, the skyline gradually declined in the older areas of Tribeca, Soho, and the West Village.

The president and the passengers on his side of the jet all stared at the familiar, always magical sight: the Empire State Building, still stunning and sleek; the Chrysler Building whose top resembled frozen lava; and the triangular heights of the modern green-tinted Citibank Building. For the first time Andrew Carter saw the new slender apartment building that rose like a needle more than ninety stories above 57th Street. It was black, so tall and thin that it was eerie.

When the jet made its final adjustment for the landing at Teterboro, the Manhattan skyline slid out of view, like a magical illusion. The president settled into his oversize seat and strapped and snapped on his seat belt. To his right was Roger Fitton, the secretary of defense whom Carter had privately decided to fire just a week before the assault on Manhattan. On the president's left, in full formal military clothing, was dour, determined General Malcolm Foster, that scrawny native of West Virginia the president completely trusted even though the two men couldn't have been more different. Carter was naturally eloquent; Malcolm Foster spoke only when he had a fact to convey. Secret Service agents sat silently in the rows of seats behind and in front of the president of the United States.

The perfectly engineered Bombardier was as quiet as a glider plane when it was two miles from Teterboro. Suddenly Roger Fitton, who had taken a three-minute call on his cell phone, said, "Mr. President, your favorite mayor just finished a press conference."

Carter smiled. "He's the only man in the world who loves those cameras more than I do." He lapsed into silence. "So tell me what he said about Gina Carbone's resignation?"

"Not word one."

"Didn't Lazarus get my order to him?"

"That was Lazarus just on the cell with me. He did give your order."

"Before or after Fortune's press conference?"

"Before."

"Before?"

"Right, before."

"So what did the motherfucker say at this press conference?"

"Fortune praised Commissioner Carbone as if she were the Ulysses S. Grant of the twenty-first century. He said that because of her effectiveness he was ordering the immediate lifting of the lock-down of Manhattan. The city, he said, is now safe enough for that."

Carter's moods and reactions had always been a mystery to Fitton. Carter and Fitton had known each other for the few years their careers in the Senate overlapped when they had adjoining office suites and both served on the Foreign Relations Committee. As Defense Secretary, Fitton had met with Carter at least twice a week over the last three years in the Oval Office and conference rooms in the Pentagon and elsewhere. Fitton had never once been invited to the legendary basketball games Carter held at the White House gym.

As the Bombardier leveled with the sureness of an arrow, with the flat New Jersey terrain racing on both sides of the slender craft, Andrew Carter said nothing. Whoever the pilot was had the expertise of an astronaut. The wheels of the jet made a velvet contact with the old and somewhat rutted runway of the small airport.

Even when the Bombardier stopped completely, its flawless engines subsiding into silence, no one in the cabin moved; there were no snapping sounds of seat belts clicking open and loose. This was because Andrew Carter, ordinarily as vigorous and fast at fifty-two as he had been decades earlier as a college, and briefly a professional basketball player, remained motionless. The only sound, the only movement, came two minutes after the jet halted when the pilot opened the cockpit's sealed door. The pilot, who had close-cropped blond hair, was a woman. Andrew Carter and the other people in the luxurious cabin hadn't known that because the door to the cockpit was closed and sealed when, less than an hour before, they had quickly scaled the stairs to the inside of the plane. The pilot and copilot, a large man in a Navy pilot's uniform who left the cockpit only when the attractive woman was at the front of the cabin, hadn't made any announcements during the flight.

Without unfastening his belt, the president leaned closer to Roger Fitton, asking, "Rog, how many Army and Marine soldiers do I have in the city?"

"Between fifteen and twenty thousand troops."

"Where are they primarily?"

Fitton shrugged. "All over Manhattan."

"Roger," the president said, "those are not really adequate answers. In fact, they're lousy answers."

Roger Fitton had an almost inflexible cheeriness, a quality that enabled him to win by huge margins every election he ran in Ohio. The president had picked him as the secretary of defense because he felt he needed at least one bright face among the sour collection of men and women, including Harlan Lazarus, who ran what the press always called the president's "national security team." And Fitton also carried at least an aura of military service: as a young man he had enlisted in the Army Reserve, spent four months on active duty and then twelve years on almost nonexistent reserve duty, leaving with the rank of major, the reason why some soldiers in the Administration addressed him as "Major." Andrew Carter knew it was a joke. Fitton had entered the Army because he always intended to be a politician and believed, correctly, that a claim to military service would give him some intangible edge, a credit, particularly in a state like Ohio.

"I don't understand, Mr. President. That's the best information I have. I can get you exact numbers and locations in two seconds."

The president glanced at him with unveiled disdain and, after the tense beat of two or three seconds, he turned to his left. General Foster was staring straight ahead, as if at attention. "General?" Carter said.

Without hesitating, the general said, "Twelve thousand three hundred and seventy-five, sir. They're located at every street corner in Manhattan. There are an additional two thousand nine hundred troops on Naval and Coast Guard craft on the rivers and in New York Harbor, all ready for specific deployment."

"General, I want your reserve troops to concentrate at every bridge and tunnel leading into and out of Manhattan. Your commanders must make sure that no one, absolutely no one, leaves or enters Manhattan until *I* give that order."

"Mr. President," the grim general said, "those access points are currently under the control of the NYPD."

"So?"

"If we deploy in the next hour, my soldiers will come face to face with those police officers. I understand that the rank and file of the NYPD are remarkably loyal to that commissioner, Ms. Capone or whatever her name is. She must already have directed her people that the mayor has announced the lifting of the lockdown. They see themselves as working for the mayor, not you."

"General, let me say it again. United States soldiers are to be posted immediately at every entrance and exit point in Manhattan. No one leaves or enters Manhattan unless *I* say so."

"What is it exactly, sir, that you want my troops to do? We soon will have armed men and women facing each other at bridges and tunnels, with directly conflicting orders. Tempers will flare. In Afghanistan I had many situations where soldiers, the Afghans and my troops, nominally allies on the same side, came into direct contact at times when they were under competing orders. And the results often were not pretty."

"Listen, General. I am the commander in chief. My orders are that Code Apache stays rigidly in effect until *I* say otherwise. How you and your people implement those orders is your business."

Carter then finally reached for the buckle of his seat belt. The unfastening sound of the click sharply resonated, followed immediately by a series of identical clicks as everyone else unfastened theirs.

Malcolm Foster stood first to give Carter access to the aisle. He saw the president put his hand on Fitton's wrist just as Fitton was about to stand.

"By the way, General, I'm certain the major here, with his deep reservoir of military experience, can help you."

* * *

The silver blades of the green Army helicopter already flashed like a million swords in the bright sunlight as Carter led a small entourage through a cordon of Secret Service agents on the skillet-hot tarmac of the Teterboro runway. At six four, Carter was not only the tallest person in his entourage, he was taller than the sixteen men and two women in the Secret Service detail which suddenly materialized around him.

The Army helicopter carrying President Carter was indistin-
guishable from the dozens of other green helicopters that were airborne at the same time over the Hudson River and the amazing
spectacle of Manhattan, and, in the distance, the glittering expanse
of New York Harbor. Carter could see the Statue of Liberty, as distinct as the miniature models of it displayed in the shops and kiosks
of every airport in America.

Behind him in the thunderous interior of the helicopter, the president heard the clipped voice of Malcolm Foster on a cell phone,
but couldn't hear the words. Carter was certain that the homely,
hard-bitten general was giving out commands to follow the president's order. As Carter had expected, the general hadn't spoken to
the secretary of defense, who sat quietly on the hard metal bench in
the helicopter's belly. Those benches were benches made for soldiers
and not for the president of the United States.

A thousand feet below the helicopter was the dazzling perfection
of the grid of midtown Manhattan. It had the straight lines of criss-
crossing streets and avenues and the tops of buildings that made it
look like a gigantic chessboard with all the pieces in their precisely
ordained places. Carter had flown over every small and large city
in America, and there was no sight like this anywhere else in the
country.

The helicopter suddenly dropped hundreds of feet as it approached
the glimmering green tower of the United Nations Building at the
far end of East 42nd Street. The president had been told that for
security reasons the ungainly craft would descend straight down to
the UN helicopter launch pad on the East River. The sudden descent
frightened him; it was like a free fall, as if the engines suddenly and
unexpectedly failed. He gripped the rails of the steel bench on
which he sat. His scrotum tightened, the universal reaction of men
dropped by helicopter into dangerous landing zones.

Once the helicopter had settled on the floating UN heliport, its rotors still turning and throbbing, Andrew Carter deftly jumped down the three feet from the open door. Fitton and the general needed the outstretched hand of a burly Secret Service agent to guide their jumps. Soldiers with M-16s formed a straight alley down which Carter jogged from the heliport to the plaza that surrounded the still modern-looking UN building constructed in 1947, several years before he was born. At the end of the long cordon of soldiers were iron-plated black SUVs and a limousine. As often happened, he slipped into one of the SUVs and a stand-in who closely resembled him sat behind the tinted windows of the black Lincoln limousine in which the president of the United States was always expected to ride. He was a decoy.

The convoy sped uptown on First Avenue. Startled people on the sidewalk stopped to stare at the convoy. Not only were there SUVs and the gleaming limousines there were also two dozen helmeted soldiers in Hells Angels-style helmets on Harley Davidson motorcycles both leading the convoy and following behind it.

First Avenue was, even on a cloudless day, dreary. The street-level shops were primarily nail salons, stationery stores, bodegas, a McDonald's, three Dunkin' Donuts outlets, retail banking offices with ATMs, and bleak concrete plazas surrounding equally bleak high-rise apartment buildings. The Secret Service had picked First Avenue as the convoy's route because it was the most direct way to Gracie Mansion from the UN building. The ride would take twenty minutes. The avenue was closed to all other traffic.

And then it happened: the stunning sound and the incandescent flash on the sidewalk next to the urban children's playground that ran from 65th to 68th Streets. Andrew Carter, feeling the wrenching jolt of the SUV, glanced out the tinted window to his left, the direction of the explosion and the startling starburst of fire. Before he was shoved to the floor of the SUV by three Secret Service agents who covered his body, like players in a rugby scrum, Carter saw several of the Marines on motorcycles blown down, already drenched in their own blood while the motorcycles, on their own momentum, continued forward for yards as they wobbled crazily like spinning tops and finally fell.

Andrew Carter, his face pressed against the SUV's floor, his large athlete's body entirely covered with the tense bodies of Secret Service agents, was groaning.

CHAPTER THIRTY-NINE

"Do you want to know, Mr. President, why you're still alive?"

Andrew Carter arrived at Gracie Mansion exactly four minutes after the explosion. Within that time, dozens of armed men and women, some of them Army soldiers, some New York City police officers, some Secret Service agents, some in uniforms that were unrecognizable because they bore no insignias, had swarmed over the ordinarily peaceful streets of the neighborhood. Gracie Mansion had first been built in the 1800s, when most of Manhattan above 14th Street was farmland. The mansion, originally a farmhouse, was a security nightmare. Its main entrance was less than thirty feet from the edge of East End Avenue. A tasteful brick wall and a tall wooden fence surrounded the mansion on all sides. No barbed wires, no electrified fences, no concrete barriers. The mansion was in effect part of Carl Schurz Park and of the quiet neighborhood.

Roland Fortune had learned within seconds about the explosion on First Avenue. But he had only learned a few minutes before that the President of the United States had landed, unannounced to anyone in Roland's administration, at the UN building and that a fast-moving motorcade was speeding uptown to Gracie Mansion. Roland believed he had sensed or felt or intuited the explosion, just as some people believe they felt, sensed, or intuited the first tectonic shift of an earthquake.

In that four-minute interval, no one had told him definitively that the president's damaged motorcade was speeding to Gracie Mansion. He simply knew that dozens of armed men and women had suddenly materialized on the quiet nearby streets and in the usually bucolic park. Gina Carbone had ordered him to sit in the only space in the old building that did not have windows. That was the colonial-style foyer at the main entrance to the Mansion.

Andrew Carter was uninjured. He didn't have any visible bruises. By the time his SUV had stopped five feet from the mansion's main door, a female Secret Service agent had given Carter several slightly astringent baby wipes and said, "Sir, you need to wash your face with these." She held her makeup mirror to his face. Long experienced with the politician's skill at cleaning and freshening up, Carter used all the wipes to remove grime from his forehead and the dirty streaks on his cheeks.

Repeating the first words he spoke to Carter when the president walked through the front door, Roland asked, "Do you know why you're still alive?"

Carter's expression was not just puzzled, it was angry. He said nothing.

"Commissioner," Roland suddenly called out.

As if appearing on cue through a side door on a stage, Gina Carbone entered the hallway. Roland knew that Carter had only seen newspaper, magazine, and television images of Gina. He'd be impressed by how tall and striking she was in person.

The foyer in the mansion was small. It was crowded: Andrew Carter and Roland Fortune, both large and powerfully built men; slender and malevolent-looking Harlan Lazarus with at least two of his aides, both wizened men who resembled their boss; and four bulky, pumped-up Secret Service agents, all of them black and with the size of comic book characters.

Yet Gina Carbone, the only woman, dominated the narrow space. She projected absolute confidence and calm.

"This," Roland said, "is Gina Carbone."

She said nothing. Likewise, President Carter didn't speak to her although he glanced at her.

"Why is she here? What was it," the president icily asked Roland, "about my message to fire her that was unclear?"

Roland was close enough to Carter in this densely packed space to detect, faintly, that distinctively acrid odor of sweat the president shed on the basketball court during those times Roland had been invited to play in the White House gym—which was constructed over the old pool that was legendary for years as the place where President Kennedy used to swim in the nude every afternoon cavorting with secretaries, actresses, socialites, and prostitutes. Unlike Kennedy, Carter was a happily married man with no need for afternoon trysts with hundreds of women. One of his first orders as president was to have the long-neglected fetid pool ripped out and replaced with the basketball court.

"And what is it," Roland asked, "about my question that you won't answer?" He paused, calmly defiant. "Do you know why you're alive?" he repeated.

Harlan Lazarus interrupted, "Do you know who you're talking to, Mr. Fortune? Does the word *respect* mean anything to you?"

There were at least ten seconds of utter silence. The only sound was the faint sibilance emanating from the earpieces the Secret Service agents each wore.

Roland said, "Listen to me carefully. Commissioner Carbone learned that a man and a woman were on the sidewalks near the city playground your convoy was about to pass. She was informed they were suicide bombers with enough explosives to take down a building. One, a woman, was on the east side of 62nd Street and

First Avenue, and the other, a man, directly across the avenue. There must have been dozens of children and young parents there who were killed or hurt in that playground. Within three minutes of learning about the suicide bombers, and about your sudden, miraculous arrival and route, the commissioner had two sharpshooters in place. The woman was hit in the head and died before she could do whatever these people do to detonate themselves. Your convoy was less than half a block away. The other sharpshooter was slightly off target. The male suicide bomber was struck in the middle of the chest. Hence the explosion. But had that explosion happened at the same time as Mata Hari was supposed to explode five seconds later, as these people had planned, you would have been the first assassinated president since 1963."

Andrew Carter's face was impassive.

Shrilly, Lazarus said, "Why wasn't I told about this?"

Roland turned to him. They were two feet from each other. "And why the fuck, after four days of begging this man to come to New York, weren't we told he was on his way here? You know how the commissioner found out? Can you guess? She had taken down a suspect half an hour earlier who, after a few minutes of very uncomfortable hesitation, found it necessary to tell her people that the President of the United States was in an Army helicopter over Manhattan and about to land next to the UN building and get into a convoy to drive up First Avenue to see me to tell me to fire her. There wasn't any fucking time to waste."

Roland had a powerful voice. His shouting resonated in the hallway. And then in a whisper he said, "So there was no time to tell you, Mr. Lazarus. There was only time for the commissioner to let me know what her people had learned and for me to tell her to do whatever she needed to do to save this man's life. If I'd been spending my time firing her, on your say-so, the president would be dead." He stopped. "Do you get that, you fucking jerk?"

President Cater raised his hand, signaling Lazarus not to respond. "Everyone leave this room, except the agents. My friend the mayor and I need to have a heart-to-heart, locker-room kind of talk."

CHAPTER FORTY

THE BLACK, ANONYMOUS Impala stopped in the middle of the Holland Tunnel. Except for officers dressed in riot gear—men and women in bulletproof vests, combat helmets and all carrying M-16s, the black weapon that even as a doctor in Iraq and Afghanistan Gabriel knew so well and had from time to time carried—the tiled, yellow-illuminated interior of the tunnel was empty. As soon as the rear door of the car opened, Gabriel, still in the painful plastic handcuffs, was pulled from the back seat. He was led up a narrow flight of steps into a cage-like structure, similar to the kind of booths in the subway system in which clerks once sold tokens and now sold shiny plastic MetroCards. He had seen these booths many dozens of times over the years in which he had driven through the tunnel. He assumed the booths were small stations where traffic was monitored. He spent fewer than two seconds in the booth before he was pushed through a rear door and into a long, brightly lit corridor. It smelled of urine and ammonia, like a bathroom at the Port Authority bus terminal.

The level of fear he felt was far more intense than the fear he experienced in the several times he was under fire in Afghanistan and Iraq. At those times he knew his exposure to danger was only momentary, even if those moments lasted ten to twenty minutes. He was, after all, a doctor, not an infantryman, and he was a healer whom other soldiers were trained to protect and serve.

But now, in this long and utterly unfamiliar corridor under the Hudson River, he had no reason to believe the strange men who were pushing and pulling him had any interest in protecting him. To them he was not a healer with the special skills needed to save wounded people. He was something else, or some other type of person, to these men. They all looked like superbly trained infantry soldiers.

Gabriel knew from all of the years in which he'd lived in New York that both the Lincoln Tunnel and the Holland Tunnel were linked by underwater corridors to blocky stone structures that rose out of the Hudson River. Most people had no real idea what they were. They were anomalies. The stone structures were odd. They were ugly. As a boy, Gabriel learned they served both as air vents for the long tunnels and as escape destinations for people trapped in the tunnels. But there had never once been a disaster in either tunnel.

At the end of the corridor was an open space that resembled the innards of a towering factory floor. It was filled with dark men chained to one another, all sitting on the damp concrete floor. Some glanced at him. He was, after all, a white man, as were all the guards. But there was something different about him. He was a white man in handcuffs.

Disoriented, in pain, Gabriel Hauser heard a man with a Midwestern accent say, "Take the cuffs off him."

A small key in the hand of a woman officer unerringly entered the lock, which clicked like the sound of two marbles gently striking each other, and the plastic cuffs fell off his wrists. Freed, his hands and arms were momentarily useless, filled with that feeling of innumerable pins and needles that he knew was the result of blood suddenly freed to flow into constrained muscles. Involuntarily, his arms rose upward because of the sudden free flow of fresh blood, as if he were a puppet.

Still in the blue blazer, blue button-down shirt, and red-and-black regimental tie he had worn for several days, Roger Davidson stepped in front of Gabriel. "Do you want to know who I am?"

Gabriel quietly said, "Not really."

"Doesn't matter. Because you'll never know."

Regaining his focus as the pain subsided, Gabriel asked, "Who are these men?"

"What men? I don't see any men here. I see lying animals."

Gabriel was a brave man. He stared into Davidson's eyes. It was Davidson who finally disengaged, glancing to his left. Gabriel said, "Raj Gandhi was right, then. You stole these men."

"Come on, Dr. Hauser, I want you to see an old friend of yours."

Gabriel followed Davidson to a far side of the chilly concrete floor. Lying face up, utterly motionless, almost naked except for a dirty towel spread like a loincloth, was Silas Nasar. He was dead. Gabriel calculated that he had seen more than two thousand dead people, most of them men, in his life. This was the first time he shuddered.

"This," Davidson said, "is a shame. I really wanted you to be able to talk to him, Dr. Hauser. He was a friend of yours. You cared for him. But the poor fucker had a heart attack before we could get you here. It's a shame."

"Bullshit. You killed him. Those are dried bullet holes on the side of his torso."

"Make my life easier, Dr. Hauser. Who is this man?"

"He was a patient of mine. Patient X52. There's no reason he should be dead. Certainly not from the wounds I treated."

"Let me tell you something," Davidson said. "I get to decide who lives and who dies. His name was Silas Nasar. You know that."

Unblinking, Gabriel stared at him. "You're just a simple butcher. Why are people like you even born?"

Davidson didn't react. "Let me ask you something. The very first time you saw this man was when, as the Angel of Life, you ran to the museum steps on Sunday to begin saving lives, right?"

Gabriel said, "What planet are you from? I'm a doctor."

"I want to show you something. Maybe it will give you your last chance to tell the truth and save your own life." He reached into an interior pocket of his sports jacket. He held his cell phone to Gabriel's face. "We took this information from your laptop. We found this selfie of Mr. Nasar taken three weeks ago. He sent it to you. And you sent this selfie of yourself back, with the text message, *Can't wait to meet you tomorrow.* Your words, not ours."

Gabriel said nothing.

"So," Davidson asked, "what did you talk about? Cut the shit. What did you do? What did you plan? This man was completely preoccupied with the planning for all this . . ." Davidson paused, waving an arm broadly. "All this jihad carnage. Don't, don't just tell me you were interested only in his chocolate dick. Same taste as his cousin's?"

Gabriel continued to stare at him.

"Your time is running out, Doctor. I need information. I need to save lives. In my way, not yours."

And suddenly a recollection crystallized for Gabriel. "You were in Iraq. I saved your life."

"What's that they used to say in New York?" Davidson asked. "That and a subway token will get you a ride."

"You had a gut wound from a roadside bomb. Men usually die from gut wounds. I cured you."

"I have another friend of yours even if unfortunately you can't talk again to Mr. Nasar," Davidson said.

There was a single bathroom in the underwater fortress. It had an iron door on iron hinges. Both the door and its hinges were more rusted than the rest of the spare, austere place. Like a kid in a school yard, Davidson pushed Gabriel in the direction of the bathroom. Gabriel resisted the impulse to push back. He had met men like Davidson before, one of them, in fact, was Roger Davidson himself. Gabriel knew Davidson was not a Marine, Navy SEAL, or a regular Army soldier, but a killer attached to some federal agency like the CIA, NSA, FBI, or an utterly anonymous group. Gabriel was strong, but not trained in the ways to kill. Davidson was.

When Davidson pulled open the iron door to the bathroom, Gabriel saw Mohammad Hussein. He was sitting on a chair next to an open latrine. Mohammad stood immediately, and just as immediately, Gabriel rushed forward to embrace him. Mohammad was even more slender than he had been in Afghanistan when they had hugged for the last time, in those last hours before Gabriel was taken out of the country. "It's been so long, Gabriel," Mohammad said in that slightly accented, almost perfect English that had made him such a valuable translator.

As Davidson was filming them with his cell phone, Gabriel said, "Where did you go? Where have you been?"

"I'm sorry I've caused you such heartache. All I can say is that I've been here, in this bathroom, for three hours."

"How are your children?"

"Well, thank Allah."

With his cell phone camera still running, Davidson said, "Don't be shy, Mr. Hussein. Tell the doctor why you're really here."

"Gabriel, I was devoted to the Taliban. And now to ISIS. I am who I am, so I became an interpreter. I was trusted. I knew you were a special doctor, that you had permission to treat generals, colonels, CIA people even if all they got was paper cuts. My job was to get information. I had contact with you, with generals, State Department people, CIA, everyone, through you. Americans have an aversion to learning our language. I love English."

Gabriel said, "I don't believe you."

"Even before you left, I found out that people like Mr. Davidson here were—how do you put it—alert to me. So after you left Kabul I was arrested by Mr. Davidson and his friends. I didn't like it. They let me continue to e-mail you for a while as if nothing had happened. Then Mr. Davidson and his friends got the idea that if I *escaped* from the Americans I would find my way to ISIS. Mr. Davidson liked to beat me in the prison camp, his people raped my wife, they terrified my children. But all of them were still alive. I learned to listen to Mr. Davidson."

"This person I hear you describing, the person I know as Mohammad Hussein," Gabriel said, "isn't you."

"I was promised that if I was allowed to escape the detention center and went to Syria to join one of the rebel groups my wife and children would be safe. Mr. Davidson said I had a lot of value. I knew the languages, and I hated Americans. It would take time, he said, to establish my credibility. I might not succeed, but if I tried, he said, my wife and children wouldn't be harmed again. He had his ways, he said, of tracking me and my sincerity. I was even given courses on tactics and ways of acting with groups like ISIS. I'm a good actor."

"You're lying to me now."

"No, Gabriel, not now. In the past, yes, I did."

"Did you love me?"

"I'm not sure what that means when that word comes from you."

"Why did you just hug me?"

"Why not?" Mohammad shrugged, the inelegant movement of a man Gabriel had always seen as innately, naturally elegant. "I found my way to ISIS. I found love there, mission, revenge. I was the only one there who knew English."

"Why are you here?"

"I was sent back by ISIS to Kabul. Mr. Davidson was gone. I never found my wife and children. I still had my American credentials as a loyal translator. I still had your e-mails urging Americans to let me come to the U.S. because of all the service I had done for you as a nurse. And so I came to America." He gestured casually at the dead man. "Silas Nasar was my first contact here."

"Was he your cousin?"

"Of course not. But I knew you would love him. And I knew, Gabriel, how much you hated what America had done to you. A match made in heaven, you and Silas."

"This man you are pretending to be now," Gabriel repeated, "is not the person you are, Mohammad. I know you. You're not a hater, you're not a killer, you're not a liar, not a pretender."

"I never made you any promises. You never made any to me."

"That's enough," Davidson suddenly interrupted. "Enough of this girlie talk. Let's just get this done."

Davidson then climbed a small circular iron stairwell. As though responding to a prearranged signal, Mohammad Hussein followed him. The woman who had unlocked Gabriel's handcuffs reattached them and in an almost gentle tone said, "Follow them." With no physical prodding, Gabriel too ascended the iron stairs.

A small door opened. Suddenly he was in the open air on the top of the strange building just above the flow of the vast river's waters. Three men were already there, each with professional cameras and audio equipment. They wore ski masks revealing only their eyes. They wore black gloves. The cameras and audio equipment were off. Davidson led Gabriel into a makeshift, chain-link cage, large enough so that Gabriel could only stand and not bend over or turn. And then Davidson, too, put on a full-size ski mask and black gloves. He took off his blue blazer and white shirt and tossed them down the door into the stairwell. He dressed in the kind of white robe with a loose belt Gabriel had seen on thousands of normal civilian men in Iraq and Afghanistan.

Slender Mohammad Hussein, also wearing a ski mask he had pulled over his head and face before emerging into the open air, squeezed into the cage with Gabriel. He draped a heavy, professionally printed sign over Gabriel's neck and chest. In Arabic, a language Gabriel could fluently read but barely speak, the sign read *The Angel of Life and Death Defiles Islam.* It read the same in English as well. Mohammad, without speaking to Gabriel, slipped out of the cage with a cat's agility.

Beneath Gabriel's feet was a slippery, viscous substance. But his keen mind and sensitive body focused on other things as the men with cameras, speaking in English, gave theatrical directions to Mohammad at the side of the cage and another man, unrecognizable to Gabriel, standing on the other side of the cage, also in a full mask.

Once the camera's eye began to shine, Mohammad spoke: "What you are about to witness is the consequence of disloyalty to Islam. This man, called by infidels the Angel of Life, who in Allah's eyes is the Angel of Death, joined the slaughter of the faithful in Iraq and Afghanistan. He kept alive those who killed us."

This is when and how I die. Gabriel suddenly sensed a profound spirit of ease, as he listened to Mohammad's familiar voice. It was a glorious summer day. A light breeze tinged with the scent of ocean water swept over the Hudson River. During his childhood and teenage years this powerful river had been part of his life, like the Mississippi in Mark Twain's life. Gabriel had seen it every day from the slender and grimy window in the kitchen of his parents' apartment. And during those wonderful years when he had loved Jerome Fletcher every room of that large apartment on Riverside Drive had views of this ancient, all-powerful river. Gabriel had learned the exuberance of running on the miles of the esplanade that bordered the Hudson. He knew its scents, its moods, the qualities of light on its surface. Now he was about to join its eternal flow and become a part of it.

"Now the Islamic State is here," Gabriel vaguely, almost serenely, heard Mohammad say. "Allah is a God of love and a God of vengeance. We have just taken the life of the president of this evil nation. And we now take the life of this betrayer. Allah will do with him as Allah sees fit."

All of this, Gabriel knew in the last seconds of his life, was being broadcast on YouTube, Twitter, Snapchat, television, every device able to deliver sights and sounds as they happened around the globe. But they could not deliver his ecstatic inner sense that he was now part of the river, the flow of air, the scent of fish and the plants that had always thrived on the river's life-giving waters.

As the fire engulfed him, he made no sound. *Ashes to ashes. Dust to dust.*

CHAPTER FORTY-ONE

THEY STOOD IN the middle of the pastel-painted hallway. Each of the four Secret Service agents was in a corner, one as close to the oak door as possible to make sure it was secure and stayed that way.

Andrew Carter spoke first. "She's a remarkable woman."

"She has balls."

"Apparently more than that, Roland. How else can you explain this Garafalo guy? He couldn't have been interested in her balls."

"It's her personal life, Mr. President. I knew about her and him."

"Did you tell her it didn't show good judgment for the commissioner of the biggest police department in the world to be the playmate of a Gambino family member who'd served several years in a federal prison?"

"No, I didn't. And she didn't give me advice about my personal life."

"Well," Carter said, "the personal is now political. Lazarus has a great deal of power."

"Is that so? He hasn't done much to impress that on me in the last four days."

"He has many friends in the courts and the justice department. There is already a grand jury investigating her, and Garafalo, and the tape that crazy doctor made, and the murder of a *New York Times* reporter. Who knows? I'm not a lawyer. She could be indicted and arrested in an hour. All Garafalo has to do is talk."

"Mr. President, he went to jail for years because he wouldn't talk." Roland was so close to the president that he smelled the man's rancid, fear-tinged breath. "Let me make it clear," Roland continued, "I'm not firing her. And we have more important things to talk about. There are millions, probably billions, of people in the world who think you are dead. It was the explosion heard around the world. Whoever those people are—Boko Haram, ISIS, the evil spawn of Timothy McVeigh—billions of people saw on Twitter what was happening half an hour ago on First Avenue."

"My people," Carter answered, "are setting up a press conference right now, in the dining room. There will be a curtain hanging behind me, with American flags all over it. Roland, you should be flattered. I'm taking a cue from your stage acting when people thought you were dead at the Met. The only difference is that no one will know where my broadcast is coming from." He stopped, as if deciding whether to say what was on his mind. Then he said, "I admired you, by the way, when you went to the Museum the day of the first explosions. It took courage. I admired that."

"Or," Roland answered, "it was just stupid. I didn't imagine at the time that these attacks would continue."

Carter's expression changed, from near admiration to something more somber. "You had no authority to order the lifting of the lockdown. That's my authority."

"It is? Really, the silence from D.C. was stunning. You and Lazarus and that bizarre general talked a great deal. But nothing happened. You don't know this city. Garbage piles up quickly here. Millions of people move around all the time. They're not really obedient. There's more and more chaos. I knew that. You didn't. And you still don't. A ride in a motorcade from the UN building along scenic First Avenue is not going to reveal much to you."

"Roland, you knew about the plan for a lockdown almost from

the day you became mayor. My sources told me you never once voiced an objection."

"The people, including Lazarus, who briefed me about this always seemed to be living in a fantasy land. He was always with these anonymous, white, obsessed men and women from Tulsa, Oklahoma, or outlandish places like that. I listened and said nothing. They knew less about Manhattan than they know about Neptune."

"Why didn't you say that? Leaders ask questions, they probe, they ask, *what if?*"

"Are you telling me, Mr. President, what leaders do?"

"I'm telling you that this lockdown will continue until I decide it will end."

Roland said, "We barely know each other. You learned how to play basketball at Stanford. I learned on a cracked tar court on 106th Street that had hoops but no nets. I learned that if some guy elbowed you, you elbowed him back. You learned that when gentlemen played every elbow throw was accidental and called for an apology. So what I know from what I learned as a kid is that in this city if this lockdown continues several hundred thousand people will start to move and overwhelm the tunnels and the bridges."

"I've ordered General Foster to place Marines and Special Forces troops to take over all exits and entrances to Manhattan."

"I can't tell you how idiotic, dangerous, that is, Mr. President. You're living in the world of *Alice in Wonderland.*"

At that moment a heavy hand, forceful and persistent, slammed against the closed door. One of the enormous agents pressed the earpiece more deeply into his ear. He listened intently. "Mr. President," he finally said, "it's Judge Lazarus. He says it's essential that he see you."

Without glancing at Roland Fortune, Carter said, "Unlock the door and let the scarecrow in."

Lazarus carried an iPad. Without speaking, he held the iPad between the president and the mayor. On the screen was the image, as clear as a Hollywood production, of an Arabic-accented man speaking perfect English saying that ISIS had just exploded to infinity the president of the United States. And next on the screen was the stunning image of the extraordinarily handsome, troublesome Gabriel Hauser, in a wire cage, as he was immolated above the Hudson River.

Wordlessly, Carter watched the whole scene as transfixed as a teenager by a horror movie. With the scene unfolding, Roland first wondered if he too was watching a Hollywood movie scene. And then he dwelt on how Gabriel Hauser didn't make a sound. As a teenager in high school studying modern American history, Roland had seen a film of saffron-dressed Buddhist monks on fire in Saigon to protest the Vietnam War. What had struck him most about the newsreels was that, in all-consuming flames, the monks, too, had never made a sound. Now, in this horrific image, Gabriel Hauser also was silent even as his body first became a torch entirely on fire and then diminished. It soon became a smaller and smaller mound of ash as the flames had less and less to consume.

Roland, squeezing with both index fingers the corners of his eyes so as not to cry, said, "Just four days ago I wanted to meet this man to thank him for his bravery."

"The gods of fortune," Lazarus said to Roland, "were on your side that that meeting never took place. The Angel of Life worked with the people who just torched him."

Carter, who had no visible reaction to the video, said, "And, Mr. Mayor, this just happened in the very city you now want to open, is that right?"

"You don't know very much," Roland answered. "What you just so calmly saw didn't take place in Manhattan. This island's borders are broken. These men took this doctor to a blockhouse in the Hudson River hundreds of yards from the Manhattan waterfront. It's equally accessible from New Jersey. You've never lived here, so you've never noticed those blockhouses in the river near the Holland Tunnel and the Lincoln Tunnel."

"At the moment, Mr. Mayor, I'm more concerned about my authority to act. I will *not* let you take that away from me."

"That's crap, Mr. President. People are dying. What are you going to have General Foster's soldiers do when hundreds of thousands of men, women, and children begin to walk and drive to the exits at the Triboro Bridge, the 59th Street Bridge, the Queens Midtown Tunnel? Push them back? Fire warning shots? Use tear gas? Why not just shoot some? Hosni Mubarak thought that was good strategy."

At that moment, Lazarus held his iPad aloft between the two angry men. "Are you two worried about authority? Take a look at this. We have a rogue woman who is showing the world she has more authority than either of you."

* * *

The iPad's screen displayed Gina Carbone while she spoke, standing at the curved iron railing that ran along the high edge of the esplanade of Carl Schurz Park. Behind her was the gleaming light on the surface of the East River. Much further beyond her were the dense, dark, low-lying expanses of the Queens waterfront.

Surrounded by high-ranking uniformed NYPD police officers, she said to the dozens of reporters who were kept behind an impenetrable barricade ten feet in front of her, "The first point and most important by far is that the president of the United States is alive and completely unharmed. For obvious reasons he is at an undisclosed location in Manhattan."

Even though her face was in intense sunlight, Gina neither blinked nor squinted. She spoke and bore herself steadily with the utter repose of a news broadcaster.

"Elite snipers of this great police department were put in place on First Avenue as soon as Mayor Fortune and I learned that terrorists had information that President Carter was making an unannounced visit to Manhattan to witness firsthand the steady, lethal degradation of the evil forces that have terrorized this besieged city since Sunday."

"I want to arrest this woman," Lazarus said to Carter and Fortune as he steadily held the iPad for them, "right now." Gina was speaking no more than one hundred yards from where they stood in the foyer. "This," Lazarus said, "is treason. Who does she think she is?"

Gina continued, "What I can tell you at this moment is that suicide bombers, a man and a woman who we believe were experienced U.S.-grown ISIS terrorists, stood directly opposite each other on First Avenue waiting for the decisive moment when the unmarked presidential convoy was to pass between them. At that point, at that moment, their tactical plan was to detonate enough explosives strapped to their ankles, legs, stomachs, and chests to create an inferno.

"One of our snipers, when the convoy was just a block away, dispatched a single round that struck the female in the head, killing her instantly and without igniting the weapons of mass destruction she wore. Our second sniper, who as a Navy SEAL in Iraq had made at least ninety long distance kills, fired at the male suicide bomber on the east side of First Avenue. For reasons that are not entirely clear to us, that kill shot also hit the bomber, delivering a mortal round, but the remarkable quantity of explosives he wore somehow detonated."

A shrill voice rang out from beyond the barrier: "When will we see the president?"

"That is the president's decision."

The same insistent voice called out: "Then, Commissioner, how do you know what you've just told us?"

"I saw him. He's a remarkable man. Calm, determined, undisturbed. He's a consummate leader."

Gina paused. Confidence and beauty radiated from her, a powerful presence. "I have more information for you, for the world. But first, as a former soldier myself, and because at the outset of these awful days I promised you only truth, I do have to report that at least four brave men who were part of the motorcade were killed. We know who they are and will give you that information when their families are notified.

"And there are other truths I'll share with you. When the second suicide bomber, a human death machine, exploded, there were also severe losses in a popular playground near where these animals were standing. Dozens of innocent children and their parents were killed and maimed. I will have more information for you on that when, as I've assured you from the start, I have the truth about this unspeakable, cowardly brutality."

Gina then gripped the stem of the microphone as if it were a weapon. "Cowards make mistakes. You all witnessed the brutal immolation of Dr. Gabriel Hauser just minutes ago. Immensely brave elements of the NYPD's Special Forces know who these killers are and are incapacitating them even as we speak. This is not Syria. This is not Iraq. This is not Yemen, Libya, Nigeria. We now have these people in our sights. They will face swift and certain justice. The nightmare is coming to an end."

She paused. The cameras tightened on her powerful face.

"That is the truth I promised you."

CHAPTER FORTY-TWO

THE CONFERENCE ROOMS inside the ugly, Soviet-style brick U.S. attorney's office at One Saint Andrew's Plaza in downtown Manhattan were utilitarian and windowless. There were many of them. There were no water containers in any of them, no wastebaskets, no coffee, no pens, no pencils, no paper. They each had identical furniture: long laminated tables whose surfaces were lacquered to resemble dark wood and seven or eight lightly upholstered chairs on four ball-bearing shaped wheels.

Yet despite the identity of the rooms, Tony Garafalo had the sensation that this was precisely the same one he had sat in seven years earlier when he was first arrested before he was convicted and sent to jail. Just as now, he was placed in the chair at the head of the table, but then, unlike now, separate handcuffs affixed his wrists, hands, ankles, and arms to the frame of the chair. This time, for some reason, he had complete freedom of movement. He could roll the chair backwards or forwards. He could lean into the table or away from it. He could make gestures. The one thing he was not allowed to do was stand and walk around.

And then, as now, there were at least eight other people in the room. Two of them were assistant U.S. attorneys, the lawyers who were just assigned to lead the investigations of Gina Carbone and Tony Garafalo. Seven years earlier, the assistants were both men in their mid-thirties. Like almost all assistant U.S. attorneys in

Manhattan, they were graduates of Ivy League law schools. They had then spent two or three years as law clerks to federal judges, and then another three or four years with huge New York City law firms before moving for another four or five years to assignments as assistant United States attorneys: a standardized sequence of credentials that each of the assistants hoped would end in the ultimate lifetime prize—partnerships in their early forties in one of the legendary New York City law firms.

And then, as now, the other six or seven people in the room were anonymous law enforcement agents, all armed with visible holstered pistols. Seven years ago the only law enforcement agent who was a woman was Gina Carbone, with the rank of inspector. Tony Garafalo had known her since he was ten. They were raised on the same working-class block on Staten Island. Each winter both their parents' lawns were decorated with identical smiling Santa Clauses in red stocking caps urging on identical, bulb-illuminated plastic reindeer.

And both of their uncles were soldiers in the Gambino family.

For two years, when he was thirty and she was in her early twenties before she unexpectedly enlisted in the Army and Tony Garafalo had long ago earned the nickname "Tony the Horse" because of the heft and size of his penis, they were lovers. When Tony was manacled in this same room, he first learned that Gina was a member of the team of FBI, IRS, Postal Service Inspectors, and NYPD officers who formed the combined squad that had investigated and taken him down. He didn't acknowledge knowing her; and he mentioned nothing about the fact that the last time he had fucked her was as she leaned against the trunk of his Corvette the night before she left for Fort Knox to start her Army basic training. He also kept to himself that years ago when she came she was a screamer, not a moaner.

In fact, seven years ago, despite volleys of questions from everyone in the interview room, he hadn't said a word to anyone. Nothing, *nada*. There were hours of questions about what he knew, what he had said, what he had done, where he lived. He didn't even concede what his name was. The only words Gina spoke were, "That's Tony Garafalo."

But today, in what may have been the same ugly and sterile room, he wanted to talk. The two assistant U.S. attorneys, both in their mid-thirties, weren't the same as those from seven years earlier; those two had left to whatever rewards or fates they reached. Tony, handsome as a movie star, stared at the two new assistants with nothing but the contempt that was bred into his DNA and his life experience, just as he knew that Gina Carbone had the same breeding and background, only that she had skillfully learned to conceal them and only at times glaringly, laughingly, revealed to him when they had been alone many times during the last two years. One of the new assistants who faced him was a dapper young black man, caramel colored and with effete steel-framed glasses. Incredibly to Tony, the other assistant was an Asian woman: Tony thought for a minute that he would break the ice by asking her for an order of lemon chicken and noodles.

"Mr. Garafalo," the African American assistant said, "I'm obligated to tell you that you have a right to remain silent and to have a lawyer present. And that anything you may say to us can and will be used against you."

"Let me ask you a question, Mr. Clark? That's your name, isn't it?"

Horace Clark nodded. "Same name that I had when I introduced myself to you three minutes ago."

"Haven't you guys learned how to use tape recorders and video equipment and all that stuff? I don't see anything like that."

"We don't record interviews," Clark answered.

"Even the Podunk PD records interviews these days. Andy of Mayberry would be doing it. Fuck, even cops wear cameras when they're out on the street."

"It's federal policy not to have recording devices during interviews. You must surely know that, Mr. Garafalo, you've had experience with this process before."

"So you still rely on the miracle of 302s?" Tony asked.

Form 302 was the government form, in use since the era of J. Edgar Hoover, on which FBI and other government agents wrote in sometimes vivid narratives the results of conversations they had with witnesses, defendants, and others. Tony used the words *the miracle of 302s* because, even though he had once sat for hours with FBI and other agents without ever saying a word, there were at least five agents who testified against him at trial who used their 302 reports to recount his incriminating statements.

During his trial, Tony had whispered to his lawyer, the legendary Vincent Sorrentino, "This is all made-up shit. I never said a word to those fuckers." In return, Sorrentino, cupping his right hand over Tony's left ear, had quietly said, "That's why we call them form *302F*, with *F* as in fiction." Sorrentino had added, "Don't worry, I'll rip up their asses and their 302s on cross." And Sorrentino had.

"Doesn't matter to me," Tony told Horace Clark. "It'll give you guys all day tomorrow to pick up some overtime when you write your 302s." Tony Garafalo through the years had built up a way of fostering camaraderie with law enforcement agents, many of whom were born and raised in the same kinds of neighborhoods in Brooklyn, the Bronx, and Staten Island in which he had been raised. Tony was a man of many roles—if he'd become an actor, he could play convincingly a suave gangster, a compassionate priest, a lawyer or the leader of one of those evil empires in the action movies with computer animation that had become so popular in the years since his prison term ended.

All of the agents, men with Italian, Irish, and Polish names, either smiled or laughed when they heard him say "the miracle of 302s." The two assistants didn't laugh or even smile.

Gently adjusting the thin frames of his glasses, Horace Clark asked, "Mr. Garafalo, do you know the name Gina Carbone?"

"The name?" Tony smiled at the serious Horace Clark. "I know the person, too."

"Do you know the Gina Carbone who is the current commissioner of the New York City Police Department?"

"Sure I do."

"How long have you known Commissioner Carbone?"

"My math isn't great. I'm fifty-four. I was ten or so when she was born. Our families lived on the same street. I even remember going to her baptism." Tony glanced at the Asian Assistant, whose only words so far had been to introduce herself as "Assistant U.S. Attorney Yvette Yang," a name that had tempted Tony to think of her as *Yo Yo*. "You know what a baptism is, don't you?"

She ignored him. In front of her at the table was a yellow legal pad at the top of which, as Tony could see, the only words were "Interview Notes with Anthony Garafalo" and the date.

"Did there come a point in time when you and Commissioner Carbone became friends?"

"That's a really complicated word, Mr. Clark. She was my friend when she was baptized. Our families were, as I told you, close. I saw her almost every day for years. I do remember that when I was eighteen or so I played a lot of heavy-duty American Legion baseball. I told the coach to get a uniform for her and make her the first girl bat boy. She really, really wanted that. She kept on asking me to help get her that job. So the team made a little uniform for her that was just like ours and she became the first bat girl, not just for our team but in all of the other American Legion teams we played from all around the country." Tony paused and smiled. "The coach, you know, would have made my eighty-five-year-old grandmother the first bat grandmother if I asked. I was so good I was being seriously scouted by the Pirates, the Red Sox, and the fucking San Diego Padres at the time. Gina, by the way, was a great bat girl from day one. She got to loose foul balls and picked up dropped bats faster than any bat boy I ever saw."

"So you were friends then, too? She was about ten when you were twenty or so," Clark said.

"Well," Tony said, "there's that problem with the word *friend*. She wanted to be on the team. If I hadn't been at her baptism, if I didn't know her and her family, if she had just been a little girl from the neighborhood begging the star of the team, which was yours truly, to be the first bat girl, I'd have ignored her." Tony glanced around the room. "In my world *friends* help *friends*. Does that happen in your world, Ms. Yo?"

"My name is Ms. Yang, Mr. Garafalo."

"Hey, sorry. You can't imagine the things I've been called. The name Garafalo confuses a lot of people. Ask these other guys around the table, especially the good-looking Polish guy over there, what people have done with their names. You gotta get used to it, you gotta have a sense of humor about it."

"Thanks for the insight, Mr. Garafalo," Horace Clark said.

"No problem."

"Let me ask you this, sir," Clark said, "what happened to your baseball prospects? I'm just curious."

"I decided there was another line of work I was going to like better."

"And what was that?"

"Gangster."

Three of the agents laughed aloud. Yang glanced disapprovingly at them, the censorious expression of a grade-school teacher. Their laughter slowly, defiantly subsided.

"Why," Clark asked, "did you make that choice?"

"Who knows? But my baseball training came in real handy. I always had a bat nearby. Hitting a head is a lot easier to hit than a speedy baseball. So before I went to jail I had two names, Tony the Horse, Tony the Batter."

"What," Horace Clark asked, "did 'The Horse' mean?"

Garafalo glanced at the Asian girl. "I've got a dick the size of a Louisville Slugger."

Yvette Yang, unblinking, stared at the yellow legal pad.

"Ask the commissioner," Garafalo said. "She's known that for a long, long time. She knew it when she sat here seven years ago when our *friendship* was so hot again, but I didn't know until that minute that she was part of the hit squad that wound up with me spending years at the Supermax in Colorado. At the trial they ended up playing tapes of me talking to Gina Carbone, my *friend*, who used to wear a wire when we drove around or went to restaurants together."

Again adjusting the right joint of his slender glasses—in what Garafalo now understood was a nervous tic—Clark asked, "Are we to understand that from time to time you and the commissioner are in an intimate relationship?"

"Good guess."

"When was the last time you and Commissioner Carbone were *friends*?"

"We've been good *friends* for two years."

"How," Yvette Yang asked, "did the most recent *friendship* begin?"

"Our families still live close to each other. Italians on Staten Island like to have barbecues in the summer. I was out of Supermax for two, three weeks. The barbecue was at her parents' house. They have a nice patio. I just walked over with my family, like we'd been doing since I was a kid. Gina was there. She was already the police chief. She had a security detail. I guess she was really surprised to see me because she and her people began to leave."

"What happened next?"

"I called out 'Gina.' She stopped. She looked great. She let me walk over to her. I said, 'Gina, no hard feelings, please. It was your job, you did what you had to do.'"

Yvette Yang asked, "Did you mean that?"

"Not one fucking word. I wanted to kill her. She had even had the tapes going when we were in bed. They, by the way, were useless, hundreds of hours of them. All you could hear was an hour or so of me banging her and her screaming, *More, more, yes, yes!*" He paused. "My lawyer, Vinnie Sorrentino, wanted to play one of those tapes for the jury. Vinnie's a great guy, a great lawyer. When the judge asked what the point was of letting a jury listen to an hour of pornography, Vinnie said, *Prosecutorial misconduct.* Even the judge, an old woman, laughed, but she said no. Ms. Yang, do you scream or moan?"

Serious-faced, Clark asked, "Did you, at this barbecue, say anything else to the commissioner?"

"'I was only doing my job, too.' That's what I told her. 'No hard feelings,' I said."

"What happened next?" Clark asked.

"I had gotten a job as a salesman at the Mercedes Benz place on Queens Boulevard. I knew I was a good salesman. Back in my ball-playing days some writer for the *Daily News* said watching me play was like watching a top-of-the-line Mercedes racing on a high-speed track. I still have a copy of the article."

"That," Yvette Yang said, "is a very rapid period of time for someone just released from Supermax, the highest security prison in the United States, to find work at a prestigious auto dealership. Is the owner of the dealership part of organized crime or connected to it?"

"That's none of your fucking business."

"Let's return to Commissioner Carbone," Clark said. "Tell us the next event."

"At the barbecue I said to Gina, 'Wow, now you're the chief, the *capo di tutti capi.*' And I told her what dealership I was working for, just casually. And then she left with her security detail, but not before kissing my eighty year-old mother and father. Just like *friends* do."

"And next?"

"Next, just a few days later, I'm at my desk at the dealership, and it's a slow day, and my desk phone, with caller ID, rings. The little screen that tells you whose calling says *Pay Phone.* That's really unusual, I think. There must have been six pay phones left in all of New York. But I'm a salesman and, hey, you never know.

"And so I take the call and it's Gina. She obviously didn't want to use her phone at the PD or her cell phone. A pay phone call is untraceable. Right away I think *Fuck, this is great. Bingo.*

"And Gina bullshits for a little while. How's the job going? How are your kids? Bullshit like that. And then Gina, who was never shy, asked if I can get together with her at that coffee shop near LaGuardia off the Grand Central Parkway. It's just a silver-sided coffee shop, no name on it, just a red neon sign on it that says *Diner.* The kind of place where limo and cab drivers stop off for coffee and hamburgers at all hours of the day and night. Transients, people tired from long flights, taxi and limo drivers on breaks."

"What did you say?" Horace Clark asked.

"I joked. I said to her, 'You gonna be wearing a wire this time, Gina?'"

"And?"

"She said, 'Come on, Tony, those days are long over. I'll let you take me into the bathroom first and I'll strip completely so you can check for wires.'"

Tony had noticed that Yvette Yang's eyes blinked very infrequently. She said, "You do realize, Mr. Garafalo, don't you, that Mr. Clark and I are law enforcement agents of the federal government. As are all the other officers in this room. Lying to us is, in and of itself, a federal offense punishable by five years in prison and a fine of $250,000."

"Not a problem, Ms. Yang. I'm not lying. Ask Gina. Ask Commissioner Carbone." Tony Garafalo knew that the other agents, all men, all trying not to smile, were having the time of their lives as they listened to him.

Smooth as a dark marble, Clark asked, "Did the meeting at the diner take place?"

"The next day. Middle of the afternoon. She came in a little Toyota one of her brothers owned. She wore an oversize Mets baseball cap. She was already famous, she didn't want to be recognized. If she had security with her, I didn't see them. There were a few guys at the counter who were already there when I got there a few minutes before her. They didn't necessarily look like limo or cab drivers taking a break." Tony glanced up at the male agents at the far end of the table. "No, I didn't take her to the bathroom to check out whether she was wearing a wire."

"What did you discuss?"

"Discuss? We weren't there to talk about a nuclear treaty with Iran. After half an hour or so she wrote down on a napkin what her address was—it's an apartment on East 79th Street and East End Avenue near one of the downtown entrance ramps to the FDR so that she has an easy time getting downtown to One Police Plaza, and she said she wanted to cook for me that night."

"What did you say?" Clark asked.

"Maybe she's not your type, Mr. Clark, but Gina was, and is, a real good-looking woman. Besides, not once in my life have I ever said no to a woman who asked me to dinner in her house. That's always a *bingo*."

One of the agents at the far end of the table suddenly said, "Tony, you must need a bottle of water by now, right?"

"Sure, thanks."

The agent walked to Tony and put a bottle of water in front of him. "Thanks, guy," Tony said.

Clark, who didn't appear to approve that one of his agents had offered water to Tony, asked, "And next?"

"I went over. We ate. And I fucked her. Or she fucked me. Or we fucked each other. I guess it depends on how you look at it."

Yvette Yang asked, "And how long did this relationship, as I would call it, go on?"

"For two years. Until last night. I don't think she has plans to see me again."

"Did she," Horace Clark asked, "tell you anything about her work?"

Tony, with a twist of his heavy, powerful hands, snapped open the sealed cap of the water bottle.

"Listen to me real careful now. We spent at least three nights a week together for two years. She had this thing about the city being vulnerable. What pissed her off even more was that the Feds, the Homeland *Insecurity* shitheads she called them, didn't understand New York. She said the mayor was a great guy but a garbagehead, a pill user; Xanax, Vicodin, that shit, and that he thought the Feds were idiots, too, but he was too busy with other stuff, particularly the *Masterpiece Theatre* girlfriend he had, to ask too many questions about the Feds' plans for protecting the city.

"So Gina put together her own plans. She had this huge budget. She told me the number once but it was so big it was like what
we used to call a telephone book number and it didn't really mean
nothing to me. She started telling me she was using chunks of the
budget to hire guys, tough guys, who'd been in Afghanistan and
Iraq to organize special groups that would know what to do if any
part of the city got attacked."

"Why," Horace Clark asked, "did she tell you these things?"

"Ask her. Pillow talk, I guess. She had always loved for me to
screw her. When I finished her off each time, she got tired. And she
talked. I heard about the hit list. I heard about state-of-the-art secret prisons on piers that looked like they were crumbling into the
East River. I heard about something she called Code Apache. When
I asked her whether she had hired Tonto and the Lone Ranger for
Code Apache, she thought that was funny and said no, it was her
plan to lock down Manhattan if an attack happened here. She told
me about a guy named Davidson, a real killer, someone we really
could have used in the Gambino family."

"Why," Yvette Yang asked, "are you telling us all this? You have
no immunity from prosecution, you have no lawyer, and you are
saying extraordinary things about the commissioner of the New
York City Police Department and even the mayor of the city."

Refreshed by the water, Tony said, "Did you ever hear of revenge?
Payback? I was at her baptism. I took care of getting her what she
wanted—bat girl—when she was a kid. I was her lover when she got
to be old enough to have lovers. We lived on the same street. Our
uncles were in the same business. I drove Gina Carbone to the airport when she left for basic training. I screwed her the night before
she left."

Tony stared only at Yvette Yang, who was obviously afraid of him
or had nothing but contempt for him. "We were *friends*. For life.

And then eight years ago she decided to work with a group of you people. They knew she knew me. They knew we were—what's the right word—dating? She taped everything I told her.

"And then she sat in this same room. She could have warned me off, given me a heads up. Like a *friend* would do. And then she testified at my trial." Tony sipped more water. "Anything else you want to know, Ms. Yang. Or don't you have friends?"

Suddenly Clark said, "We could use a bathroom break. If you want to use the bathroom, Mr. Garafalo, we'll have to handcuff you as we walk through the hallways."

Tony Garafalo waved a hand and stayed seated. "Go enjoy yourselves. I'm good."

* * *

"Who is, or was, Raj Gandhi?"

"I read lots of newspapers. It got to be a habit in prison, where I read the fucking *New York Times* in that dirty newsprint that got all over my hands. Now I've even got a Kindle. I had no idea in prison that there was such a thing. I read the *Times* there."

"And?"

"I started seeing the names of reporters I hadn't seen before. When I was on trial I hated the two reporters from the *Times* who were there all the time. They were supposed to be experts on the Mafia. They didn't know shit from Shinola about the families. Everything they knew was from the movies. Both Jews. They studied the *Godfather* movies. That, they thought, made them experts. When it came to my trial they were hanging reporters, just like in the old Western movies there were hanging judges.

"But when I came out of Supermax, where, believe it or not, I got to know the Unabomber, a pretty sweet guy actually, those two reporters were gone. Retired, fired, dropped in the East River. Who the hell knows? Over the last two years on my gorgeous little Kindle I saw mainly new names of reporters."

"And one of those was Raj Gandhi?" Yvette Yang asked.

"Very perceptive, Ms. Yang. I liked the name, I liked his articles. I looked him up on Google, another thing I never saw or heard of at Supermax. He was new to the city. I read his articles about the wars in Iraq and Afghanistan.

"So I started calling him. I wanted him to know about the hit list, the prison on the piers, Gina's secret army, what she thought about Homeland Security."

"Did you tell him who you were?" Clark asked.

"Tony Bennett." From somewhere in the room one of the agents laughed, briefly. "Come on, Horace, grow up. I gave him information. I wanted him to work. I'm a salesman, an actor. When you've got a guy from Queens in a Mercedes show room, you talk Queens. When you've got a twenty-five year-old kid from Harvard Business School and Goldman Sachs who wants a Mercedes convertible you talk his talk. I've got this God-given skill of imitating accents and voices. I know how to do these things. Remember, I'm a criminal."

"So," Yvette Yang asked, "why should we believe anything you say to us now?"

"That's your choice."

Clark asked quietly, "Did you kill Raj Gandhi?"

"Of course not. Never saw him. I only talked to him. I used a wiseass Queens accent. Once he let the world know what I wanted him to know, I was happy I had picked out such a smart dothead. I had no use for him any longer. He did what I wanted. No need to hurt him."

Yvette Yang said, "We have videotape of you entering and leaving his building."

"I knew where he lived. It was right in the phone book. There's a gorgeous thirty-year-old in that building. She's one of my other girlfriends. Her name is Gloria Kopechne. She's something like the grandniece of that girl Teddy Kennedy killed on Martha's Vineyard in, what the hell was it? 1969? Take a look through all your video-tapes. Go talk to her. There are probably thirty videotapes of me going into and out of that lobby. I was fucking her. She is kind of a rich kid. No job. I had an open invite to go there to screw her any-time I wanted. I was even in the elevator with her and Mr. Gandhi the day he did his blog-heard-round-the-world. He had no idea who I was. But I'll tell you this. He was a very polite little dothead."

Tony drank more water. "Go ask the commissioner. My guess is she had one of her boys hit him. Gina always had a bad temper. She believes in revenge, payback, anything you want to call it, as much as I do."

Tony had, in fact, been naked in Gloria Kopechne's bed ten minutes after his perfectly aimed shot had entered Raj Gandhi's forehead.

Clark removed his glasses. He looked at the far end of the table where the agents sat. "Take this gentleman to his cell. And two of you go visit Ms. Kopechne right now."

CHAPTER FORTY-THREE

CAMERON DEWAR, AS soon as he was unexpectedly and miraculously released from the conference room on the thirtieth floor of
the new federal office building that overlooked the cluster of new
and nineteenth-century courthouses on Foley Square in downtown
Manhattan, walked the eight miles to the apartment on 82nd Street.
He knew that after this one last time he would never return to it
even though it had been his beloved home for years, because when
the two unknown agents had suddenly told him he was free to leave,
they had already turned on a vivid, wall-mounted video screen that
displayed, as it was happening, the burning of his lover and best
friend in a cage on the windswept Hudson River. Cam threw up in
a wastebasket. The anonymous agents in suits didn't flinch. One of
them casually said, "That's the door. Get out. We don't need your
sorry, worn-out ass anymore."

And the other agent said, "And thanks for letting us know about
the soup kitchen. It made it easy to find the Angel of Life."

When he opened the oak door to the gorgeous old-world apartment, Cam was overwhelmed by the silence, the stillness, darkness.
The wounded Oliver was in the hospital. Gabriel was dead. They
had made this home vivid and vital. It was now only a collection of
objects which he had selected and for which Gabriel had paid: the
Chesterfield sofa, the vases, the wall sconces that suffused all their
space with seductive light.

Literally uncertain how he would go about closing down this phase of his life, Cam stood in the kitchen and cried. This was grief, and he knew it. The sense of total loss and destruction. When he was a boy in the Deep South, his father, a Baptist minister who never forgave the fact that Cam was gay, often read that passage in the Gospels in which Peter, expressing his undying love for Jesus and that he would lay down his life for him, was told by Jesus that he would three times deny ever knowing him. And Peter did make that denial three times on the night Jesus was arrested. And Peter, too, had cried.

Cam saw on the rattan coffee table the pile of printed sheets with the e-mails Gabriel Hauser had exchanged with his Afghan lover. Cam saw from the way the papers were organized that Gabriel had taken time to read them all, one of the last acts of his life. As a doctor, Gabriel was a methodical man. He had separated the pages with meaningless e-mail chatter from those pages that suggested Gabriel's love and determination to bring Mohammad to the United States.

In one much smaller stack of papers, as Cam saw, Gabriel had assembled those e-mails that in any way referred to Mohammad's "cousin," Silas Nasar, and his family. Some of those e-mails had grainy, black-and-white images of Silas, images in which the evidently handsome, bearded cousin had traces of a seahorse-shaped birthmark on the left side of his face.

Cam went to the kitchen and took out one of the big, black opaque garbage bags he used for trash. He stuffed the hundreds of pages containing all the e-mails into them and neatly tied the twisted neck of the bag when it was filled. Then, because he and Gabriel were frequent travelers, particularly to Paris, Cam went to the large closet where they stored their suitcases. He opened them on the bed with the elaborate quilt on which they had so frequently made passionate or tender love, depending on their moods or needs.

Cam carefully laid in the suitcases his own newly laundered shirts and pants, socks, and underwear. Although he still suffered through gusts of grief and fear, he made certain he took nothing that belonged to Gabriel.

Once the suitcases were packed, he carried them one flight down the bannistered wooden stairwell to the apartment where Gloria and Everett Jordan lived. They were married and in their mid-thirties. Neither of them worked and they made no secret of the fact that they were both trust fund babies who spent eight months of each year at apartments they owned in London and Rome. They were friendly, open and engaging. They liked Cam and Gabriel, and left the key and the codes to their security system with Cam so that he could water their plants, replace those that had died, and just generally watch over their small, beautifully decorated New York home.

At that moment Cam had only two specific plans in mind. One was to leave his luggage in their bedroom, and the other was to return for one last time to the apartment in which he and Oliver and Gabriel had so happily lived until less than a week ago and take the doctor's prescription pad that Gabriel kept for emergencies in a drawer in the kitchen. Cam precisely and carefully tore six prescription slips from the pad.

He left the apartment with the heavy plastic bag into which he had placed all the printed pages with the e-mails Gabriel and Mohammad and Silas Nasar had written. Even on elegant East 82nd Street there were mountains of identical black plastic bags. He dropped his anonymous bag into the center of the mountain range of bags. Since most of the other bags contained a pervasive odor of the rotting of household stuff—food, diapers, all the other detritus of daily living that except for the lockdown would have been picked up virtually every day by the big white city garbage trucks—he was certain no one would ever go near the bag filled only with pages of paper.

He knew that in the city's attempt to return even to the rudiments of normalcy that the century-old, quaint pharmacy at the corner of 90th Street and Madison Avenue was open. After years of living with Gabriel he had developed, for no particular reason, a passable facsimile of his lover's handwriting, a kind of skill at draftsmanship that, when he was a little isolated boy living in the Deep South, gave him the dream of becoming an architect who would design antebellum mansions. Besides, imitating a doctor's script was not an art.

Cam prescribed thirty Vicodin. He dated the slip a week earlier. The pharmacist knew Gabriel and knew Cam, and Cam was concerned that the man might have seen or heard that Dr. Hauser had been put to death in a cage in a fire on the Hudson River just an hour earlier. The pharmacist, bald and bland and friendly, simply glanced at the script and said, "This'll take about ten minutes. You can come back or wait."

"I'll wait," Cam said. There was an old leather chair, its surface all cracked from years of use but still intact, near the front of the store. He sat in it, tremendously comforted by its all-encompassing softness and the view, through the window, of the beautiful intersection of Madison Avenue and 90th Street. He had often walked Oliver here. And he knew he would never see it again.

And there was something else that he loved during the quiet ten minutes he waited. Old pharmacies, like old hardware stores, all somehow retained the unique comforting odors they must have had a hundred years ago.

Finally, he heard George say, "It's ready, Mr. Dewar."

"Do me a favor, George, I'll pay for this in cash."

George knew Cam had insurance. "It's one hundred and twenty dollars that way. Ten dollars only with your insurance co-pay."

"It's fine, George."

He took the bottle and placed it deep in the right pocket of his pants.

Ten minutes later and fifteen blocks further downtown, he walked into one of those awful, fluorescent Duane Reade stores. He always avoided them. They had become, in his eyes, the scourge of the city, the steady conversion of Manhattan to a suburban mall. He walked past rows of paper towels, headache and sinus medicines, and beauty and makeup products to the pharmacy area. He handed a script for thirty Xanax to a beautiful Punjabi woman who was the pharmacist on duty. She asked whether the Duane Reade stores had his insurance information. He said no. He wanted to pay in cash. He had always expressed a hostility to the computerized world in which, he believed, every movement and transaction and event of his life could be instantaneously tracked. Cash was not only the coin of the realm. For him it was the coin of anonymity.

Cam handed her the one hundred and forty dollars for the Xanax bottle. He stuffed the brown circular bottle deep into his left pocket. He felt fortified now: that he had the ability to choose between life and death. When he was a boy his father, the Baptist pastor, had a large plaque in the kitchen. It contained the words from Deuteronomy in which God says each morning, "I put before thee life and death, blessings and curses. Choose life."

Cam took an hour to walk to the homeless shelter near Tompkins Square Park which he quickly disclosed, when asked, as a place where Gabriel might be. It was one of the very few places in Manhattan where Gabriel Hauser regularly went—the hospital, the Boat House in Central Park, the Angelika Theater and the Film Forum, both on West Houston Street, the Three Lives Book Store at the quiet intersection where, oddly enough, Waverly Place intersected with Waverly Place. But, Cam had told the agents, given the state of the city, the homeless shelter and the chaos and pain, the shelter was the most likely place where Gabriel would be.

The big basement room in the old church wasn't crowded. It was getting dark. Some of the ceiling lights were already on. As Cam knew from his sometime visits with Gabriel, the huge basement room was usually dark even on the brightest days.

The only sounds were the sounds children made—cries, laughter, chatter. He'd never had much tolerance for children. He'd never regretted for a minute that he had never and would never have kids—his father had once thundered that it was God's will that men have and raise and nurture the young.

The adults in the room for the most part were quiet and seated on the cots. Only half the cots were occupied. Everyone was alone, except for the mothers of the noisy kids.

Something else Cam had never imagined was that he'd lie down in one of the cots. Gabriel had told him the cots—the steel frames, the mattresses and the sheets, blankets and pillows were clean, although sometimes torn. Cam knew that Gabriel often used his own money to replace the torn bedding.

In the kitchen, as big and clean and orderly as it always was between mealtimes, Cam found on the scrubbed steel counter one of those tall amber-colored plastic glasses that New York City diners used. He filled it with water. He carried it to what appeared to be the darkest area of the big basement. No one spoke to him. He carried nothing but the brimming glass of water. He realized that to anyone who saw him he must have had the look of one of those stranded suburbanites who had literally been locked in the island of Manhattan for more than three days and had finally decided to use one of the long-established homeless shelters rather than the makeshift encampments in the city parks. Those were now out of control with garbage, overloaded mobile latrines, every imaginable type of debris.

Cam found the cot, its blanket, pillow, and sheets clean—one of the cots that Gabriel, just hours earlier, had cleaned.

The corner of the church's vast basement was cool and comfortable even on a hot evening. There was no one in the nearby cots. As he lay quietly on his back, with his wrists and hands under his head, he recalled for the first time in many years words his stentorian father had frequently quoted from John's Gospel in which Jesus said, *I have the power to keep my life and to lay down my life.*

So do we all, Cam thought, nothing unique about Jesus in that or anyone else. *We all have that power.*

Somewhat furtively, Cam sat up on his cot although he knew no one in this place could care what he did or didn't do. He shook from the brown prescription bottle fifteen of the Vicodin tablets into his right palm and from the other bottle fifteen of the pills. Then he took up from the floor next to his cot the big glass of water and in twenty seconds swallowed all thirty pills.

*   *   *

Nothing in his life had ever granted him such bliss for the few minutes he stretched out on his cot. *I chose death*, he said in a whisper, *not life. The right choice, my choice, unlike Gabriel, who was not blessed with the choice.*

Cam had the sense that he was afloat on his back in a warm, only slightly undulating ocean. And finally, still on his back in that ocean, he drifted below the surface of the benign and all-enveloping water.

CHAPTER FORTY-FOUR

JUDGE HARLAN LAZARUS was waiting alone for Andrew Carter in the ancient basement of Gracie Mansion, over two hundred years old and unchanged in all that time, and rose to his feet as Carter, alone, stepped down the creaking wooden stairwell. Carter, with the aid of his speechwriters who were in the Executive Office Building in Washington and linked to him by a large video screen, had finished preparing a five-minute speech that was to be broadcast around the world. He had just been told by one of the Secret Service agents that the director of Homeland Security had "absolutely vital information" he needed to give the president before he demonstrated to the world that he was unharmed and still completely in charge of the freeing of Manhattan and the defeat of the ISIS onslaught. "The judge," the agent had said without a trace of irony, "is alone in the basement. And the basement is completely secure, a medieval fortress."

There was only a single unshaded 75-watt bulb in the basement. It had the odor of old cold stone. Lazarus looked liked a spectre as he emerged from the semidarkness to the foot of the stairwell. Carter waited for him. Even under the light bulb, Lazarus' face looked like a death mask.

"So what is it now?" Carter, annoyed and somewhat apprehensive, asked.

"Two assistant U.S. attorneys and some of my agents just had a long, tell-all interview with Tony Garafalo. They have enough information now to go in front of a grand jury and have Gina Carbone and Roland Fortune indicted today."

"Why," Carter asked, "would I let that happen?"

"Because justice is important."

"What the hell are you talking about?"

"Mr. President, the police commissioner of the largest city in the country has been having a two-year affair with a serious mobster. And that commissioner has since Sunday been engaged in secret arrests. And she has for years developed a cadre of what, in effect, are mercenaries, some of them once Blackwater mercenaries, and put them on the NYPD payroll as community liaison officers whose only real work has been to illegally, without warrants or court approval, put wiretaps and secret surveillance devices on people her mercenaries believe are security risks, people, by the way, who as I've just had my experts check, are not on any suspicious persons list—in my department, the CIA, or the NSA. She had a high-tech, off-the-books detention facility built on what, in effect, is a camouflaged and abandoned pier. And she has told all this to a mobster who has been her lover for several years. They were together as recently as last night. And it is obvious to us that her unusual confidante passed this information along to an investigative reporter for the *New York Times*. And that this lifelong gangster shot that reporter to death last night."

"And you are telling me this," Andrew Carter asked, "for what reason?"

Lazarus, who from the skeletal sockets in which his eyes were deeply set, looked at the president with the same skepticism and contempt with which he had glared at Ivy League law students when they had given him the wrong answer. He said, "Mr. President, she's the hub of the wheel of a kidnapping and murder syndicate. At a minimum, a grand jury in two hours could, given what Garafalo has confessed to two experienced assistant U.S. attorneys and several seasoned federal law enforcement agents, indict her for these things, and she could then be arrested on that indictment in fifteen minutes."

"Judge, do you have any idea how fundamentally off base you are?" Carter stared at him. "And what is this about indicting the mayor? Where did you get that idea? Is it against the law to be so good-looking?"

"Mr. President, the mayor is a drug addict. Garafalo on his cell phone had dozens of YouTube-style films secretly taken by Fortune's security detail of Fortune taking and paying for deliveries of banned opiate substances from known drug dealers during all the years he has been in office. The security detail gave the live recordings to Carbone, to whom the detail members are extraordinarily loyal. The recordings were transferred to her cell phone. She either transferred them to Garafalo for the love of the game—maybe they learned those kinds of games when they were kids in the same neighborhood on Staten Island long before Steve Jobs gave the world cell phones— or he just roamed through her cell phone for the fun of it when she was sleeping. Whatever the way, he has the images. And now I do."

Lazarus removed his iPhone from the internal pocket of the loose fitting suit he wore and held it up before the president. Lazarus said, "They're both criminals. She has no respect for the Constitution. And she spends all of her spare time with Garafalo, who is a walking crime wave. And the mayor has enough banned substances to open a warehouse."

Andrew Carter reached out and took Lazarus' cell phone from him. Lazarus said, "I'll cue up some more of the images for you. You can see for yourself."

And then Carter deliberately let Lazarus' cell phone drop from his hand. It hit the old stone of the basement floor, which was cobbled together two centuries ago. The phone was intact. Thinking that Carter had inadvertently lost his grip on the sleek silver object, Lazarus, in an uncommon gesture of cooperation, began to lean over to pick up the phone.

And it was then that the heel of Andrew Carter's two-thousand-dollar shoes covered Lazarus' cell phone and ground it into splinters.

"Here is what you'll do, Judge, beginning immediately. *First*, if a grand jury is already sitting, disband it. Make sure if it is sitting that all of the people on it are told to disregard whatever they've heard so far and have them reminded that grand jurors are bound by law to total secrecy. If they've heard anything at all from the government lawyers or the agents they will be indicted themselves if they repeat anything they heard.

"*Second*, if any of the government lawyers have any of the tapes that were on this phone they are to turn them over to your people immediately and then your people are to bring them to my Secret Service agents. I will tell my agents to give me any of those devices."

Lazarus was utterly motionless, like a medical school skeleton suspended in midair. He didn't say a word.

"*Finally*, and most important, you are to fly back to Washington and stay in that little bachelor apartment you have in Anacostia and not leave it until I tell you to, and at that point I'll have my press secretary announce I've received your resignation and accepted it with deep regret. And you will remember forever that before you took the job you signed an agreement *never* to write about or speak about anything you ever learned while serving as Director of Homeland Security. If you do I'll have *you* indicted, since you seem to get such pleasure from indictments."

Carter turned and began walking up the creaking stairs. "And don't ever let me see your face or hear your voice again."

CHAPTER FORTY-FIVE

THERE WAS NO need for Gina Carbone and Roger Davidson to speak again since they had many times, in the isolation of her office at One Police Plaza, spoken about strategies to follow depending on how what they called "war games" developed. One of the endgames had now happened in the Holland Tunnel. This was one of the possible scenarios they had discussed. They had known that if they ever had to seize the men on the hit list it might be necessary to move them from Pier 37 to another secure location. One of those was the never-used labyrinth, built in the Depression, that connected the tunnel to the huge, eerie complex that was designed as a "safe" place in the event of a disaster in the tunnel. Davidson and his crew had taken the prisoners in sealed NYPD vans to the tunnel complex as soon as Davidson learned that Harlan Lazarus had ordered a cadre of Homeland Security agents to invade and search Pier 37.

Gina had given Davidson—a name she knew was not his real one although she knew everything about his background from the time he first landed as a United States advisor in Afghanistan to train local Afghan fighters during the failed Soviet invasion in the 1980s—the power to use Plan A, Plan B, or Plan C of Code Apache. He was to decide when the end game had been reached and that there was no longer a need for the eighteen or so men on the hit list who had been taken down in the immediate aftermath of the first bombings at the Met.

Plan A was simply to return the men to the small houses and apartments where they had been when they were seized in the first hours of Code Apache. Of course the men would be likely to speak out if Davidson put Plan A in place, but he and the commissioner were certain no one would believe or care about their stories.

Plan B was to bring them into the standard criminal justice system, booking them at several different precincts in Manhattan, as if they had been separately arrested on weapons charges, putting them in holding cells, and then several hours later bringing them in front of different judges for arraignment; they would all be denied bail and then held in separate cells at the sprawling Rikers Island prison complex. And, Gina and Davidson also agreed, no one would believe their stories.

But both of them tacitly knew Davidson would opt for Plan C, the "Charlie plan." And that when the Charlie plan ended Davidson and his corps of ten men whom he had recruited over the last two years and the only men, all with fake names, who knew the essence of Code Apache's details, would themselves just disappear to different places around the planet.

* * *

Plan C began as soon as Gabriel Hauser became a black, utterly misshapen skeleton at the bottom of the cage in glimmering light over the Hudson River. Davidson addressed the members of his team who had been with him on the roof of the blockhouse, the men who had filmed Mohammad speaking and then Gabriel Houser in flames. "Throw the equipment into the river and let's get downstairs fast. Keep the masks on." More gently he told Mohammad, "Good work. Come down with us."

They raced down the iron stairwell, ripping off their black masks now that they were out of the sight of the outside world. On the factory-like floor of the blockhouse the prisoners were still in clusters of five or six, each cluster guarded by other members of Davidson's crew armed with M-16s and various German-manufactured pistols. "Let's get them all back in the tunnel," Davidson ordered. The sullen men moved, some of them reluctantly, responding to the commands of the three men in his group who spoke Arabic.

Once inside the tunnel the prisoners were again separated into small groups spaced about thirty feet from one another. "This," Davidson said, "is Plan C. Let's get it on."

At those words from Davidson, volleys of rifle and pistol shots resonated through the inside of the tunnel. Davidson, too, was shooting. He and all of his team wore bulletproof vests and lay prone on the tunnel's floor to minimize the risks of ricocheting bullets. Within thirty seconds all eighteen men who had been on the hit list were riddled with bullet holes. All were dead. Mohammed, too, was dead.

Davidson's men then took out of the sealed vans the hidden supplies of ISIS-style weapons, primarily AK-47 rifles and Ruger pistols. They placed those weapons and spent bullet casings from them in the inert hands and near the bodies of the dead. As his people worked methodically through the well-rehearsed ruse of Plan C, Davidson ran down the corridor through which he had, less than forty-five minutes earlier, calmly walked with Gabriel Hauser. At that time Davidson had known exactly what would happen to Hauser.

Davidson walked deliberately to Silas Nasar's body. He shot Nasar seven times. Wearing plastic gloves, Davidson put the Russian-made AK-47 in Nasar's right hand.

All that remained of Plan C was for the man known as Roger

Davidson to disappear, to slip into anonymity. He was in the back of one of the windowless vans when it emerged from the Holland Tunnel. He was in plainclothes. All of his other special team members were in the uniform and helmets of the NYPD Counterterrorism Unit.

No one on Canal Street, that southern border of Chinatown now teeming with oblivious Chinese immigrants, noticed Roger Davidson as he stepped quickly from the rear door of the van.

* * *

Andrew Carter stood in his exquisitely tailored suit in the middle of the stage in the small press room in Gracie Mansion. The stage was covered in black carpet, and behind him was a big, vivid American flag. He had rejected the idea of standing behind a podium with the presidential seal or a desk with the seal. He was now perfectly composed, convinced that the simple act of standing would convey better to the world that he was well and unhurt by the horrific explosion on First Avenue. And he had no notes and no prompters. A tiny microphone was attached to his lapel. Reporters were excluded from the room, just as they had been excluded from the mansion itself.

The president began, "As you can see, I am alive and well. I came here to see for myself the condition of this largest and most important urban center in the United States.

"Obviously the route of my travel was discovered by the ever-contracting remnants of the people who have been attempting to carry out a reign of terror here. Because of my presence, the brave men and women who traveled with me were the targets of yet another cowardly attack. But it was a desperate one, a man and a woman strapped with explosives. One was killed by a highly skilled sharpshooter. That was the woman. The man, too, was shot at the same time by another sharpshooter, but unfortunately the massive amount of explosives strapped to his body detonated. The cowardliness of this attack is demonstrated by the fact that he had placed himself next to a playground.

"My heart goes out to the brave men and women on motorcycles who accompanied me on this trip. Five of them are dead. The sixth is in a nearby hospital, where her condition is critical, but she is expected to survive her wounds. I know well all of these brave people. They protected me and the office I hold for years. More important, they were my friends.

"At the same time, my deepest sympathies are with the children and their parents, all of them totally innocent, who were trying to bring this city to its vital normalcy. We will soon release the count of the dead and wounded in the playground."

Andrew Carter as he spoke moved slightly with the grace he had learned as a college and professional basketball player. They were slight movements, but fluid, natural. It was a Steve Jobs performance, unadorned, confident, and direct. He intended the movements to reveal that nothing had harmed him, that he was healthy and intact. "There is positive news. Thanks to the efforts of United States Homeland Security agents, thousands of brave United States soldiers, and the heroic counterterrorism tactics of the New York City Police Department, the tide has immensely and successfully turned against these terrorists. They have been weakened immeasurably, and, as to the few who are left, we know where they are and are hunting them down. They will soon pose no threat.

"Along with Mayor Roland Fortune, we will soon announce that this essential, and successful, lockdown of Manhattan is coming to an end. The mayor, although severely injured during the first explosions, has led this city through this crisis with his characteristic charisma and care."

Andrew Carter paused. "Thousands of brave men and women have met and thwarted these attacks. Much of the credit for that goes to Gina Carbone, the commissioner of the police department of this great city."

CHAPTER FORTY-SIX

THE METROPOLITAN DETENTION Center was a surprisingly small building with a brown brick exterior. The MDC was built in the 1970s and it was anonymous, with no signs announcing its name or purpose. Only its narrow and widely spaced windows with wire meshing suggested from the outside that it might be a prison.

Internally it was an extraordinary building. Its official purpose as a prison was to act as a short-term and secure facility for three hundred men and as many as fifty women who were federal prisoners and who, because a judge had determined that they posed a risk of danger or a threat of flight, were denied bail. Anyone who was in MDC was not guilty; men and women were held there, often for months, because they had been indicted on serious federal crimes and not released on any form of bail while waiting for their trials.

MDC was attached by an intricate series of tunnels, suspended walkways and other outwardly invisible avenues to the three closely adjacent federal courthouses and to the adjoining building, the office of the United States attorney for the southern district of New York, so that the prisoners could easily and secretly be moved to the courthouses for appearances before judges or trials. As soon as a person was convicted, he or she was bundled out of the MDC and sent to one of the more than seventy regular prisons around the country that kept the thousands of people convicted of federal felonies.

There were traditional conference rooms in the MDC where lawyers could meet with their inmate clients. They were not comfortable rooms but they were well-known to the lawyers who used them. But there were a few other, entirely unknown rooms, even more medieval than the rest of the prison. They were known as the "rubber hose rooms" and only a few of the federal marshals who ruled MDC knew where they were. They were only the size of large closets.

And they were nothing like the more conventional conference rooms in the adjoining, far more comfortable U.S. Attorney's office where Tony Garafalo had one day earlier met with the two government lawyers and the six or seven bemused federal agents. Instead, in this secret room, Tony Garafalo stood against one of the walls, his hands and feet shackled to the wall.

He waited in the almost total darkness for two minutes. Nothing like this, not even several weeks in solitary confinement at the Supermax prison in Colorado, had ever happened to him. And, in these two minutes, probably for the first time in his life, he felt fear.

Tony heard the three iron locks to the door slide in quick intervals from left to right. Gina Carbone entered the cell. He knew that only because for the briefest moment her tall shape formed a black silhouette against the empty dim hallway. She slid the iron door closed.

Gina turned on the small halogen flashlight she carried. She trained the beam, which was as bright as the sun, into his eyes.

Tony said, "Hey, babe, didn't know you were into S and M."

"Once a wiseass always a wiseass."

"You talk too much."

"Think so? I never said a word to you about my company business," she answered. "Somehow you got into my cell phone and computer. Where did they teach you to get to be a computer genius? Not at Supermax, right?"

"You gonna unlock me from this shit? It is unconstitutional. Right there in the Eighth Amendment. No cruel and unusual punishment."

"Now you're Alan Dershowitz?"

"At least stop shining that friggin' light in my face."

"Don't worry. You're still as good looking as ever."

She kept the intense, single focus beam on his face. "You didn't get away with it, you know?"

"I did, and you know it, babe, and you know why."

"I have great forensics people. You're too stupid to know that. They're issuing a report to the world that the tape the little Indian put out was a forgery. He spliced it all together. It was phony—like you. You know those Indians? And those Indians, unlike a cheap bum like you, are geniuses when it comes to tech stuff."

"You're dreaming this all up, babe."

"And the Indian reporter never laid eyes on Gabriel Hauser in his life. The guy on the bench was one of my people, a great actor and look-alike of a guy, the Angel of Life, Mr. Gandhi had only seen on TV."

Garafalo laughed.

Gina Carbone laughed, too, the sardonic laugh, the mocking chuckle she had learned from her Gambino family uncle. It was, Tony realized, the chuckle he'd learned when an order was given from a family consigliere to do bad things to someone. This was the first time in his life he felt, and knew he felt, real fear.

"Babe," he said, "we've fucked in a lot of different places. How about here? Nobody's looking."

"And those agents you talked to yesterday. Never happened. You know the drill. You never left your cell. Not yesterday, not today."

"You know, Gina, you were always a crazy broad. I'm going to keep on talking. Maybe I'll write a book. Make a million bucks."

"With your heart condition? I don't think so."

Tony closed his eyes. But the membranes that were his eyelids could not stop the glare. "What the fuck are you talking about?"

"Don't tell me all those good doctors at Supermax didn't have all those long talks with you about how your heart valves were shot to hell? How they told you they would have you flown to that prison hospital in Texas for surgery to replace the valves? I just had all their reports e-mailed to me. I felt real bad for you. I never knew anything was wrong."

"Gina, you're full of shit. That fucking Usain Bolt guy wishes he had my heart."

"That's what you kept on telling the doctors. You said, and it's in their notes, that you had the heart of Usain Bolt."

"You should know that. I could pump you for two hours easy without breaking a sweat."

"I got the notes, Tony. They're the only notes, all copies are deleted." She paused and turned off the intense flashlight. "You won't be the first fifty-four-year-old inmate to die in the federal prison system of a heart attack. You were always a stubborn Wop who thought he knew everything."

* * *

Two hours later, in the solitary confinement cell where John Gotti and other celebrity prisoners were held while awaiting trial, Tony Garafalo was dead of a heart attack. There was nothing the two new prison doctors could do to save him.

CHAPTER FORTY-SEVEN

"I HAVE AN important announcement," Gina Carbone, dressed in her customary black pants and shirt on which the traditional patch of the New York City Police Department was sewn with only the word commissioner on it to differentiate her from the 40,000 other cops who wore the patch, stood at the simple wooden podium in the small press room at One Police Plaza.

"We believe that we have eliminated, either through capture or deaths in firefights, all the significant terrorists who through the last several days created as much chaos and death as they could.

"Within the last half hour elite and courageous members of the NYPD have killed as many as eighteen of the fanatical jihadists who somehow gained access to the Holland Tunnel. These were the people who, in a despicable display of cowardice, burned to death Dr. Gabriel Hauser in a cage on top of the building that for years has served as the most visible part of the ventilation and emergency escape route of the tunnel.

"To anticipate a question one of you is likely to ask, and I will take some questions, we do not at this moment know when and how these eighteen members of what we believe to be ISIS gained access to the tunnel's interior system. There is some evidence that they were members of a sleeper cell that in the three days before the attacks began had steadily gained access to the intricate and very large and almost never used or patrolled ventilation and escape system."

Deftly, Gina adjusted the slender and flexible microphone. "We do not yet know why ISIS selected Dr. Hauser for this horrible display. In fact, to be completely direct, we are investigating how Dr. Hauser came to be in the tunnel in the first place. His presence may have been voluntary. It may have been involuntary. Let me say this as well. Although the doctor was originally praised for his courage, we have, as you know, developed and are investigating his possible involvement in the planning or prearrangement of the attacks. And his familiarity with some of the people who participated. All of this, of course, is not meant to detract from the horror of his murder."

She stared into the camera's glowing orange eye. "More important than anything else I've said is this: the president and the mayor will soon lead a march over one of the city's bridges. Traffic will begin to flow into and out of Manhattan, all in an orderly way. No one will be hurt, no one injured. The lockdown which has inconvenienced so many of you has been a success. As difficult as it has been, the people of this city have sustained this hardship and it has allowed us to hunt down, isolate, and incapacitate murderers. Within hours the streets in all parts of the city will be clean, traffic will flow, bars and restaurants will be open, as will schools, hospitals, all those things that have made this city the vital center of the world.

"But for a time, and it will be a time that the president and the mayor will decide with me and my people's assistance, there will be soldiers and armed NYPD officers on the streets and in the subways and in almost every public space. If a person means no harm, there will be no harm to you or to him or her. We are not vigilantes, we are not racists, we do not profile people because of their ethnic or religious status. We are law enforcement officers. But if you do mean harm, you will be stopped by any means necessary."

CHAPTER FORTY-EIGHT

IN ALL HIS forty-seven years of living in the Bronx and Manhattan, Roland Fortune had never walked on the Triboro Bridge. In the past, as he drove either on his own or, more recently, surrounded by black SUV police vehicles for his protection, he had always gazed out the window at the immense view of the island of Manhattan, that Emerald City, and its extraordinary skyline, as extraordinary in daylight or at night, in rain, fog, snow, or clear sunshine.

And in the three years he had lived in Gracie Mansion, with its unobstructed view of the bridge's almost two mile long expanse, it had taken on an almost totemic significance for him, from the sunrises that seemed to originate from and through and under the bridge's structure as he sat quietly for a few minutes on the flagstone outdoor patio to the nighttime views when thousands of lights etched the bridge's fantastical curved outline.

Today, toward the center of the bridge with only the president of the United States, the day at noon was awash with full sunshine, as it had been since Sunday. Both Andrew Carter and Roland Fortune were in business suits. Carter wore a colorful tie. Roland's white shirt was unbuttoned at the neck.

Behind them, at a distance of thirty feet, were the symbols and objects of America's awesome military power, tanks, armored personnel carriers, unsmiling Marines in full battle gear. On the long, bridge-spanning walkways that Roland had never seen anyone use, rows of New York City police officers, also completely armed, stood like the Praetorian Guard. Helicopters were suspended in midair over, above, below and at the sides of the bridge. The East River waters were dazzling.

Fifteen feet ahead of the handsome WASP president and the equally handsome Hispanic mayor as they waved, smiled, and nodded were the five television vehicles with cameras broadcasting to billions of people this scene of two jubilant and confident men walking across the major bridge that linked Manhattan to Queens and to the rest of the world. Behind the television vans and their cameras was another dense phalanx of armor and soldiers. The surface of the bridge quaked slightly beneath the feet of the two smiling men as they waved at the cameras.

On the inbound side of the bridge leading into Manhattan was an endless stream of empty white city garbage trucks. All of them had been inspected for explosives and cleared. Not a single Arabic man or crew member was in the trucks. The mayor and the president had decided hours earlier that the first and most important steps in the restoration of the stricken city was to remove the mountains of black garbage bags and strange, often inexplicable other debris that had filled the sidewalks for days.

CHAPTER FORTY-NINE

JOHN HEWITT-GORDAN, WHO had arrived on the second flight
into the reopened LaGuardia, was driven in one of the mayor's
unmarked, all-black SUVs over the same bridge that the president
and the mayor had crossed two days earlier. But the retired British
major didn't glance out of the window as the SUV made the long
and curving sweep on the upper roadway from the dreary Queens
neighborhoods to the view of the celestial city.

Today there were mist and rain for the first time in more than
a week. But, even in the midday gloom, the eastern skyline of
Manhattan was still visible.

His thirty-year career in Her Majesty's Army had brought him to
the city only three times. The utilitarian and homely Twin Towers
of the World Trade Center were still standing then, and his beloved
Sarah had been studying at Cambridge.

Instead, as this over-powered vehicle Roland Fortune had insisted on providing him sped over the wide surfaces of the renovated bridge, John absentmindedly thumbed through worn copies
of popular magazines that had accumulated in the elastic pouches
along the sides of the rear doors. Utterly coincidentally, he picked
up a worn copy of *People*, a magazine at which he had never once
glanced before. The frequently thumbed pages were flexible and
dirty, almost distasteful.

He was about to slip it back into the elasticized pouch at the moment he saw a large picture of Sarah Gordan-Hewitt and Mayor

Roland Fortune. They were radiant, life infused, in evening dress. Never, he thought, had his daughter, this flesh of his flesh, looked so beautiful, a woman obviously in love with the man holding her hand, and with life, with all the years she was entitled to believe she had before her.

The SUV didn't make the customary turn to the left as it approached the Manhattan side of the long bridge beyond the tollbooths. Instead, it took the direction to East 125th Street, to the heart of East Harlem, and as it sped down that wide street to the West Side, its sirens began to blare and its police cruiser lights flashed. Other traffic stopped. The mountainous bags of garbage had already been removed from the sidewalks. The loud, light-flashing SUV did not stop at any of the red lights. At the end of West 125th Street it turned onto the West Side Highway and sped downtown.

Given all he had heard over the last several days on the BBC, John Hewitt-Gordan expected to see a scarred city. So far, to the extent he sometimes stared out of the tinted windows, the city was unmarked, unharmed, intact. To his right the Hudson River flowed gently seaward, to New York Harbor, as it had done for thousands of years. To his left were the staid, monumental buildings lining Riverside Drive.

The van exited the West Side Highway at West 14th Street. The closed, steadily deteriorating St. Vincent's Hospital was only five minutes from the exit. Standing on a concrete platform, just as he had promised, was Roland Fortune.

As soon as the van's door was opened for him, John Hewitt-Gordan, agile and graceful, stepped out effortlessly even though he was nearly seventy. He embraced Roland, the first time this had happened instead of their customary and formal handshake.

John asked, "Can we see her?"

"She's inside."

Together they walked through the white industrial doors that had once served for deliveries to the now decaying hospital. The big room was far cooler than it had been when Roland was brought there a day after the first explosion, when the rows of bodies lay under blue tarpaulins. Now, although the warehouse room still served as a temporary morgue, the rows of the dead were in identical silver caskets. Roland noticed that the space was cooler, and he noticed too that the unique, unmistakable odor of rotting human flesh had largely dissipated, although it was still there in traces.

"My God," John whispered, "how many people have died?"

"More than fifteen hundred. This is one of at least thirty temporary morgues."

"Where is my daughter, Roland?"

The huge black nurse who had first taken him to Sarah, and who had warned him not to pull back the tarpaulin to look at her, was still there. Roland wondered how many breaks the dedicated man had taken in the last four days.

Someone had alerted the nurse to the fact that the mayor was returning. Just as a few days earlier when there were no names on the tarps but only seemingly random combinations of numbers and letters, today the metal coffins also were marked with letter and number combinations. Only in the last twenty-four hours after the lifting of Manhattan's siege had dental and DNA samples been brought to the city from all over the country and the world so that the long process of identifying the unknown dead could start.

But the immense nurse, the man with earrings and tattoos who could just as easily have been a boxer or a wrestler rather than a caregiver, stood patiently in one place. Roland knew it was the area where Sarah had been laid out days earlier on the damp concrete floor. He was certain that the nurse stood at the aluminum casket that contained her body.

For the first time ever, John Hewitt-Gordan looked suddenly distracted and old as the moment of seeing Sarah approached. He followed while Roland walked deliberately to the immobile nurse. John glanced up at the industrial-style ceiling. Naked light bulbs without even metallic shades hung from the ceiling. Along one wall was a row of seven forklifts designed to carry the caskets. As a one-time commander of a supply battalion in the British Army, he knew how to drive the ungainly machines.

And then he was brought back from his mental world of pure disbelief when he heard the nurse say, in a Bronx accent totally new to him, "This is the one you're looking for, Mayor."

The top of the silver coffin bore the large handwritten words, in black magic marker, "Sarah Hewitt Gordan."

Standing over the coffin, John said, "That's not how her name is spelled."

Roland said, "It is, John, for these people."

"The hyphen. The hyphen is missing."

The nurse, saying nothing, rolled his eyes up to the ceiling. He knew from ten years of this work that the living often refused to believe in the deaths of children, husbands, wives, or lovers even when the inert bodies lay in front of them.

"Roland, may we ask to have the lid raised?"

"John, it's Sarah. Trust me. I saw her myself. This wonderful nurse was with me."

"How long ago was that?" John asked. "Wasn't it four or five days ago when we spoke? Mistakes can be made."

"I don't remember exactly, John. I've been too confused to count days. I do know that the woman in this casket is Sarah. This nurse warned me not to look at her. But I did. It was not a good idea even then, days ago."

"Let me see this person." There was the steely edge of the voice of command Major John Hewitt-Gordan must have used thousands of times in his long career.

The nurse spoke to the mayor, "Like I said before, that ain't a good idea."

Roland said simply, "Open it."

The nurse leaned forward and snapped open the two steel latches that held in place the upper half of the casket lid, which he raised. As soon as he did, an overpowering odor of dead flesh rose from the box, so powerful that it was almost palpable. Roland put his hand over his nose and mouth; he gagged.

John Hewitt-Gordan stared into the casket. He didn't flinch. Almost involuntarily, Roland, too, glanced inside, and immediately regretted it, searing into his memory a vision he knew he would never forget. Death had worked its terrible magic swiftly. Dozens of lines had formed over Sarah's upper lip, which were drawn down over her upper teeth. Her open eyes seemed to have disappeared. Her hair looked like straw. Her skin color was an unnatural white. A death mask.

Roland looked away. The nurse simply waited, holding the lid open for as long as John wanted. Then John finally said, "Thank you."

The nurse lowered the lid.

* * *

Roland Fortune and John Hewitt-Gordan stood on the cracked cement loading platform. The mist and fog had now turned to rain. There was a tin roof, with many rusted fissures, above them. They managed to stay dry. On the sidewalk near the loading dock were five unmarked black SUVs, including the one that had brought John here from LaGuardia.

Roland said to the suddenly frail man, "I have you scheduled for the nine p.m. Flight 767 on British Airways to London. Sarah's coffin will soon be taken to LaGuardia for that same flight tonight."

"Thank you," John said. He wasn't moving. The rain droned on the tin roof. Finally, he said, "I had hoped, Roland, that one day you would be my son."

"I am your son," Roland Fortune said.

They stared at each other. Without touching or embracing, they both cried, quietly, their faces contorted.

CHAPTER FIFTY

AT SIX THAT night, in much steadier rain that made the early summer day prematurely dark, like a century-old Stieglitz photograph of Manhattan, Irv Rothstein said, "No one will worry about not seeing you, Mr. Mayor, in the next thirty-six hours."

They were in an unmarked police van driving to the same heliport at the UN building where President Andrew Carter had landed and from which he had already left for Washington hours earlier. "I'm still not sure," Roland answered, "that this is the right thing to do."

"I hate to burst your bubble, Mr. Mayor, but no one in Manhattan or the world will give a shit that New York City's mayor has gone quiet for a day and a half. Bloomberg used to fly to his island in the Caribbean every weekend, come hell or high water, and nobody complained. Besides, the public is overloaded with you. It's natural, as we've announced, that the mayor of the City of New York, wounded as he was in the first minutes of the attack before bravely ignoring his injuries, brought the city back to life. The dancing clubs are packed, the movie theaters are open. Nobody can even make a restaurant reservation because they're filled. Gina Carbone has everyone's back covered, and a grateful president has said you and the commissioner will be given special Presidential Medals of Honor soon. So it makes all the sense in the world that for the next thirty-six hours the mayor, with a team of doctors, is resting quietly, healing."

Irv smiled, relishing as always his role as comedian, court jester, and the wizard of public relations. "And," he said, "it's never good to disappoint Carolina. She made us promise."

Carolina Geary was the chairman of Goldman Sachs. She had early on in her rapidly expanding career recognized Sarah's talents and was her "godmother" at the firm. Carolina, the first woman to lead Goldman Sachs, was all business. She had twice met Sarah's boyfriend, the mayor of New York City. Geary had been at her estate in East Hampton when the first explosions at the Met detonated, and she had stayed in East Hampton. When the siege was lifted, one of her key assistants contacted Irv Rothstein and said Carolina would have her private helicopter fly Roland directly to the secluded, oceanfront estate for a day or two of rest.

At first, Roland had hesitated. "Irv," he had said, "I'm no Bloomberg. I barely know Carolina. And how will it look if the mayor of the City of New York, with all this shit going on, suddenly decides it's time for a vacation getaway?"

But Roland relented. "Let's go," he said.

The interior of the Goldman Sachs corporate helicopter resembled one of those immensely expensive entertainment rooms that people with enormous wealth built into their Fifth Avenue and Park Avenue apartments; plush seating, an ultramodern television screen, even two nineteenth-century Impressionist paintings. There were two pilots who didn't know that the chief passenger they were carrying for the one hour flight was Roland Fortune. The three flight attendants were long-term employees of Goldman Sachs who, given their salaries and the rules of the firm, had for years learned the artistry of complete secrecy, a kind of corporate *omertà*.

It was already dark when the helicopter rose from the UN heliport and, in the rain, flew southward over the East River. Roland was in a seat next to a large window. Because of the tilt of the helicopter as it gained altitude, he was able to see, even through the shroud of rain and mist, the sights that were so profoundly familiar to him: the southern end of Roosevelt Island where the broken, eerie, nineteenth-century, long-abandoned insane asylum was; the stone outcropping in the middle of the East River on which was placed the powerful lighthouse that warned the river traffic; and the heights of the now heavily traveled Williamsburg, Manhattan, and Brooklyn Bridges. Dimly, too, he could see through the rain and fog the millions of lights that filled the Manhattan skyline.

The helicopter's flight path was to reach the Verrazano Narrows Bridge between Brooklyn and Staten Island and then abruptly turn left to fly over the edge of the ocean on an almost straight course along the south shore of Long Island to Carolina's estate in East Hampton.

Spread out below him were the rigid grids of light from the myriad small homes in Brooklyn and Queens, as well as full views of LaGuardia to the north and the larger terrain of JFK airport to the south. And, of course, there was the vast blackness of the Atlantic Ocean. There were ships at sea, with their toy-like lights; freighters, Naval and Coast Guard ships, pleasure boats. It seemed there were hundreds of freighters for ten to twenty miles near New York Harbor, backed up and immobilized during the days and nights before the lifting of the lockdown.

When Roland checked the time, he realized that, if it was on schedule, British Airways Flight 767 at LaGuardia, with the body of Sarah Hewitt-Gordan in the cargo compartment, was about to leave or was already airborne. He thought of the usually stoic John Hewitt-Gordan, who had once to Roland appeared to be a caricature of a British officer, on the same plane. Now, Roland thought, he and they might be in the air at the same time flying east, with

John in the first-class compartment and Sarah's casket in the baggage area in the British Airways plane and Roland in a powerful helicopter. Just as the ocean was filled with the lights of hundreds of vessels, so, too, the sky was filled with the twinkling lights of many aircraft suddenly freed from the lockdown.

* * *

Fire Island, a fragile enclave of land that somehow had survived millennia of geological change which had submerged hundreds of other similar land masses off the south coast of Long Island, glimmered below the helicopter. He knew the island well and quietly gazed out at its peaceful outlines. The summer season had just started, the parties were under way, men were meeting men, women were joining women, and young men and women were coming together, too. To them, the siege of Manhattan must have been a riveting nightmare, but it was over now, and now was the time to party.

Just as the sight of Fire Island receded, Roland heard the pilot's voice. It was a startled command, "Look at that."

Ten miles away and fifteen thousand feet higher, a fireball like an exploding star illuminated the sea. In the vivid light, the waves resembled molten lead, suddenly frozen.

The object in the sky that created the spectacular glare was a British Airways Airbus. Roland watched as one of its immense wings, all enflamed, detached itself from the body of the plane that, although it was now gradually descending toward the ocean, continued its forward motion on its powerful momentum. Irregular fragments of the plane spun away, all in flames.

What a sight, Roland thought. *This can't be real.* And then he was jarred into reality as the calm pilot said, "Traffic control wants to know if any of you saw a rocket or an object hit that plane."

No one answered. The Airbus had just been one of the many planes in the air, in the beauty of the immense night as they flew above the low-lying cloud cover. Roland had certainly seen nothing rise to or toward the Airbus. It was only when the pilot first spoke out that he became transfixed, horrified, mesmerized.

Without the severed wing that was still dropping, spinning, to the ocean's illuminated surface, the remainder of the Airbus revolved slowly. The cockpit was gone, plummeting faster than what remained of the plane. The crazed thought occurred to Roland that now the burning, shredding plane could not be saved because the two men or women who knew how to control it were in free fall, doomed.

The burning remnants of the Airbus rolled yet again as it descended into almost an upright, normal position. And then, incredibly, the tail separated from the rest of the fuselage, as if it were made of frail balsa wood.

Then another blast exploded from the bottom of the fragmented airplane, and the contents of the cargo compartment were released from the blazing plane. Hundreds of objects fell like confetti into the ocean.

The helicopter pilot announced, "We have word now that the plane was British Airways Flight 767 to London."

* * *

At that moment, the helicopter tilted radically, as if it was struck. Only the seat belt Roland wore kept him from being thrown from his plush seat and smashed against the other wall. *Is this how I'm going to die, too?* he thought, *near her?*

The calm pilot, using his skills to straighten the reeling helicopter, said, "The commissioner of the New York City Police

Department has ordered us to return to the city and fly over the middle of Long Island itself, not the shore. Ms. Carbone said a flight over the ocean might not be safe. Don't be alarmed: you'll soon see Air Force fighter jets over us, to our sides, behind and ahead of us. The mayor is safe."

Am I? Do I want to be?

Roland Fortune strained to his side to look out the window again. In the distance, all he saw on the remote ocean surface was a faint glow from the remnants of the destroyed plane, like ashes that the ocean would soon absorb.